Praise ~~for~~ author Michele Hauf

"With action-packed excitement from start to finish, Hauf offers an original storyline full of quirky, fun characters and wonderful descriptions. And the sexual tension between CJ and Vika sparkles. Readers won't want to put this one down."
—*RT Book Reviews* on *This Wicked Magic*, Top Pick!

"This quirky story has a fair amount of humor and a lot of heart as well."
—*HarlequinJunkie.com* on *The Vampire Hunter*

"*Kiss Me Deadly* is an addictive read, one that won't be put down until the final page is completed."
—*Examiner.com*

Praise for Jane Godman

"The relationship between Cal and Stella is unique, complex and deeply sensual. Their forbidden romance keeps the tension ratcheted high."
—*RT Book Reviews* on *Otherworld Protector*

"A beautifully written spell-binder, with dashes of the occult and a climactic ending. Set between wars, this exceptional book also has a supernatural touch. It is captivating and very steamy."
—*Goodreads* on *Valley of Nightmares*

Chapter 1

Ethan Pierce stood before a steel-barred cage in the Acquisitions department's clean room. He was the director of the department, which was responsible for hunting, collecting and containing objects of magical nature, dangerous curses and talismans, even volatile creatures that may prove harmful to common humans if left unmonitored in the mortal realm. Ethan sent retrievers out on jobs that canvassed the world, and those adventuring professionals returned with the items.

This latest acquisition, brought in hours earlier by the retriever Bron Everhart, was needed to help locate an even more important item. For what Acquisitions ultimately sought was the blood demon Gazariel, who had stolen the code for the Final Days. If that code was to be activated, all the angels from Above would fall and smother the mortal realm with their smoldering wings. Literally. And the only way to find the demon was with the one thing in this world that wore its sigil.

"A witch," Ethan muttered as he paced before the cage.

Behind the steel bars, which were warded to keep in the subject, yet also wired with electricity to keep her docile and hamper any magic she should attempt to use in defense, stood the witch. She was a head shorter than Ethan, thin and dressed in clingy black leggings, fierce-looking black ankle boots with high heels and a silky black shirt that revealed a toned abdomen. Over it all she wore a heavy coat made of what looked like fake gray fur, which was studded with silver and black spangles. Her long white hair spilled forward, concealing one eye, and fell messily over one shoulder to her waist.

The other eye held him intently. It was a blue eye, the iris circled with black as if someone had drawn those eyes to be colored in. And on her eyelids, black shadow granted plenty Gothic melodrama. All together the look was…

Wicked, Ethan thought.

Hatred was too strong a word to apply to his feelings about witches as a species. Not all witches were evil or malicious. Yet he'd never completely get over his dislike for witches. They'd once held a murderous reign over his species, vampires, when their blood had been poisonous. One dip of the fang into a witch's vein could bring an ugly and permanent death. That was no longer. The Great Protection Spell, which had turned all witches' blood poisonous, had been broken decades earlier.

Rationally, Ethan knew not all witches were dangerous. And besides, it was the twenty-first century.

Things had changed. He worked with a few witches here at Acquisitions and the overseeing department, the Archives. For the most part, witches of the light were safe and trustworthy.

But the dark witches, such as the one standing in the cage before him? A shudder traced Ethan's spine.

The witch didn't move, only held his gaze, as if breaking it might arrest her breathing. And he wasn't about to look away. He must show her his dominance. In order to work with the witch to find the demon, she must be kept under control. Subdued. Yet her magic should remain accessible, which would keep the sigil she supposedly wore somewhere on her body open and ready to lure in the demon Gazariel.

Capturing this specific demon would prove a challenge. All perfunctory means of tracking him through Acquisitions' database had turned up nothing, though intel revealed that he was definitely in Paris.

Upon receiving orders to obtain the missing Final Days code—from a highly unprecedented command—Ethan had considered all the dozens of retrievers he had on staff. Who could do the job? Most were currently on assignment. None were stationed in Paris at the moment. But that wasn't the problem; any retriever was available and on call 24/7, able to move about worldwide.

The problem was that blood magic may be required to hold the demon once found. And the best one to deal with such magic? A vampire. Of which Ethan had been since his birth in the 1500s. Of course, he wasn't willing to give his own blood for this mission, but he didn't expect he would have to. He'd learned once that his blood could have a devastating effect on another being.

He never made the same mistake twice.

It had been decades, maybe even close to a century, since Ethan had gone out on a job. He'd become complacent, sitting behind a desk, clacking away at reports on the laptop and ordering others around. He loved his job. He did it well.

And yet, the call to adventure, to get out and actually participate in life again, was too strong to resist. He'd once stood alongside his fellow warrior vampires in the Blood Wars of the sixteenth century, defeating werewolves and slaying random witches who would deign to assist the nasty wolves. Then, he had been undefeatable, powerful and virile. He still was. The urge to exercise his soul beyond the paperwork and office politics was strong.

So Ethan had assigned this job to himself. His knowledge on the various demon breeds was minimal, yet he knew Paris, and more importantly, had the determination to root out the target. And he was the perfect partner for a witch. He wouldn't fall under her spell or forget for one moment who or what he was dealing with.

A dark witch who wore the demon Gazariel's mark.

The deflecting vibrations coming off the steel bars were strong, electronic in nature, but Tuesday didn't allow that to bother her. Yet. What was more disturbing was how she'd just been sitting in a bar, nursing a pink Panty Dropper cocktail, and then the world had gone black. And now she was standing in a cage.

Had someone roofied her? She always wore protective wards to deflect any silly human trick. And a clasp of the obsidian crystal that hung from a leather cord around her neck and above her breasts confirmed they hadn't removed her grounding and protective wards. That could only mean someone with power greater than hers—and was aware of who and what she was—had been able to drug her, kidnap her and cage her.

And while that realization was humiliating she had to remain calm and focused. She wasn't about to let the vampire see her sweat. *No weakness here, buddy.*

She knew the man was vampire because his red, ashy aura gave him away. Very few witches had the Sight— an ability to see vampire auras. Tuesday found it more of a nuisance. There were so many vampires walking the world. Sometimes the frequency of red glows in large, overcrowded cities annoyed her. Seriously. The biters were everywhere.

Not that there was anything wrong with vamps. Every once in a while, she didn't mind the occasional bite with a side of no-strings sex.

The vampire had been observing her for a few minutes. Hadn't said a word. He'd strode into the large, steel-walled, hexagon-shaped room, which only contained the cage and her, and had turned on the lights, which were blue LEDs along the floors and one blindingly white overhead spotlight.

He shoved his hands in the front pockets of his clean black jeans, which fit well, and were tucked into his combat boots. His shirtsleeves were rolled up to the elbows to display muscled forearms dusted with dark hair to match the slicked and cropped hair on his head. From under the shirt, a glimpse of a gray T-shirt hung over his pants. He looked to be strong, a force. And his carriage screamed of discipline, perhaps even military.

A smartly trimmed beard hugged his jaw and a neat mustache framed his solemn mouth. Sprinkled under his lower lip were gray strands amongst the dark brown. His face was expressionless, yet his gray eyes saw everything.

Her unprofessional assessment said that he looked world-weary. Like he'd been doing this far too long and needed a break. Although, what it was that he'd been doing, exactly, she had no clue.

"I'm Ethan Pierce," he finally said. His voice was deep and not unfriendly, and while he used English, he had a noticeable French accent. Tuesday had known a few Frenchmen in her lifetime. She'd visited France a couple times over the centuries.

"And you are Tuesday Knightsbridge," he stated.

He didn't score points for knowing her name. Unless kidnapping random witches was a thing nowadays.

Maintaining her stance, Tuesday held his gaze. But now he swept his eyes back and forth, and his hands slid out of his pockets to clasp before him. Classic villain hand-twist pose? Check, please!

"Do you know where you are?" he asked.

She wasn't ready to speak. Of course she knew where she was. She stood in a frigging cage.

"Not talking? I can deal with that. For now. You are in a holding cell at Acquisitions. We're a division of the Council's Archives."

The Council? That was a supposedly nonviolent ruling board that oversaw the actions of the world's paranormal nations, and was composed of various species to represent most. But they were watchers; they never interfered.

Guess that was a myth.

"In Paris," he said.

Paris? What the—? She'd been flown across the

ocean, from her current residence of Boston, Massachusetts, to France?

Anger rising, Tuesday lunged forward, gripping the steel bars. Vicious electricity zapped at her fingers, and she released them, taking the brunt of the shocking force through her body. She was violently tossed backward to land on her ass in the center of the cage. Legs splayed, she shook off a shiver. Her fur coat slipped down her shoulders to her wrists. She sucked in a gulp of air.

The man smirked. "By the way, those bars are activated."

Tuesday flicked up the sign of the Devil and growled, "Be taken to Beneath!"

"She speaks. And with a curse, of all things. I would expect nothing less from a dark witch. But the cage is warded. As is this clean room. No magic can get in or out. Nice try, though."

Oh, he wanted a curse? Utterly incensed, Tuesday spread out her fingers and focused a stream of magic at the man's crotch. *"Languidulus!"*

While normally invisible, once her magic hit the cage bars, a shot of violet light bounced off and splintered in dying pink embers onto the cage floor.

"What was that?" The vampire's smirk was annoyingly sexy. "Another curse? Did you try to give me a tail?"

Tuesday smiled nicely and tilted her head. "Actually, I cursed your dick to forever remain limp. And my magic is much stronger than you can imagine. I'd invest in Viagra, if I were you." She winked at him.

The slightest flinch moved the corner of one of his eyes. Bull's-eye. She could get under the man's skin.

With mere words. This predicament was going to prove an easy escape. She just had to dig under his outer machismo to access the key.

But Paris? That meant she'd been out, at the very least, for eight or nine hours. And moved around according to this bastard's will. Not cool.

"What the hell is the benevolent Council doing sending someone to kidnap me?" she asked. Standing, her heels clicked on the cage floor. She shook out the alpaca fur coat she wore over black leggings and a comfy shirt. The coat was spangled in warding designs. A Tibetan monk had initially made it for her. A glitter sidhe-witch had sewn on the wards a few years ago. "And who the fuck is Ethan Pierce?"

"I'm the director of Acquisitions. We acquire things that need to be locked away. Behind chains and wards."

"And you think *I* need to be locked away?" She flipped him the bird. Yeah, so it wasn't a hex. Some common gestures were much more to the point.

"Actually, Acquisitions needs you to get to what we really want."

"Which is?"

"The blood demon Gazariel."

Tuesday's hand slapped across her chest, below the obsidian crystal. Though rarely spoken, the sound of that demon's name always provoked such an action. She could feel his sigil burn her skin under the silk shirt.

"We know you wear the demon's sigil," Ethan explained. "Got it in the seventeenth century, if our records are accurate. Will you show it to me?"

She wouldn't give him anything. Not until she heard what weird and strange plans he—they; Acquisitions?—had for her.

"The sigil is some kind of blood curse, yes?" He paced a few steps to the side then turned back to her. "Doesn't matter how you got it. Or what it does. But I've been told, because of your connection to the demon, it makes you one of the darkest of the dark witches. I don't like dark witches, by the way."

"Would have never guessed. Your hosting skills are severely lacking. And I don't care what the hell you are, Pierce, I don't like you."

"I'm vampire."

"I knew that." She sneered. "A flesh pricker. Who is also a Richard."

"A... Richard?" The man narrowed his eyes and shrugged in question.

"Think about it a bit," she offered. He'd get it, sooner or later. "So you think you have the right to pluck any old witch off the streets and force her to do your bidding?"

"I wouldn't use the word *force*. But you are old, aren't you?"

His self-satisfied smirk did not rile her. Too much. Age was relative when a person had immortality; he should know that. She snapped the rubber band she wore about her wrist. The man would not like to see her dark magic in all its wicked glory.

"You have been brought to Paris to assist us in locating Gazariel."

The sigil she'd worn since the seventeenth century burned over her skin. "Quit saying that name," she insisted. "You only grant the demon more power with each utterance. Do you know that?"

Apparently he did not.

The man hung his head for a few seconds, then

looked up at her. "I know my demon lore. Basically. The saying a name three times thing generally only works with Himself. Demons are much more slippery when it comes to summoning them. Which is why you are here in Paris."

Paris! She could not believe this.

"Now, you'll serve to lure the demon to us—me, since I'm in charge of this mission—and then I will obtain from him what we seek to contain."

"The demon has something you want?"

He nodded. "It's dangerous to all. In the demon's hands, the world could be destroyed."

Tuesday scoffed. Always so dramatic with the end-of-the-world crap. It was never a small portion of the world, but the whole thing. What kind of villain would even think to destroy a world he would like to remain on to rule? The demon couldn't rule anything if he didn't have followers to bow down to him. End of the world, her ass.

But then she considered what she knew about Gazariel. He was a trickster. His title was The Beautiful One. Because he was a pretty bit of charm and allure. Vain and self-serving, as well. And deadly. He liked to take advantage of a person when they were at their lowest, defeated. But most importantly, he was an asshole. And she didn't want to get any closer to him than she already was. Wearing his sigil did not make her his bitch—so long as she kept her distance from him.

"So let me get this straight." She walked up to the bars until the shock waves from the wards teased at her skin and lifted the hairs in her pores. Must have been warded by another dark witch with a tech edge. It messed with her personal vibrations, so she took a step back and, with a thought, pulled a white light over herself. All she could manage in this damnable cage was a weak veil, but it gave her some solace. "You want to dangle me before the demon as bait?"

The man tapped a finger against his jaw, then nodded. "Yes, that's about it."

She turned and paced in a half arc, hands to her hips, head down in thought. A glance to the man's face found him stoic, trying to show her he would not back down, no matter what. Tough guy, pushing around a helpless woman. Been there, done that. Never going to let it happen again.

If she should refuse him, he would force her. And enjoy it. Typical male.

But he didn't know Tuesday Knightsbridge at all. Helplessness was not a condition she had ever ascribed to. And that would give her the upper hand.

"Sounds like fun," she said cheerily. "Let's do it."

Chapter 2

Another man entered the clean room and Tuesday immediately felt familiar vibrations flow off of him. Another dark witch. He was tall and lean, and everything about him was black, from his long straight hair and thin mustache to his clothing. Spell tattoos covered his hands and exposed neck. A coil of thin rope was attached to his hip holster à la the Wild West. Weird. Also, he wasn't wearing shoes.

"You've got her in a cage?" he said to the vampire. "What the hell?"

"She's dangerous," Ethan said.

Yeah, and don't forget it, buddy. But Tuesday didn't say that.

Instead she crossed her arms and stood in the cage center, taking in her opponents. The dark one was on alert in his movements as he walked around the cage as if sizing up an animal. Shame threatened to rise up in her. She'd been made to feel like less than dirt many times before. Always by those who claimed witches were foul and evil things, and who would seek to allay their shortcomings and misguided beliefs by harming her. But that had been centuries ago.

Would this world never get a clue and drop the old, ingrained prejudices?

"This is Certainly Jones," Ethan said to her. "He's head of the Archives and our resident dark witch."

"Are you okay? Have you been treated well?" Certainly asked her. A touch of British accented his voice, and his tone felt calming.

"I've been kidnapped. Most likely drugged. I'm hungry. And I have to pee," she offered. "How's tricks with you?"

He stopped before the front of the cage and looked over his shoulder at the militant vampire. "You should feed her. And let her go to the bathroom."

"As soon as we've shackled her, she can do whatever she desires."

"Shackle?" Tuesday closed her eyes, fisting her fingers at her sides. "What the hell is going on?"

"We need you to work for us. You've agreed, saying it would be fun," Ethan said. "But in order to work alongside me you'll have to be out of this cage. And I can't risk you running off or using your magic against me. CJ here has a simple shackle spell that'll keep you subdued."

"You are a—" She lunged, aiming to grasp through the cage bars, but too late, she remembered it was electrified. The jolt sent her flying backward again to land on her back in a sprawl. "I hate you!"

"I don't need you to like me. I just need you to help me find Gazariel."

"Stop saying that bastard's name," she said from her position on the floor. Humiliated and utterly exhausted, she wasn't about to pull herself up until he gave her a good reason to do so.

"Saying the demon's name won't invoke him," Certainly said.

"I know that. I just hate his name. You think the two of us were friends? That's why I'm wearing his sigil?" Letting her head fall back, she flipped them both the bird from the floor.

"She's definitely going to be a handful," Certainly commented. "Open the cage and let me in. I've got this rope bespelled to shackle her."

The dark witch was coming inside with her? Well… she wasn't in the mood to fight him. And he thought to shackle her with a rope spell? That wasn't going to go as successfully for him as he expected. Tuesday decided to play along. Just for giggles.

The bars suddenly flickered with static and then Tuesday felt the electric energy shut off. The cage door swung open with a creak. She remained splayed on the floor as the dark witch stepped up into the cage and padded over and stood above her. The door closed and she heard the vampire twist the lock then tap in a digital code.

"I'm sorry about this," Certainly said. "I know you didn't ask for this, but sometimes things have to be done to ensure worse things don't happen."

"Now you're going to tell me not to blame you and that we can all get along, right? Peace, love and 'Kumbaya'? Get it done with, witch. I do need to use the facilities."

"Will you stand, please?"

Tuesday held up her hand and gestured for him to grab it to help her stand. As he did so, she felt his magic jolt against her own. He was strong, but not as powerful as her. But he was cute, and she had a plan, so she was going to let him off easy. Mostly. And hell, she wasn't sure she could even invoke her magic inside this crazy warded cage. But she wouldn't be Tuesday Knightsbridge if she didn't give it a go.

She slapped her palms to his temples and fixed her gaze onto his intense jade eyes. Before he knew to look away she fixed onto his soul. It was a witch's skill, to hold a soul fix on another witch. She felt his inner struggle, his need to close his eyes and lock her out. But she had been doing this far too long to allow anyone escape from her delving soul gaze.

The witch's soul was dark to the core. Less than two centuries old, he'd walked a free and defiant path. He was…connected closely to another. A twin? Yes, he had a twin brother for whom he held great love and respect. He'd once carried dozens of demons within him after a trip to Daemonia. Some of those demons had made him hurt himself. Others had taught him to care more deeply than he could have fathomed. And…the man loved deeply. Another witch, who was mother to his one-year-old twin sons.

That feeling, the emotion of unconditional love that flooded the man's system, pricked at Tuesday's willpower. She winced, fearing what may happen should she allow herself to linger in his eyes. To fall into the deep and devastating emotion of love.

Tuesday released the man and he stumbled backward, catching himself before he hit the bars.

"What did she do to you?" Ethan asked from outside the cage.

"I'm…fine," Certainly said, catching his hands on his knees and huffing. It took a lot out of a person to have his soul tapped. "She just…"

"I looked into his soul," Tuesday explained to Ethan. "I like this one. He's strong." She pointed at the vampire. "You. I do not like."

"We've already discussed our mutual lack of admiration for one another. *Like* isn't a requirement to work together. You going to be okay, CJ?"

The dark witch nodded. "Yep. Just gathering back my wits." He straightened and snapped the simple rope before him in warning. "You going to behave?"

Tuesday nodded. "I saw your wife. You love her very much."

"I would die for her," Certainly said with an ease that tugged at Tuesday's hardened heart. Because she believed that he would. What a lucky woman.

Romantics and silly sops would have a person believe love was the be-all and end-all. Whatever.

"Get on with it."

She held her hands before her, wrists together, waiting to be bound. The rope wouldn't impact her movement or physical health. It would keep her from performing any sort of magic, hex, spell or charm. But if the rope was damaged after the spell had been cast…

"On second thought," she said, "it'll work better if you drape it across my chest."

"Across your heart," Certainly said. "Good idea. And you will need the use of your hands." He lowered the lariat over her head and rested it on a shoulder, then draped it across her heart to fall between her breasts. "You're going to have to remove the crystal."

"I never take it off."

"The spell won't fix otherwise."

She shook her head and clasped the cool obsidian.

"Do you want to get out of here?" Certainly asked.

"Did they drug me?" she asked quietly. "Just tell me what they used to incapacitate me."

"I don't know for sure. Henbane, possibly?"

Tuesday nodded. Henbane, when mixed with a vile adjuvant, could take out a witch for the better part of a day. Damn it! Her wards should have caught that.

Certainly Jones could prove an ally if she played her cards right. But for now she must submit in order to gain freedom. She pulled the leather cord from around her neck and handed it to him. "That must be returned to me immediately."

"It will. You'll be able to wear it after I've cast the spell." He tucked the crystal in his front pocket, then jumped a little in reaction.

"It's not yours to possess," Tuesday warned. "It will come back to me quickly."

"I get that." He tapped the rope. "This will shackle your magic only against Ethan Pierce. You will still be able to wield magic in all other instances. It may be necessary to protect yourself against the demon."

"I appreciate that. What the hell is that guy?"

Certainly looked over a shoulder. Ethan paced, arms across his chest.

"Vampire."

"I know that. I mean, what's his deal? He's so… angry."

"Really? This coming from the angriest witch I've ever met?"

"You guys *did* kidnap me."

"Point taken. Don't give Pierce such a hard time. He generally works behind the desk telling others what to do. But I think this time it's personal."

"How so?"

Certainly shrugged. "Not sure. And even if I did have a clue? That's for him to give to you, not me. Close your eyes."

Tuesday did so because she was tired and wanted to get out of this stupid cage. Much as shackling her magic against anyone would piss her off, at the very least he wasn't completely disabling her.

The witch chanted a spell that caused the rope to suddenly squeeze about her. She felt the sigil beneath her shirt warm and reach out for the rope. It didn't like being controlled. Which was a good thing. And she counted on its retaliation.

In a matter of moments the witch said, "So mote it be."

And the rope fell slack again, as if an ill-hung necklace. Tuesday let out a breath. Her skin tingled, but otherwise, she didn't feel any different. In the next instant, the obsidian on the cord flew out from the witch's pocket and landed smartly in Tuesday's grasp.

The cage door opened and Ethan asked, "How will we know it worked?"

"It worked." CJ stepped out of the cage. "My magic always works." He winked at Tuesday. "I'm sorry, but the rope is the shackle. You'll have to figure out your own style for that." He turned to Ethan. "You going to take her upstairs for a bit, then…off to adventure?"

The men shared a look that was a few seconds too

long for Tuesday not to wonder what had gone unspoken.

"Right," Ethan suddenly said. "I've got some things to finish up in the office. Come on, witch."

"Really? You're going to let your new pet out on a leash?" She flopped the lariat around before her. "Aren't you the kindest master ever."

"Good luck," CJ said and wandered out of the room.

"Get out of the cage, witch."

She stepped up to the threshold. "My name is Tuesday. Treat me well and I will return the kindness."

Ethan nodded. "Lead me to the demon and I'll be more than grateful."

"I'm not going to lead you anywhere without cold hard cash."

"What?"

"You think I'm going to do this for nothing? Slavery went out last century. If you want me to cooperate we need to talk money." She jumped down onto the concrete floor, blessedly relieved to have left the smothering confines of that magic-busting cage. With a shiver and a flip of her hair over her shoulder, she walked up to the man.

He stood a head higher than her, but she was accustomed to looking up to people, mostly men. Her stance spoke louder than her lacking height.

"How much do you want?" he asked, surprising her that he hadn't argued.

"A million. US dollars, not your freaky French euros."

He broke out into throaty laughter that, in any other circumstance, might have grasped her by the lusting heart and teased her to flutter her lashes at him. But this was not any other time. With a flick of her forefinger, Tuesday tossed a beam of pain at the vampire. The magic burst into a spray of violet sparks just inches from his face and dispersed.

Damn shackle.

"Good to see CJ's spell works," he said. "Tough luck, witch. I'm impervious to your magic now."

Only so long as the shackle stayed in place. And her sigil was so hot that it could burn through pretty much anything right now…

"Half a million then," she said.

"Ten grand."

Tuesday spun and jumped up into the cage opening. "I think I'll stay here then. Apparently, I'm the only one who can do what you need done. I'm worth more than a few bucks. You think about it, then get back to me."

"I've got a budget, witch."

"And I've got all the time in the world. Do you?"

He rubbed his stubble-shadowed jaw. Tuesday rather liked it when a man tickled his stubble over her skin, as his gaze journeyed down her stomach and lower. And his beard was frosted with a touch of grey in the dark brown, which added a delicious seasoning to his appearance. If the man wasn't so obstinate he'd actually be sexy.

"A hundred thousand," he offered. "That's as high as I can go."

"Deal." Tuesday jumped down again and marched past him toward the door. She would have taken the ten grand. "Let's get out of this dungeon. Did you forget I need to pee?"

The witch had gone into the private bathroom attached to the office Ethan occupied in headquarters.

There were no windows in the small washroom for her to escape through, so he trusted her to shut the door.

Meanwhile, he checked his email. No new orders waiting for retrieval assignment. And he'd sent details regarding his taking this particular mission to the Council. No reply, so far, was good news.

He glanced to the maple-wood bathroom door. He and CJ had only planned things so far. And that plan hadn't quite come to complete fruition. It would, soon enough. He wasn't sure how he was going to work with the witch.

She was obstinate. A smart-ass. And he hadn't expected her to be gorgeous. Utterly beautiful. In a weird, silver Goth sort of way. Behind her defensive, smart mouth and angry rubber band-snapping machinations he felt sure a sensual goddess inhabited the irresistible curves and gemstone blue eyes.

He raked fingers through his hair and shook his head. What was he thinking? He needed to do this right. He was the boss. And he wasn't about to show weakness or failure to his employees by letting his thoughts stray from the task at hand.

He'd handle the witch with a strong hand and command. He had to stay on guard with her. To set an example for others. But it would prove a challenge, not only because of her odd appeal, but also because it had been so long since he'd actually worked a mission. If she learned that he was questioning his own abilities— and thus had taken the job to prove he wasn't washed up and was physically capable of handling such a mission—he'd never succeed.

They headed out, Tuesday following Ethan's sure gait. It was a confident walk. A sexy walk. After many turns and an elevator ride down four floors, the sight of a door up ahead gave her great glee. Soon.

She pressed her hand over the shackle rope, which she'd been holding snug against the sigil. The rope fibers were hot and smoldering. It was working.

"I don't live far from here. We'll walk," Ethan said.

He'd mentioned they would discuss a plan for capturing the demon. Why they didn't simply do it in his office was beyond her, but she appreciated the opportunity to get out of the building. And away.

He opened a heavy steel door. Bright daylight filtered in, making Tuesday blink. She had lost all concept of time, and even though her muscles were dragging her downward from exhaustion, the crisp winter air, inhaled deeply, worked to lighten her. And keep her focused. Tugging her coat closed, but keeping one hand inside on the shackling rope, she followed the vampire outside.

They exited into a narrow, cobblestone alleyway. Ethan turned left.

Tuesday turned right and started to run. She made it ten feet, pulling away the rope that had burned apart thanks to the demon sigil, and dropped it behind her. But as her speed increased and she began to pump her arms, her body collided with an invisible wall, slamming her backward to land in the arms of Ethan Pierce.

"I expected as much," he said. A flash of his bright smile did not give her any mirth. "So did CJ. The rope was merely a distraction until CJ had time to work up a stronger spell."

"Bastard," she muttered, and collapsed in his arms.

Chapter 3

The steel door through which they'd exited opened and the dark witch swung out with urgency. He lifted his hand, exposing the glowing spell tattoos that covered his palm. As he approached, he asked Ethan, "You sure about this, man?"

"Nope. But someone's got to do it. So do your darkest."

"Oh, no." Not knowing what was coming, but not stupid, either, Tuesday struggled out of Ethan's grasp.

The vampire stretched back an arm toward his approaching cohort while he managed to hold her by the coat with his other hand. She wasn't going to let whatever might happen...happen.

She began to speak a deflection spell, but a slash of Certainly's hand caused Tuesday's words to suddenly jumble and drop in the air. He'd deflected her deflection. He was stronger than she'd anticipated.

With his full body, the vampire crushed her against the brick wall. She kicked, unwilling to be contained. Suddenly, she smelled blood. What the—? The dark witch grabbed her wrist and an icy pain seared the center of her palm. A coppery scent filled the air. He was invoking blood magic?

"No!"

Kicking, Tuesday hit Ethan's gut, but the vampire lunged forward and slapped his hand into hers. Heat from his blood mingled with hers. The dark witch held their hands together and recited a simple incantation that she recognized as a binder.

Tuesday growled, but the exhaustion from what she'd been through since sitting in the bar—back in the United States—had depleted her magic. The blood spell coursed through her system, and she felt it bite at her neck from the inside. Certainly Jones's dark and masterful magic bound her to the vampire. They would not be able to leave one another's side, nor would they be able to harm one another.

"This is the only blood you'll ever get from me," the vampire said on a low, accusing tone.

With a shout for survival, Tuesday pushed away from her captor with a shove of her free hand to his chest. The dark witch stepped away, allowing her to stumble against the wall. She caught her hands flat on the rough brick behind her, cursed, then watched as the knife wound sealed in a glow of violet on her palm.

"Had to be done," Certainly commented.

"How close do we have to stay to one another now?" Ethan asked, as if he'd only been given a simple handshake.

"Not sure. Try it out."

"Try running off," Ethan said to her. "See how far you get."

"Try fucking yourself, vampire."

"Like I said, she's going to be a challenge," Certainly said.

"Challenge accepted. I'll start walking home," Ethan said. "We'll see how far I get before you have no choice but to follow." He slapped a hand into the dark witch's. "Thanks, CJ."

Ethan strolled off down the alley. And Tuesday tugged her coat up and adjusted her hair. She pointed an accusing finger at Certainly. "You, Jones, are on my shit list."

He shrugged. "I honor your power, Tuesday Knightsbridge. You are an old and strong witch. But I can feel your darkness is even greater than mine."

"Yeah? Warlock's looking pretty good right about now." If she grievously harmed another witch the warlock title would be slapped on her. "That would really put you in your place."

"As well, it would put you in a place you don't want to stand. Don't let it overwhelm you, Tuesday. Remember what you once were."

Really? The man was trying the New Age-y bullshit on her? "You know nothing about me."

"No, but I saw into your soul when you were looking into mine." He bowed his head toward her. "I am sorry for the things you have suffered because of what we are."

Yeah, so witches had been a favorite cat's-paw over the centuries. She'd survived, and she would continue to so do thanks to her hardened heart.

Suddenly, Tuesday's body jerked forward. Certainly stepped aside and they both looked down the alley. Ethan stood about fifty yards off. He gave them a thumbs-up.

And when he started walking again, Tuesday was pulled after him.

"Shit list!" she called back to Certainly, who had the decency to place his palms together and bow to her in reverence.

Ethan chuckled to himself as the witch reluctantly followed him down the street to his place in the eleventh arrondissement. He lived in a third-floor loft close to Père Lachaise cemetery, which boasted an excellent view of Sacré Coeur up on the hill.

He left the front door open behind him, not feeling the need to wait on the witch. She'd stand back just to piss him off, surely. He tossed his keys onto the gray granite kitchen counter and kicked off his shoes, then wandered through the living area. With a few words to the electronic house butler—"Stuart, modify for sun"— the electrochromic shades fixed between the double windowpanes that looked out over the city adjusted to a soft white that would allow in light but not the UV rays that gave him the most caution.

The layout of the loft was open—no walls, save the ones enclosing the bathroom. Strolling through the living room, around a corner and through the bedroom, he went into the bathroom but left the door open behind him. "Stuart, warm water." Ethan splashed water on his face, then manually twisted off the faucet and took a few deep breaths.

He opened his palm. The cut CJ had given him had already healed. Sharing blood with the witch hadn't been as horrible as he'd expected. Remnants of fear over the once-poisonous witch blood remained. He'd have to get over it. And fast. If the demon was a blood demon, surely much blood would be spilled in the coming days. The witch's. And the demon's. Ethan wasn't willing to give any more than the few drops he'd provided today.

He liked blood. As sustenance. But he never drank witch's blood, even since the Great Protection Spell had been broken. It couldn't harm him now. And there were even some vampires who liked drinking from witches. If you added in sex and a specific spell for bloodsex-magic, the vampire could steal some of that witch's magic for himself.

He had no desire to own magic. But to taste the witch's blood? He couldn't shake the scent of her blood as it had trickled into the air in the alley outside head-quarters. It had roused him so much in that moment that he'd used violence and had shoved her roughly to hide his burgeoning desires. He hoped she wouldn't bleed near him again.

That would prove a challenge.

"Honey, I'm home!"

He shook his head, but no reflection in the mirror showed his exasperation. CJ had warned she would be a struggle. But that was a challenge he welcomed. Now, to work with the witch.

Tuesday had shucked off her coat and now reclined on the leather sofa that sat against a rough brick wall. She'd kicked off her shoes and waggled her bare toes—the nails were painted bright blue—as she stretched out her arms and yawned. The black shirt had a but-ton below her breasts and was open from there down, revealing abs. And much more skin than he wanted to notice right now.

"Tired?" he asked.

"Unlike vampires, we witches do need a little shut-eye now and then. And after all the torments I've endured?"

"Why don't you take twenty minutes to rest? Stuart, close the shades completely."

As the windows darkened, Tuesday sat up and glanced over a shoulder. "Who the hell is Stuart? A house brownie?"

Ethan chuckled. "A bit similar. That's the name of the electronic house butler. This place is high-tech. If you need something, Stuart can usually get it."

"Stuart, book me a flight back to Boston, STAT," Tuesday said.

As the butler began to confirm, Ethan canceled that request. "And ignore all requests from any voice but my own," he ordered.

"Of course," Stuart replied.

"That's creepy." Tuesday lay back down and crossed her arms over her chest. "And so not fair."

"While you rest I'm going to make a few calls. Plan our first move."

"You don't have a plan?"

"Of course I do," he lied. Sitting before the kitchen counter with his back to her, he pushed aside her spangled coat. A pad of paper and a pen waited near the phone. He was all about the high-tech, but he'd never give up the landline. "You want a blanket or something?"

"Fuck you, Richard." And she turned over on the sofa and snuggled up in a ball.

Again with the Richard? He thought about it a few seconds. Ah. Richard shortened was… All righty then. He shouldn't expect her to think very highly of him after having one of his retrievers kidnap her and fly her across the ocean. And then forcibly bind her to him.

He may have to find a means to cozy up to her in order to get her to trust him or he'd never get anywhere with her. At the very least, he needed her to want to trust him.

Pulling out his cell phone, he scrolled through the contacts. He knew the person he had to speak to first to learn anything about any demon in Paris.

Edamite Thrash was a sort of demon overlord with a penchant for niceness. But Ethan didn't tell anyone that, or Thrash would scratch you with the poison thorns that grew from his knuckles. The man was a corax demon, which meant he could shift into an unkindness of ravens and take to the skies. He also made it his job to oversee the demons of Paris, knowing who was where, and when and why. He kept a loose rein on his species, and enforced punishment only when one of them threatened to expose their kind with their foolish actions.

Ethan knew most of the major players in the paranormal realm who inhabited Paris. That was his job, to know whom he could trust and with whom he had best watch his back. Ed was trustworthy.

The dark feather tattoo on Ed's neck always drew Ethan's eye. He wore many sigils tattooed on his skin, and combined with his standard dark business suit and smartly parted and slicked black hair, he looked dangerous yet disturbingly *GQ* stylish.

He shook the man's hand, noting he always wore

black leather half gloves that exposed his fingers. He needed only cover the thorns on his knuckles to prevent an accident.

"Good to see you, man." Ed nodded over Ethan's shoulder. "Who is this pretty?"

Tuesday, who had followed Ethan into the building at a distance, was acting petulant, yet she strolled forward and offered her hand to shake. "Tuesday Knightsbridge."

Ed clasped her hand. "The witch. I've heard about you."

"You have? From who?"

"My girlfriend, Tamatha Bellerose."

"Bellerose? Oh, yes, her mother is Petrina. I know that witch." And the quickness with which Tuesday pulled her hand from the demon's clasp clued Ethan she probably didn't have a good relationship with the family. "Just in Paris for a visit," she added. "Forced, as it is."

Ed looked to Ethan for explanation.

"Tuesday is helping me to locate a demon. That's why I wanted to check in with you. See if you've any information that may lead us to him."

Ed leaned against the desk behind him and crossed his arms over his chest. "Which demon?"

"The Beautiful One," Tuesday said before Ethan could say the name.

"Ah. Gazariel." Ed winced and rubbed his jaw. "I do know he's in town. But haven't a clue where. He hasn't been making much noise so he's not on my give-a-fuck radar. Why is she helping? You only require a witch when you need to summon a demon from Beneath or Daemonia."

"I'm bait," Tuesday said, tossing out the words at the same time Ethan said, "She's my lure for the demon."

"You two don't get along very well, do you?"

Ethan kept an eye on Tuesday as she walked about the demon's office, looked over the marble conference table and then wandered to the wall where various artifacts were displayed on small individual shelves.

"We had to take her away from her home to get her to work with us," Ethan offered.

"Kidnapped me," Tuesday called over her shoulder as she peered into a glass container that likely held faery dust. The contents sparkled in all colors from the afternoon sun beaming in through the windows.

"Sounds on par for Acquisitions," Ed said. "So, a lure, eh? Why would Gazariel be interested in that witch?"

"She wears his sigil. Or that is the information we have."

Ed stood and now he gave Tuesday his full attention. She turned from her curious seeking and splayed her hands. "Yep, I'm the demon's bitch. I carry his curse. And Einstein here thinks that'll draw him to me. Idiot."

"He'll come to you. We just have to get you close enough he puts up his head and notices," Ethan said. "Give him a sniff of the witch's scent."

"He's not going to be attracted to the one who wears his curse," Ed said. "Why would he? I know a bit about The Beautiful One. He put an unwanted curse in her many centuries ago when he had the opportunity. And now he's done with it. I'm not sure of the nature of the curse, but if the demon wants it gone from him, there's not a thing in this world that would incline him to set one foot near her now. She's useless."

"Hey! I can hear you," Tuesday called. The blue glass sphere she had touched wobbled and rolled off the shelf. She caught it just before it hit the floor. "Oops. Good save, though, yeah?"

"Don't touch the breakables," Ethan said, chastising the overly curious witch. And to Ed he said, "Are you serious? But we need her to open that curse and hold Gazariel so he will submit."

"Why do you need him to submit?"

"He's got something that Acquisitions wants."

Ed lifted an eyebrow.

"It's a book of angel names and sigils. A muse wrote it. It holds the code for the Final Days."

"Is that thing back in circulation? I thought the angel Raphael had taken it underwing, so to speak?"

"It made a series of exchanges before Raphael secured it from a vampire intent on populating the world with nephilim. Let's just say it's been in so many hands, even the Archives' records are confused as to where it was last seen before landing in the demon's hands. But I have good intel that The Beautiful One currently has it."

"Doesn't sound like a party."

"It's not. The list of angel names, when ordered correctly, holds an ancient coded word, or words, that when spoken, will send all angels plummeting to earth to smother mankind with their multitudes. Their wings will burn human flesh, young and old. Paranormals are not exempt, either. The earth will become an ashy cemetery of the mortal, the paranormal and the divine."

"Whew!" Ed ran a gloved hand through his slick hair. "That's something you want to stop. But your challenge will be getting the demon to come to you, *without* knowing you've got the witch, and then surprising him with her at just the right moment."

Ethan's temples had begun to pulse. He hadn't expected this particular complication. If he would have known before the demon didn't want anything to do with the witch, he wouldn't have bound himself to her until after they'd secured Gazariel. Of course, he needed Tuesday to bring the demon to him. This was a mess. Had she known as much?

Her self-satisfied grin answered that one for him.

"Keep her out of sight until you need her," Ed suggested.

"Too late. I bound myself to her to keep her close and protect myself from any retaliatory magic."

"Then you've got a problem, Pierce."

No need to state that one out loud. Tuesday's soft tsking sounds riled him and Ethan fisted his hands. Yet when he saw her smile beam at sight of his anger, he relented the knuckle-whitening clutch. The witch would not get under his skin. He was smarter than this. And he didn't need to snap a rubber band to remind him of that.

He turned to Ed. "Can you help by telling me where Gazariel might be?"

"I haven't a clue."

"But you keep tabs on all the demons—how can you know he's in the city and not have a location on him?"

"It's a feeling, Pierce, not an exact science or even a map. Believe me, I would help you if I could. The Beautiful One is from Beneath, so you might start at l'Enfer."

The Devil Himself's nightclub. It was frequented by demons, vamps, werewolves and most any sort looking for dark and devious indulgences. Just the place Ethan wanted to visit. Not.

"Hey, how much you want for this?" Tuesday waggled a pearlescent alicorn she'd found on a shelf.

Ed shrugged. "You can take it."

"What? Are you serious?" The witch actually tittered with glee. "You do know how valuable this is?"

"It's…" Ed winced. "I should have never obtained that thing. It was taken from innocence. It's not something I have a right to own. I've been meaning to get rid of it for a while now. You'd be doing me a favor by taking it."

"Nice!" Tuesday stabbed the air with the thing. "I can so use this."

Ethan could but shake his head and wish the day would get better.

"I guess you'll be clubbing then?" Ed offered as he extended his hand to shake.

"Sounds like it." Ethan thanked the man and started out of the room, knowing Tuesday would have to follow. Sooner or later.

As he got on the elevator, the witch entered, twirling the alicorn gaily. "I got a prize," she teased.

"What the hell can you do with that thing?"

"You'll find out soon enough. By the way, I'm going to need some magical supplies. You whisked me away from home and cauldron. I need certain items to work magic, put up wards and generally survive."

"Like what?"

She shrugged and tapped the alicorn against her jaw. "This is a start. There's got to be magic shops in the city. And you'll have to pay, sweetie, since my kidnapper decided against bringing along my purse. And I'll be needing some clothes as well. Can't go clubbing looking like this, can I?"

"You like fine. All black and perfectly witchy? You'll fit right in at l'Enfer." Ethan checked his watch. It was around six in the evening. A few more hours before the club opened.

"Can a chick get pizza in this town?"

Rolling his eyes, he strolled out as the elevator doors opened. The witch had no taste whatsoever.

Chapter 4

At the plain black metal doors to the club l'Enfer, they stopped before the bouncer with red eyes. A sign over his high left shoulder stated, in Latin, what basically translated as "no funny stuff" and "you take your own chances entering." Tuesday boldly met the bouncer's gaze and focused her intent toward him. The demon looked down, chastised by her audacity. Served him right. He was young and needed to learn to show respect for his elders.

Blowing him a kiss laced with pizza sauce and some kind of cheese that had not been mozzarella—the French really liked their weird cheeses—she then glided down the dark hallway. The music thudded in her heart and veins. Not worrying whether Ethan gained access, she picked up the beat and danced as she walked.

She sensed the brooding vampire was behind her, and

felt his hand go to her hip, as if to guide her through the darkness, but he quickly removed it. Tuesday smiled. Had he forgotten himself for a moment? Thought of her as an actual desirable female he might get close to? She could work with that.

Much as she had developed a liking for clubbing over the last several decades, Tuesday preferred less crowded venues, and with more upbeat tunes. L'Enfer had not invested any expense in color. Everything was black, with hematite and silver metallic bits and trim here and there. The lighting was red, and flashed across the inhabitants and dancers, who also wore mostly black.

Tuesday was dressed for the part, right down to her matte black nail polish and eye shadow. Yet she felt naked without some lip gloss; a deep violet would be perfect for this Gothic milieu. As it was, she felt virtually exposed without any magical accoutrements to hand, and bound to a freaking vampire. Yet she wasn't powerless. Her simple mastery over the bouncer had proven that. And she did have the alicorn stuck in her waistband. She felt it tremble. This was not a place for such a thing. The demon hadn't wanted to possess innocence? Interesting.

She wouldn't test the alicorn's power here. The place was owned by the Devil Himself, and the sign on the door had clearly stated no funny stuff. The bouncer should have frisked her for weapons. Idiot.

On the other hand, a place like this probably thrived on the illicit use of weapons and how much damage could be done before a person was kicked out. If that would even happen. Again, the sign mentioned taking one's own chances.

"You see him?" Ethan shouted next to her ear.

Tuesday leaned away from him. "I can hear well enough over the noise, vampire. And I just got here. Let me look around, will you? You want to dance?"

"I'm not a dancer. And I'm on a job."

"Right, all work and no play. Should I call you Jack?"

"Just keep your mind on business."

"Can I at least have a drink? We should try to blend in. Look like we're here to party and not jack up some asshole demon, yeah?"

Ethan sighed then reluctantly nodded. "What do you want?"

"Anything that doesn't contain a live entity. I suspect that's on the menu here. And I prefer vodka."

"Live entities," he muttered. With a frown, he headed toward the long, black quartz bar that was edged with a cut-in of red crystals that seemed to glow like LEDs.

Tuesday allowed her body to inhale the beat. Despite the fact this club was owned by the rather dour Dark Prince, the music wasn't too terribly dirge-like. The Goth singer with a string of spikes embedded down the sides of each bare arm sang about his friends being heathens and suggested she should take it slow. All righty, then.

Tuesday swayed to the beat as a crimson-haired faery with violet eyes matched her with a smile and a shimmy. If she was going to be forced to work for some rogue organization to capture a pompous, yet also vicious demon she had no wish to ever see again, at the very least, she could enjoy herself. Lifting her arms, she spun onto the dance floor.

Below her, the Plexiglas floor flashed red and black and then segued into flames. It was a realistic effect, and she almost fancied to feel the heat. A brush of fur tickled her right hand, and with a spin she eyed the tattooed back of a thin person who moved a little too jerkily not to be demon.

A guitar solo screamed and coaxed the crowd to pump their fists and jump in a pounding stomp of fraternity to whatever dark gods were the current rage. Tuesday preferred Loki. The one portrayed in the movies by the handsome dark-haired actor, most specifically. As she spun, arms swaying above her head and hips shifting, she spied Ethan standing at the edge of the dance floor, holding a red glowing drink. His grim look spoke much louder than the music.

"Spoilsport." She wandered over and took the drink, then tilted back a healthy swallow. Instead of the expected burn, she felt a distinct icy grab at the back of her throat, which then melted into a blaze of heat down her esophagus. And it tasted of cinnamon and chocolate. "Whew! That is some good stuff."

"I thought it would be the drink for you. It's called The Devil's Bitch."

"Oh, Ethan, you can hate me all you need to." She fluttered her lashes at him. "I'm not going to crack under all that loathing. You know your emotions only reflect back onto you? Also makes it easy for a witch to use against you. That is, if the witch could drop some magic on your vampire ass. Ditch the frowny face and let's agree to disagree, and then get on with things, shall we?"

"So you've decided to stop pouting and work with me?"

Yeah, she was being as much of a problem child as he was. And if she didn't get to work now, she'd never be free of the man and his brooding grey eyes. And could his teeth be any whiter? She wanted to see his fangs. To touch them and feel them pierce her neck…but no. She would not bone up this task by falling all puppy-eyed over the vamp. She was better than that. Because she had no choice.

"We're partners." She held out a hand and he shook it, holding it for a few seconds longer than was proper. She could feel his heartbeats in that hold, and they were sure and confident. Powerful. And, yes, controlling. The man would not relent. "Good then. I'll take a look around. You probably wouldn't recognize the demon if he was choking you, so you just…"

His eyes took in their surroundings. He put off a very militant, I'm-ready vibe. "I'll stay close to you."

"Sure, keep close. I'll protect the big bad vampire from a suggestive side glance or a dance-off. Ha!"

She strolled off into the clove-scented shadows that edged the dance floor, knowing the man would follow. It wasn't as if she could get any farther away from him than fifty yards. Nothing like having a puppy dog on her tail. Of course, she liked puppies. Had once owned one, until the local troll had stolen it and— She tried never to imagine what had become of her sweet Nugget after that. Long time ago. Always avoid trolls, had been the lesson.

Noting every face she passed, Tuesday pulled on her Sherlock cloak. It was easy to tell the demons, as their eyes were generally red, although some demon-possessed humans' eyes gave off a dull blue glow. Most natural demons who did not require a human meat suit could disguise their irises, but when out at the club they apparently let their freak flags fly. Red irises everywhere!

Thinking of freaks…

She strolled toward a tall sliver of a demon who looked like a walking skeleton, yet he wore thin, clear muscle over those bones. A wraith? They were usually dangerous and she was surprised one would put himself in a social situation. But when the creature turned to cast her a violet gaze she realized it was faery. And faeries could be even more vicious than demons.

Propping her palm over the alicorn at her waist, Tuesday detoured from her approach, wisely dismissing the oddity. With a flick of her fingers she could reduce them all to gibbering sycophants. But she would not because she didn't want to call attention to herself.

Finishing off the drink, which still cooled then burned, she set the empty goblet on a table and eyed the flashing red-and-silver staircase leading up to the balcony. She skipped up the steps, edging past a couple who made out carefully, for the woman's spiked bra looked quite deadly. Blood tinted the air. Hmm… Perhaps the bra served the exact purpose its wearer desired.

Tuesday glanced back to see Ethan following and noticed his expression when he neared the couple. He winced and shook his head. The man was discerning. Points for him.

Stepping up into the dark and smoky balcony, Tuesday was immediately surrounded by three tall men, all of them demons. The one before her flashed a silver-toothed grin, punctuated by curved fangs, and his nostrils flared and put out little wisps of black smoke. It wasn't cigarettes or weed producing the smoke, but rather the thickness of demons here above the crowd. "A tasty witch has dared to broach our private balcony?"

"I wasn't aware it was private." She lifted her hand,

prepared to repel the demon, when suddenly Ethan gripped her wrist and eased himself around to stand before her.

"She didn't know, gentlemen," he offered. "Demons only up here?"

"You got it, vampire. But if she wants to stay—" Silver Tooth let his gaze creep over Tuesday's skin "—we want to play."

"Oh, yeah?" Tuesday reached around Ethan with her free hand and he turned to clasp both her wrists. "Don't restrain me before them," she said. "I can stand up for myself."

"Hear that, vampire? She can take care of herself. Why don't you leave the tasty little witch to us?"

Now Tuesday did feel a shiver of caution, and the touch of someone's fingers from behind, sliding across her ass, made her jump. Right against Ethan's arm, which slid across her shoulder and directed her back toward the stairs.

"We're leaving," he said more to her than the randy demons. "But before we do…" He cocked a look over his shoulder at the silver-toothed leader. "Any of you familiar with Gazariel?"

"He means The Beautiful One," Tuesday quickly amended. It was not cool to call demons by their names, especially around others.

"Get that witch out of here," Silver Tooth said.

"But the demon I'm looking for—" Ethan began.

"No pretty demons in this club, vampire. And if you don't take your pet witch and leave we'll make sure no one ever calls her pretty, either."

Ethan clasped Tuesday's hand and led her down the

stairs. The couple was still making out. Blood beaded in various spots on the man's chest and neck. Ethan quickened their pace.

When they landed on the main floor, he directed her toward a wall, where a private moment could be found behind it, as it was set off from the frenzy of dancers.

"I had no idea that was a demons-only area," she said. "But you don't score points for rescuing me. I was fine."

"I know that. But no funny stuff, remember? And I like to take care of my assets. Make sure they survive the length of the job."

"I'm an asset to you? I don't know if that's a good or a bad thing. I'm guessing not especially good."

"You are valuable. What's so bad about that?"

"My value, as determined by what I can do for you, is a very bad thing. Any man who tries to put a—" she made air quotes "—'value' on a woman is not a man at all."

Feminism was her right, and she would never stop to point out the patriarchy's misguided beliefs and lacking empathy for those who were their equals. She strode off toward the front hallway, where they had entered. "He's not here. Let's blow this joint."

Once outside on the street, she walked swiftly away from the nondescript doors, but abruptly hit an invisible wall and couldn't press onward. Curse that vampire! She cast a glance over her shoulder. Ethan stood a good distance away, unmoving, giving her a sly wave.

"Such a Richard," she muttered. "Well? What are you waiting for?"

"I'm going this way." He pointed over his shoulder, then turned and walked off.

And the pull of the binding dragged Tuesday along after him.

"It was a stupid thing to do anyway," Tuesday muttered as she followed Ethan down the quiet, dark Parisian street toward wherever he was headed. She hadn't a choice in the matter. "Going to that club? Why would The Beautiful One hang out at that depressing place? Do you even know who you're after? That demon likes to shine. To see and be seen. He's vain and all about pleasure and self-gratification. He thrives on attention. Adoration. Love. He's not for darkness and murk. That's why he pawned off his curse on me."

Ethan cast a glance over his shoulder at her, then resumed his pace.

"What kind of sorry adventuring detective vampire are you?" she called. "Don't you know how to do this stuff? I mean, let's go to the least likely place the dude is going to be and feed the witch to the demons, why don't we?"

She smirked to think about getting hit on by those nasty demons. The one with the silver teeth had to have doused himself in body spray for the young and bepimpled. Ugh. And then Ethan had felt the need to intervene. Like some kind of rescuing hero? She could have taken care of herself. But how often did a man step in to try and help her? So rarely, she couldn't think back that far.

"I'm hungry!" she announced in frustration. "That pizza was terrible. Who sells pizza slices out of a freezer? That's like 7-Eleven stuff. So wrong. I thought

Paris was classier? Let's get something to eat. Do you have to walk so fast? It's not as if we're going to find the demon now. I'd guess he's more of a day kind of demon. All the better to allow others to admire his beaming gorgeousness. Are you even listening to me, Pierce? Bueller?"

With that, the vampire swung round, marched up to her, bracketed her face with his hands and…

…kissed her.

For no reason. And with no grace. He planted a firm, seconds-long kiss on her mouth. And for those few seconds Tuesday's heart thundered and a tickle-thrill shimmied up the back of her neck. She didn't mind the kiss. In fact, it proved a scintillating connection. The vibrations between them shivered haphazardly, but then quickly started to harmonize. To actually blend—as if they were meant to come together. How weird was that?

But the kiss ended as quickly as it had landed on her mouth. And she hadn't time to determine why it had felt so right.

Ethan stepped back, hands splaying outward. With a sexy wink, he then said, "I knew that would work."

Tuesday touched her lips, stunned that he'd taken her by surprise, but even more stunned that she wasn't upset about the attack kiss.

"I figured a kiss would get you to shut up," he said. Turning, he marched onward.

Really? He'd employed the kiss to make her stop talking? Of all the nerve! She was not one of his victims he could subdue with persuasion or a plunge of fang into vein. And so what if she had been talking? It wasn't as if he'd shown an eagerness to converse with her. She was alone in a strange, foreign city, being led around by a bossy vampire who held her captive with a magical bond. Damn right she was going to chatter away nervously when the mood struck!

On the other hand, she wasn't about to let some cocky vampire feel he had gotten the upper hand with her.

Tuesday raced up behind Ethan. "You want to use kisses as weapons?" She shoved him and he spun to face her with a questioning gape. "One thing you need to know about me—I'm always cocked and loaded."

Grabbing his coat lapel, she pulled him in and planted a kiss on his mouth. This one was as unwarranted and desperately seeking as his had been. The man stumbled backward and his shoulders hit a brick wall, and it gave her the opportunity to move in and deepen the kiss.

His hand caught at the base of her spine under her coat, and he pressed her closer to his hard abs and hugged hip-to-hip. And Tuesday forgot that she was angry and let the lust and want rise and play out.

The man's mouth was incredible. His lips were warm and firm, and when their tongues danced she couldn't imagine doing such a tango with anyone else. And she had tangoed with many in her lifetime. Cinnamon mingled with his clean taste, brewing a cocktail more heady than any weird concoction served in a demonic dance club.

But she was kissing him to make a point. And she'd hate to let him think she actually *wanted* this kiss. She did not. Mostly. Yes, she did!

But that was not how she intended to play her hand.

Shoving away from him, Tuesday swept her hair over her shoulder and assumed a cocky stance. "I won that one, vampire."

If a smirk could get any sexier, she didn't know. A few fine wrinkles creased the corners of his eyes, and she even noticed glints of gray strands silvering the hair at his temples. So sexy. Urm, in a completely uninteresting way, of course.

"Sounds fine by me," Ethan said. "You can have the win, partner."

"Right. Partner." She wrinkled her nose at that one. She *had* suggested they could be partners, hadn't she? "About that food?"

"Just up the street, there's a cheesy little bar that might still be open. It's owned by a couple of expats. They serve American food."

Intrigued beyond what she wanted to convey, Tuesday muttered, "Lead the way."

An hour later, Tuesday was full from pulled-pork tacos with pickled jalapeños, and a fruity drink that had a lot of alcohol and even more sugar in it. She would not even require magic to fly now. And Ethan had watched her gobble the food with little more than that constant smirk and a gleam in his eyes.

They were pretty gray eyes, and added a touch of niceness to his usual dour expression. While he was a handsome man, she could tell he dared not show too much. He had been honed and hardened over the centuries. Much as she had been. And she well knew it was never wise to let life play out on her face for others to interpret and use to their advantage.

"How long have you been walking this seriously whacked planet?" she asked as she noisily sucked the last bits of the red slushy drink through the straw. She wasn't drunk, but she was feeling fine.

"Conversation now?"

"Yes. I'm finished stuffing my face. I'm feeling relaxed for the first time since my captivity—" She caught his scoff. "I was in a freakin' cage."

"Fine. I'm sorry, okay? It had to be done. But now you're out, so get over it."

It took a snap of the rubber band not to flip him off.

"What did you ask?" he said. "How old am I?" He lifted his feet and propped them on a nearby wicker chair, leaning back against the wall in the stuffy bar that had announced last call ten minutes after they'd arrived. "I was born in…the 1500s."

"Can't remember the exact year?"

He shrugged. "Early part of the century. We weren't known for marking our birth dates back then."

"Yeah. I was born in the 1640s, give or take a few years. Or decades. I remember at the time it was the great Puritan migration. They sailed to the New World by boatloads from England. All kinds of religious rabble, preaching and condemning. Fur traders and fishers, too. I dated a fisherman once. He smelled. So! That makes you the old man and me the sexy young thang."

"Which should grant me wisdom and you…?"

Tuesday shimmied confidently on the chair. "A chick with a whole lot of experience on every single thing you can imagine."

"It is interesting walking through the ages, isn't it?"

"It is." She teased a finger around the rim of her glass. "You ever get tired of it?"

"Not yet. Immortality suits me."

"Save for the part about drinking all that blood?"

"Coming from a witch who must have consumed how many vampire hearts to keep her immortality over the centuries?"

"Five," she said proudly. In order to maintain im-mortality, a witch had to consume a beating vampire heart once a century. Split the rib cage. Reach in. Feast. And try not to wretch. "Each one of those bastards de-served to die, too."

"And what qualifies as deserving in your book?"

"Assholes. Murderers. And general idiots."

Ethan quirked an eyebrow. "I shall endeavor not to be an asshole or an idiot. At least, not too often."

Tuesday yawned. "You've had a pitiful showing in the trying department. But I won't hold that against you."

"I thought you intended to hold everything that made you uncomfortable against me?"

"Pretty much. But you're lucky I'm tired now. I only got about two winks on your couch. Can we go back to your place? I need to seriously crash and recharge. If I can get some good sleep then I'll be able to think clearly and maybe even stir up a demon-tracking spell."

"Then here's to a well-rested witch."

The witch nodded off within five minutes. Ethan had offered her his bed. It was around the corner in the loft. None of the rooms had separating walls, save bathroom, and he could see the end of the bed from the kitchen. The city lights beamed in through the floor-to-ceiling windows that lined the bedroom area. He'd bought this place for those windows. The view was incredible. He'd wanted to point out Sacré Coeur to her, but she had literally dropped onto the bed and rolled into a snore.

Now, he wondered what their next move should be. And if more kisses would be required to make her com-ply with his wishes. She hadn't needed provoking to kiss him back after he'd initially kissed her. A retaliatory kiss? Bring them on.

And in his next thought, he frowned. He'd kissed a witch. And…he'd liked it.

Chapter 5

A shower had never felt more welcome. Tuesday dried off in the steamy room. The floor and walls were grey marble that was deeply streaked with clear quartz. Gorgeous stonework. And she could feel some of the earth's energies remaining in the stone when she pressed a palm to it, though they were weak. The manufacturing process tended to rape natural stone of most of its essence, but if she took her time, and had the inclination, she could restore its vital energy with an earthing spell.

It was a hell of a lot more than Stuart could do, that was for sure.

"Take that, Stuart."

It was weird to think that an inanimate object was listening in, all the time, waiting for a cue to turn on some function in the apartment. Electronic witchcraft was not her thing. But apparently Ethan was one of those spoiled rich bachelors who could afford life's luxuries. But he didn't seem to flaunt it, with million-dollar wristwatches or fancy suits, so he earned credit for that.

The bathroom was attached to the bedroom, which was open to the rest of the loft. A nice setup, and she suspected the view out the picture window was awesome, were the shades not blocking the bright sunlight now. She hadn't realized how dead tired she had been last night. Her face had hit the pillow. Snores had commenced.

Now she didn't hear Ethan puttering about in the kitchen, but then, why should she? The guy was a vampire. He didn't eat food. But she certainly hoped he played the charming host and either ordered in or found something for her to nosh on.

Fingering her black silk shirt, which revealed a nicely toned tummy, she sighed. She'd worn it for two days straight *and* a long flight across the Atlantic Ocean. She needed clean things to wear. And at the very least, some basic magical accoutrements.

Combing out her hair with Ethan's comb, she then snapped her fingers and whispered, "Dry," and a whoosh of air fluffed up and through the wet strands, instantly drying them. Sometimes Latin wasn't necessary to kick in the magic. Keep it Simple, Stupid was a motto she followed with her spellcraft. She wove her thick hair into a loose side plait and left some in the back hanging free.

Without makeup or a toothbrush she felt out of her element. Not quite in top form. She scanned the insides of the medicine cabinet and spied the wood-handled toothbrush. Nah. She wasn't going to use a vampire's toothbrush. She squirted a blob of toothpaste on her finger and scrubbed the old-fashioned way. Centuries ago, this had been her only option to dental health. That, or use a bit of twig or the corner of some rough suede. It worked. But her kingdom for a dash of dark eye shadow and lip gloss.

"Ugh. Nature witch," she muttered to her reflection. "I should concoct a makeup spell." She tapped her fingernails against the mirror, thinking it odd that a vampire even had one in his home. "Yeah, I'll worry about the lacking glamour later. I've got bigger problems to solve."

Putting the obsidian crystal around her neck, she held it a few moments. Grounding herself. Finding a calm tone for her personal vibration.

Now ready to face whatever adventure the vampire with the attack kisses had in mind for her, she wandered out into the living area. Seated on the leather sofa, Ethan was focused on an iPad, but he nodded over his shoulder and said, "Ran down to the creperie an hour ago when you were still sleeping. Got you some croissants and *pain au chocolat*. Fresh juice, too."

Points for the vampire. But she wouldn't tell him that.

"You mean Stuart is incapable of such errands? Not sure you got your money's worth with that guy," she said gaily.

Sliding onto a bar stool and tearing into the paper bag, Tuesday bit into a still-warm pastry loaded with gooey chocolate. Crisp, thin layers of pastry engulfing sweet, dark chocolate? By the seven sacred witches, it was amazing.

"What are the plans for today?" she asked around chews.

"Thought you could summon the demon. Witches can do that, right?"

"Right, but I can't summon a demon who has marked me. Just doesn't work that way. I can track him, perhaps even locate him, but he's not going to come when I call like a little bitch."

Ethan's sigh echoed across the room. "I thought you'd be more useful."

"Way to boost a chick's confidence. Besides, Edamite Thrash confirmed The Beautiful One wasn't going to come when I call. So get over it, will you? I know what is first on today's list of adventures."

"What's that?"

"Shopping! I can't wander around in this same getup. I mean, I can work it, but I seriously prefer clean clothes. And I need some lip gloss and eye liner. I feel naked without the black stuff."

"Is that going to help you to locate the demon?"

"It will." She turned and fluttered her lashes at him. "Don't you know a woman's power is all in how she feels about herself? When I look good, I do my best."

"I think you look great."

"You're a guy. Guys always say dismissive things like that."

He shook his head and set aside the iPad. "Shopping it is. And then?"

"And then, I also need to pick up some spell supplies. Outfit myself with a makeshift hex-and-spell armory. Then I should be able to set up a grid to map the city of demons. And hopefully, by incorporating the sigil's power, The Beautiful One will stand out on that map."

"Hopefully? I'm going to need more than that. I require assurance."

Tuesday shrugged and bit off another piece of chocolaty pastry. "You get hope from me for now, vamp. Say, do you mind that I used your comb?"

"As long as you didn't use my toothbrush, I don't care."

"What if I did use your toothbrush?"

"We're stopping at a pharmacy, first thing."

The witch could work the tight black jeans and floaty flowered shirt. Her vibe was definitely bohemian, with her thick white hair braided down one side and the furred spangled coat topping it all off. In the pharmacy, she tore open the makeup packaging and performed a quick makeover on herself, fluttering her newly blackened lashes at him and pursing her deep violet lips.

Ethan nodded approval because the sooner she served her personal needs, the quicker he could be done with this stupid stuff and get on to the important work. But he had to admit the deep color she wore on her lips stirred his desires. The violet lipstick emphasized her plump, heart-shaped mouth. He couldn't take his eyes from them. They might taste like sweet grapes warmed under the Tuscan sun.

Yikes. Ethan checked himself. What was he thinking? He was not attracted to a witch. Yes, he was. And what the fuck was that about?

"Come on!" Tuesday skipped ahead, obviously on some kind of spending high.

Ethan kept his credit card handy. Whatever made the witch happy.

Now, she had managed to find a dusty candle shop that opened to a private room in the back that was filled with all the witchy accoutrements he imagined she'd ever need. And while he suspected the shop owner was one of those kitchen witches who spoke incantations from books she'd bought on the internet and thought she was casting spells, she wasn't a real born witch like Tuesday Knightsbridge. And if she knew that the woman buying smudge sticks and candles from her really did possess natural magic, she would be in awe.

Tuesday popped her head out from the back room with a bag full of goodies and winked at Ethan as she wandered by. "Homeward! Stuart waits for us!"

At the very least, he'd gotten a new toothbrush.

Back at his place, Tuesday dropped her shopping booty on the floor by the sofa, tossed her coat on the chair and beelined to the bathroom while he picked up the mess.

Setting her heeled boots on the rug by the door, he then placed the bags neatly on the kitchen counter. He liked a clean, organized home. Which was probably why his few attempts at living with women over the years had failed. Also, the lack of privacy was jarring. Sharing a home with another person was hard work. And since he could have a relationship without moving in with the woman, he chose to stick with what worked.

Although a few relationships here and there, over the centuries, had worked for him. Most had been so long ago he'd forgotten what it felt like or how it had lasted. That wasn't exactly true. A man never forgot the women who had passed through his life. And the current one was moving through like a hurricane intent on settling and spinning about for a while.

"Stuart, be sure to send the vacuum through when next I leave."

The home butler confirmed with a blip on the wall panel and a solid green light. Ethan had programmed it not to return voice reply unless necessary. It wasn't like he needed to talk to the artificial intelligence to make conversation. He used it merely as the maid he liked to have available at all hours of the day, yet didn't want a human stumbling around in his life discovering that he didn't need to sleep and eat. And he'd bitten a maid once. Early nineteenth century? It was best not to drink from the help.

Tuesday returned, flipping her hair over a shoulder, and stretched out on the sofa. "Where's my stuff?"

"On the kitchen counter. You can't leave a trail of bread crumbs wherever you walk."

"I don't need to. We're attached at the hip. If you should lose sight of me, you'll find me soon enough. Bring me my bags."

"Get them yourself." He settled onto the big leather chair with the wide wooden arms. The wood was worn from decades of use and connection to life. And more than a few frenzied bang sessions. "Dazzle me with your witchy magic and this demon map you said you could conjure."

"I don't dazzle on command." She wandered over to the counter and pulled out things from the bags.

"Then how do I get you to dazzle me?" Ethan asked. "Is there a magic word?"

"*Please* seems to work most of the time."

He pressed his fingers to his forehead. He should have left the witch in the cage.

On the other hand, she couldn't hex him and he did need help with this case. He had absolutely no clue how to lure in the demon otherwise, so he would take her sassy mouth and… Well, he'd kiss her again if need be. Heh. That kiss had set her off-kilter.

But the return kiss had surprised him. And then he'd accepted it for the retaliation it had been. *Now* a kiss from those grape-stained lips would give him what he wanted from her. Another taste. A teasing test of his abilities to remain completely unaffected by her charms and attraction.

She had some. Somewhere in that scatter of spangles, sass and black eye shadow.

"Black salt and raven's ash." She waggled between them two vials of a dark substance that she'd purchased from the candle shop. "This will do the trick."

She wandered over and pushed the narrow coffee table up against the sofa. The wide dark-stained plank flooring was the original from when the building had once been a millinery factory. Ethan liked it because he'd known a man who had worked here in the 1920s. He'd taken immense pride in the cut of a woman's hat, or even the specific froth of a silk flower adorning a sweeping brim. He'd also asked Ethan for vampirism after learning that the mercury used to cure the felt for his creations was driving him insane. Ethan had convinced him an insane vampire would be worse than a human prematurely dead from bleeding out.

In all his centuries, Ethan had never created another vampire. And he didn't intend to do so anytime soon. It was too much power to simply give away as if a holiday gift. And besides, he was blood-born, not a created vampire. His breed were superior to those who had been transformed in a back alley or at a lover's lusty request. And he wasn't about to tarnish the line. If he ever desired to procreate, he would have a child, who, depending on its mother's lineage and paranormal species, would very likely be born vampire. He preferred to mate with another vampire, but he wasn't rigid in that stance. Love was actually his key requirement to a happy, lasting relationship.

But love was fickle and…well, he'd take it if it came his way, but he wasn't on a quest to track it down.

Ethan leaned forward to rest his elbows on his knees and watched as Tuesday sprinkled black salt in a pattern before her on the floor. He was curious about witchcraft, and knew it was powerful. No man should mess with a witch. But he was feeling cocky with the protective bind against her. So long as it lasted until they found the demon.

Leaning over the scattered salt, which designed a pentagram inside a circle, Tuesday closed her eyes and spread her arms wide. She chanted words that Ethan would never try to decipher. Witch words. Dangerous words. Yet he could feel them forming sentences in his veins, warning that she could take him out if he dropped his guard.

With a snap of her fingers, the salt suddenly illuminated and jittered on the floor, moving, ordering and aligning. The tiny grains jumped and crackled. The scent of salt tinged the air. And when it settled and continued to glow, Tuesday sat back on her heels, hands propped on each thigh.

"A map of Paris," she said with a gesture over the salt. "What do you think?"

Ethan leaned over to inspect the map. It included both the right and left bank, and the Seine and the main island. It even showed faint demarcations for the twenty arrondissements. "You've dazzled me, witch. Now where are all the demons? Or just the one in particular?"

"That requires more intense chanting. And an elemental callout. You stay there. Don't move, because I don't want the bond between us to tug me out of concentration. Deal?"

"I am a captive audience."

She looked at him a moment, and he couldn't decide if she thought she was peering into an idiot's eyes or, in fact, seeing beyond his irises and into his very soul. He'd witnessed it when she'd peered into Certainly Jones's soul. Was it a skill they could only perform on other witches? Or need he worry, too?

"What?" he finally asked.

"There's something about you, Ethan Pierce. Something that keeps me from stabbing you through the heart with this athame." She twirled the knife she'd bought from the store. The hilt looked to be carved from opal. That was why the bill had registered in the hundreds of euros. "I'm not sure what that is, though, so I'm going to keep the blade close."

"Whatever works for you. You couldn't harm me if you tried."

"Probably not. But you are racking up the points against you for when the bond is lifted. Know that."

"I'm not afraid of a witch."

Her head tilted and her gaze narrowed as she said simply, "You should be."

And Ethan realized she was right. But he wouldn't show his anxiety.

Casting her focus over the salt map, she moved up on her knees, spread out her arms and began to chant.

* * *

Tuesday felt the presence of every demon inhabiting the city prick at her skin. It wasn't pleasant, but it wasn't painful, either. Rather a sort of vehement and inner knowing. The elemental spell had been successful. She opened her eyes and looked over the map.

Ethan kneeled on the opposite side of the map and scanned the results as well. "What are all the glowing red salt crystals?"

"Demons," she said.

"There's so many. Thousands."

"Are you surprised?"

"No. But how is this going to help our search?"

"Hold your horses, big boy. The real magic comes next."

Tugging loose the ribbon ties at the bodice of her new shirt, Tuesday tossed the obsidian crystal over her shoulder and then pressed her fingers against the sigil between her breasts. She lowered her other hand over the map, moving methodically as she silently thought Gazariel's name. The sigil warmed and she could feel the tendrils of it creep through her chest and toward her extremities. It noticed her.

And that was not a good thing.

Wanting to abruptly end the spell, she suddenly noted the violet glow at one edge of the map. "There! Where is that?"

Ethan turned his head to assess the map. "Looks like the Bois de Boulogne. A big, forested park at the edge of the city. Is that purple spot The Beautiful One?"

"It is. And now I'm cutting the connection before he catches on."

"Wait!"

Tuesday pulled her fingers from the sigil. The violet light snuffed out.

"If you would have held on longer, I could have marked the exact location," Ethan protested. "That would have made our job easier. Are you helping me or hindering me, witch?"

"What do you think I'm doing? You think I enjoy being your captive? I want this over as quickly as possible. But I will not call the demon directly to me. He could manifest within me. And then what will you do?"

"That can happen?"

"It's likely. But remember what Edamite said. If he's smart he's not going to come near me. And he is."

"Sorry. I, uh… I don't intend to place you in harm's way. I just want to utilize your expertise."

"And this, eh?" She tapped the sigil.

"Can I take a look at that?"

She studied his curious gaze. He wasn't aware that a childlike wonder could overtake his normally serious expression. Nor could he be aware how much that relaxation of his outer shield attracted her. Because it made him everything he probably didn't want to be— soft, kind, accepting.

Tuesday nodded her consent.

Ethan reached over and pressed two fingers to the sigil. It was an intimate touch and her skin warmed. Her breasts hugged his knuckles. He flicked his wondrous gaze onto hers.

"I can feel your fear," he said. "I don't want you to be afraid. I will protect you."

Tuesday wrapped her fingers about his wrist, holding him there at her breast. "There's nothing a vampire can do to protect me that I can't already do myself. You're going to have to make a better plea for my continuing to work with you than that."

"All right. How about this?"

And with that, he slid over the salt map, smearing the left bank of Paris, and cupped the back of her head as he pulled her in for another sudden kiss.

His mouth warmed against hers and demanded she not ignore him. That she allow him to protect her. And at the same time, it teased her to submit in a way she generally didn't care to with a man. It was the surprise of their connection, their easy manner of locking lips, that excited her, and made her want to not break it.

On her knees, Tuesday scooched closer. He slipped one hand down her hair and clasped his fingers into it, easing her forward, into his arms. Into his interesting acceptance. She'd thought he didn't like witches. So why was he kissing her?

Did it matter? Not in this moment. She wanted to taste every sensual, hot bit of him. Inhale his cool, fresh-air scent, and every breath that he greedily gave and took from her. Moaning into his mouth, she grabbed at his shirt and straddled his legs with hers. They kneeled there on the scattered remains of the city map, a strange fusion of opposites who couldn't resist the pull to experience one another.

And when he put his hand again on the sigil, she moved his fingers to cup her breast. She hugged up against him, giving him permission to touch her, wanting to own the vampire's desire… To control him as he sought to control her.

Ethan broke the kiss and pulled his hand abruptly from her skin. "Uh…"

Appearing befuddled, he probably wasn't sure why

he'd kissed her. And had manhandled her boob. So she wouldn't let him consider it too long. Because if she had to use normal skills instead of magic to control him, it was best to keep him unsure and wondering.

"Feel like a walk in the park?" she asked.

"Sure. I um…"

She stood and knotted the ties of her shirt into a bow. "Then let's get to it before I shove you down and have some hex with you."

She'd let him ponder the use of that word for what she really wanted to do to him. The man had ignited something within her. And she had never been a witch to deny herself the pleasures life offered.

Chapter 6

Parked at the curb, Ethan waited for Tuesday while she purchased food from a stand. He didn't use the BMW often because he walked to work even in the winter. Vampires could easily regulate their body temperature. But the trip to the park would prove long on foot, and he didn't want the witch to suffer the cold, especially walking in those high-heeled boots.

Tuesday slid in and closed the door and settled back to chomp on a savory-smelling crepe.

"You want a bite? It's got weird French cheese and ham in it. This is amazing."

"I'd rather suck dead blood," he muttered.

"Oh, yeah? What's wrong with a little taste once in a while? I know vampires can eat small amounts of food."

"I don't have a taste for meat. I get enough of the flavor when I drink blood. And you just dripped fontina onto the leather seat. Would you be careful?"

"Fontina, eh? Don't tell me you don't steal a taste every now and then." She swiped a napkin over the seat and then leaned forward, pointing. "That's the— What is it?"

"The Louvre," he pronounced carefully.

"Louv-ra, with the ra-ra shout at the end," she mocked. "You're not French, are you?"

"I'm English. Born in London, actually, but I didn't stay there more than a decade. I've lived everywhere. Spent some time in the Americas in the 1700s. Right around the time Massachusetts became a state."

"Good times," she said, sitting back. "Puritanical shame, Indian genocide and witch hunts. Go, witch hunters! Not."

Ethan shouldn't have brought that up. If she knew about the travesties he'd committed against witches when he had been a young vampire only set on impressing his tribe leaders? He'd be very thankful for the binding spell that prevented her from using magic against him.

"Have you been in Paris before?" he asked.

"Once or twice. Never for longer than a month or two. And never in a mood to do any touristing. Once I was here looking for a bastard imp who stole my voice. Little creep isn't singing or snickering anymore. What's that?"

"The Luxor Obelisk." Ethan drove by the seventy-five-foot-high yellow granite obelisk placed in the center of the Place de la Concorde at the end of the Tuileries Garden. "Originally located at the Luxor Temple in Egypt—a gift from Muhammad Ali Pasha, the ruler of Egypt at the time."

"You know the city's history."

"I've lived it. Of all my centuries, I've spent the most time in Paris. And up ahead is the Champs-élysées."

"Oh, I know that's a good shopping street. Should have waited to get my togs up ahead." She scanned the signs screaming for customers to come in and spend their precious euros. They passed luxury-car dealers and high-end clothing retailers. And… "There's a Mc-Donalds on the classy upscale shopping street?"

"And movie rental stores," Ethan said. "Go figure. It's all a big tourist trap. But then, this street has been ever since Napoleonic times."

"More good times," Tuesday offered. "The Inquisition was still around then. You gotta love a self-righteous maniac intent on destroying that which he does not understand. And if it's a woman, then even more reason to put her in her place."

"Do you remember any good times that were actually good?"

"Oh, sure. I loved the late nineteenth century. So bohemian. We witches really got to shine then. The seventies and the hippies also welcomed us with open arms. What's that? Wait! I know this one."

Ethan stopped the car at a light before he would enter the roundabout before the monument.

"The arch of triumph, right?"

"Right." He wouldn't correct her too harshly. "Napoleon's Arc d'Triomphe, erected to honor those who served in the Revolutionary and Napoleonic wars. There's a tomb of an unknown soldier beneath it. If you go to the top it offers a great view of the whole city."

"Then let's do it. Yeah?"

"After the demon is found you can take all the time you like for sightseeing."

"Because then you'll cut my leash and set me free?"

He didn't like hearing it put that way, but it was the truth. "Exactly."

Ten minutes later they pulled in to the park, which was massive and filled with sports areas, a zoo and playgrounds, housing and entertainment complexes. And yet there was still a preserved forested area, an oasis set at the border of the big, cosmopolitan city. A light dusting of snow clung to the trees, giving the forest a faery-tale touch as sun twinkled on the snow.

Ethan parked in a lot before a hiking trail. He kept the car running because the witch would probably appreciate the heat. He pulled on his blue-lensed sunglasses. He could walk in direct sunlight a few minutes without feeling the burn, and much longer in the winter sun. And these lenses were also charmed to view wards, which served as more than a means to protection from sizzling retinas.

"What's the plan?" Tuesday asked. "Are we going to tromp about the park and call 'Here, demon, come on, demon!'"

"Won't that sigil you wear lead us to him?"

"Right." She touched her chest and closed her eyes. "Or him to me. Not that he'd come running with arms wide open to embrace me."

Ethan sensed she plummeted to some place very low whenever she touched the sigil. He had to ask. "Tell me how you got the sigil? It could be helpful to know what I'm dealing with here."

"*Now* you decide to ask about the stakes? You are so not a romantic, vampire."

"What does romance have to do with anything?"

"Nothing." She crossed her arms over her chest and averted her gaze out the window. "Kisses don't have any place between us, either."

"I beg to differ. They have proven a useful tool for me."

"Again, not a romantic bone in your body, eh?"

"What? Do you require emotion, some feeling next time I kiss you?"

"You think you're going to kiss me again?"

"Probably."

She turned on the seat to look at him. "Why? Do you like kissing me?"

"It was pleasant." He sounded like an asshole, but what was she angling for right now with that teasing question? The woman was a curiously complex mixture of opposites. One minute she was trying to put a hex on him to make his dick limp, the next she wanted to make out. "Do *you* want to kiss me again?"

She sat up, lifting her chin haughtily. "You haven't been kissed by me yet, vampire. When I kiss you properly? You'll know. And you'll never have to wonder if you want another again. Because you will. You'll crave my kiss, my touch. You'll want to hex me every chance you get."

Ethan offered a shrug. "Have to say, that does sound intriguing."

"Damn right it does. So we heading out on the demon quest?"

"First, I need the details." He pushed back his seat

and tilted to face her comfortably. Taking off the sunglasses, he asked, "Tell me how you got Gazariel's sigil."

Boston, MA—1680

Finnister McAdams was going blind. He wore a black strip of sack cloth across his eyes now because he had explained to Tuesday how the light bothered him. Made him blink and gave him headaches. 'Twas as if the devil was prodding his eyes with his mighty pitchfork.

Tuesday knew well the Devil Himself did not wield a pitchfork, but to correct him would only put her in danger. She'd prepared Finn an herbal tincture in his morning tea. Rosemary, black salts and feverfew. Had cast a healing spell…without him knowing. Even laid mustard plasters over his eyes. Nothing proved efficacious.

Now she considered calling up a demon to aid in healing her lover's eyes. Such creatures did possess healing powers. At least, a few of them did so. If only the witch summoning them could find a beneficent demon. And that was the challenge.

Tuesday loved her man, Finn. From the moment he'd settled next to her in the lavender field and compared her eyes to the sky, she had loved him desperately. Three months they had been sharing her tiny cabin at the edge of the village with one another. Finn was strong and proud, and very handsome. His hair was copper, his thick beard as well. His skin was ruddy and pale, so he always wore a wide-brimmed hat when outside. He was fashioned of flame and earth. And when he held her in his arms it wasn't tentative or rough. He knew how to hold a woman. And Tuesday's heart fluttered when he kissed her.

But if he knew she was a witch he would be displeased. The man was Puritan. His family had sailed across the Atlantic Ocean from England six months earlier. His father was seeking a congregation to share and spread the word of God. And Finnister, while a godly man, seemed more inclined to craftwork that involved turning wood into beautiful creations. He even fashioned lovely knife hilts, and had skill with a blade.

With the witch trials and all the heinous accusations running rampant of late, Tuesday did not dare reveal her truth to her lover. Because even if he could accept her, she risked the townsfolk putting him on trial for harboring her secret.

But she could no longer bear to see him stumble about the house, seeking wood for the stove and instead stabbing his fingers into the log pile and yelping as slivers cut through his skin. Or to watch him try to piss in the chamber pot and instead spray the stone floor.

She would care for him. Because she loved him.

But she must try one last thing before giving up on his healing. And that required she summon a demon. She wasn't schooled in demons, didn't know which to summon for the healing of sight, but would take whatever beast she could conjure. Surely, even a lowly demon might have some healing skills. And she had a way of winning a man's trust with her gentle confidence and attentive manner.

Shouldn't be so different with demons.

So just before midnight, on a hot summer's eve, she kissed Finn's forehead as he snoozed before the window, and snuck out with her cotton bag of charms and potions under her arm. Her wood-soled clogs took the soft red earth in quick strides and she was thankful for the fast-growing moss that muffled her steps. She would avoid the gatekeepers, and slip into the forest half a mile from the village. It was a haunted forest, or rumors told, so that kept out most villagers.

All except those who knew better. Like her. The forest was a thin place where the realm of Daemonia overlapped this mortal realm. Summoning a demon would be as simple as snapping her fingers. And having the fortitude to do so.

Tuesday had lived nearly forty years, and had honed her magical skills in privacy and under the tutelage of some powerful aunts and good women. She had eaten a vampire's heart to secure immortality and a youthful appearance—at least, for another century—and had cast down the moon and summoned healings and utilized the natural elements to move through life.

She was not like those women who were being accused in the trials. Women who had knowledge of female anatomy and tried to heal and teach others. They were merely humans who sought to educate and save. But the menfolk would not condone a smart woman living in their midst. Females were to submit and serve. And they used them as cat's-paws and accused them of witchery. Anything to subdue and make them submissive.

Of course, Tuesday could be thankful for the distraction of that wayward and unprofessional witchery. It kept most eyes from her, a true witch. And she was wise enough not to share her skills with anyone who had not been vetted to her by a witch elder. Even when Finn slyly questioned if she would ever attempt witchcraft, she laughed and told him he was silly. It was something she imagined most every woman in the village had been asked. Men were suspicious creatures. Their fear of losing control to what they deemed a *mere* woman made them so.

A woman would do well to learn how to control such irresponsible creatures—men. And she was teaching herself that by learning all that she could about herself, her body, nature and the universe. Strength came with wisdom and knowledge.

But tonight she would reach beyond her own capabilities in a quest to save her lover's sight.

Once deep in the forest, she did not light a candle. She didn't wish discovery by hunters. Drawing out a pentagram with black salt on the leaf-crusted forest floor, she spoke the invocation to summon a demon. The surprise she felt when one appeared made her step back and clutch the smoky quartz she wore from a leather strap about her neck for protection. He stood within the circle, but posed gallantly beside a thick oak, elbow propped high to lean against it.

His eyes glowed red, so she knew he was demon. But otherwise he looked a human, dressed in a fine blue silk frock coat, shot through with silver threading, and with lace dripping around his wrists and at his neck. Such finery belonged only to royalty. She had seen Pandora dolls imported from Europe wearing such elaborate silks. And his hair was long and wavy and black as midnight. He smelled...of lilacs. A pretty man—demon—if she was to size him up. And that notion startled her. Should not demons be more creature-like? Horned and possessed of red or black skin with claws? This demon's handsome appearance was disconcerting, to say the least.

"Who are you?" she asked, a bit too timidly for her comfort. So she set back her shoulders and lifted her chin. Courage hummed in her bones. "Have you come from Daemonia?"

"You don't even know who you've summoned? What a sorry witch you are!" The demon tugged out the lace from the end of one sleeve. "Daemonia is the last place I should ever tread. I am of this realm. And I am Gazariel, The Beautiful One."

Tuesday knew demons often went by monikers, and that one was right on the nose. Beautiful, indeed. And he seemed to believe it himself, judging by his mannerisms. Primping and preening. Not a wrinkle to the silk, nor a hair out of place. Was that rouge on his pale cheeks?

She tested the binding on the summons and did not feel a weakness in the air. He could not approach her, and if he tried, the circle should keep him in check.

"I need your help," she said. "With a healing."

The demon rolled his eyes and shook his head sadly. "Bother. Always with the sicknesses! And here I thought you might request I attend the next village soiree and impregnate a dozen virgins with my demon babies." He gestured dismissively. "You're boring, witch."

"My lover is going blind. You can kiss his eyes and give him sight."

"Of course I can." He rubbed his fingernails against the embroidery edging his silk lapels. "We demons have such skills. Most of us, anyway. I would not dare to ask a wrath demon for some delicate brain trephination, though, mind you. What is this lover's name?"

"Finnister McAdams. His sight is almost completely gone. He is a kind man. And so young. He is strong and contributes all that he can to the village. If you could see to healing him, I would be ever grateful."

"Release me," the demon said.

Tuesday's spine stiffened. She was no fool. "Not until you give me what I ask."

"I can't go near the man unless you unbind me, now can I?" He splayed his lace-encircled hand toward the circle on the ground.

That was true. He did need to move about freely. And she could hardly lead Finn here to the forest to receive what healing magic the demon could provide. Such had to be managed with cunning.

"You'll follow me home and attend to him while he sleeps?"

"He doesn't know you're a witch? Of course not. You may be a bore but you are not stupid. Take down the circle. I'll see what I can do. And in turn, I'll ask a favor from you."

"Which is?"

He shrugged and flipped out a hand to display the lace grandly. "I'll decide on that after the task is complete."

A favor to a demon? It was only fair to reciprocate. But she wasn't sure what she could do for him. And she had no intention of having one of his demon babies. Well. She could not. Her womb was barren. She'd known that for decades. A condition she'd been born with, according to a wise witch who had gazed into her soul and seen her birth.

With trepidation, Tuesday slashed a foot through the salt circle. The demon disappeared instantly, leaving her alone in the dark woods. An owl hooted, chastising her with his repeated tones.

"I have been a fool! He will never give me what I want. I should have offered him a gift immediately. Given him reason to want to help me."

And what would the creature demand of her should he serve her wishes? It would never be good, she felt sure.

"It is a sacrifice I am willing to make," she muttered and turned to wander back to the village.

By the time she returned home, she saw the demon standing outside her door. His pale blue frock coat was an unwanted beacon in the darkness, and in a village where the only colors worn were black, brown and gray.

She rushed up to him. "What are you doing here? You can't be seen!"

"Oh, Tuesday Knightsbridge, you sad, pitiful witch." He placed a hand over her chest, right between her breasts, and Tuesday felt a searing pain but she could not step away from the demon. "Your lover lies to you. I came here to find him returning from the forest. He followed you. Watched you and I. He knows. And he is not going blind. His sight is as perfect as yours or mine."

"No, that's—"

"That's a foolish witch for you," the demon said piteously. "And you have fallen in love with a witch hunter. Ha!"

The searing at her chest now burned as if in flames.

Then her front door opened, and Finn spilled out with hell blazing in his eyes. He looked right at her. Saw her for what she was. Finn snarled, "Witch!"

The torture began the next day. The water chair was the one that siphoned all Tuesday's gumption from her.

She was tied to a chair on the end of a seesaw and repeatedly dunked into the filthy, muddy river. Each time she was lifted above water, gasping, choking, pleading for Finn to stop, she was commanded to confess to being a witch and consorting with demons.

She would not. She would survive this. Somehow.

Later, the whip that flayed at her skin left deep gashes, and caused Tuesday to pass out more than a few times. Hot pokers to her hips and between her toes almost made her confess. Almost.

After four days of suffering her lover's vicious, hateful punishments, Tuesday was lying on the cold, hard dirt floor on a tiny cell at the edge of the village. No moonlight on this night of the new moon. On the other side of the building, the village pigs snorted and rooted, and filled the air with a nauseating odor that she breathed as if a toxin.

All vitality had been beaten out of her. Even the will to live had been vanquished with a humiliating search of her private body parts in search of devil's marks. Finn had done so before a dozen village elders. All men. All leering. If she'd the strength she would have cast a spell over them all, reducing them to stupid, foul, snorting pigs like those outside her cell. Alas, she'd expelled all her energies with a breathing spell during the dunking.

She would be dead by morning. Her tattered heart told her as much. And she sighed with acceptance.

When the flash of red light flickered in the cell and she scented a brief fragrance of lilacs, she tried to lift her head to look at the demon, but the flay marks along her neck pained her with every subtle movement.

The demon's silk, red-heeled shoes were but inches from her face. "Men are terrible, yes?"

Indeed. And yet, she was not prepared to condemn them all. Her father had been a good man. And the village baker, who she knew was married to a witch whom he protected, was also kind. "Not all of them."

"You're right. It is love that is so vile. Can't be trusted. Merely a means to trick and use innocence. And you have been thoroughly used, my witch."

Indeed. Why had the demon returned? To rub her failures into her open wounds? Or did he still require she serve him something in return? He hadn't healed Finn, for the man hadn't required any healing.

The demon bowed low and the tickle of his hair across her cheek smelled sweet and too luxurious. "I can give you something that you'll find most useful."

"Leave me to die, demon."

"Do not address me so. It is vulgar. I am The Beautiful One."

She could but close her eyes tightly and wish death would quicken its pace.

"I carry a curse," Gazariel continued. "But I don't need it. Or want it. And you can have it if you'll willingly accept it."

A curse? Why ever would she ask for a curse?

By some means, Tuesday managed to roll to her back. The red light surrounding him illuminated her cell. Her tormentor looked down over her. Pity from a demon? She'd thought being held under the river waters for long minutes had been her lowest. Gazariel's pouting mouth reduced her to less than that low.

"If I am dead," she whispered, "curse or not, it will not matter."

"Oh, you're going to live, witch. I will make sure of that. The question is, do you want to walk this earth a wise, smart, powerful witch who will never again be defeated by love?"

The demon placed his palm between her breasts. And Tuesday felt a darkness tickle into her heart.

"What is the curse?" she asked.

He leaned in and whispered in her ear, and his voice was melodious and warming. "You will never know true love again. Your soul will repel it, and even should it occur, the moment your lover realizes he loves you he will suddenly hate you. Perhaps even suffer a cruel malady or some such," he added offhandedly.

Such a curse actually sounded sweet and tempting. She was lying here, near death, because of love. Fickle, cruel love. And she wanted the demon to save her. No one ever wanted to die. And she wasn't singular for wishing it so. Even for the sacrifice of accepting such a deal. To never again know love? To feel the pain of what love could do to her?

To live so that she could walk away from the bastard Finnister McAdams and all those men who had wounded her soul deep?

With a nod, she said, "I'll take the curse."

The demon lifted her under the chin, dragging her body to sit up. With a forceful shove, Tuesday's back hit the cell wall and she screamed at the pain as the sigil seared into her skin.

Gazariel apported out of the tiny cell. And she did not see him ever again.

Chapter 7

That was a heavy past to carry in one's baggage. Ethan rubbed his jaw and shook his head. "I'm sorry."

A smirk to send away the horrible remembrance of the pain she had endured at her lover's hand was all Tuesday could manage. "Don't be. I took the curse willingly."

"To never have love?"

She shrugged. "It was a means to escape the torture and to live."

"But you can't still want such a thing?"

She shrugged and looked aside. Ethan's heart shivered as it had when she'd described the awful torture she'd endured at the hands of a witch hunter, a man she had loved.

He knew what it felt like to wield the whip. Never against a witch, of course. Their blood could have killed him back in the days when such violence had been acceptable, a means to survival. As a young vampire in his tribe, he'd been tested, asked to prove his alliances, most especially during the Blood Wars that had seen his tribe fighting the werewolves. Never had he regretted those acts more than now. Yet to mention it would not win any trust from the witch.

Could his actions since she'd arrived in Paris be construed as a subtle torture, a form of control? Surely. Hell, he didn't want to think about this too much. It would only stifle the mission. He had to focus on the task at hand. Her tale was sad, but she had survived, and seemed the stronger for it.

She'd been punished for caring about another man. By a seemingly selfish and narcissistic demon, who had cursed her only because he could. And yet, she had willingly taken his dark curse in a moment of such weakness she could not have known the impact it would have on her. No one would wish to never know love. Even he, who was jaded by love, would take it if the time was right and his heart leaped.

"We can't wander about the forest calling out for the demon," she said as a means to indicate she was finished talking about her history.

The demon had taken advantage of her.

Now more than ever Ethan wanted to find that bastard, and once he gave up the book with the code, then Ethan would banish him to Daemonia, never to return. Was there a possibility he could have Gazariel take back the curse from Tuesday? With the forced expulsion to Daemonia, all curses, hexes and otherwise foul doings would be erased in the demon's wake. She could be freed if he found the demon and kicked him the hell out of the mortal realm.

"You're right about wandering around without a clear direction." He started the engine and the car heater roared up again. "Tell me what to do."

With a heavy sigh, she pointed behind her. "I think he's probably living in one of those fancy apartments we passed. I mean, he's not living in a tree. The man can obviously walk and live amongst the mortals without suspicion, like all the other demons that showed up on my map. They hold jobs, they live and love, they pass for human."

"As we all do."

"Exactly. So, I need to cast a GPS spell and that should lead us in the right direction."

"A GPS spell? Like the map you cast at my place?"

"This one is more advanced. A witch has got to evolve with the technology, yeah?"

A witch, a vampire and every other paranormal species. The mortal realm was not designed for their sort. At least regarding being out and vocal about who and what they were. His species did what they had to do to survive.

"What do you need to cast such a spell?"

"Your cell phone, and the demon's sigil. And a couple drops of blood."

About to ask why they couldn't use *her* phone, Ethan remembered she'd been taken from a bar in Massachusetts, with little more than her clothes and shoes. She probably didn't have a phone.

He tugged the phone from his pocket and before he handed it to her, he asked, "Is this going to brick my phone?"

"Nah." She grabbed it and tapped the home button. "Maybe? No. I don't know. I've never tried it before. I'm only just learning tech spells. But you're rich. You can afford another."

"What makes you think I'm rich?"

"You're driving a Bimmer. And that apartment with the stunning view had to set you back a couple million."

So he was well off. That happened when a vampire took care to invest over the centuries and kept a healthy portfolio across various international markets and banks. Tech stocks were a gold mine. His accountant was a vampiress who lived near the Eiffel Tower, and she was a gem.

"Just don't set it on fire," he said.

"I won't. I think. Maybe?" She winked at him. "I do have water magic in case of emergency."

Her mood had lifted since she'd told him her tale, and he was grateful for that. Though he'd never discount anyone's suffering. There had been occasions he'd been hunted over the centuries—by slayers and werewolves—but nothing could compare to being caught and tortured. And to live to tell about it.

Tuesday set the phone on the raised center console between them and opened up her coat to tug free the ribbons at her shirt front. Those full breasts were a sweet tease, and Ethan had to remind himself he was on a mission. His attention swerved from her breasts to her lips, and back again.

Hell yes, he'd kiss her again. But thinking that made him wince as he sensed a swift boner could give him up. And the last thing he wanted to do with this witch was prove to her that he was the Richard she'd accused him of being.

"Got a knife?" she asked and extended her forefinger toward him. "I left my athame at your place."

Ethan stared at the finger and all lusty thoughts were replaced by sudden horror. Maybe that limp-dick spell had a delay set on it because he was no longer hard. Because what she asked...

She needed blood for the magic. Blood magic was wicked and he'd known a lot of it might be needed on this adventure. He knew better than to challenge it, or try to interfere with it. But what should he expect from a dark witch?

"No knife," he said.

"Then take a bite, yeah?" She waggled her finger before him. "I just need a couple drops."

"Take a bite?" Aghast at her moxie, he shook his head in bewilderment. "What the hell?"

"Seriously, vampire? Just prick my finger with one of your fangs. Come on, you want to find this demon or not?"

Tonguing the insides of his upper teeth, he met her assessing stare, which wasn't so much aggressive as impatient. She was trying to cast a spell with the tools she had to work with. Yet a taste of blood could do *things* to him. Things that would bring up his erection again. He shouldn't make a big deal out of it.

Fuck, this woman challenged him on so many levels. He'd not expected this mission to become fraught with...emotion and utter mental challenge.

But he would not reveal his consternation. If he'd learned anything about Tuesday Knightsbridge, seeing him in a quandary would make her too happy.

Fangs lowering, he grabbed her wrist and pierced her finger with the pin-sharp tip of one of them. Blood scent curled into his nostrils. It was more alluring than the usual quick bite's coppery, chemical-laced blood. This blood was deep, thick and steeped with the centuries.

He quickly shoved her hand away so the temptation would not drip onto his tongue.

Tuesday squeezed a couple drops onto the iPhone screen. She glanced at him. "You okay, vamp? Not going to attack me in a raging blood hunger?"

"I am perfectly capable of being around blood without turning into a monster." Turning into a horny flesh-pricker, on the other hand? When had he last smelled such…tempting blood?

"Good for you." She stuck her finger in her mouth and sucked at it. "Holster those fangs then, will you? Makes me nervous."

"Really?" He leaned forward, brandishing his fangs boldly. "You scared I'll attack?"

"No, I just like the bite too much."

Startled by that reply, he sat back. Was she a fang junkie? He'd thought only humans succumbed to such base lust for the bite. It was the orgasmic sensations the bite delivered. Such highs could become a drug. Some humans could not get enough.

She winked at him. Ethan willed his fangs to rise to their normal positions.

"Hey, it's as good for the bite-ee as it is for the biter," she said. "You know that. So! Let's get this spell going, yeah?"

Sure. But it was difficult now *not* to think about clasping her long white hair in his hand as he breathed against her neck, dripping with blood. It would taste like the world and all he had lived through. And such memories were both sweet and sour.

Tuesday drew the demon's S-shaped sigil on the phone screen with the blood. A line was drawn through that, connecting both curves. The GPS app was open, he noticed, and now he found it easier to turn his attention to what she was doing instead of slipping into a lusty fantasy of slurping at her neck and making her come with nothing more than the bite.

Pressing her bloodied finger to the sigil between her breasts, Tuesday bowed her head and began to chant. The air in the car grew throat-clutchingly humid, and then it took on an icy chill that hardened his sinuses before returning to normal. Ethan coughed. The phone jittered. The blood purled and rose in droplets, reaching for the hand Tuesday held but inches from the phone. And the scent swarmed Ethan's senses and pushed him headfirst into the unavoidable fantasy.

She would taste old and ancient, laced with centuries of experience. He could sup at her, drain her of her magic... A vampire could steal a witch's power by enacting bloodsexmagic. It required having sex with the witch while drinking her blood and enacting a spell. He'd never thought to do something so wicked. Until now.

A snap of fingers stirred Ethan back to the now. "What?"

"Where were you, vampire?"

In a heated embrace with a witch who could give him so much more than he'd ever dreamed to have.

"Sorry, got lost for a minute there."

"Oh, yeah? Are you aroused?"

He tilted his head, sneering. "You think a few drops of blood is enough to get me horny?"

She shrugged. "I do. Truth be told, I'm feeling it. I mean, like I said, fangs do it for me. Seriously."

Ethan ran his tongue under the tip of one fang. Oh, the serious action he could show her. But he wasn't a fool. And he was a man on a mission. "Did it work?"

"I got a hit." She tapped the phone. "Looks like he's north about a quarter of a mile."

The twosome got out of the car. Ethan scanned their surroundings. Beyond a copse of ancient oak trees rose a gated community that likely sheltered old money and self-made tech millionaires.

"You ever break and enter?" he asked.

"I don't think I should answer that one." Tuesday shrugged up her coat and then shook her hands out at her sides as if preparing for a gunfight. "But whatever fun you're planning? I'm in!"

Attempting to enter a gated community in full daylight was probably not the wisest move, but Tuesday was in it to win it. Besides, she wanted to see if Ethan had a plan. He didn't have a plan. She knew it. But she'd give him the benefit of the doubt. Until he failed, and she'd have an argument for her release and could be done with him.

Telling him about her past hadn't been a problem. She held no emotion for the stupid witch she'd once been. Smarter, wiser, she now did better because she knew better. And she hadn't been looking for sympathy from the vampire, though she'd felt it rise off him in the car. Whatever.

She'd revealed her curse, but she would never tell him the ridiculous means to break that curse. That was a secret she'd take to her grave. Besides, knowing it would keep it from ever happening.

They'd parked a block down from the black wrought-iron gates and now strolled casually along the hornbeam hedgerow that grew eight feet high. Hands shoved in his coat pockets, the vampire kept a keen eye from behind the sexy blue sunglasses. Not many were out walking because the day was chilly.

One small reason to be thankful—when she'd been kidnapped she'd been wearing her alpaca coat. She loved this thing, and it was warm.

The vampire looked…cold. His coat was short, stopping below his waist, and revealed a nice tight ass that was emphasized perfectly by the dark jeans. If the fangs in the car hadn't started her engine, that view certainly revved it to a wanting purr.

To do the guy or not? Everything about his controlling authority screamed *no, run away!* And everything else, from the fangs to the sexy smile, begged her to give him a chance. One more kiss. One good fuck. A no-strings hex-fest of nudity, fangs and orgasms unending.

Tuesday suddenly bumped right in to Ethan, who had stopped walking for some odd reason.

"Really?" he murmured. "I thought witches had a built-in sixth-sense kind of thing. Were you walking with your eyes closed?"

"My sixth sense isn't tuned to idiots," she responded. Good save. She'd been thinking about his fangs in her neck and how strong of an orgasm that would give her. If her tale of taking the curse wasn't enough to remind her what a fool she could be for a handsome smile then…whew!

The entry gate was twenty feet ahead. Time to pull on her stern witch and focus. "What's the plan?"

"I don't have a plan."

"I knew it."

"Why not just stroll in?" Ethan asked.

"Awesome. The direct approach, it is. Let's see you work your skills, vampire."

"I've got skills." And with that he strode toward the small, freestanding office situated next to the entry gate. He cast her a smirk over his shoulder.

And Tuesday was all in with the tease. She hastened her steps, following him like a witch to the lying witch hunter.

Inside the outhouse-sized office situated before the gate, a man pushing ninety lifted his chin and eyed their approach. He shook his head, obviously not recognizing Ethan, and said, "We don't allow solicitors, monsieur. Move along."

Ethan slid his hand through the small space beneath the protective Plexiglas window and smiled charmingly. "This won't take long."

The old man shoved at Ethan's hand, but then all of a sudden his fingers shook and he dropped them onto Ethan's palm. The vampire clasped his fingers and said calmly, "We're here to visit friends. Won't be long. You won't remember us, nor will you consider anything out of the ordinary. Open the gates, please."

Dropping the old man's hand and stepping back to stand next to Tuesday, Ethan waited while the gates swung inward.

"Nice." She marched forward, giving the gatekeeper a thumbs-up as she did. "Persuasion?"

"I can convince a man to jump into flames," he said

as he passed her by and wandered along the edge of the curbed and curved drive.

The road was bare of snow and Tuesday assumed it had heat coils beneath, for she could sense the electric vibrations as she walked it. Ethan's steps moved faster and all of a sudden she was tugged along against her will.

"Damn binding spell." She picked up her pace.

There had to be a way to crack the bond open. For as intriguing as it was to follow Mr. Tight Pants, she could not abide this humiliation for much longer. This was one curse she had not asked for.

Ethan paused before the garage entrance. To each side of the underground lot stood a massive four-story complex that stretched longer than a football field in each direction.

"Now what?" she asked.

"What's your tracker say?"

She checked the GPS on his phone. One tiny blood drop moved over the screen as they had walked. "He's to the left."

And her heart dropped as she realized she could be so close to the one demon she'd tried to avoid and had done so successfully for centuries. Why was she walking into a grand old reunion now?

"Wait, Ethan."

He turned and waited for her to speak.

"Maybe you can take it from here," she said, hating her sudden rise of worry and weakness. She stood up to demons all the time. She was witch! Hear her cackle!

But Gazariel?

The image of the demon's silk shoes with painted red

heels standing but inches from her face was the most heart-wrenching memory.

"You think he's going to hurt you?" Ethan asked. "I don't know why he would. It sounds like you took the one thing from him he least wanted. He should welcome you with open arms."

"Yeah? I don't think so. He probably thinks I can return the curse back to him."

"Can you?"

"No! The only way to break the curse is…" Yeah, that part about a true love willing to die for her? Ethan didn't need to know about that. "Like it or not, we are connected. He probably knows I'm close right now."

"Which means we should hurry. Whether he's happy or angry to see you, we'll find out soon enough."

She grabbed him by the coat. "Give me a plan, yeah? I mean, when we do find him, what then? Are you going to slap a pair of handcuffs on him and hope the steel doesn't instantly melt, and in turn, the demon melts us?"

He took the phone from her. "I've got a containment crew on speed dial. They'll be here five minutes after my call. Can I, uh…use this now?"

"Yes, sure." She wiped off her blood from the screen and he started to scroll. "But what are we going to do while we wait out those very long and most likely painful five minutes in the demon's presence?"

"Certainly Jones gave me a demon manacle." He patted his pocket. "It'll contain the subject."

"Let me see it."

"Don't you trust me? Do you think I'd walk in on a demon ill-prepared? I've done this before."

"Have you?" She wasn't feeling it. He hadn't seemed

to have a plan yet. Why all of a sudden should he be prepared?

"Don't worry, Tuesday. I've got this one."

She sighed and dropped her shoulders. Wasn't as if she had a right to argue. She was merely the lure. And she did want to get this show on the road. The sooner they found Gazariel, the quicker she would be freed.

Ethan talked to someone on the line, confirming arrival in five minutes.

Time to let the guy show her he was the man and that he had everything under control? In her experience that never seemed to go quite as spectacularly as the man thought it would. And she was always left to sweep up the bloody pieces.

He smiled at her as he conferred with whomever he was talking to.

Why she should let Ethan take the alpha route was beyond her, but she submitted because…that ridiculous charming smile did possess a magic of its own.

As did the wanting, needy witch who had been willing to summon a demon to save her fickle lover's eyesight.

"Let's do this then," she said as Ethan hung up. "But don't say I didn't warn you in advance. This is not going to go well."

Chapter 8

Ethan did not appreciate that the witch had no trust in him. Before taking the cozy seat of director of Acquisitions, he'd been a retriever for a century. He knew this job and had chased every artifact, magical spell and creature in existence. Demons were easy enough to subdue if a man had the proper bind. And CJ had promised the manacle he'd given him would work.

He checked his pocket for the small iron pod, which he need only toss at the demon to bind him. And at his wrist he'd drawn a demon protection spell with a felt-tip marker before leaving his loft. He would be able to approach Gazariel, but it should deflect any demonic magic until the subject was securely bound.

Proceeding onward, he strode toward the elevator in the building lobby. Tuesday followed. He probably didn't need her from this point on. The phone GPS spell had taken them as far as it could. The demon was some-where in the building. But the fact she wore the demon's sigil, and was feeling the demon's presence now, could not be overlooked.

And as long as she was with him, he could protect her from Gazariel. "Up and to the left," Tuesday reported as they stepped onto the elevator and the doors closed behind them. Barry Manilow's "Mandy" hummed out of the speakers while they slowly rose two floors.

"You're tracking now from a...feeling?" Ethan asked.

"It's the sigil. It senses the demon. As I'm sure he feels me. And that is not a pleasant feeling, let me tell you."

"You can wait outside."

"Don't think so, vampire. I'm not a pussy. I'm in it to win it. Besides, how do you intend to enter a private residence?"

Vampires could not enter a private residence unless invited. It was something that didn't ever cause Ethan concern because he'd developed ways to get around that detour over the years. "I'll call out the demon."

"Not going to happen. He's too smart. You'll have to follow me inside." She looked upward, then closed her eyes. "Must be the top floor. Yep." The doors dinged and she strolled out, heading left down the hallway. "You should probably call in your containment crew right now."

"They should already be on the grounds." Ethan took out his phone. He dialed and gave the team leader direc-tions to the building and floor. Estimated arrival time was less than five minutes.

"I feel like it's...just ahead," Tuesday said as she

pressed her fingers between her breasts. "Must be that door at the end of the hallway."

"Must be?"

The witch stopped and tugged apart her blousy shirt to reveal the glowing sigil. It was faint but glowed red, as if it burned. Definitely working.

Ethan nodded. "All right. It's that suite. I suppose if a demon is going to live it up in the ritzy part of town he should go for the best. Let me take the lead."

"Why? You got magic to keep back the demon?"

"I've got the manacle and demonic wards."

"That's sweet." She stopped before him, hands to her hips. "But what are you going to do when the bastard charges us and then smokes out of sight? You can't manacle smoke. We need to catch him unawares. Which I'm guessing is going to be impossible thanks to your bait."

She suddenly hissed and swore, pressing her hand to her chest. Actual smoke tendriled between her fingers.

"He's close. I gotta ward myself." She stretched out her arms over her head, then swung them down along her body to her feet. A whoosh of cool air prickled across Ethan's skin. "You want in?"

Ethan didn't have to consider it. "Hell yes."

She slapped her hands to the top of his head, then dragged both down along his shoulders and his length to his feet, drawing around him with what he felt as a tightening tingle that briefly squeezed his skin. He'd never submitted to witchcraft before, but this adventure was offering up a slew of new challenges.

"What will this do?" he asked.

"Hopefully, keep the demon from peeling our skin off too terribly quickly." She noticed his gape. "I don't know. Maybe he's not the skin-peeling type."

"I thought you knew this demon?"

"I do, but it's not like we had coffee and got to know one another. Last time I saw him was in the seventeenth century. And he placed his hand on my heart and filled me full of yuck."

"A yuck that you asked for."

"Stating facts isn't going to win you points."

"I know. You were near death. Anyone would have taken what he offered just to stay alive."

"Right, I wasn't thinking with all my faculties. And hey, I'm still alive, so I guess I should be thankful. Now. You take the lead. Knock on his door, why don't you?"

Ethan stepped up and took a moment to consider what he was doing. Casually knocking on a demon's door? Perhaps a team fully armed with semiautomatics and full assault gear? His days of knocking down the door to a werewolf pack's lair with a battering ram were long gone, but he never lost the skill or the caution.

Of course, the witch was right. If entry was required, he'd need to follow her in.

Ethan knocked on the door. The containment crew would be armed to the extent that they could hold the demon and some powerful spells. Where were they?

Tuesday hissed and clutched her chest. The demon had to know she was near. If they didn't act now they might lose him. She stood beside him. And he strangely felt like they were two door-to-door salesmen, hawking their mundane and ridiculous goods to complete strangers. Tuesday winked at him.

Her winks always made him feel a twinge of promise. The job did have some high points, after all.

"He's gone," she said with a gasp.

"What?"

"I don't feel him anymore. The sigil has gone cold. Look."

Indeed, the mark between her breasts was now merely dark gray, as if a faded tattoo.

Ethan reacted. He stepped back and lunged a kick at the door right beside the lock mechanism. The door swung inward and slammed against the wall. Tuesday walked over the threshold and said, "I invite you to enter, vampire."

Didn't matter who offered it, the invite was the key to breeching that nuisance vampire deterrent.

Ethan strode into the apartment, which opened into a vast room, gaudily furnished with a leopard-print sofa and chairs. The entire opposite wall sported floor-to-ceiling windows that looked out over the snow-dusted forest below. He had the option to go left or right. Right was a kitchen, so he turned left and raced down the hallway.

Tuesday stayed behind and began to chant some witchy incantation. It tightened the ward about his skin. *Good call, witch.*

The bedroom was empty, though the bedclothes were rumpled and the sheets pushed to the end. He held a hand over the mattress but didn't sense any warmth. In the bathroom the gleam of silver fixtures advertising ridiculous wealth blinded him, but no one hid in there. He rushed back out to the kitchen, where Tuesday stood surrounded by a glowing violet light.

"What are you doing?"

"He's coming," she said from within the violet aura, and turned toward the kicked-open front door.

Charging down the hallway strode a tall, dark-haired

man—demon—with fire in his eyes and wicked curved blades in each of his hands.

Tuesday felt her violet protective ward crack and fall away as the demon crossed the threshold into his own home. She was the intruder, and she felt a wicked tug at her energies because of it. As well, her initial white light began to shiver. It wouldn't hold for long. Nor would Ethan's.

Yet at the same time her chest lifted, her hands reached as if to caress, and her body wanted to walk toward the man. Demon. The one who had cursed her. Who had tricked her and set her on the path toward a loveless life. But as much as she embraced her choice to take that curse—at the time it had been her only option to survive—she did not want to embrace Gazariel. She had too much fight in her to succumb to anything else he should wish to put upon her.

But did Ethan? The vampire stood before the demon, shoulders back and in a defensive stance. He held the manacle bind in one hand, but had yet to toss it at the demon. Because he could not. The demon's power filled the room.

Gazariel clanked the curved blades together before him. Brilliant sparks scattered to the floor. He then splayed out his arms, not quite ready for battle, more a show of power. "So my curse taker has returned for more? Long time, no see, witch."

His voice was liquid and compelling. And indeed, the man was beautiful beyond compare. Dark hair spilled like diamonds past his shoulders. His face was perfectly symmetrical and his eyes glistened like blue gemstones.

A mouth that any woman would dream to kiss curled in wicked satisfaction.

"Idiot," Tuesday admonished herself as she shook herself out of the stare. That was exactly what the demon wanted. Her adoration. "I didn't return of my free will," she said to Gazariel. "I would never purposely seek you again. Never."

"And yet you have." Gazariel glanced at Ethan. "Vampire. Can't release the manacle?" The demon blew him a kiss. "What do you want from me that you would enter my home without permission?"

"You have the book of angel names and sigils written by the muse. Give it to me and we'll leave without incident."

Gazariel's laughter echoed like dulcet chimes throughout the room, but ended on a deafening snarl that coiled in Tuesday's lungs and tightened her breaths. Her white light wisped away, leaving her vulnerable. And the wanting rose. He was so attractive. And his voice…

"I don't know what you're talking about." The demon strolled casually toward the windows. With a flick of each hand the curved blades aported away from him and disappeared.

Taking his chance, Ethan flung the manacle toward the demon. Gazariel put up a hand, stopping the manacle in midair.

Startled out of the ridiculous pining, Tuesday snapped back into focus. She threw her own magic into the mix and asked the bind to find its victim. The small black hexagon manacle shuddered in midair, struggling against the demon's magic and her own. It cracked, emitting a beam of green light, and then dropped to the floor and shattered.

Ethan spoke into his phone. "Now!"

"The cavalry?" Gazariel glanced out the opened doorway. He shook his shoulders and spread out his arms, great black wings suddenly emerging behind him, wide enough to stretch the width of the room. "I don't think so."

With a bend of his fingers, Gazariel tugged Tuesday across the room, her feet dragging on the marble floor and toes tilting backward. She couldn't stop the movement. And when she landed in the demon's arms, he turned her back against his chest and clamped a hand up under her jaw. The icy prick of his fingernails to her skin pushed her back four centuries to that dreaded night he had touched her heart. And had taken love from her life ever after.

A forward sweep of his wing glanced across her face. It burned yet smelled sweet, as if flowers mingled with the most delectable treats. Lilacs. Oh… He was a wicked beauty.

The sigil on her chest burned brightly and she cried out at the pain of it. And at that moment Gazariel cried out, too, releasing her and shoving her to the floor.

"Damn it!" Wings folding down and dusting the floor, he shook out the hand that must have touched the sigil. "I forget we are inexplicably bound. And that was a curse I did not want to ever feel again. You, witch, are an imposition."

"And you are an asshole. But nothing has changed in four centuries, eh?"

"The containment team is on their way up," Ethan

announced. "Hand over the code now and we won't have to use force."

"Force?" The demon laughed. As his wings assumed full, shiny display behind him, he lifted his head regally. "You don't know what you're dealing with, do you, vampire? You, who would ally yourself with a powerful dark witch, yet are completely unaware of how her connection to me is forged. I might have put the curse inside her, but it will forever be rooted in my bones. It is why I have chosen to avoid Miss Knightsbridge for all this time. I can feel that bedamned curse. It wants back inside me." He clutched the fingers of one hand before him. "And know that for as long as she wears my curse, whatever I feel she will feel when we are in proximity."

Ethan glanced to Tuesday, who pushed up from the floor and backed away from the demon. She wasn't about to use any more magic when she knew it would be ineffective. Expelling such would only drain her.

"I think that means that if you hurt him, you hurt me," she said. "Peachy." Especially since she knew the retrieval of the book probably meant much more to Ethan than protecting her.

"She may carry the one thing I least want in this realm," the demon said. With a discerning tilt of his head, he appeared to sniff the air, perhaps take her in a bit more deeply. "But I must admit, it is attractive the longer I stand in its presence. Love can be so…heart-wrenching." He pursed his lips at them. "Oh. Sorry. You don't know that, do you, my witch? Or at least, you don't know anymore."

"If you're having relationship issues, then take it back," Tuesday said. "The curse is yours for the taking. I've had enough of it."

"Is that so? Does the pitiful witch now desire love? Perhaps you wish to fall head over heels with another witch hunter. You wore the gashes in your skin so beautifully." Gazariel chuckled and shook his head. "I will never have enough of the mortal pleasures I am able to enjoy thanks to not being shackled by that curse. Love and adoration are my oxygen! And I have tired of the two of you."

Out in the hallway a crew of three appeared, approaching cautiously.

Gazariel shook his head. "Too little. Too late." With a jaunty tilt of his head, he winked at Tuesday. "Let's have a little fun."

Spreading his arms out wide, Gazariel recited a demonic incantation. His wings closed about him, circling him, yet still kept a border of four feet around him. His own summoning circle, Tuesday guessed. From within the circle it began to glow blue, and a flurry of blue light wavered and then shot out to disperse into the ceiling, walls and floor.

Suddenly the building began to shudder. Tuesday had never experienced an earthquake but this must be what it felt like. Her body jittered. The floor tremored beneath her feet. A lamp toppled and Ethan stepped before her, as if to protect.

The demon smiled wickedly. In his hand he held a glowing blue light. "I will bring this building down if you do not take your minions and leave, vampire."

"He's serious," Tuesday said through a tight jaw. She could feel the demon's intrusion into her very being. He was using her magic, the darkness that coiled in the sigil, to enhance his own magic and spread it out as wide as the building. "Get out of here!"

"I'm not leaving you." But when Ethan tugged her arm, she felt as if she was planted on the floor. Her legs were leaden. She could not move.

The walls began to crack.

"I can't move. You've got to get everyone out of the building. Save them! Now!"

The containment crew shouted to Ethan for orders. Ethan commanded them to evacuate the building—knock on all doors to get everyone out. He caught Tuesday's gaze and didn't ask her anything, but she understood. He would protect innocent lives first and foremost.

"I'll be fine," she said. "If this bastard takes me out, he might take himself out, too. He won't let that happen. Just hurry. Get the people out of this building!"

Ethan dashed off.

And Tuesday growled at Gazariel. "You dare play with the lives of innocents?"

The demon chuffed. He tossed the blue ball of light through the open doorway and down the hall. "Always."

A painting fell off the wall and the window shattered behind him. Tuesday tried to conjure up the shards and send them back at the demon, but she couldn't focus beyond merely standing upright and not screaming. She felt as if he touched her heart. Again. And then a sudden tug at her entire body, similar to when she'd walked too far away from Ethan, briefly knocked her off balance.

Had the bond been severed? Ethan wouldn't be able to run through the building otherwise.

The demon winked at her. "I did that. You're welcome."

She acknowledged the sudden release, a freedom she'd desired since arriving in Paris. That was a good thing. For more than her. It would allow Ethan to clear out the innocents and escape the shaking building.

"Don't harm anyone," she pleaded. "Please, Gazariel."

"You surprise me, witch. With all the darkness I can feel within you, such an incredible lack of love, and still you plead for the lives of innocents. Something wrong with that. You're but one step away from warlock. Why not let it happen?"

"Is that what you want? Wouldn't that then give me power over you?"

Speaking it made her realize suddenly that maybe it could be so. If she went warlock could she control Gazariel? She'd never had a reason to do so—for centuries—until Ethan had gotten her involved in chasing the demon down. Warlocks were witches who had gone against their own, and often committed terrible acts against humanity. But they were so powerful.

Was it worth the sacrifice of her last remnants of light to subdue this threat? Gazariel held a book that could destroy so many innocents.

All of a sudden Gazariel fisted a hand before him and Tuesday was pulled across the room toward him. She slammed against his chest and he spun, gripping her against his body. The final window smashed out and he soared through it and over the nearby treetops, landing her on the snowy ground with a spine-crimping thump.

Tuesday lay on her back with Gazariel kneeling over her. His wings coved them in a private embrace. The demon pressed a palm over her chest. "You have been such a good girl, keeping this wicked curse from me. But the vampire has drawn up your naughtiness. And... do I sense you really *do* seek love? Poor, pitiful witch."

"I get the feeling you are having love troubles yourself. Did someone jilt you? Why not take back the curse so you won't be bothered by such foolish human emotions? If only for a little while?" Desperation did not suit her, but she'd not been able to stop speaking her hopes.

A curl of his fingers felt as if he was gripping her very heart. Tuesday moaned at the pain.

"Ethan just wants the code," she blurted out. "Give him the book and we'll leave you alone. Why do you want to destroy the world when you're having so much fun in it?"

"The book isn't for me. It's a gift for…a woman."

"What? Did you give it to someone else? Someone you love? No. You're trying to win someone's love? Is that it?"

"Enough talk about a stupid book."

She'd guessed right. "So not everyone loves you, eh?"

The demon was not having it now.

"You, witch, are going to leave me alone. Because I promise…" He bent forward, his hair dusting her face. A dark wanting desire melted over her skin as he whispered against her ear, "If you follow me, I will take out your loveless heart and devour it."

With that, a force whisked Gazariel away from her in a beating of wings and a swirl of snowflakes from the ground.

Gasping and panting, Tuesday rolled to her side and coiled up into a ball on the cold, snowy earth. He'd touched her heart again. And each time it left behind a mark that she would never feel heal over.

The demon had plans to give the code book to a woman? Why? And who was this woman? Had to be a lover, someone he was trying to win, as she had guessed. It made little sense. She couldn't imagine Gazariel stooping so low. Couldn't he have love with but a flutter of his thick, black lashes? And he was not a demon who could condone the ending of the world. Who, then, would remain alive to worship and adore him?

Through the wide-spaced tree trunks Tuesday saw a man's legs running toward her. Ethan plunged to the snow-littered ground and leaned over to embrace her. He'd left her alone with the demon.

She shoved him away. "Don't touch me!"

Ethan reared back and put up his palms. "I'm sorry. Everyone is out of the building. The shaking has stopped. I've called in the fire department and the police. Where's the demon?"

"Gone." For good, if she would only stay away from him. Which, at the moment, felt like the safest and smartest thing to do.

"Let me help you up. Get you to the car so you can warm up. Did he hurt you?"

Only for centuries. And so deeply, even she could not have foreseen the depth of such wounds. Something Ethan could never understand.

Tuesday pushed up and stood, backing away from the vampire. She put up a hand and focused her repulsive energies toward him. She was tattered and weak, but she did manage to topple him backward a few feet.

"The binding between us has been broken," she said. "Time for you to let me go."

"We haven't gotten what we want."

"It's what *you* want, not what I want." She sighed and winced. This whole mess was because some demon who had an abundance of love wanted even more? What the hell? "Just let me go, Ethan. Gazariel is…too strong. I need to be away from…this."

"I still need your help."

"As your prisoner?"

He inhaled through his nose and splayed his hands before him. "I'm sorry, Tuesday. You're right. I've gone about this wrong. You should… Yes, you're free to go. I still need your help, but I won't force you. If you feel the desire to stop Gazariel from harming so many, you know where to find me." He stepped back, but then stopped. "Let me at least get you a ride. A place to stay."

"Leave me," she said. A shiver of cold traced over her skin. A hug would feel welcome. She didn't know how to ask for it, though.

Ethan nodded, then turned to stride off. It was too easy for the vampire to walk away from her.

And Tuesday exhaled and held her breath as she watched him slip between the trees and back into the commotion surrounding the evacuation. Police cars had arrived. Red and blue lights flashed. The building had not collapsed, but she suspected it was so structurally damaged it would have to be condemned.

He was needed there in the midst of that chaos. The man had chosen the correct fight, instead of staying and holding her. Because…she did need someone to hold her right now. Her body felt ready to tumble onto the ground and melt into the snow. To surrender.

The demon had taken so much from her today.

She cast a look up into the sky. She did not know where Gazariel had gone. And she didn't want to know.

Chapter 9

Ethan had paced the loft for hours. He'd not been able to get leaving Tuesday alone in the woods out of his mind. Now as he strode the halls of headquarters, destined for the Archives, he wished he would have tried harder. To make her understand that he needed her help and that she could trust him.

And beyond that, to let her know that his initial feelings for her had changed. They'd shared much in the past few days and he'd developed a real understanding for the witch. He genuinely cared for her.

The binding CJ had conjured between Ethan and Tuesday had been a mistake. It hadn't given her a reason to trust him. And she had been a good sport, going along with every request he made of her.

But he'd felt her terror when they'd stood in the apartment and Gazariel had begun to make the walls shake. The demon had connected with Tuesday. In a terrible and painful way. And then to find her lying in the snow outside, looking so defeated and frail, his heart had cringed.

The witch had been cursed to never know love. What sort of hollow, empty life had she lived? He couldn't fathom such a lack of love.

Yet she deserved more protection and respect than he could give her. So he'd let her go. He'd find another way to track Gazariel. He now knew the demon was in the city. And if he had been in Paris for this long, then what reason had he to leave now? Unless they'd spooked him.

Ethan needed to learn as much as he could about the demon. The knowledge could only enhance his search efforts.

The vast Archives was located many stories below ground. It was a repository of all things, from books and ancient artifacts, to histories of the various paranormal species, and related ephemera. It basically housed all the information about the paranormal nations that could be contained. There were also catalogued weapons, shackled magics, volatile items placed in containment and even a few creatures that were much better off—for the humans' sake—locked up than out running loose in the mortal realm.

As director of Acquisitions, Ethan had seen to placing a good majority of the contents of the Archives there. Acquisitions was often referred to as the Archives' dirty little secret, for their methods were brutal and unforgiving. And if the Archives needed to contain an ancient evil—or merely wanted it to study—they asked Ethan to deploy a retriever.

As well, if a mysterious stranger showed up in his office with information that a certain book of angel sigils and names had gone missing, Ethan was charged to react appropriately. At all costs, the mortal realm must be protected from discovering there were creatures and magics that existed beyond myth and fable.

Secrets. It was always about keeping secrets. He knew too many of them. And some days he wished he could erase them all from memory and start anew. Other days, it was good to know exactly what the world could—and did—deal him.

Entering the Archives' office, Ethan spied Certainly Jones sitting behind an ancient wood desk, his feet propped up on the desk as he sipped tea. The man rarely wore shoes, which always startled Ethan. He liked to maintain a certain business decorum at the office. But the Archives was not his domain. And CJ possessed mysterious ways and a manner that was ever polite but also secretive. However, the man was trustworthy, and that was what mattered most to Ethan.

"How'd the containment go this afternoon?" CJ asked, not bothering to sit up from his relaxed posture.

"Do you have a new demon behind bars?"

"Nope."

"Then you know how it went. I need your help, Jones."

"Where's Tuesday Knightsbridge?"

Ethan gestured with a vague sweep over his shoulder. "I let her go. She'd served her purpose."

"Uh-huh." CJ sat up, giving Ethan that I-know-you-better-than-you-know-yourself look. Witches and their looks. A man had to be cautious around them.

"The demon broke the binding between us," Ethan

said. "It didn't feel right to make her stay unless she wanted to actually help."

"And she did not. Makes sense. You did kidnap her."

"I did not—" Ethan knew an argument over semantics was senseless.

The witch stood. "What help can I offer? I can provide knowledge, but as for hands-on, you know I'm not much for taking on demons. Not anymore, you understand."

CJ had once gone into Daemonia, purposely, and had returned from that despicable, demon-infested realm. Actually, his return had been an orchestrated rescue by his twin brother, Thoroughly Jones. The trip there had changed CJ, made him miserable and dark and... he'd come near to death. But another witch—a pretty red-haired woman named Viktorie Saint-Charles—had helped him to escape the psychological torments of those demonic hosts and now he avoided demons like the proverbial plague.

"I need all the information you have on Gazariel," Ethan said. "Specifically, what you can tell me about the curse he had. The one he gave to Tuesday. And if there's a way to break it."

Because if they could break the curse then he need not fear that Tuesday would be harmed when finally he did capture Gazariel.

"I'll have to search the records." CJ gestured toward the silver service by the wall behind Ethan. "Tea?"

Tuesday sipped the thick hot chocolate and tugged the alpaca coat snugly around her shoulders. She was still cold even though she could feel the heat blast through the nearby vent that was level with her ankles. She sat before the front second-floor window of Angelina, having been drawn to the chic yet touristy café because she'd once heard they served the best hot chocolate ever.

Truth. But it was also rich and so sweet she was already flying high on a sugar rush. Good thing she'd foregone checking out the decadent pastries. With but a clasp of her waitress's hand, she'd assured the bill was paid and that no one would remember her sitting here for two hours, staring out over the snow-frothed horse-chestnut trees that edged the Tuileries Garden across the street. And wondering.

What to do now?

Ethan had released her from duty. Well, she would have walked away from him no matter if he'd given her leave or not. Wasn't as if she'd volunteered for the mission. She'd had no choice. It hadn't been duty, but forced servitude.

But now that she did have a choice, she wasn't sure what came next. Her intention was to hop a flight back home. That was the logical decision. Maybe do a little touristing before hopping on that flight? That option was a little less safe and she risked the vampire deciding he needed her again and finding her.

Or she could walk back into the fray and put up her fists and show the demon her teeth.

All her life she had stood up for her beliefs, ever since she'd been given a renewed chance at life thanks to the dreadful curse the demon had put inside her. But if she couldn't know love then she'd be damned to sit around and pout about it. She had not once felt regretful for her decision made in that dark cell outside the pigpen.

And yet, she wasn't feeling so strong or powerful at the moment. Her chest ached from Gazariel's touch. He had touched her heart. And should they meet again he wouldn't pause to rip it out. That was a truth she inexplicably knew.

Back in the seventeenth century, the demon hadn't wanted the curse he'd put inside her. But this afternoon, she'd seen the glitter of desire in his eyes as he had recognized the tease of lacking love. He'd wanted it. And he had not.

Something was up with Gazariel and his love life. He'd not been able to hide his reaction to her guessing at that. Of course, it was possible not everyone would love him. Yes? Maybe? Tuesday couldn't fathom being loved by everyone she met. Was The Beautiful One growing weary of unending love and devotion? It did sound tiresome.

And yet, a small taste of love seemed too delicious to Tuesday right now.

Yes, she'd been near death, wishing to die, when she'd accepted the curse. Over the centuries, she'd made it her own, embracing the utter lack of love. How easy it was to never have to worry about love and all its ridiculous predicaments.

And she'd been fine with fleeting romantic relationships over the years. Just when the man started to get all doe-eyed and she suspected he was falling in love, he'd suddenly notice something about her he hated, or he'd simply leave. She had expected those reactions, so they hadn't bothered her. Too much.

But now she wasn't so sure. Gazariel's touch had given the curse new life. Had strengthened it. Ethan had walked away from her with ease. And that was because of the curse, surely.

Suddenly the thought of not having love in her life was tangible and real. A hole in her heart. And she couldn't be a strong powerful woman if part of her had a hole in it.

Did she want to shuck off the curse and allow love into her life? Could she be so brave? It wasn't as if she was in love with Ethan Pierce or he with her. But she wanted that option. She really did.

"Just leave Paris," she whispered over the cup of chocolate. "You know it's the right choice. The vampire has no interest in you beyond what you can do for him."

And what she could do for him might bring back the demon. And that would see her bloody heart dangling from Gazariel's fingers. One way or another, she would not survive if she didn't leave the city today.

She snapped the rubber band.

Yeah, it was the only choice.

Pulling out the cell phone she'd slipped from Ethan's pocket while lying on the snowy ground, she downloaded an airline app and checked the schedule for flights leaving for the US. There were four this evening. And each one still had remaining seats.

The Archives had a room for virtually every species of paranormal that inhabited the mortal realm. The room on witches was the largest. The unicorn room was the smallest due to a lack of information. But Tuesday did wield an alicorn, Ethan thought, as they passed by that room. Just what sort of trouble could a witch get into with that thing? He wanted to know.

He really did.

As Ethan followed CJ into the demon room, he felt a cool chill fall over his skin and he adopted a militant need to scan the room and look over his shoulder. Nothing followed him down the aisles of dark, dusty bookshelves, nor did he see anything flying above near the two-story-high ceiling. But he was not mistaken that pairs of red eyes seemed to flicker here and there from within the books and haphazardly stacked artifacts.

"Tamatha has been rearranging," CJ said. "It's a bit of a clutter right now. The inner chamber is neater."

CJ pushed open a heavy steel door. It looked like something that should front a bank vault. The dark witch's casual manner relaxed Ethan's tensions. He followed him inside the massive annex room, taking in the musty odor and the many aisles that boasted boxes or small cages with creatures inside. Books papered an entire wall that stretched the length of the chamber.

"Ignore the blaggert," CJ offered as they filed past a small glass-barred cage, secured with electronic locks. Inside, a diminutive red creature with tufted ears bent and waggled his bare ass at them as they passed.

"The *Bibliodaemon* is up on that dais," CJ said. "As with most species, there is a book, or bible, that describes them all, and is constantly updated."

"Like the *Book of All Spells*."

Ethan knew that book was like a living archive of any and all spells created by witches. If a witch was speaking a new spell right now, it was magically being written into that book. There was another for vampires, *The Vampire Codex*, though he'd never been curious about it. Weird, to think that now. Of course, he lived the vampire's life; no need to have it explained to him in text.

"Yes, like that book." CJ skipped up two steps to a

steel dais, where a table displayed a huge book that was about three feet high and two feet wide. It sat open to some pages that looked like time-stained parchment. With a sweep of his hand and a mutter of Latin, followed by the demon Gazariel's name, CJ sent the pages fluttering. "It'll take a few minutes to bring up the records. Kind of like the internet but slower and more interesting, eh?"

"Your job must never see a dull day," Ethan commented as he pulled up a stool to sit and watch the book pages move rapidly in search.

"It's a kick, that's for sure. But we could use more help. I've only got Tamatha as my assistant. She's off in the harpie room today. Maybe? I don't know. It's quite the labyrinth down here. A couple more hands would be helpful. We've such a backload of stuff from your retrievers."

"You mean it hasn't all been catalogued?"

"Who has the time? I have a holding room that's warded to the nines. Tamatha and I are working as fast as we can to keep up with the acquisitions."

"You should put in a requisition to the Council. I'm sure they'd approve you hiring more help."

CJ nodded. "Thing is, I'm very particular about who I work with. And I don't have time to vet someone new. So I guess I either lighten up or shut up, eh?"

"Seems to be the case."

The pages stopped moving and CJ leaned over the book and read. "'Gazariel, master angel of the First Void, Creator of Vanity, fallen to Beneath where he became known as The Beautiful One, and was cast out by the Devil Himself.'"

"That demon was once an angel?"

"Many demons were originally angels," CJ said. "When they Fell, those who landed in Beneath assumed demonic form. Others became the Sinistari, who now hunt the Fallen."

"I thought the majority of demons were from Daemonia?"

"They are. Yet you'll not find a former Fallen One who is now demon who would ever set foot in Daemonia. While Daemonia has its own version of royalty, the Fallen Ones deem themselves highest of all demons since they originated in Above. Daemonia is, literally, beneath them. Looks like your guy has a reason for being called The Beautiful One. Creator of Vanity, eh?"

The demon had been primping when he'd stood before them in the apartment complex. It was as if he couldn't *not* flaunt his beauty.

"Does it say why Himself cast him out of Beneath?" Ethan asked. "Isn't that odd? I thought The Old Lad was always looking for more minions."

CJ leaned over the book and read silently for a while. "Himself was jealous."

"Why, because Gazariel is pretty?"

"Exactly. So he cursed Gazariel with an evil that would not allow him to own love and cast him out to the mortal realm."

"To own it," Ethan repeated, thinking, trying to work this out. "But not necessarily to never know it?"

CJ shrugged. "I suppose. But I assume if a person would have fallen in love with the demon, while he still wore the curse, something terrible would have happened to that person to make them stop loving him."

"Yet Gazariel himself could actually love still." Which would mean that Tuesday could still love. Maybe.

"So the curse came from the devil…" Ethan did not repeat Himself's name. Say the name three times in a row? You've invited the devil for a visit. Not something he ever intended to do. "And obviously Gazariel didn't want that hanging on him, so he pawned it off on a witch."

"Interesting that he was able to so easily give it away."

"Tuesday said she asked for it."

CJ lifted an eyebrow.

"She had been beaten and tortured by a witch hunter, whom she loved, and was very near death."

"Then some demon offers to take love, which hurt her, from her life?"

"Exactly."

"Poor thing." CJ propped his arms akimbo. "Tuesday is dark but she doesn't strike me as evil incarnate."

"If the curse is designed to keep away love, maybe that's all it can get out of her? If she is innately good?"

"Possible. But how is learning this going to help you get a hand on the demon? If he's slipped through your hands once already?"

"I'm trying to gather as much information as I can. And whatever happens I don't want Tuesday getting hurt. She and Gazariel are tied together. He told us if we hurt him she will feel it."

"That makes things difficult. But if she's left the city? She could be at a safe distance."

"But how to know what that safe distance is?"

"Why is Gazariel in Paris?" CJ asked. "If he's got the Final Days code, why not use it? Or is he holding it for someone? Waiting to hand it off? Or has he already done so? There's a reason he's not running far."

"Right. And now that he knows I want what he has…"

"Then he'll make himself scarce."

"Or will he? I'm not sure." Ethan crossed his arms, considering what he'd learned. "There is the connection between him and Tuesday. She is key to calling the demon forth. And there was a moment when I'm sure I saw the desire for the curse in the demon's eyes. When he touched Tuesday, he could feel that darkness calling to him. He said something about love not being what it was cracked up to be. I think he would take the curse back if given the right conditions."

"Which are?"

"I don't know. A bad love affair? Can you perform a tracking spell like Tuesday did? I need to know where Gazariel is right now."

"I'm sure she was using the sigil as a direct conduit. Do you have something from Tuesday that I might use to call up the demon?"

"I…no. Maybe? She was at my place for a bit. I'll have to go see if she left anything behind."

"If you could find some hair strands that would be optimal. That still won't guarantee I can get a fix on the demon. I'll give it a shot, though."

Ethan slapped a hand into CJ's. "Thanks, man."

"Have you considered calling in a reckoner for when you do find Gazariel? Perhaps as a threat?"

A reckoner consigned demons to Daemonia. To threaten Gazariel with going to that place, which he must fear as most mortals feared Hell, could provide some leverage, perhaps even get him to confess about where the book was.

"Good call. I'll have to look up Savin Thorne."

"He's living in the fourteenth. Bit of a hermit. But yes, I'd recommend the man."

"Thanks. I'm heading home to see if I can find traces of the witch. Can I get a copy of that page?" He pointed to the oversized book.

"Why do you people think I'm some kind of a copy machine?"

Ethan shrugged. "You're not?" Then he chuckled. "Have your assistant send me a digital file of it, yes?"

"I can have it to you in a few hours."

"Thanks." Ethan patted his jacket pocket. No phone. Had he lost it in the scuffle at the Bois de Boulogne? Damn. "Send it to my office email," he said. "I seem to have misplaced my phone. Er, will you show me the way out of here? We took so many turns I don't want to end up in the werewolf room."

"Why? Not keen on the dogs?"

"Not so much that as not in the mood to relive some rather sketchy history."

"Blood Wars?" CJ asked.

Ethan nodded.

"I completely understand. Just being in this room creeps me out. Too many memories of an experimental magic excursion to Daemonia gone awry. Let's go."

Tuesday stood in line behind a family of six, who waited with shoes in hand to pass through security at Charles de Gaulle airport. The flight took off in an hour, and she was ready for the eight-hour sleep she would sink into as soon as her butt landed on the narrow seat.

But for perhaps the fifth time, she glanced over her shoulder and gazed out the windows at the stream of cabs letting off travelers or picking them up. Was she really ready to write off this adventure and mark it as defeat? That wasn't like her. She reveled in a good challenge. And if it involved getting down and dirty with some bastard demon? Bring it on. She could stand up to the most powerful of them and win. Every time.

Yes, even the one demon who wanted to rip out her heart.

And there was a certain sexy vampire who had sparked her interest. Was she simply going to walk away from the man without having gotten more than a few kisses? Didn't feel right. Even if she returned, fucked him and left, at least she'd have had that pleasure.

To leave or not?

She knew Gazariel would rely on her fear, on not wanting to lose her heart. And the idea of shivering before the demon did not sit well with her. She was stronger than this. And the demon was messing with her. He wanted to end the world because of…unrequited love? Sounded like a bad romance to her.

It was time to seriously consider transferring this curse back to Gazariel. If he wore the curse, he'd fall out of love and lose the desire to hand off a dangerous gift to goddess knew what kind of malicious entity.

Love? Tuesday clutched her shoes tightly against her chest. Yes, she was ready to welcome it into her life. She wanted it. And if that wasn't reason enough to turn and aim for the exit door, she wasn't about to let that ridiculous fop of a demon tell her what to do. It was time to stand up and show it her teeth.

"Mademoiselle?"

She turned to find the security guard waiting for her to remove her coat then step forward through the X-ray machine. She'd never liked those machines. Something wrong with peering inside a person and seeing their very bones.

"Right." She took one step forward, and then...one step back.

Chapter 10

Ethan opened his apartment door to discover a yawning witch waiting outside in the hallway.

She snapped her mouth shut and put up one finger. "I've got one more idea for a tracking spell on that bastard demon."

"Okay."

"But first, I need a shower." Tuesday strode inside, passing him by, and rummaged through her bag. She tugged out his phone and dropped it on the couch. "Yeah?"

He gestured toward the bedroom, which led to the bathroom. "You know where it is."

She didn't say another word. Didn't explain why she'd returned, or for how long. And he felt it best to let things play out and see what she'd offer him. Because he hadn't found anything of hers to give to CJ for a summoning spell, not even a single strand of hair.

He needed her. In more ways than he was willing to admit to himself.

But this time around, he'd play things closer to the vest. Not go all director-in-charge on her by forcing her to comply. This time, he'd follow the witch's lead. It felt right. It felt as though his heart demanded it.

After a shower, Tuesday pulled on a T-shirt that hung to her thighs, then looked in the mirror. Emblazoned across the shirt were the words, Surely Not Everybody Was Kung Fu Fighting. She'd found it in a vintage store while shopping with Ethan. Ha! And yes, there had been occasions in the nightclubs during the 1970s disco frenzy when everyone had been kung fu fighting. In dance mode, of course. Good times.

She was ready to pull out all her moves against Gazariel. She had no clue how to give the curse back to him, but she would not relent until it happened. If he was in love, maybe she could use that against him. She had to find out who his lover was. And how much she meant to him. Apparently enough to give her a trinket that could end the world.

Tuesday did a few kung fu moves in front of the mirror, then gave it her best fighter's face. That demon wanted to threaten her?

"Let's see what he does when love is taken away from him." And she delivered a knockout kick to her absent opponent.

Grabbing her bag, which she'd filled with a few more magical accoutrements thanks to her rushing around on a hot-chocolate high earlier, she wandered out through the bedroom and set down the bag in the corner between the bed and the living area. An old wood vanity held a record player and a neat stack of albums sat beside it. And on the other half of the vanity a crystal decanter with dark alcohol in it sat surrounded by three wide-bowled glasses.

Ethan sat on the sofa, legs up on the coffee table, bare feet tilted outward. He gazed idly at her.

"Let's do this spell before I fall asleep from utter exhaustion," she said, taking a few items out of her bag. "Get me something to write with. Like a felt-tip marker. Take off your shirt. And lie down in this big ol' salt circle I'm about to make."

She began to pour the bag of ordinary table salt she'd bought at a local market onto the wide plank flooring before the vanity.

Ethan, meanwhile, got a pen from the kitchen and tugged off his shirt. She did notice those washboard abs, and at that moment her circle took a distinct swerve inward.

Shaking off the alluring sight, Tuesday redirected the salt and closed up the circle. It was big enough to contain a very sizable vampire and his nekkid abs that screamed for some hella licking. She gestured toward it. "Lie down."

Ethan scratched his head, then pressed his thumb and forefinger close together. "Just a teeny bit of info first?"

She propped her hands on her hips. Fine. The man was cute enough that he could command that of her. "We want to catch The Beautiful One, yeah?"

"Agreed."

"I am the one who alerts the demon we're near. Not cool. So you need to become the bait or lure or even the GPS. With this spell, I'm going to make you into a tracker. You should be able to turn it on or off when needed. It'll be like you borrowing some of my magic but without having to perform bloodsexmagic."

He shrugged, then stepped inside the circle. "This doesn't require blood?"

"It does, but yours this time."

He put up a hand. "I'm a vampire."

Tuesday gave him a droll look. "I got that. First try, even."

"I don't give blood," he said. "I only take it."

"Get over your bad self."

He crossed his arms. "I refuse to give blood."

Tuesday inhaled through her nose and met the vampire eye-to-eye. All seriousness in those pretty gray irises. For all that she had given thus far, a few drops of blood shouldn't be a hardship for him. And yet, she looked down his face, to his neck, which was tight with tension, and along his arms, that ended in fists. Something was bothering him. And it had to do with the blood.

"It's not going to hurt. Promise," she lied. "And besides, you did give blood for the binding between the two of us."

"That was different. You were a mere...witch. And I was desperate."

"And you're not now?" Though she had caught the vitriol in the way he'd said *witch*. He had not liked her very much when she'd first arrived. A mutual feeling. But her feelings had changed. And she'd thought he was starting to come around as well.

"Why can't we use your blood?" he asked.

"Because you'd get turned on and toss me on the end of the bed before I could finish the spell."

He smirked and shook his head. Not the reaction

she'd been hoping for with the gibe, either. "We've been through this, witch. I don't go from calm to horny with the sniff of a few drops of blood."

"You were aroused by my blood in the car."

He closed his eyes. And Tuesday had to keep herself from leaning forward, moving in to smell his fresh outdoors scent. She wanted to kiss him. Damn her, the stupidest witch of all time. He had a certain allure, not unlike Gazariel's strange pull. But with Ethan it felt honest and even promising.

"The last time I gave blood I killed a woman," he stated plainly.

Tuesday leaned back and met the man's gaze. Stoic and calm, as he had been that first time she'd woken up in the cage to look upon her captor.

"You...killed. You're a vampire—"

"We don't all kill to survive," he interrupted. "I've never killed merely for blood. It is beneath me. It is unnecessary."

"But you have killed before. Many," she said, knowing it to be the truth. For she had walked through the same centuries as he had. No one lived that long and got out of it untouched by foulness or evil.

"I fought in the Blood Wars," he said. "Of course I've killed. It was kill or be killed then. But what I'm talking about is the voluntary giving of blood that results in loss of life. I can't do it. I won't."

"Ethan." She grabbed his hand and held it with both of hers. "Help me to understand. You killed someone by giving them blood? Were you...trying to transform them?"

He made to tug out of her grasp, so she pulled his hand closer and held it firmly. "Talk to me. I shared my ugly stuff with you. I've done desperate things at desperate times. Tell me why donating a few drops of blood is such a big no-no for you."

"A few drops? That's all you need?"

She shrugged. "Yeah?"

He lifted an eyebrow.

"It's not going to be a lot. I need it to trace the spell on you. I'm not going to take it into my veins, if that's got you worried. I don't intend to die today. Swear it by the seven sacred witches."

He studied her, and as he did she suspected he wasn't going to explain to her the whole deal behind his killing someone with a blood transfusion. She wanted to know about that wackiness. But really, this spell did not require a surgical operation or large amounts of the red stuff.

"There's no such thing as the seven sacred witches," he finally said.

Tuesday shrugged. "You got me. Now can we do this? Just a tiny donation is all I ask of you." She pinched her fingers together before him. "I won't even need an athame. Just…" She spun and leaned over to shuffle around in her bag, pulling out the alicorn. "This will be perfect. Yeah?"

"Just a small amount?" Ethan asked. And when she nodded, he sighed and sat down.

"All the way down," she directed, and the vampire lay on his back. "This won't hurt a bit. Maybe a little. You're a big boy. You got this."

But what she wouldn't give to have heard about the person he'd killed. It bothered him enough to freak him out over a little blood ritual. She would learn about it. Soon enough.

With Ethan prone in the circle, Tuesday remained outside the line of salt, and took a moment to admire his physique. What was it about vampires and how they didn't need to work out, yet they all seemed to have the abs and pecs of a bodybuilder? Wasn't easy to disregard. But she would.

For now.

Kneeling, she leaned in and placed a palm to his chest. "Just go with it, okay?"

"I do owe you this much. Thanks, by the way."

"For what?"

"For coming back. You had every right to leave."

"Yeah, well I'm not going to let that asshole demon shove me around and make me feel like the weak one. If he's have relationship issues, ending the world is not the way to resolve them."

"Relationship issues?"

"Yeah. I think the demon wants to give the book to some chick to win her love. Or maybe he already has. He wasn't clear. I just knew with certainty that whoever the woman was, she wasn't in love with him."

"I thought everyone adored him?"

"Do you?"

"He was kind of handsome."

Tuesday couldn't stop some head-shaking laughter. "Right? I mean, it's crazy, but I thought the same."

"That's what makes him so dangerous," Ethan said.

"And why we need to be vigilant. We're strong. We can do this. Together…" She uncapped the red marker he'd found and checked the writing on the plastic tube. Water soluble. Good for him. He'd be able to wash this off later. "We make a pretty decent team. Now I'm going to draw a tracking grid on you."

Ethan put his hands behind his head and closed his eyes as she drew a circle on his chest, and within it, a pentagram. She marked the four compass directions. A copy of the sigil she wore was placed at the spirit peak of the pentagram. Gliding the marker under his pec, she couldn't help but slow down and study the rigid nipple and the sudden goose-bumping of his skin. He was aware she was studying him.

The man would jump if she dashed out her tongue and licked his skin. He wasn't overly hot. Vampires never were too hot, but weren't cold, either, as one might expect. The flesh and muscles beneath her hands were solid and hard. And oh, so delectable. And as the red line journeyed over one abdominal ridge and then the next, she pressed her lips together.

Didn't want to start drooling on the guy. That would be so not cool.

"Are you thinking what I'm thinking?" Ethan asked softly.

She finished her line work with three short dashes above his navel and set aside the marker, but remained leaning over the salt circle and close to his body. "What's that?"

He nudged up a shoulder. "That I like you touching me."

Tuesday lifted an eyebrow. He still had his eyes closed. And from her vantage point, so close to his ribs and looking up over that hard pectoral landscape, she thought she saw his smile grow.

"I am thinking the same thing," she answered truthfully. "You make for a nice drawing board."

"Your breath on my skin is making me uncomfortable."

She glanced down toward his jeans and…oh, yes, he was growing hard. Well, she didn't need him aroused for this spell—nor did she want to spend too much time considering his arousal because that would only do the same to her—so she gave his stomach a quick smack with her fingers and sat back.

"What the hell?" He lifted his head to seek her.

"Had to be done. We've got to focus. No silly stuff."

"If that's the way you want to play it." He put his head down and closed his eyes again. "But I wouldn't call what I was thinking of doing to you silly."

Mercy. Had he really needed to say that? Because now Tuesday wanted to know what had been running through his thoughts. And how not-silly it might have been. Surely it had involved lots of skin-on-skin contact. And more of his devastating kisses. And if they were forced to do it inside the salt circle without upsetting the perimeter, they might have to get into all sorts of weird yet tight positions.

Hell, she must be overtired if she was slipping into random moments of sex fantasy. What the hex? She shook her head and grabbed the alicorn. The quicker she finished the spell, the sooner she could find out the answer regarding the silly stuff.

Waving the alicorn above the man's chest, she told him to be quiet.

"When will you need my blood?" he asked.

"Oh, uh, soon." She didn't want to freak him out and have him running away before she even got this going. "I'll use this." She waggled the alicorn. "Now. Silence. Just focus on the tone of my voice and drawing in the vibrations that I send to you, yeah?"

He nodded and closed his eyes again. Moonlight

gleamed through the big windows to their sides, and
fell across his face as if lighting a Hollywood vampire
in the big redemption scene. Oh, what a pretty man.

She'd returned from the airport for more than one
reason, and she would not forget that.

Soon enough.

Standing, Tuesday first walked the circle widder-
shins, enclosing it in a permeable violet light that would
allow her access to the inside, but wouldn't include
her as part of the spell. Stepping inside, she straddled
Ethan's legs. She wore only the long T-shirt, but his
eyes were closed and she—she had to keep it together
and rein in her lusty thoughts. Just for a while longer.

Holding the alicorn in one hand, she spread the fingers of her other hand and leaned forward, focusing
her energies toward the sigils drawn on his chest. The
words to the spell came by rote and she chanted them
over and over, changing her tone to a deeper resonance
after a few successions.

The red marker began to glow white and appeared
as if it opened Ethan's skin, though it did not. It was a
deep and luminous glow. It allowed in her magic. Pointing the alicorn in each direction—north, east, south,
then west—she then drew a line down to the center of
the pentagram.

Then, with a forceful stab of the alicorn's point, she
punctured Ethan's chest.

Chapter 11

Something ice-cold pierced his chest. Ethan gasped, winced. Slapped a hand to his chest, but the witch pushed it away immediately. She'd...staked him?

"Just go with it," she said calmly. "It's only in a quarter of an inch. I need blood, remember?"

She...needed blood? Fuck. Just...what the fuck?

As he felt blood drool from the puncture, Tuesday quickly used the tip of the alicorn to draw with his blood, tracing the sigil over his chest. She'd freaking staked him with a unicorn's horn!

Closing his eyes and letting his head fall back to the floor, Ethan then smirked and snorted. What the hell kind of whacked adventure had he tumbled into? He'd let a witch stake him and...he'd survived. He was still here. Not ash. And she was speaking her witchy voodoo words and humming above him.

When she'd asked for him to give blood, memories of the time he'd killed another with a blood transfusion had almost stopped him from doing this. That had been a different time. A completely different century. Medicine had advanced greatly. And…he hadn't wanted to give her details. To expose his broken heart to her. So he'd dropped his nervous worries and succumbed to Tuesday's wishes.

The witch didn't need to see into that soft and weak part of him. Because apparently she was more into stabbing a man than sympathizing with him. Bloody hell.

Opening his left eye, Ethan spied Tuesday as she kissed the blood-tipped alicorn. Then, kneeling and still straddling him, she bowed to blow across the wet blood. Her magic stirred up a violet fog and with her hands she coaxed it into a malleable cloud over his body, stretching it to encompass him from head to toe. And with a single clap of her palms, the fog dropped over his body and permeated his skin with a sizzle that made him hiss.

Tuesday stood, looking over her work. "That was it. You're such a big boy," she cooed as if he was a child. "That wasn't so bad, was it?"

He would not reply to her mocking tone. Even if he sensed she was teasing him. But it was difficult not to admire the view from where he lay. The woman wore but a T-shirt that was long enough to cover everything, but short enough to make him want to lift his head and take a closer look.

She just staked you, idiot. Right. Ethan pushed up to his elbows and looked over his bloody chest.

Fool that he was, he'd had the thought while in the Archives earlier that he'd like to see what she was capable of when wielding the alicorn. And now he knew.

Twirling the bloodied alicorn, the witch waggled an eyebrow. "Remember when you shoved me against the wall in the alleyway before the dark witch bonded us? You said that was the only blood I'd ever get from you." She shrugged. "Guess you were wrong, eh?"

"I'm doing this to help the mission. Unlike you, who seem to merely want to gloat about taking advantage of a man's kindness. You fucking staked me, witch!"

"And now you can tell everyone you've survived being staked. You don't have to mention it was with a unicorn horn and resulted in you looking like a glitter-bombed clubber."

Her giggle was enough to make Ethan mentally snap a rubber band at his wrist. But he wouldn't get angry at her. He was doing this to help the mission. And if he had gained some sort of magic out of the deal? So be it.

"Now you should have a sixth sense about the demon's location," she said. "You just have to learn to tap in to it. Focus inwardly, keeping the demon's name fore and your intent to find him as the guide. Shouldn't be too difficult for a vampire who has used persuasion on humans. Yeah?"

He had mastered enthralling humans centuries ago. He'd been born innately knowing how to control others with but a tweak to their thoughts, a subtle whisper after the bite, or even a gentle caress that would send a shiver of compliance through their system along with memory loss or even altered thoughts.

"Sounds good to me." Ethan touched the blood on his chest. It sparkled with violet. Was that a condition of using the alicorn? Interesting, and yet a bit too night-club-glitter for him.

"You can get up. But it'll take a bit for it all to soak

in, to really get a fix in you. What would be helpful is…" Tapping a finger to her bottom lip, she stepped out of the circle and gripped the obsidian crystal that hung about her neck from the leather cord.

"Is…?" He stood behind her, and brushed some of the violet dust off his jeans.

"Is what?" she asked.

"You were about to say something would be helpful?" He dismissed the query. "Whatever. Can I wash this off?"

"No, leave it on. The marker, anyway. It'll disappear when the spell has set. But you can wash off the blood that dribbled down the side of your ribs. You got a broom?"

"Stuart, vacuum the living area," he said and wandered into the bathroom.

Tuesday stood aside and watched as the Roomba vacuum cleaner appeared from out of a closet and scurried over to sweep up the salt and random drops of Ethan's blood. Skipping to avoid being attacked by the tenacious thing, she sat on the chair to stay out of the way.

A glance to the bathroom door made her smile. She had freaked the fuck out of the vampire by stabbing him with the alicorn. He might have thought she'd been staking him. Ha!

She shouldn't gloat over that sneaky triumph, but— Yes, she would. She'd caught him unawares, and yet, he hadn't overreacted or tried to push her away. He'd complied and had allowed her to finish the spell. He earned points for that. Not many vamps would do the same, she felt sure. Especially the ones with a bossy, controlling complex.

Yet, he had been not so eager to order her around since she'd returned from her near escape from the country. More points to the vampire for that restraint. Was it a new tactic to get her to ultimately work with him? Probably. Yet he'd given her a clue that there was more between them than mere spellcraft and demon chasing.

He wanted her.

And she was the witch to let the vampire have what he wanted.

When he returned to the room with a blood-free chest, but a few sparkles still in his hair and on his back, he wandered over to the vanity by the wall and poured himself a snifter of brandy. The city lights gleamed against a gray sky, highlighting his physique with a golden glow. He wore nothing but jeans, which he must have unbuttoned to clean off the blood—and he'd forgotten to rebutton them—and tufts of dark hair were visible.

Comfortable? Check.

Sexy? Mercy, could a witch get a break?

"You want some?" he asked as the vacuum rolled off to its closet and shut down.

Hell yes, she wanted some. "Uh…" Turning on the leather chair and pulling up her legs, Tuesday asked, "Oh, you mean brandy?"

"Yes."

"Ugh. That stuff makes me gag."

"Then you haven't tried the good stuff." He held up the goblet and strode over to the window, which was parallel to the bed. An outside light flashed crimson in the glass, winking at them. "A man can drink worlds in brandy. I've tasted Greece and Armenia, Turkey and

Chile. Stravecchio is one of my favorites. It's distilled in copper pots."

"I may have once dated a winemaker," Tuesday said.

"A vintner?"

"Yeah, that's what he called himself. Maybe *date* is too technical a term. More like fucked once or twice. Or a dozen times."

It was either that, or she'd dated a dozen different vintners and fucked them once or twice. Details. He didn't need to know everything about her life.

Ethan leaned back against the brick wall, where the window frame began; the massive pane was but inches from his left shoulder. The moonlight mixed with city lights gave his face a stark quality that Tuesday admired. While vampires as old as he could often look as young as teenagers or twentysomethings, Ethan had a certain seasoning to him that appealed to her centuries-gained sensibilities. He was not young and the years had imprinted on his face. In the line that cut down between his eyebrows when he flashed her the serious look, and in the silver hairs that dashed through his brown hair and beard stubble. A wise toughness deepened his gray irises to a cunning yet knowing stare.

He would be called classically handsome by those who cast Hollywood movies, and probably pigeonholed into the widowed or divorced single-father-with-an-edge role. The man was solid. Physically aware. And comfortable in his skin, muscles and bones that wrapped and formed him into a startlingly exquisite physique.

Washboard abs? Check.

"So, you fucked a lot of men over the centuries?" he asked, as he stared off through the window.

Now he was getting to the interesting conversation. Of course, she had mentioned the vintner.

"A dozen or hundreds. I don't record notches. You?"

"Fuck men?" He shrugged. "Not as often as you, I'm sure."

That nugget of info swirled a deep, hot thrill right between her legs. She could entirely see the man swinging for either women or men. That was sexy to her. A man who was not afraid of his sexuality and who lived his life the way he chose.

"I know the world is vast and coincidence rare," she said, "but if I ever learn we've fucked the same man that would so rock my world."

He chuckled and sipped the brandy. "I never kiss and tell."

And now she really wanted to delve into his love life. The fantasy of him bedding another man put a tight pull at the base of her throat and heated her breasts. And... oh, yes. She shifted on the chair, squeezing her thighs together to catch the flutter of want in her pussy.

"Sex becomes different the longer you live, yes?" he asked.

She nodded. Because it had. In ways no mere mortal could ever imagine.

"It's not so much about the romance and roses," he continued. His gaze was fixed on some point out the window. His rugged profile teased Tuesday's sense of control. "Nothing like what you see in the movies or read in those romance novels."

"Have you ever read a romance novel?"

"No."

"Then don't knock them. I even like the ones about the vampires and werewolves, despite the authors getting their paranormal attributes wildly wrong most of the time. But you're right. As the years, decades and centuries glide by, sex becomes less about the physical. And yet, at the same time, the meaning of it becomes more."

"Exactly," he said with a tilt of the brandy snifter toward her. "It's less about an emotional bond and more about…" He gave it some consideration. "It's about finding yourself in someone else, yet not getting lost there. Knowing that you both are a part of something much bigger. And also, surrendering to the moment, and being able to focus completely on that other person and yourself. Love has nothing to do with sex. It's too messy, and too much thinking is involved."

"I agree. Though—" Now that she'd decided she might welcome love into her life, Tuesday wasn't one-hundred-percent certain anymore what, exactly, sex did mean to her. Though she did know one thing. "It's definitely a soul thing."

"Yes. It's…well, it's worlds." He tipped the glass to his lips for a swallow. "So are we going to avoid the obvious?"

"Which is?"

"That we need to discuss what is going on with us moving forward."

"Honestly? I wish we would avoid it. For now. I'm tired." She pushed her hands through her hair and let the heavy tresses drop over her shoulders. She was aware it was a sensual move, and took all the leisure in drawing her hair back over a shoulder for him to watch. "I just want to sit here and watch you drink your brandy."

He shrugged, then took another sip. That the conversation had turned to sex only spurred her on. She had been thinking the man needed to have sex to make the spell sink in, and had almost said as much earlier, but had wisely stopped herself. And she was very willing to volunteer to assist in the said process of spell-sinking-in.

"Worlds, eh?" she asked.

"Yes, indeed."

"Worlds in the brandy and in sex." She leaned forward, a hand to her knee. Lowering her lashes, she looked up through them. "I bet you've seen worlds unending."

"That I have." He turned to face her. The sleek line of his body stretching his long torso, down his hips and the length of his legs to bare feet screamed out "sex" to Tuesday. "Do something for me?"

She shrugged. "Anything. As long as it's interesting."

He crossed the arm he held the drink in over his chest and eyed her for a moment. That gaze could strip a woman bare. And Tuesday felt it move over her skin as a warm breath that tickled and tightened her nipples. It traced along her side and shivered down the length of each of her legs. And there at her core, it teased her to open herself, to want what she'd been cursed to never have.

Finally, Ethan said, "Show me your world."

Chapter 12

Tuesday lifted an eyebrow. Show him her world?

Now that request was interesting enough to make her want to comply. She had been waiting for this moment. It was time the two of them, indeed, peeked into one another's worlds. Or even went for a running dive.

Yeah, she favored a good splash that would land her all in.

She settled back against the cushy leather seat that she imagined Ethan must have lived in, sat in, perhaps even fucked in for decades. It was so comfortable. And she felt at ease sitting before his soft gaze.

Drawing up her knees, she let them drop apart and to the sides, exposing herself to him. The T-shirt inched above her trimmed patch of pubic hairs, teasing him with the view.

His attention was easy and yet focused. As he tilted

a hip forward, she noticed his erection bulged beneath the dark jeans. He'd been hard for much longer than the few seconds she'd taken to get comfy. It was a good thing for him her limp-dick spell had not succeeded that first day when he'd held her captive in the cage. Good for her, too.

Tapping a finger against her lips, she eyed him teasingly, yet the promise was true. She licked a fingertip and kissed it. Gliding her fingers down between her legs, she watched Ethan as she slid that wetted fingertip along her heated folds. Slowly, deeply, she traced up a slick wetness and skated across her clit, which now hummed with a greedy need for attention. A delicious, erotic thrill shivered in her core and loosened her shoulder muscles.

This was her world, as Ethan had put it. A woman who knew how to gratify herself. She knew what made her squirm, what strokes could make her hum with pleasure, what pressure, speed and the length of time to gauge each touch. And knowing that about herself made her strong and wise. It was a knowledge she had tried to teach those women she had healed over the centuries. The body was theirs to understand. Treat it well, and they would be well. And that included self-care. Which meant jilling off.

Because really, what woman could ever teach a man what she did not first know herself from experience and practice?

Ethan watched without a lusty gape or a smirk. It was his calm, gleaming gaze that made the tease more exciting for her. Everything about him called to her on a sensual song. The relaxed curl of his fingers cupping the brandy snifter. The liquid flame scent of the golden brown liquor. And the tilt of his head that caught the moonlight in the silver strands near his temples. Mmm…

Tuesday moaned appreciatively. The man was something to admire. She didn't need to see fangs to get off on his sexy. Her finger stroked faster and firmer, focusing where she was most sensitive. Wet, swollen and tingling, her body stepped forward to sing its alluring wisdom.

She could do this quickly or draw it out, and prolonging it won the vote.

Ethan tilted his head, turning to study her with more intensity. His upper teeth eased over his lower lip in a tense but wanting slip. The man's abs, still marked with the tracking grid, flexed. And a wince signaled her he was feeling the intensity of the moment in the tightening of his erection. It strained against his jeans. And his fingers curled about the brandy glass more possessively.

Her motions quickened. Tuesday closed her eyes briefly, falling into the sensations, the tightening in her core, the promising jitter of release that seemed to reside at every place within her body at once. And yet… she slowed, easing up on the pressure so that the high began to simmer. Too fast. Never too slow.

"Is this a world you want to learn more about?" she said in breathy gasps. "Ethan?"

"Fuck yes."

"I'm so close." She moaned sweetly. But she wouldn't get herself off. Yet. Not until he joined in on the fun. "Take your cock out. Let me see your world, vampire."

He unzipped and his cock, granted release, sprang up against his tight belly. Still holding the glass, the fingers of his other hand curled about his sizeable hard-on and squeezed, then stroked.

"Turn and face the window," Tuesday directed. "I want to see you from that angle."

He did so, setting the glass up on a jut of wood that was part of the design along the brick wall to his side. He placed the heel of his palm up high on the window, and with his other hand he stroked up and down, slowly, measured, and tightened then loosened his grip. He knew exactly what worked for him. He also knew his body, and so she paid attention to his motions, the pace and the intensity.

"I can't watch you when I'm facing this way," he said.

"You've seen me. It's my turn to watch. Your cock has an inward curve. That's sexy."

He glanced aside at her, smiling briefly, but then his jaw tightened and Tuesday knew he had hit a sweet spot with his pumping motions. She sucked in her lower lip, biting it lightly. Her own motions synched with his, moving faster, more firmly.

"Come over here," he said. "I need your wet pussy to slick my strokes."

She obliged with a teasingly slow stroll over to the window. Leaning her shoulders against a thin connecting steel column, she eyed him from his shuttered eyelids, to his pulsing hard abs, down to his cock. The head of it was red and swollen. Angry and virile. The color of his want and of her desire.

"Take off that shirt," he said.

The T-shirt was abandoned as she flung it to the bed. Ethan moved his gaze over her body, and Tuesday leaned her shoulders back against the cool windowpane, the action lifting her breasts. The nipples were so tight and her pussy demanded touch. Yet she could stand there and soak up his adoration for however long he would give it to her.

Ethan gestured his stroking hand toward her mons. "May I?"

Strangely pleased by his polite request to enter her wanting heat, she nodded and tilted her hips forward. Keeping his gaze pinned to hers, Ethan slid his fingers into her folds. He groaned, and slid them within her moistness. The tease of it, of his welcome invasion into her, was enough to make her gasp.

A glint in his gray irises stole something from her. She gave it willingly.

His didn't remain within her long enough to give her more than a heart-pounding tingle and a wish for him to move deeper. The man returned to the task literally at hand; her wetness gleamed on his length as his strokes about his erection increased velocity.

Sex without the commitment or relationship expectations was exactly the way she preferred it. And it seemed Ethan was completely on board with that. This night was going to be a hell of a lot more interesting than an eight-hour flight to the States.

Slipping her fingers between her folds, Tuesday matched Ethan's rhythm. They held eye contact, mouths slightly parted, gasps punctuating the brandy-tinted air. A dare was volleyed between them with the curl of a lip, or the lift of an eyebrow. Then of a sudden his strokes slowed. His grin revealed bright whites. And in his eyes a question alighted.

Tuesday turned toward him and tapped her finger on his lips. He lashed out his tongue to taste her salty sweetness. She glided it in deeper, skating his tongue, then slipping it under each of his pointed fangs. They were not lowered, but that didn't matter. She knew touching a vampire's fangs was an erotic act. Like touching his cock, it produced the same titillating sensations throughout his system.

He grasped her hand and sucked in her finger, slow, hard... He dashed his tongue firmly at the base, where it met her palm. An exhale heated her skin and she felt the prick of his fang—but he didn't break skin.

"Taste me," she dared. "You know you want to."

He shook his head. "That's not how we're doing this."

"Oh? Is there a guidebook I wasn't allowed to read?"

"There might be."

He kissed her finger and placed her hand about his cock. He moved his fingers to squeeze over hers and show her the speed he liked for her strokes. Tuesday was a fast learner and she took over immediately.

The man cupped her jaw and slid his palm over her cheek. His thumb rubbed her lower lip. With a lash of her tongue she tasted his musky flavor twined with hers. She pulled him closer by his hard-on and touched the head of him to her pinnacle, where she was achingly wet and slick. Leaning into him and lifting one leg to hook at his hip, she hinted at allowing him entrance.

Ethan bowed his head to meet foreheads with her. "Tease me, witch. Don't make this easy."

She gripped his rod tightly, pushing him away from her. Then she lifted her mouth toward his but didn't quite connect, save for with a wink. She liked the tease, too. It was filled with heartbeats and breaths, and silent pleadings that were so loud she felt them racing in her blood. Heated sighs mingled. Skin, moist with desire, slid against skin. And their worlds opened wide, coaxing one another to explore. To learn. To know.

"Kneel," she boldly commanded.

The vampire kissed her lips. A smirk formed behind that kiss, curling on her mouth. A secret he wouldn't allow her to do more than taste. Then he began to lower. His lips brushed her chin, his tongue dashed the pulse on her neck. He held there, scenting her heat, drawing her in, content to indulge himself in her. She wanted to force him lower, but instead she closed her eyes and took in the frustratingly delicious shiver of Ethan taking his time.

Finally, he kissed lower, slowly, and lingered over her breasts, breathing across them—*hush, hush, hush*—but not touching for more than a second. And on his path he veered toward her heart chakra, the center of her being, and kissed the sigil, which didn't glow or pain her in any way. His tongue traced the *S* shape of it, then followed the straight line that dashed from curl to curl. The tickle of his beard on her breasts tightened her nipples. Another *hush*.

The man's journey took him down her stomach. Hot breaths circled her navel. He kneeled and looked up to her, his mouth but inches from her pussy.

Tuesday ran her fingers through his short, spiky hair, reveling in the luxurious softness of it. Yet it looked rough, stalwart. Manly. He begged her permission with his gray eyes. And with a tilt of her hips, she invited him closer.

The first stroke of his tongue to her clit roused a chuckle of affirmation from her. Oh, yeah, the man was on a mission. And his focus did not veer. It required but a few more careful and firm strokes to lift her from the denial she'd been forcing herself to maintain and set her free.

Tuesday came with a throaty growl and a slap of her palms against the window glass behind her. "Yes!" She clasped her fingers tightly against Ethan's scalp. "Oh, you perfect, nasty vampire."

The moon highlighted their naked antics, and she realized that the neighbors were probably getting a good show.

Let them watch.

She bowed forward over her lover as the shivering effects of the orgasm tickled through her system and made everything so much brighter, crisper and fanfreakin'-tastic.

"You taste like many worlds," Ethan whispered against her wetness. "And you come like no world will ever contain you. Powerful witch."

He kissed her there, and there, and then he slid his fingers inside her and groaned with pleasure. "Fuck." He tilted his head against her belly, lashing out his tongue across her skin, then looked up to her. Another request for permission gleamed in his eyes.

"I want this—" she toed his cock "—inside me." She lifted his chin with her fingers. "Now."

He moved backward toward the bed. Tuesday followed, her fingers still under his chin. With a lift, she directed him up and onto the inviting soft bedding. She then straddled him and crawled forward to position herself as if upon the siege perilous. She may not find the Holy Grail, but she would invade Ethan's world tonight.

The man spread his arms across the bed and closed his eyes, giving her the control, the freedom to explore his world. He would take what she would give him.

Ethan slid his palms up her arms and then around to cup her breasts. He thumbed her nipples and pinched them gently, then not so gently. That erotic twinge pulled her forward and hastened her need to feel him within her. Gripping the control stick, Tuesday mounted his thick cock and slid onto him slowly, inch by hot inch, taking him into her feminine power and granting him that secret.

The vampire groaned and squeezed her breasts, but without any purpose, for he was falling into her. Filling her. Being owned by her as she squeezed her inner muscles to hug him tightly. His hips rocked. He swore and insisted she go faster, but she kept her pace slow, lingering, enjoying every hot, thick measure of him.

Bending her knees she settled completely onto him and leaned back, catching her palms beside his thighs. He tilted his hips forward, deepening their connection. She may have opened her world to him, but right now the world slipped away. Only they two existed. Rocking, engaged and finding a harmonious rhythm. Such luxury to feel so full and powerful.

Yet the power was shared. And Tuesday didn't mind that at all.

As the moon slowly glided across the inky night sky, together they rose to a climax that made their bodies shudder. Ethan's chest muscles and biceps flexed into steely ropes. His abdomen clenched. His hips tremored as he spilled inside her.

Shivering with exquisite orgasm, Tuesday flung forward to hug her lover. Nestled in his panting embrace, she smiled with satisfaction.

Tonight she had entered the vampire's world.

Chapter 13

Tuesday rose with the sun, or rather what she expected was early morning. The window shades had drawn down while she had been slumbering. Good ol' Stuart. She could get used to a home butler like that.

"No, never," she muttered. There was something creepy about a robot tending the household duties. She'd seen the movies. It never ended well.

Shaking her head, she wandered into Ethan's kitchen to pour some orange juice. On the kitchen counter, she found one stale croissant in a brown patisserie box so she gnawed on that, thinking to leave the vampire to sleep.

Settling onto the sofa and pulling the bag of supplies she'd purchased onto her lap, she again eyed the bed for movement. That had been some good sex last night. But she didn't intend to sew any strings of attachment between the two of them. It had just been sex. Leave it at that.

Because she didn't belong in Paris, and she most certainly was not in the frame of mind to begin an affair with a sexy vampire who knew how to touch her in all the right places in all the right ways.

Even if she had decided getting rid of the love curse was most important.

She blew out a breath and shook her head.

She wasn't a romantic. Romance had gotten stale for her somewhere around the mid-eighteenth century. Hell, it had been earlier than that. The four days and nights Finnister had tortured her relentlessly had pretty much banished all her idiotic desires for love and romance.

Sex was as she and Ethan had discussed. More than romance, it was a world. And if a person went into a relationship expecting it to fulfill and complete them and make them happy, then they were doing it wrong. Happiness could only come from within. And recognizing that Ethan made her happy—but wasn't the source of that feeling—was key.

However, there was nothing wrong in reveling in the afterglow of a night having been well-fucked.

Pulling out items from the bag, she decided the Tibetan quartz points might come in handy for a summoning spell. She really needed some shungite, something powerful to shield her from the demon's awareness, but the shop had been out. The obsidian she wore was strong and attuned to her body, but it tended to shiver when attacked.

The tracking magic she'd given to Ethan with last night's spell might work. And it might not. Surely, the sex had settled that magic into his very bones. Now, it was all in how he worked with such power. And much as she felt he was a smart guy who could handle this mission on his own, she didn't want to be left standing on the side. Seriously. She liked to participate. And she owed the demon a smackdown that would make his heart crumble and fall from his chest. He'd gotten all the love over these centuries. It was time to tilt the scales in her favor.

"Time to let the witch reign," she murmured, and sipped the orange juice.

Another glance to the bed found the sheets pushed away and the mattress absent of a slumbering vampire. He must have slipped into the bathroom. And she hadn't even noticed. Vampires were shifty like that.

She could only smile at the thought.

Ten minutes later the shower stopped and Ethan wandered through the bedroom with a towel wrapped about his hips. Water droplets glinted on his chest and shoulders, and he scrubbed his hair with a smaller towel until it stood up all over. A slick of his fingers over each side of his head left it styled perfectly. He noticed her watching him and winked at her.

Tuesday experienced a sudden desire to kneel before him and give him whatever he may ask of her.

But she didn't. That would be pushing it. Was she all of a sudden so wishy-washy simply because she'd been considering romance? Silly witch.

"You're an early riser. For a vampire," she commented as he padded into the living area and stood before her.

Tossing the towel he'd used on his hair back to land on the end of the bed, he shrugged. "Never need much sleep. And it's supposed to rain today around noon. I'm getting ready to go out."

"Yeah? You got a date?"

His smile was quick and easy. And it held all the answers to the secrets she'd given him last night. "I'm going to test out this tracking magic you gave me." He splayed a palm down his chest and abs. The red marker was gone, washed away in the shower. The sex had quickened the spell sinking in. The man was now a walking demon compass. "Can't sit around hoping the demon will come knocking on my door, can I?"

"Does that mean I have to stay here?"

"You do know the danger of coming along."

"It's not so much a danger as me being the plague the demon wants to avoid. Do you have your crew ready to go this time?"

"I will." He sat on the sofa next to her, and the towel parted to reveal his muscular, dark-haired thighs and a tease of penis. "Can I kiss you this morning and tell you how beautiful you are? Or are we not doing that lovey-dovey kind of stuff?"

"I'll take a kiss and a compliment any day."

"Good." He leaned in and kissed her, taking his time as he opened her mouth with his and slipped his tongue against hers. Instant recall of his tongue tasting her pussy filled Tuesday's chest with a deep and wanting moan. The vampire ended the kiss with a slip of his thumb over her bottom lip. "You're beautiful, witch."

"You're pretty sexy yourself. Want to have hex?"

"I hope that means what I want it to mean."

"Oh, it does." Tuesday plunged her hand under the towel and claimed his semi-erect cock with a firm grip. "I get a head start."

As she bowed to tug away his towel and lick up his quickly hardening length, Ethan commented, "I think I'm the one with the head start, if you know what I mean. Oh, yes, this is a good way to begin the day."

Ethan slipped on his Ray-Bans and exited the building. He vacillated on whether or not to drive on his quest to find the demon, then decided against it. On foot he could maneuver quicker and into tighter situations. As vampire he had the ability to traverse the entire city in a swift dash, leaving those he passed only wondering if it was a sudden wind that had brushed their hair across their skin. But he'd start slow as he learned to work with this magic Tuesday had given him.

The training session had been all of a few minutes as she'd explained he had to focus inwardly on his sense of direction and need to stand before the demon Gazariel, while also dividing that focus outward to pick up on signals that indicated he was moving toward that goal. Elementals would work with him, she had explained. He knew elementals were tiny creatures, like sprites, but also not. They were of the elements—earth, air, water and fire—and could resemble their namesakes or not. And they could either choose to be seen or not. A mysterious species that Tuesday had said he should trust would guide him.

So he did.

The forecasted rain was more like a mist, but the sky was clouded and that was all that mattered to a vampire. Still, he kept on the sunglasses so as to notice any wards he should avoid.

Leaving his coat open, and his shirt unbuttoned, he needed to access the invisible sigil on his chest that

Tuesday had drawn. Before he'd left, she had taken his hand and placed his forefingers to each of the compass points, between his nipples, above his navel and under his ribs on each side. He had to focus on the demon's name and his intent, so he murmured, "Take me to Gazariel, The Beautiful One."

With a touch to the north direction on his chest, he felt nothing. He slid his fingers down to the south and an inexplicable tug turned him toward the Seine. Had that been the elementals?

"Trust them," Ethan muttered, and he began to walk, following the minute but definite sensation that seemed to keep his feet on track and his eyes on the prize.

If tracking a demon was this easy, he should consider staffing a dark witch to train his retrievers. On the other hand, none in his employ seemed to have too much trouble locating a mission target. It was the adventure and the hunt that fueled a retriever, and he was feeling that old yet invigorating thrill again. He wondered why he'd ever thought settling behind a desk was for him, and now challenged his idea of where, exactly, he wanted his future to go. Perhaps he should participate in fieldwork more often?

When he reached the river and crossed the busy street to lean over the stone balustrade and peer into the inky waters, he touched his chest again and turned his attention inward to divine his next move. This time he was drawn across the Pont de Sully and into the fifth arrondissement to pass before the Arab World Institute. It was a favorite building of his. The facade was paneled with metal squares that were light-sensitive and could regulate the amount of light that entered the building.

They mimicked an element of Arabic architecture, the *mashrabiya*. It was gorgeous, plain and simple.

Pulled now with more urgency, he walked swiftly down a curving street, and turned this way and that until he'd broached the depths of the fifth and the traffic slowed and the number of pedestrians decreased. He dodged to avoid a cyclist on the sidewalk, then abruptly turned to the right.

He stood before a three-story white stucco building hugged by a small patio area with outdoor dining tables capped by red-and white-striped umbrellas. The aroma of roasting meat appealed to him, and he also picked up the delicious caraway scent of baked rye bread. A four-star restaurant?

He supposed demons did have to eat. And the place was large and spacious, so Ethan could enter without being noticed. But also, it was filled with humans. He couldn't risk taking the demon into captivity here. He'd have to get him outside.

He buttoned up his shirt so he wouldn't stand out in such a tony place. At the hostess station, Ethan explained he was looking for a friend and wanted to take a look around. The receptionist with emerald eyes and too much red lipstick started to explain that wasn't the policy and that the place was reservations-only. So Ethan touched her hand and traced his finger along her wrist right above the vein, making sure she felt his persuasion.

She suddenly nodded and gestured him to walk inside. With a sigh, she then turned back to her black leather book of names and tables, instantly forgetting Ethan had been there.

The main room, which hummed with low conversa-

tion, was vast and spacious and walled completely in
windows, such as in a Victorian conservatory. Massive
plants grew up along the walls and hung from the ceiling, and were positioned to give privacy to most tables.
It smelled like summer, too. Ethan wouldn't be surprised to see a parrot or even a snake gliding amongst
the greenery, but he quickly reined in his wonder and
scanned the room from his discreet position beside a
tall, bushy ficus.

The pull he felt in his chest was unmistakable. Tuesday's magic had worked. The demon had to be in here.

Methodically, he scanned over every table until he
spied a head of dark hair sitting before the far window.
A man was talking animatedly to a woman whom Ethan
couldn't quite see, for a frond of greenery obscured the
view. Didn't matter. He'd found Gazariel. Dressed in an
elegant business suit that gleamed when he moved. Like
hematite catching the sun, his wavy dark hair looked
styled and ready for a magazine photo shoot. Indeed,
he was beautiful, and Ethan could admit that.

Now, how to get him out of the restaurant and in position for capture?

He tugged out his phone and texted the containment
team leader his location. Five minutes and they'd be
outside near the hornbeam shrubbery that demarcated
the edge of the property.

Whoever the woman was that the demon spoke to
could be a girlfriend or lover. The one he had given the
book to? Or had he yet to give her the gift? What sort of
gift was a book of angel names and sigils? The woman
had to be paranormal. Ethan didn't see the point in a
human wanting something like that. Or knowing the
value of such a gift.

On the other hand, there were many humans who genuinely Believed, and those sorts could be the most dangerous to his species, to all species.

A waiter neared Ethan and cast him a curious look so Ethan sent out some more persuasive vibes. He needed to remain unremarkable to those around him.

On the other side of the room, the demon clasped the woman's hand from across the table and she leaned forward, a spill of coal-black hair falling over her cheek and veiling her face. Dark lipstick emphasized her narrow mouth as she spoke. Yet when she stroked her hair back with a hand, curling it over an ear, Ethan saw clearly what she looked like.

And he recognized her.

"Holy—what the hell?"

He knew the woman's name. Anyx. She was not human, but rather vampire.

And she was his ex-wife.

Chapter 14

Outside the restaurant, Ethan stalked over to the containment crew waiting for action and told the leader the grab had been called off.

"Not today," he said at the crew leader's inquiry. "There's been…a glitch. Sorry. Thanks for being prompt. But we can't take the demon in hand just yet."

The crew left, and Ethan ran his fingers back through his hair, hoping he'd made the right call. Gripping and ungripping his fingers into fists, he paced before the shrubbery.

Why was Anyx with Gazariel? And how did that change things? He could have taken Gazariel. But without knowing whether or not the demon had given her the book—or Gazariel may have given the book to someone entirely different—Ethan had decided not to move in.

Because what if they grabbed the demon and the vampiress got away?

He could take them both into custody. The vicious yet vain demon with a flair for taking down buildings by stealing a witch's magic, and a vampiress whom Ethan had once shared his bed with for decades. Their marriage had lasted sixty years.

Punching the air in frustration, Ethan strode off toward the street, then paused and turned back to the restaurant. This was not how the director of a black ops team that collected dangerous objects from across the world must react in the face of adversity. If he intended to continue with fieldwork he must get this right. Stand up to the challenge. As strange and perplexing as that new challenge had become.

He would wait and track them both. He had to know what connection Gazariel and Anyx had and then he would decide how to deal with this.

Of all the women in the world the demon could be having a relationship with, why did it have to be that particular vampiress?

Tuesday was listening to one of the jazz albums Ethan owned. Having never been interested in the musical style before, she warmed to it now. Swaying to the saxophone's mournful cry, she wrapped her arms across her chest and closed her eyes. She'd dated a musician once. More than once. A handful of musicians over the centuries. But the one she remembered with a self-indulgent smile had been an '80s hair-band drummer. Those guys could keep a steady rhythm going. For a long time.

Smirking, she turned to find Ethan standing before

her, smiling widely to have caught her in a personal moment.

She stopped swaying. "I didn't hear you come in."

"The music is on."

"You don't mind? I'm starting to like this stuff."

He tossed his coat aside to the couch and approached, taking her hands in his as if to dance. And then he did start to dance with her, slowly, turning her and finding the beat.

"Billie Holiday is one of my favorites," he said. "I never missed a concert when she performed in Europe."

"Really? You were a fanboy?"

"I suppose. I dated a musician or two."

She chuckled. "I was thinking the same. Two or three, or maybe a dozen. It was all good."

"That it was. We who have lived so long have time on our hands. Time that needs to be filled. So I adventure. Try new things. Keep an open mind about what I encounter. And fuck a musician every once in a while."

"Good life goals, if you ask me. Yeah, settling down in one place, or with one person, only stays interesting for so long. I move around a lot." She tilted her head onto his shoulder because it felt a natural thing to do. He smelled like the cool outdoors. "Just returned to Boston a few months ago after some world traveling."

"You have a permanent residence there?"

"I've owned the place for about forty years. I was thinking I'd open up a New Age shop and sell candles and crystals. Maybe. It sounds…kitchen witch. Yet it gives me something to do, you know? I've lived in the city off and on over the centuries. I always gravitate back to home."

"Never had a hankering to settle in Paris?"

She shrugged and hugged up against him and their footsteps slowed as they swayed. "Too cosmopolitan for me. I like slow-paced and homey. I live in a little suburb at the edge of the city that hugs a forest. We witches do need nature to survive."

He bowed his head and nuzzled his nose beside her ear. The tickle and his warm breath sent a shiver across her skin. A good shiver. But as she looked up at him, she remembered where he'd been and what for.

"How did it go? You're in a good mood, so…?"

"I, uh…" Ethan broke their clutch and walked to the window, his back to her. The shades had risen completely to let in the clouded light. He raked his fingers through his hair. "I didn't apprehend The Beautiful One today. There was an issue."

"But you found him?" Tuesday plucked the needle off the vinyl and set the arm aside, then turned off the record player. "Where did you find him?"

"I tracked him to a four-star restaurant in the fifth. He was lunching with…a woman."

"A lover? I wonder if that's the one he told me he was going to give the book to."

"Do you think he's already given it to her?"

"I don't know. I got the impression he had or would soon. And if he knows we're after it, then he probably wants it out of his hands. What happened? Why didn't you capture him? Did they see you? Was your containment crew late again? Ethan?"

"Tuesday, just—" He turned and took her hands.

And suddenly, heart dropping to her gut, Tuesday felt as if he was going to lay some great confession on her and, whatever it was, she wouldn't like it. "What's going on? You could have had him."

"I made a judgment call. Didn't think the time was right. I want to learn more about the demon's connection to the woman. She's, uh… Tuesday, I recognized the woman Gazariel was with. Her name is Anyx. She's vampire. An old and powerful vampire."

"Yeah? What kept you from taking the demon in hand? You afraid of a vampiress? Didn't want to hurt her feelings by capturing her lover?"

He bracketed her face with his hands and said, "Anyx is my ex-wife."

Tuesday shoved out of his reach. His ex-wife? But that meant he'd once been married. Which—okay, after five hundred years the guy could have been married a time or two. Or even four or a dozen. Shouldn't bother her. Some paranormals who lived a long time had a tendency to collect spouses. And yet…

"Tuesday? I know that's some freaky information to out with, but what's this about?" He gestured toward her stiff posture and open jaw. "Are you…angry? I've lived a long life. There's a lot you don't know about me."

"I know that." She put up a palm as if that could block all the feelings from streaming into her soul. Feelings of betrayal, rejection and downright jealousy. What was up with that? She had no right. And really, she'd decided this was just a fling with the guy. She didn't care what he did, or *who* he did, or when he had done it. Maybe? "You took me by surprise."

"You're upset."

"No, I'm not."

"You—"

He grabbed her by the shoulders and shoved her against the wall. Pinning her with his hips and hands, he kissed her soundly. It wasn't sweet or tender, nor lingering or heady. The man was kissing her in punishment. And as quickly as it started he ended it.

"You don't get to do this," he said. "You have a past, too, witch. Don't go all raging, jealous lover on me. It's beneath you."

He shoved away from her and walked in a half circle, shoving his fingers through his hair. A side glance delivered her a stern reprimand.

Tuesday exhaled. His words were not wrong. But. Just…but.

"Will you let me explain?" he asked. "Or are you going to start calling me Richard again?"

Well, it had been a dick move to slam that one on her.

And yet. Fuck. What *was* up with her? The man had done nothing wrong. Except let the demon get away. Because of his ex-wife.

"Yeah, you'd better explain things to me," she finally said. "I'm having a hard time figuring why some chick could keep you from capturing the one demon you've been jonesing for these past few days. End of the world, remember? That's kind of important."

"I know!" he shouted.

Tuesday toned down her accusatory voice. "Did she see you? Recognize you? Why did you two break up? Ah, shit. I'm sorry, I don't have a right to those answers."

"Yes, you do. And I'll give you those answers. Sit down. I'll get you something to drink."

She could use the whole bottle of brandy right now. Even if it did taste nasty to her. Instead, Ethan returned with a glass of orange juice. She pressed the cool glass against her cheek. When Ethan sat next to her on the sofa, she shifted and pulled up her legs to face him. And also to put some distance between them.

With a nod, he accepted the defensive move. "Fine. The witch is mad at me. But you haven't managed to bespell my dick limp yet, so... I can deal."

"I would never. I mean, I *can*, but I won't. Promise?"

"You're not so sure about that one. But I'll deal with that challenge if and when it comes my way. And no, Anyx didn't see me, nor did Gazariel."

"Quit saying his name. And hers, for that matter."

Ethan sighed. "Are you really going to do this?"

Ready to swing up and punch him, Tuesday stopped her fingers from curling into a fist by wrapping them around the glass of juice. She reasoned with her shivering inner self that had wanted to believe in the man. To believe that they had started something. She'd wanted love, but maybe this was the universe telling her to back off. Keep the curse. Her heart was safer that way.

When had she begun to think in such a way? Really? She was asking to be let down.

"I was married to Anyx in the sixteenth century," Ethan said. "Right out of my parents' home. The marriage was arranged. We were both vampire. My tribe wanted to form an alliance with another tribe. It was a mutual decision, though. I knew her and had my eye on her before the proposal was even suggested."

Tuesday sighed heavily. She didn't want to hear all this romantic bullshit. Or did she? By the seven sacred witches, she'd listen. He did deserve that much from her.

"We were married for sixty years before we decided to part ways. A couple can only remain together so long before they grow apart and develop different interests. Interests that may oppose one another. And the indifference that grows slowly yet deeply—it's a strong divide. The institution of marriage is not something that lends well to monogamy. We'd both discovered that. We parted amicably."

"Then why the sudden horror at seeing her today? It's been four hundred years. You seem to be over her. Why didn't you march up and take Gazariel out of there?"

"First, because it was in a public place. I required a means to lure him out, and with Anyx there…well. And also, I'm not sure what's going on between Anyx and the demon. And I think learning about that connection may be important. One of the main reasons we parted ways was because she developed a dark obsession with death."

"Coming from a vampire? That doesn't surprise me."

He flicked her a stabbing look. "Really? Is that what you think of me?"

She shrugged. "You're not like that."

"But all the rest of the vampires are walking purveyors of death? You sound worse than I do when I was initially cursing you a witch."

He was right. And she was giving this vampire bitch too much power by hating her for merely having been in Ethan's life. As his wife. For sixty freakin' years. But they'd been apart four and a half centuries. And that did mean something.

"Sorry." Tuesday clasped one of Ethan's hands. "All vamps are not like that. I know you don't kill to survive. It's a stupid myth only made stronger by movies and fiction. I shouldn't buy in to the hive mind's vampiric beliefs. And I don't. It's just a shocker to hear all this. You know?" Bowing her head, she winced and looked up through her lashes. "I gotta know, though… Was she your only wife?"

"Yes." He kissed her forehead, and she lifted her face up to meet his small smile with one of her own.

"I soured on the whole institution of marriage after we parted ways. It falls in the same category as sex with regard to what it should mean and what it really means. A piece of paper uniting two people until death parts them is nothing but trouble waiting to happen."

"So I've heard." She set the empty glass on the floor beside the couch.

"What about you? Any exes I should know about?"

"I've never put on a ring." She waggled her bare fingers. "Never will."

"A ring means so little. A man or woman can have a lover, for years, decades, and it can be a stronger relationship than some marriage certificate could ever forge."

"We are in agreement on that. But love, well…"

"I'm sorry. It must be hard for you if you've never known love."

"Maybe. I don't know. How can one know to miss something they've never had?" She swallowed. That was a lie. "Well, I did have it once. At least, I thought I did. Asshole witch hunter."

And yet, her soul sighed and uttered a longing cry for such an experience. Love?

Best not to think about it right now.

"Okay, I learned something new about you today and I didn't fall apart because of it," she said. "Not yet, at least. I guess I would be stunned if you'd *not* been married. You're quite the catch."

"Why, thank you. But it was a political thing, as I've said. The tribes eventually went back to warring against one another, even though Anyx and I remained man and wife. We did love each other, though. In our own ways."

"What tribe are you in?"

"Right now? I am unaligned. Then? I was in tribe Nava. They are still together to this day, but they've spread across Europe from our humble Parisian beginnings."

"What tribe was your ex-wife with?"

"Sarax," he said. "They disbanded last century. They'd gotten into some really dark shit. I'm pretty sure she was still with them then."

"What did you mean about her having an obsession with death?"

Ethan stood and paced toward the window, arms akimbo. He looked over his shoulder at her. "Anyx began collecting ephemera related to death spells and memento mori. She never used any of the spells—at least, not to my knowledge—but she liked to know what the spell or object could do. After she acquired a plague curse I called it quits. Yet her interest in such dangerous objects may have been what led me to the work I do today. In fact, I know it is."

"A plague curse? Sounds like the kind of chick who would be interested in a book that, when the code is deciphered, could end the world."

"Yes. No. I don't know. I mean, Anyx loved life when I knew her. She was not a vampire who would ever kill indiscriminately. I can't imagine her wanting to destroy the world."

"People change."

"Yes, and she probably has."

"Tell me this. Do you still love her?"

"I did. As I said, in my own way. It was appreciation and admiration. And we were physically attracted to one another. And then the love faded. I don't hate her, but I'm indifferent to her. She would be like a stranger to me now." He placed a hand over his heart. "She's just another vampiress to me."

Tuesday nodded. The hand over his heart had been an unconscious move. He might think that was what he believed, but if she meant nothing to him then why hadn't he walked up to Gazariel and grabbed him? It shouldn't have mattered what the woman meant to him.

"So what's the plan now?" she asked.

"I followed them out of the restaurant. The demon dropped Anyx off on the rue de Rivoli. I then followed him to a parking garage and he joined her in shopping. It looked to be a long day of retail adventure that I wasn't up for. I'll go out again. And next time, I'll take the demon in hand, no matter what. But I'll have to take measures to contain Anyx as well."

"You need me."

"I don't see how that will work if your sigil tips off the demon we're after him."

"I'll figure this one out." She pressed a hand between her breasts. "But admit you might need an uninvolved party to keep you on point."

"Uninvolved?" He leaned forward, close enough to kiss her. "I thought we were involved?"

"You know what I mean." She tapped his mouth. "I have no ties to the vampiress. You need me to keep you steady."

"You do have a manner about you that challenges me, yet also, stills me. Not sure what that is, but I don't mind it. In fact, I might even say you make me better."

"I'll take that. And I'll raise you with this."

She kissed his chin, nipping the stubble and then rubbing her lips over the rough hair. The brush of it tickled across her skin delightfully. So she played at a few more nips to his chin, along his jaw, and then landed on his lower lip and tugged it with a gentle, biting hold.

"You're feisty this afternoon," he said, and pulled her tight against his body. He still wore the coolness from outside on him, and it shivered into her being and ruched her nipples. "Mmm, I like that." He thumbed one of her nipples through the T-shirt, then pinched it, but not as softly as she had been with the nips.

Tuesday squirmed, yet arched her back to lift her breasts, and he took the hint. Bowing to her, he pushed up her blousy shirt and sucked in a nipple. His mouth was hot and his tongue firmly traced and lashed and teased her to a whimpering, clutching, wanting witch.

She shoved at his shirt, but realized it was a button-up. Wasn't going to come off without some pause to make it happen. And she needed to press her bare breasts against his hard pecs.

"Take this off," she pouted, and tugged at the shirt.

"We're going to do this right now?" he asked, plucking slowly at each button down the front of the shirt. He stepped back and pulled it off, exposing a feast to her eyes.

"Oh, yeah." Tuesday veered toward the bed, but Ethan grabbed her wrist and spun her around. She almost walked into the leather chair in the process, and suddenly, he spun her to face away from him, and pushed her forward.

She caught her hands on the back of the chair, and with a grin, leaned forward onto her elbows. A wiggle of her ass received a hard smack from his palm. He pulled down her leggings and gave her another smack that stung yet made her instantly wet.

Behind her she heard him unzip, and seconds later

his heavy cock fell against her buttocks. Ethan grinded against her, fitting himself between her legs. She reached down and gripped the head of him, squeezing the length between her thighs.

"Fuck yes," he said tightly, as he cupped a hand over her breast and leaned down to kiss her nape. His hot breath caused erotic sensations that traveled her skin from neck to toe, and danced everywhere in between with the giddy madness of frenzied desire. Turning his head, his cheek hugged her spine. He clutched her breast as an inhale drew in her scent. "Put me inside you." He rocked his hips, pleading for entrance.

Tuesday guided him inside, and he slid in forcefully, pushing her stomach against the back of the chair and pulling her shoulders against him with a hand across her breasts. He kissed her hard again on her nape and bit, but not with his fangs. Just a soft, clinging, feral bite.

He rapidly thrust in and out of her, seeking his pleasure. Yet when his hand slid around to finger her clit, she cried out at the surprising attention. He pushed into her hard while she rocked forward, meeting his finger to adjust the pressure there. Inside her and outside, the man fit her perfectly and knew how to play her to the edge.

"Now," she gasped, hoping he was close to climax. Because she was. And then she decided she didn't need to wait. So she slapped a hand over his finger, moving it a bit to the left, and that was what released her to orgasm. She shouted and gripped the leather.

And behind her Ethan swore again and hilted himself as her orgasm tightened her about him, and with a few more thrusts, he came, too.

Chapter 15

"That was good." Tuesday sat up on the bed and looked over Ethan's bare chest. The soft beige sheet barely covered his cock, yet exposed those gorgeous muscles that pointed to all the action. The window shades had darkened by half to subdue the setting sunlight, and a hazy pale light softened the air.

"Good?" Ethan whistled lowly. "What does it take to rate a great?"

"Are you competing for a better grade?"

"No. Just not sure I can live with a mere good."

"Well…" She trailed a finger along the muscle that led to his crotch.

The sex had been amazing, and it had given her an idea. Together, they could do wondrous things. And if he thought she made him better now, he might be blown away at what a little bloodsexmagic could do for them.

She'd already given him some of her magic. With the bite, he could become that much more capable of utilizing that magic. But...

"What would take this to *great* might offend you."

"There's nothing you can do that would offend me. Of course, I wouldn't mind you trying. Over and over." He winked at her.

"Very well. I'm going to ask for something. Something I've never done before but have been curious about."

"Ask away. If it leads to *great* I don't know how I can say no."

She crawled on top of him and stroked the dark hairs that trailed up from his cock to his belly button. Leaning down to kiss his chest, Tuesday lingered there and licked his skin, which had cooled considerably. Sculpted from steel, he was a new plaything that she wanted to learn more about. And she would. In every way possible.

She pushed her hair over one shoulder. "Bite me," she said. "Drink my soul, vampire. And in turn, let me feel yours in the thunder of your heartbeats as we climax together."

Ethan pushed up onto his elbows. His eyes, colored like a rainy sky, held her gaze, searing into her irises so she could feel his thoughts. No fear, yet something made him pause.

"I thought we'd already discussed my nixing the blood-giving stuff."

"I don't need your blood. Heck, I don't want it. Unless it's for a spell. But now that you bring it up, you never did tell me what was up with that. You stopped talking after saying you killed someone. What happened that you're such a freak about giving blood?"

"I'm not a freak." He laid his head back on the pillow and closed his eyes. Still, he winced. "I killed someone I loved, Tuesday, by giving her a blood transfusion. And I won't ever be responsible for another innocent's death by doing the same. No blood from these veins for any reason. Ever."

It was a heavy confession, and she wanted to honor it. Even if a few drops would never harm anyone. But who was she to judge him for something that obviously had hurt him deeply?

She stroked a fingertip over the faint spot below his left pec where she'd stabbed him with the alicorn. No scar, only a slight discoloration in the skin remained.

"This blood transfusion," she said quietly. "I thought you said you weren't trying to transform her?"

"I wasn't. I will never make another vampire. Not unless it is my own child. The woman—she was human. I loved her, but…" He sighed and stroked a hand down her hair. Still, he kept his eyes closed. "It was in the nineteenth century in a little seaside village in Scotland. We were on holiday there, and she'd gone out for a walk in the sunlight, knowing that I was back at the inn buried under the covers, still sleeping. It had rained through the night and the grass was wet and slippery. She fell down a cliff and landed on the boulders fronting the sea. It was hours before I found her and was able to get her to the hospital. So many broken bones. And she'd lost so much blood. And yet, I'd read about blood transfusions, and the medical science behind the operation. I knew there was a possibility of saving her, so I offered my blood."

"Was she your blood type?" Tuesday asked with surprise.

Ethan shook his head. "At that time, the doctors and surgeons weren't aware of blood types. They performed the operation unknowing that the type of blood was important. Unfortunately, we were not a match, and after pumping four pints of my blood into her, she seized and went into a coma. She died an hour later."

Oh, the poor man. "I'm sorry, Ethan."

"I'd been with her for a year. We never fooled ourselves that we'd marry and have children. She knew I was vampire. Had no desire for the lifestyle, either. I did have a moment of thinking I could save her if only I transformed her. But I did not. I respected her choice not to become vampire. And yet, I killed her by giving her my blood."

"That wasn't your fault. Medical science wasn't advanced enough at the time. You could never have known."

"I never should have offered in the first place. I should have let her be. She may have recovered."

"You don't know that. She'd fallen off a cliff? And you said she'd broken bones. It sounds like she would have died no matter what."

"Do we have to talk about this?"

"Of course not. But I have one more question."

"Shoot."

"Did you love her like you loved your wife?"

He wobbled his head. "Love comes in many different forms. You know?"

"Not really."

"Right. Sorry. There are many kinds of love. At least, from my perspective. I loved Anyx because it was something we learned and it grew between us over the years. A certain respect, and yes, sexual desire developed the love between us. But I would never call what we experienced a soul love."

"Even after sixty years?"

"Even after. As for the woman who died, I did love her passionately, but again, it wasn't soul-deep. And I'm okay with that. Whether we are human or creature or other, we love. It's what we do. And I wish you could know love."

"Well, I can love. I just can't receive love. Not for long, anyway. And always to the detriment of the guy who might think he loves me." She shrugged. "I'm fine."

"I don't think you are."

"Do we have to talk about this?" she said, repeating his question.

"Not right now, no."

"Good. And I'm glad you trust me to tell me about the blood thing." She kissed his collarbone and laid her head on his shoulder. "I won't ever ask you for blood. Promise. But…"

"You know when a person tosses in a *but* that means disregard everything I said before that word and only pay attention to what follows?"

Tuesday propped herself up over him. "There's nothing stopping you from biting me. And it could enhance the magic I've already given you. Bloodsexmagic, you know."

"I thought that was what vampires used to steal a witch's magic?"

"It is, but if given freely, and if I control the hex…"

"I don't want to get hexed."

"You've already been thoroughly hexed by me, lover."

He snickered. "Your use of the word has too many meanings to keep straight. I do like hexing you. But I'm not keen on bloodsexmagic."

"Fine. I can deal. But that doesn't mean you still can't bite me. You know you want a taste. You've thought about it. Don't deny it."

"I have." He stroked the hair along her cheek, and traced her neck where her carotid pumped in anticipation, but then dashed downward to tickle the ends of her hair across her breast.

"I dare you," she whispered, unwilling to back down from the challenge.

Because it was a challenge between the two of them. She'd mentioned to him that fangs got her off, but he had initially been offended by her being a witch. It was an old and innate vampire hang-up. He'd lived through the Great Protection Spell when one drop of witch's blood could destroy a vampire.

"I'm not poisonous," she whispered. "Promise."

"I know that. But you have to know I've never bitten a witch."

"Understandable. But you don't strike me as the type who would carry a centuries-old fear within you."

"I don't fear your blood. But I do think you're a fang junkie."

That was a term vamps reserved for humans desperate for more of the fang. But Tuesday didn't take it as an offense. She shrugged. "Not quite a junkie, but I do love the bite. The orgasm is incredible. Much better than good."

He smirked and humor danced in his eyes. He might buckle...

"You are cute," he said.

She nodded, agreeing.

"And your blood smells different than most."

"How so?"

"Old. Luxurious. Aged, like a fine wine."

"You are not winning points by calling me old, buddy."

"It's the aged vintages that are always best."

Ethan parted his lips and she watched as his fangs lowered. Beautiful weapons. Pearly white. Sharper than most animal incisors. Made for piercing. She tapped one, and then stroked it until the man's hips rocked beneath her thighs. It was a unique way to jack him off.

"Taste me, vampire. Dive deeper into my world."

Ethan dashed out his tongue to lick her finger and she leaned forward, putting her breasts level with his mouth. Offering herself, waiting...wishing for the ultimate connection between the two of them. Because, she'd had it all thus far in life. Sex with so many different species. Bites, blood-sharing and even magic-sharing. But never had she had the bite at the same time as sex. It was a sacred act, and could actually enhance her blood bond with another.

He licked her nipple. And even after making love and having him touch and taste her for hours, she felt it as a new and exciting tingle that shivered through her system. She arched her back, then lifted her breast, putting it in his mouth.

And then the painful pierce of his fangs entered her body. Tuesday gasped at the sharp and intense intrusion. But she didn't flinch or pull away as his tongue lashed after the blood that spilled over the curve of her breast and toward her nipple.

Cleaning it off, he then suckled at the twin pierce marks, drawing out her blood. The sensation was sweet, and wicked. Delicious and deadly. And when his fangs grazed her skin they raised shiver bumps in the wake of his formidable weapons.

"The other," he whispered, and she shifted on her hands, tilting her chest so he could get a firm hold on her other breast.

The second piercing felt as painfully exquisite, and she shuddered, and put a hand to the back of his head to hold him there as he fed from her. Sensation soared through her body, coiling at her pussy and making her instantly wet again. He had penetrated her in a different way, but the feeling was beyond that of simple insert-tab-A-into-slot-B intercourse.

All of a sudden he flipped her onto her back. His strong hand clutched behind her head and lifted her neck to his fangs. With an animal fierceness, Ethan growled and sank his fangs into her carotid. One hand clutched at her breast while he fed ravenously from her pumping life. She could bleed out if he let the blood flow too long, and he might tease at that, but the vampire's saliva was healing and wouldn't allow such to happen.

"Oh, Ethan…" She twined a leg around one of his and let her head fall back, unsupported as he followed her down. "Fuck me now. With your teeth and your cock."

As he shoved into her with his hard-on, Tuesday gasped because she felt that sensation as if…she was the one entering him. Ethan's pleasurable groan ceased his sucking at her neck only momentarily as their gazes met. "You feel that?" he asked.

"I feel...what you feel?"

"Yeah, and...damn." He slapped his chest. "That's amazing."

"We're sharing the blood pleasures. Don't stop. More!"

He dropped his mouth to her neck again and the tug at the wound ached as he touched a fang to it and allowed the blood to flow. And as he greedily took from her, he pumped his hips against hers, gliding in and out. One hand thumbed her nipple, pinching, squeezing, demanding.

Everything was different, and the same, and new, and familiar. The intense squeeze of her insides about his cock...she could feel that as if his steely hard rod was her own. The taste of her blood in his mouth—she experienced that sweet delicacy trickle at the back of her throat. And the coil of orgasm that mastered her core seemed to triple in intensity as it enveloped them together.

"I can feel what you feel," he gasped. "Tuesday... This is... I've never known this before." He hilted himself inside her and then reached down to thumb her clit. "Oh, Christ, that's...wow."

"Invoking a Christian deity's name? You're telling me." She held him at her neck, and rocked her hips upward, meeting his thumb strokes with exacting movements to keep him right where she wanted him. "Give it all to me, Ethan. With my blood you've entered me. And I have entered you."

"Is this witchcraft?" he said on a gasp.

"Call it bloodcraft. A kind of bonding that goes beyond the external. Our souls are touching."

"Yes, that's exactly how I feel it. Some kind of soul bond."

And she didn't want it to stop. But it really was too much. Her mind flew. And her body shuddered uncontrollably. Ethan's teeth had left her neck, his tongue losing its pace lapping her blood. Together they had ceased to rock into one another for they'd become bound in an inner embrace that sparkled and held them at the edge of life and death.

Ethan's jaw tensed. He growled, gasping then searching for the release. And with a flick of his finger across her clit, he surrendered and Tuesday fell into the strange but marvelous experience as her body released. Ethan bucked against her. She took it all in as the world moved through her veins and to her every nerve ending.

They froze together in that penultimate moment catching one another's gaze and peering deep into their reflections. And in that moment the twosome had never known another being so intimately.

Tuesday slid out of bed and padded into the kitchen, where she pulled the orange juice from the fridge. She poured a glass then drank it.

"Tuesday…"

She turned toward the bedroom, but shook her head. She hadn't heard Ethan call out to her audibly. Had she…?

"The bed is growing cold on your side. Come back to me."

Touching her ear, she realized she'd heard him say that to her…in her thoughts. Like a dream, but only it was happening now while she was wide awake.

Let me finish my juice, she thought.

And then she heard him chuckle. Again, not audibly. She felt Ethan's mirth warm her chest and it was almost as if she'd laughed herself. What was that about?

She set down the glass and teased the ends of her hair as she stared off toward the bedroom. They'd been so close in those moments when he'd been drinking her blood and fucking her at the same time. Truly, they had delved into some kind of blood bond.

Walking fast, she entered the bedroom and glided onto the bed beside Ethan. He patted the cooling side of the sheets, indicating where he wanted her.

"Did you just talk to me in my head?" she asked.

"I did."

"Vampire persuasion?"

"No. I mean, I don't think so. It was a thought that I sent to you, hoping you'd hear. I heard you reply when you were drinking juice."

"We can communicate silently now?" She snuggled up next to him, fitting one leg between both of his as she nudged up her breasts to hug his chest.

He pushed the hair from her neck and studied where he'd bitten her. "It must be residual effects from what we just did."

"Yes. I've never tried it before," she said.

"Really, Miss Fang Junkie?"

"It was either the bite or sex. Never at the same time."

"Wow, you do have a discerning bone."

"Richard."

"That was deserved. But you did say this would bond us and make us stronger together."

"I did say that, didn't I? It was a lark. I've heard it could work, but I was thinking more toward making us a powerful duo tracking the demon. I'm not sure how feeling one another's pleasure is going to help that. Did you feel it all? When I did this…" She reached down and fluttered his forefinger over her folds and then pressed at the peak of them, igniting a twinge of pleasure at her clit.

Ethan sucked in a hiss. "Just the right amount of pressure and, ah, witch, you really fly."

"Yeah? Well, I never knew what it could feel like to do this." She gripped his cock and squeezed, and in reaction she felt her stomach tense and her loins sing. "That is so not bad. Do you think we bonded? I mean, I've heard that vamps can bond with others by sharing blood. I didn't take your blood. And I've been with other vampires before. This never happened."

"I don't have an answer for you. It's weird, but cool. Probably it was a soul thing."

"Would that be okay with you? I mean, you said you've never felt soul-deep toward a woman."

"It's all right by me for now." He clasped her hand and leaned in to kiss her neck, which sent a shiver down her spine. He breathed on her skin, which tickled as well. "Who knows how long it'll last. Let's go with it for as long as we have it, yes?"

"No arguments from this witch."

She settled next to him, both of them staring up at the ceiling. Moonlight shone across a nearby rooftop and glinted copper outside the window.

"Tell me why you pulled a three-sixty from flying back to the States?" Ethan asked. "Was it just to fuck me?"

"That was one reason. But another was that this witch never backs down from a challenge."

"Even if that challenge threatened to end you?"

"Oh, yeah. I could feel that bastard hold my heart, Ethan. He promised to rip it out should I go after him again. But bring it on. This witch is not about to run with her tail between her heels because some pretty demon wants to play piñata with my heart."

"It's dangerous for you to go near him. I've learned more about the demon's curse. I stopped into the Archives while you must have been at the airport. CJ and I looked up Gazariel. I had no idea the curse originated with—"

"Himself." Tuesday felt a catch in her throat speaking that name. "It's something I've always known. Felt. But never articulated. Didn't want to put it into words because I didn't want to believe I was in any way connected to that asshole."

"The grand high asshole of all assholes."

"Exactly. A super Richard." She lifted her head to find his gaze. "Just because I'm primed for the challenge doesn't mean I'm not also freaked the hell out. I can't do this alone. And I know you can't do it without me."

"But now you've made me into some kind of magical tracking device. So maybe I can?"

"True." She smoothed her hand over his abs, where she'd drawn the spell and gifted him her magic. "Of course you can, but... Can we do this together?"

"You've no reason to seek the demon, Tuesday. It means nothing to you to get back the Final Days code. You're free to leave Paris. I mean that. I don't want you involved if the expense means your life."

"Seriously? It means everything to me if the result of having the code enacted means I'll be smothered by angels when they fall. I *am* affected by this, Ethan.

This is kind of a world-saving venture, and I do live in the world."

"You've got a point."

"I don't understand why Gazariel would give such a devious weapon to the vampiress. He seems to thrive living amongst the mortals. And without them, he would be left with the angels and... Himself. The very last being I imagine he'd want to associate with. There's something we're missing."

Ethan rolled to his side and absently stroked his fingers along her hip and up her stomach. "So you're in?"

"All the way up to my tits."

"They are nice tits." He squeezed one of them then gasped. "Man, that feels ten times better than when you pinch mine. Yours are so sensitive." He leaned forward and sucked one into his mouth, groaning with the shared pleasure.

And Tuesday closed her eyes, wondering when she'd lost her way. This man was only supposed to be a quick fuck and then she had planned to dash back to the States. Yet every part of her wanted to stay near him, to not lose contact with him. It was as if, with the bite and the sex, they had again bound themselves to one another with a stronger bond than even her magic could manage.

And the word *love* kept bouncing against her brain cells. Well, she didn't have to worry about that. The man couldn't love her. He could, but then it would explode and he'd leave or call her a bitch and hate her forever. True love was the key to breaking the curse? Never happen in her lifetime.

"I have a sort of plan," he said, rolling to his back again.

Missing his heat at her nipple, Tuesday laid her palm over the wet peak. "Tell me."

"First we need to capture the demon. Even if Anyx is with him. I have to add measures to contain her as well. If she's been gifted the book she could be attempting to decipher the code right now."

"So we need them both."

"We do."

"And then what?"

"Then we twist the screws to his thumbs."

"Literally? You know, I've seen people tortured with thumbscrews. It is so not pretty."

"I've seen it too. Metaphorically, we'll twist the screws by threatening to send Gazariel to Daemonia."

"Really? He would not like that place very much. They'd chew up a fallen angel and regurgitate him over and over. And over."

"You knew he was a Fallen One?"

"He told me. Creator of Vanity, remember? Just like the curse has always been inside me, and I've sensed it was birthed from the Big Bad Dude, I also felt the demon's ethereal ties before he cursed me. But how would you put him in Daemonia?"

"I know a reckoner."

"Good to have one of those guys on your contacts list."

"Exactly. So our first step is to track the demon again."

"All right, but I'm hungry, and I probably need another shower after all that sex. Want to share the water?"

"Go get it warmed up for me."

"Aha! Yeah, I don't think so, vampire. Why don't you go warm it up for me?"

Ethan sat up and gave her a mock bow. "Your beck is my command."

"Damn right it is. About time I get to tell you what to do."

"Stuart, start the shower."

And as her lover wandered into the bathroom, Tuesday decided that indeed, it was her turn at command. His plan to capture the demon hadn't worked. He was emotionally stalled by the vampiress and he didn't realize that weakness.

Now it was time for the witch to take control.

Chapter 16

Ethan followed Tuesday up the narrow, spiraling staircase to the fifth floor, where Savin Thorne lived in an apartment building in the fourteenth arrondissement. He'd texted Thorne an hour earlier, asking if he could stop by, and had gotten a return text that he was always welcome. It was evening, but not so late that the streets weren't packed with tourists and the locals were finishing an evening meal.

On occasion, Acquisitions employed reckoners in whatever locale they were needed. Sometimes demons who had broken mortal realm laws, or who were volatile and impossible to contain, required deportation back to Daemonia. That was a reckoner's job. And while Acquisitions wasn't in the business of capturing demons, sometimes that was a necessary by-blow of a job. Nasty demon attached to a toxic or volatile artifact? The retriever may be forced to take both. A helpful demon who refused to leave after the job was done? So long, Sunshine. Or a demon who had stolen a book that could end the world? The threat of Daemonia may be the only thing that could get him to cough it up.

Daemonia was The Place of All Demons. Not exactly *all* demons. But it was where the majority lived and existed. It wasn't Beneath or the hell the humans made up to balance out their religious beliefs. It was simply another realm where demons lived. Much like Faery housed faeries. It wasn't a good place. A mortal, or nondemon, would not care to go there, even for a brief visit. The dark witch Certainly Jones had gone there and returned without too much physical harm. It was the mental damage that could never be completely assessed. Or healed.

Ethan had personally called in Savin Thorne to send demons back to Daemonia on two occasions. Reckoners had a particular tie to Daemonia, yet they were not generally demons. Thorne was mortal, to an extent. Ethan wasn't sure what to call him, exactly. And he didn't want to get caught up in labels. He knew the man was trustworthy, smart, a loner, and could drink him under the table any day. And that was saying a lot, considering vampires generally didn't get drunk unless they literally swam in alcohol.

The sway of Tuesday's coat focused his attention on the reveal of her ass beneath the long alpaca fur. So tight and…he could feel it in his hands.

Using the silent mind communication they'd gained from their sexual encounter, Ethan put out a thought. *You distract me, witch.*

Right back atcha, vampire was her silent response.

She arrived at the only door on the fifth floor and turned to eye him, with a wink. Teasing her tongue along her lips, she lowered her gaze to his crotch. Where a healthy hard-on threatened to make walking difficult if he didn't steer his mind away from Tuesday's sexy curves and stunning kisses to focus on the task at hand.

Ethan leaned in to brush her cheek with his kiss. "Save it for later," he muttered, then rapped on the door.

Just now noticing the strains of bluesy guitar music filtering behind the door, Ethan smiled. The man did like to settle in with a whiskey and his guitar. He collected guitars, and even played the diddley bow, which was a one-stringed guitarlike instrument.

The music stopped and the door swung open five seconds later to reveal a big, hulking man with dark hair, an imposing beard and narrowed eyes, yet a smile that was so overwhelmingly honest he could tease even the most wicked demon to step forward and risk their chances with his unique skill.

"Ethan Pierce! Good to see you, man. Come on in. And let the little lady through first."

"Savin Thorne, this is Tuesday Knightsbridge. Tuesday, Savin."

They shook hands, and Savin enclosed Tuesday's hand with both of his and bowed to her. "Namaste, dark witch. Enter my home with no ill intent and I open my wards to you," he offered.

"Agreed," Tuesday said.

And Ethan felt a tug at his skin as, with a sweep of his hand before them, Savin released whatever wards he had up.

"That one pinched," Tuesday offered. "You're fully warded."

"Not wise to live any other way." Savin gestured for them to follow him through an industrial-style kitchen and beyond to the living area. Dark beams supported the ceiling and bare brickwork fashioned the walls. Steel shelves and wood furniture with faded and cracked leather cushions revealed the place to be the ultimate man cave. Add to that the wall of guitars behind the sofa, and the amps spread out along one wall, and Ethan decided the man could probably get lost in his music and not give a care for the world that bustled outside.

"Can I get you something to drink?" Savin asked. "I know it's still early but I've got an awesome whiskey aged to perfection. You want to try it, don't you, Ethan?"

"Hell yes."

"I'll give it a go," Tuesday said as she sat on the sofa, crossed her legs and shrugged off her coat. A battered electric guitar lay on the cushion next to her and she stroked her fingers down the strings and along the wooden body. "I can feel the power in this one. You practice musicomancy."

Savin returned with two glasses, handing one to Ethan, who stood by a thick beam that resembled a railroad tie, and the other to Tuesday. "I do. Or I'm learning it. Still don't have much control over it. You could feel it in the guitar?"

"Of course." She took her fingers away from the instrument. "Keep working on it. The guitar is infused with your efforts."

"Thanks. I will. So." Savin turned to Ethan, shoving his hands in his back pockets. "What's up? Generally if you need a demon reckoned you shoot me a call and tell me where to be."

"I don't have the demon under control yet," Ethan

said. "But I wanted to put you on call, if that's possible." He tilted back a swallow of the whiskey and winced. "Fuck, this is tight."

"Secret recipe." He tapped his temple. "Got it from somewhere I don't even want to question too much. What demon are you dealing with?"

"Gazariel, The Beautiful One."

Savin crimped an eyebrow. "Not sure I've heard of that one."

"He's a Fallen One," Tuesday offered. "Not originally from Daemonia. But you can still send him there?"

"Of course. But those Fallen bastards are a bitch to deal with. How do you plan on containing him long enough for me to get there and send him off?"

"That's still in the planning phase," Ethan said. "I was hoping you might have some suggestions. I need all the help I can get with this one."

"What's the demon done?"

"It's what he's got. And I may not need you to send him to Daemonia, but rather, offer the real threat of such a thing happening."

"A Fallen One would not want to go to Daemonia. I've reckoned one of them and it was a bitch. They put up quite the fight. But The Beautiful One? What are we dealing with here? A preening poseur?"

"Something like that." Ethan took another swig and still couldn't stop a wince at the burn. But it was a good burn. "The demon has the code for the Final Days. We need to get that from him and lock it away nice and safe."

"Yeah, I'd agree with that. Not much for being smothered by gajillions of angels. You want more?" Savin asked Tuesday.

"No, thanks. This is some powerful stuff."

"Brewed by Scottish trolls."

Ethan raised an eyebrow at that one. The man did have a habit of making stuff up. Just for shits and giggles.

"It's true," Savin defended, noticing Ethan's doubt. "Just ask the mermaid who sold it to me." With that, he laughed heartily, and Ethan joined him. "You want me to stand by for the call should you manage to wrangle this demon? I can get anywhere in the city in about twenty minutes, depending on how traffic cooperates. I assume you'll probably hold him at headquarters?"

"Yes, in the eleventh."

"And what's the witch helping you with? If you don't mind my asking? Or…is she your girl? Tagging along for the fun?"

"She's the operator to my compass," Ethan offered. "She wears his sigil from a curse the demon put inside her centuries ago. They are connected. She gave me some magic that will lead us to him. We've twice already encountered the demon, but… I wasn't prepared for the containment."

"No containment crew?"

"Yes, but…eh, it doesn't matter. I'm preparing for the third time. He won't slip away again."

"Most definitely. I always tell hunters demons are wily. They'll take advantage of everything you hadn't thought they could. So you two are connected?" He looked to Tuesday.

She nodded. "In a working relationship. And while I'm not looking forward to seeing Gazariel again anytime soon, I want to help Ethan get this weapon out of his hands."

"Noble, especially for a dark witch."

"We're not all bitches," Tuesday said.

"No, but the majority of you can't be trusted." He spread out a hand in placation. "Just my call. Take all the offense you like."

"I take no offense. I know what I am, and I don't make excuses for it. So you're on our team now. Great. What information do you need from us to get ready for your gig?"

"As much as you can give me. Though knowing he's Fallen is enough. But…you said you and the demon are connected?" Savin approached Tuesday and nodded, indicating she should stand. "Do you wear the demon's sigil?"

"I do."

"Can I take a look at it?"

With a hefty sigh, Tuesday rose and lifted her T-shirt. "Everybody wants to touch the witch. Just make sure your hands aren't cold."

Savin bent to study the dark sigil drawn between Tuesday's breasts. And with a brisk rub of his palms together, and a questioning gesture, he was given permission to touch. He put his finger on the sigil and traced the lines, then suddenly snapped back and stepped away, shaking the hand that had touched her.

"Yep, you two are connected. That's a nasty one. No wonder you're dark. That curse originated from the Big Guy."

"You know that?" Ethan asked.

Savin shrugged. "Some shit I just know. Like it or not. I wouldn't call her master The Beautiful One, but rather the Dark Prince."

"No." Tuesday pulled down her shirt. "I've never

been attached to Himself. Never felt that pull or such control."

"Whatever. It's what I feel. But, uh…" Savin glanced to Ethan. "You do know if I send the demon to Daemonia, she's going with it?"

Ethan caught Tuesday's gaping look and in his mind he heard her say, *What the fuck?*

"I didn't know that," Ethan offered. "We have to disconnect them before the reckoning?"

"Either that, or bye-bye, witch." Savin shrugged. "Unless she can ward herself to the nines. Not sure it's even possible with a sigil connected to the Dark One."

"Great. Ever since Ethan kidnapped me this whole ride has been one big party of suck."

"Kidnapped?"

Ethan shook his head at Savin's inquiring glance. "A retriever brought her in from the States. She's the only one with a connection to the demon."

"Since when does Acquisitions force others to do their dirty work?" Savin asked.

Ethan raised an eyebrow. The man knew the answer to that one, and he wasn't sure why he was being so openly obstinate.

"Yeah, I get it. Right." Savin sighed heavily. "You give me a call when you've got the demon contained. But I won't hold my breath waiting for the call. This will be a tough catch."

"Thanks for that vote of confidence," Ethan said. "Is there nothing you can offer in way of containing a Fallen One?"

Savin rubbed his jaw in thought. "The witch's dark magic should prove effective, and if you add a familiar into the mix that will only increase the power. But if she's bonded with the demon everything could blow up in your face. I'd suggest keeping her as far from the demon as possible. He could use her magic against you."

"As we've already seen," Tuesday said. "I won't give up on trying to help Ethan. The familiar is a good idea, though. Know of any familiars willing to risk their life for a long shot?"

"Actually—" Savin's generous grin poked dimples into his cheeks "—I do."

"How much does your organization pay a guy like Thorne to reckon demons?" Tuesday asked as they strolled down the sidewalk in a direction Ethan had pointed out.

The city rose around them in three-and four-story buildings, random trees sprouting in tiny courtyards here and there, and the constant car horns squawking at one another. Lights everywhere illuminated the dark streets and touristy areas like a carnival.

Ethan scrolled through the contacts on his phone, searching for the familiar's location. "I'm not sure. I requisition invoices to be paid directly to Savin. I'm not the money guy."

"Is that so? Are you telling me your promise to pay me for helping you was a lie?"

"No. You'll get what you deserve. But I won't be on the negotiating part of that. I don't like to be involved in the money."

"Aren't you going to put in a good word for me?" She turned and fluttered her lashes at him.

And Ethan was taken by that flirtatious move, even though he sensed it was more mocking than a flirt. "Are you worried about what Savin said about you going along with the demon to Daemonia?"

"Why should I be? I thought you said the reckoner would merely be used as a threat to get the demon to talk. Wait. Seriously? You're going to deport the demon with me attached to him? You ass!" She turned and marched onward, furred coat flying out in a rage.

Women! They changed moods like they changed their shoes.

Instead of chasing after her, Ethan sent her a mind message. *Tuesday, you're overreacting. I will never allow that to happen to you. I care about you.* He stopped, pausing to consider those thoughts. Did he really care about the witch?

Ahead of him, Tuesday stopped and turned around, arms swinging out at her sides. In his thoughts he heard her wonder, *Really?* Then her shoulders dropped and she shook her head, and spoke out loud. "Bad move, vampire. I'm not the kind of chick a guy should ever have a care for."

And she turned and strode onward, intent on putting distance between them. Was it because of the curse she wore? Did she believe love could never be hers? What if she did believe in it? Might she then have it?

His contacts list brought up Thomas the familiar's address, which was…in the opposite direction they were walking. Ethan tucked away the phone and ran up to catch Tuesday. She turned a corner down a narrow alley formed by the rough limestone bricks of a small church and a black wrought-iron fence that kept back the leafless branches from an overgrown shrub.

He grabbed her by the arm and spun her around, but didn't do the inconsiderate thing of pushing her against the wall and admonishing her for her silly emotional reaction.

"You don't get to tell me who I can care about," he said.

"Yeah? I thought you didn't like witches. If having sex a couple times is all it takes to turn your head I'd tell you to beware your female enemies, big-time."

"Tuesday, I know this is a wall you've created over the years—hell, the centuries—to make life easier to walk through."

"It's not a wall, asshole, it's a fucking curse."

"Right. The curse. But there's a wall, too. I know, because I do it, too. I love my walls. Keeps people at a distance, and makes it easy to ignore the fact that I do have feelings. So I've had a change of heart about a witch that I prejudged incorrectly. I like you. Get over it."

He leaned against the wrought-iron fence, crossing his arms over his chest. Yes, putting up that wall, like she had done. It was something he did by rote.

"What do you want from me, Ethan?"

"You know what I want from you."

She sighed and tilted her head against the wall, turning so her cheek faced him. "And I agreed to help you get what you want because I like to do shit that challenges me. Surprises me. Lures me out of the norm. Chasing a demon who could be my death? Sign me up."

"You think that if you find Gazariel you might get him to break the curse?"

She chuffed. "Only one way to make that happen, and I do like my heart exactly where it is." She turned to look at him and he maintained a cool gaze, arms still crossed defiantly. "This thing we accidentally created between us can only harm us both. You know that."

"Only if we have hope. And we've both lived long enough to know that hope is stupid and cheap."

"So you're saying you're just going with the feeling? That when it ends you can walk away? Wham, bam, thank you, witch?"

"Isn't that how you want it to go?"

She nodded. But he noticed the beginning of her wince before she smoothed away that regretful motion. She wanted more, he knew it. And he did, too. How could he get the demon to break that damn curse for her? She deserved love.

"Right." She lifted her chin. "In it for the ride, arms spread and head thrown back as we scream at the top of our lungs. Then let the chips fall where they may. I like you, too, vampire. There. I said it. You're right. I can do this. And when it's done? I can walk away."

She put out her hand to shake, as if they might seal the agreement to let their hearts stumble against one another, to fall into the experience of some kind of relationship, but knowing full well that it was only until they were both done using one another.

Ethan could get behind that. But not completely.

He gripped Tuesday's hand but then lunged forward to kiss her. She hadn't expected that, and she initially struggled. But he dropped her hand and cupped her head, keeping her mouth at his so he could deepen the kiss, dive in to her and taste her fears as they quickly wilted to allow in desire and want and the very same need he felt.

Her heartbeats entered his and at first they danced in a challenging standoff, but then quickly steadied and began to share the rhythm. She hiked up a leg against his thigh, drawing his hips to her body. Instant hard-on. Which he crushed against her in a moaning plead for what he suddenly needed right now.

"Yeah?" she said as she tilted her head to catch his mouth at a new angle. "We are away from the crowds."

"Can you put up some kind of shield?"

"You mean my invisibility cloak?"

Ethan pulled from the kiss, meeting her eyes with wonder. "You have one?"

She laughed and then crushed a kiss to his mouth. "No, and who wants the confidence of a protection shield when the risk of being seen is much more fun?"

He unzipped and hissed when her cool fingers wrapped about his cock. The heavy fall of her coat shielded them from curious eyes, should anyone pause at the end of the alleyway and peer down at them. But she was right. The idea of being caught out only made his cock harder.

He slid down her leggings and hugged his erection against her mons. Directing him, she tapped the head of him against her clit. He could feel the tingling curls of sensation with each tap, taking everything she felt into his system and doubling it with his own. He would never regret the blood bond between them. Not even if he had to walk away from her when the demon had been captured and the code secured.

Maybe? He'd just been thinking the witch deserved love. What about him?

No time to think about it. Nuzzling his nose along her hair and down to her ear, he licked her lobe as she allowed him entrance into her hot, wet pussy. With a growl, he clapped a hand about her ass and rocked her onto him as he willed down his fangs and bit into her neck.

She swore and her fingernails clawed at his neck. That exquisite pain heightened the pleasure, and as her blood spilled down his throat, Ethan spilled into her. He'd never tasted finer, nor had he felt uniquely connected to another.

A giggle from down the way clued him they'd found an audience. Ethan growled and retracted his fangs, but pulled Tuesday in closer, wanting to wrap her about his body until he felt nothing more than her heartbeats envelop his soul.

Chapter 17

Swinging out of the alleyway, Tuesday walked along-side Ethan this time. The man had a way of winning her when she most wanted to push him away. And it wasn't even the power of his cock and kiss. It was something innate. She was a part of him, and she had felt his truth and honesty as he'd kissed her roughly. The desperation in that kiss had made her understand her own desperation for acceptance. It was a long time coming.

But she wouldn't go all moon-eyed for the man and pledge her undying love to him. That way lay broken hearts and regret. Her heart broken. Men tended to wander off and never look back. Because love could never really fix in a man's heart for her. She and Ethan had agreed to go with whatever came their way, and she was good with that. Because life was meant to be lived in the moment, and no one reminded her of that more than Ethan Pierce.

"Is the familiar's place that way?" she asked, as he led her down the street. They passed a crepe hawker and she stopped. "I haven't eaten all day. You got some cash?"

With a smirk he tugged out his wallet and handed her a twenty-euro note.

"You want something? A coffee?"

"I just had a drink. And I'm not talking about the whiskey." His eyes glittered. It was a feeling that hit Tuesday in her very bones. And she couldn't prevent a return smile. "I'll wait over there. I want to check out the musician across the street." He thumbed a gesture over his shoulder, where Tuesday saw a guitarist performing, then wandered across the street.

The night was chilly but not too cold with her big coat to shield from the elements. The instant the hot creamy chocolate and bananas hit her belly, Tuesday groaned with pleasure. No one could tell her this much sugar was not good for her. This gastronomic nightmare spoke to her soul the way no kiss or sex could.

Standing at the curb, watching Ethan listen amongst the crowd as the guitarist performed a dazzling flamenco number, punctuated by frequent cries of *"olé!"* from the onlookers, Tuesday couldn't decide when she'd last been on a date with a man that hadn't seemed like a date. Of course, they were not on a date. They were tracking a crazy demon who was dating Ethan's ex-wife. But it felt date-ish. And certainly they had formed *some* kind of a relationship.

And then she realized she was laying claim to the man in a way that disturbed her. It was her reaction to the ex-wife all over again. What had become of the dark witch who preferred to fuck them and leave them? Who rarely trusted a man, and had been fine with her single no-commitments life over the centuries. Why was the idea of actually enjoying time spent with a man suddenly so alluring? Almost as if it was fulfilling a need she'd never thought to have.

A need she'd willingly sacrificed when at her lowest and near death.

It must be the Paris air. It was making her think. Too much. The City of Light was the city for lovers. So, yeah. Leave it at that, Tuesday. Just lovers.

Catching a drip of chocolate that ran down the side of her hand with her tongue, she traced her skin slowly, thinking to send the sensation across the street and to Ethan. She watched as he lifted his hand, shook it, then swung a glance over his shoulder, making direct eye contact with her.

She gave him a thumbs-up and a smiling wink.

He blew her an air kiss, then nodded that she cross over and join him as he wandered down the sidewalk. Hell, something crazy was going on between her and the man, but she didn't want to overanalyze it. She would take each moment for what it was, as he'd suggested.

"You didn't save me a taste?" he asked as she joined his side.

"I still have some on my fingers." She held out her forefinger and he leaned down to lick it, stopping long enough to suck it into his mouth and draw up a sigh from her. "And here I thought the crepe was awesome."

He winked at her and then clasped her other hand and led her onward. "The familiar lives near the Panthéon."

"Is that the big place with all the dead people in it?"

"It is. Alexandre Dumas is even interred there now. He was moved a decade or so ago from another spot. Much against his wishes to be buried in his hometown."

"You knew the guy?"

"Of course! Though I never could inspire him to try his hand at writing about vampires. Always the musketeers."

"What's wrong with a sexy musketeer? I knew a few in my time."

"But dating a lawman? Wasn't it difficult for you in the earlier centuries? Seems like the witch hunts have always been a constant."

"I got smart after I got the sigil."

"I bet you did." He swung an arm across her shoulders and hugged her close as they strolled down a cobblestoned sidewalk, avoiding a crowd lingering outside the massive domed Panthéon building. "I never had much of a problem with witches until…"

"Until? Until what? Did one of them look at you the wrong way? Give you the evil eye?"

He grimaced, but they maintained their casual pace. "I had a lover in the early twentieth century."

"Oh, yeah? Someone other than your wife? And the nameless woman with the tragic blood transfusion?"

"I've had many lovers. As I know you have. But this woman was different. She swept me off my feet, you could say. But we were only together six months."

"Was she vampire?"

"Yes."

"And?" They walked a few more paces, Tuesday sensing Ethan's tension tightening the muscles in the arm across her shoulders. But he had brought up this thread of conversation. So… "Ethan?"

"She bit a witch when she was starving for blood. And you know that's when the Great Protection Spell had rendered all witches' blood poisonous to vampires. I watched her die. It took less than five minutes for the blood to eat her up from the inside out."

Yeah, that had been the cool thing about being a witch before the spell had been broken early in the twenty-first century. A witch need not fear a vampire after centuries of persecution. The Great Protection Spell had been conjured to make all the blood in all the witches lethal to vampires. One bite and bye-bye vampire.

Tuesday had experienced a few occasions when a particularly vicious vampire had thought he was going to take what he wanted from her. No regrets whatsoever.

"She didn't know it was a witch she was biting?" she asked.

"No. And neither did I. We were out partying and she rushed ahead to feed. She was an innocent. And rationally, I know the witch was also innocent of the crime of murder. That witch had not asked to be bitten by a blood-hungry vampire. But at the time I didn't see it that way."

"You murdered the witch?"

He nodded. "I was in a rage. My old warring instincts emerged. I didn't kill her. I…couldn't."

"Of course not. If you would have made her bleed on you…"

"I'm not reckless with lives, Tuesday. You have to know that. But I did do some damage. Of which, I re-gret."

He must have been a force on the battlegrounds. How times had changed. Not always for the best, but the end of the Great Protection Spell had helped to ease tensions between vamps and witches.

"The past haunts us ever and always," she offered.

"That it does. But now you know about my witch thing."

"Yeah, but I'm not that witch, Ethan. And vampires have no reason to fear our species any longer. So for as much as I can sympathize with you losing someone you loved? You gotta get over it, vampire. Live in the moment, remember?"

"Thanks for reminding me." And then he smiled at her. "And I have gotten over it, apparently so much so that I've drunk from a witch twice within the last twenty-four hours."

Tuesday felt as if the something that had started between them had sunk deeply into her marrow. There would be no walking away from this man after they had dealt with the demon. And how to accept that her staying in his life, possibly allowing him to consider falling in love, could only mean their end?

"You can tell me about all your lovers sometime," she said. "If you want to. I'd like to hear about the women who captured your heart. Even if only for a day, week, month or year."

"Really? You didn't want to hear about Anyx."

"That was…" Not all that different. The man had lovers and a wife over the centuries. Wasn't as if she'd been celibate. Time to drop the jealousy. "We can share. But let's take it slow, yeah?"

"Agreed. Past lovers don't need to be doled out all at once. And they are the past."

"I can agree with that. Been there, don't need to look back."

"But you still owe me a couple lover stories. Which I will collect on later. Right now, I believe that is the familiar's building." Ethan stopped across the street from a nondescript four-story building fronted by stone mascarons and weather-stained pink granite. "I'm never sure how to go about approaching a familiar," he said. "Do I call out 'Here, kitty kitty'?"

"That would be obnoxious," a man's voice said from behind Tuesday and Ethan.

They both turned to find a short man with tousled brown-and-gold hair, green eyes and a confident stance lift a questioning eyebrow.

The familiar bowed to Tuesday, then took her hand and kissed the back of it. Tuesday was not impressed. She could recognize a charmer from a mile away.

"Ethan Pierce," the man said as he shook the vampire's hand. "It's been a few years, yes? How's bites?"

"The usual. I need your help, Thomas. Can we go up and talk?" He gestured toward the building.

"No." Thomas assessed Tuesday carefully, his green eyes narrowing, most likely reading her for powers or skills. Familiars had a thing with witches and could read them fairly well. "I'd prefer to stay outside. Was just heading out for a scamper anyway. Whatever you've got to offer me, make it quick."

Ethan said, "I need a familiar to help summon a demon."

"Nope." Thomas shook his head adamantly. "No can do. I don't do that kind of subservient shit. No witch is going to use me to channel a demon to this realm."

"The demon is already here. In Paris," Ethan explained. "We need to summon him into captivity."

Thomas quirked an eyebrow. "Why don't you go after him? Don't you head a troop of wild and crazy demon hunters?"

"We don't hunt demons. Exactly. Besides, we tried that."

"And failed? And why are you, the director of Acquisitions, asking me about this? Are you doing field-work now, Pierce?"

"I am. This is an important case. I don't want to cock it up."

Tuesday held back from mentioning that he'd already managed to do just that. She'd give the man a break. He was particularly cute, and she was still riding all the warm feelies after that quickie in the alley.

"You do have a partner that works with you, yes?" Ethan asked.

Thomas lifted his shoulders in affront. "Whether or not I do is none of your business. I won't do it. I do have my dignity. Good day to the two of you."

The familiar turned and strolled away, shoving his hands in the pockets of a summery white linen jacket.

Ethan called after him, "It pays!"

Thomas performed an agile turn—as graceful as a feline—and walked back up to them. "How much?"

Ethan shrugged. "How much do you charge?"

"A hundred thousand," Thomas said without pause.

Curious to see how the man who had explained to her that he didn't have a handle on the money would play this one, Tuesday listened avidly.

"Can't do that," Ethan said.

"Fifty grand."

Ethan winced.

"Oh, come on! What can you give me, man?"

"Ten," Ethan said.

Thomas turned and stalked away from them, but he flung out his arms and called without looking back, "Fine!"

"I'll need you after dark. Tomorrow!" Ethan called after him. "At headquarters. Ready to go."

Thomas delivered a thumbs-up over his shoulder and kept on walking.

"Ten grand?" Tuesday asked.

"His job isn't that complicated. Having sex until he's sated?" Ethan blew out a breath.

"Yeah, but it is dangerous. When the demon comes through, the familiar will shift to cat form and be left vulnerable. Not to mention whomever he works with will be in danger." Meaning, the person he'd be having sex with in order to become sated.

Familiars were conduits for demons to bridge into this realm. A witch could summon a demon via a familiar by invoking a spell at the point in which the familiar was sexually sated and open to receive that demon into this realm. Bridging a demon already in the same realm? Should be a piece of cake.

"You want me to invoke the spell?" Tuesday asked as she joined Ethan's side and they walked again. "I've conjured a demon or two in my day."

"Yes, and I've met one of them," he replied. "He almost brought down a four-story building on our heads. No, I'll have Certainly Jones do it. I don't want you anywhere near when the demon Gazariel is summoned."

"Don't you trust me?"

"Tuesday, I thought you said he'd rip out your heart if he saw you again. I'm trying to keep you safe."

"I appreciate that, but I think you'll need me to be

there. My sigil will focus CJ's and the familiar's magic and abbreviate the process. The familiar might not even have to go through all his…gyrations, to achieve bridging mode."

"You have something against watching a familiar have sex?"

"Do *you* want to watch? Kinky. The things I'm learning about you."

Ethan grabbed her and kissed her. Hard. Claiming. Just long enough to make her glad for his need to silence her in such a manner.

"I'd rather not watch, if truth be told," he offered.

"Fine. I'll talk to CJ about the possibility of having you close. But I need you to be protected. If we can't ensure your safety, you're out."

"My, how your attitude toward me has altered in but a few days. Is it my dazzling personality? Or merely that you like fucking me?"

"Both." The wink was the killer move to seal Tuesday's crazy fall into something she wasn't about to name. No, never. "Now come on," he said. "We've a little over twenty-four hours until tomorrow night. I'm going to call CJ and get the ball rolling, then set up things to ensure the reckoner is on-site as well. After that, we'll have a little time to spare."

"I'm hungry."

"Again? You just ate a monstrous crepe stuffed with an entire banana and enough chocolate to feed a classroom."

"Are you judging my eating habits?"

He laughed. "Not at all. Let me make the phone calls, then I'll take you to a place on the island. I've always wanted to taste their food."

Chapter 18

The meal featured tiny jewels of savory-flavored gelatin and a salad that would have starved a baby bunny. Tuesday had been forced to order two desserts. When the waiter delivered the cherry cake laced with rum he winked at Ethan. But Ethan's attention remained on Tuesday as she teased her fork at the decadent, moist cake.

They'd talked about familiars and what a weird life that must be. To be able to shift to such a small animal, such as a cat, bird, insect, or snakes and worms, and then to transform back to a human shape. Had to fuck with the insides and internal organs, yeah? The paranormal realm was truly wondrous.

The first bite of the cake made up for the pitiful meal. Lush, rum-soaked cherries burst on Tuesday's tongue, and she moaned in appreciation, savoring the wicked dark flavor.

Ethan leaned forward, his interest suddenly intent. "That good, eh?"

"You want a taste?"

"I think I'd rather experience it through you."

"I don't think the mutual-sexual-vibes thing works with food. On the other hand…"

She forked in another bite and this time closed her eyes to really enjoy and experience the flavors. Sweet and tart, dense and creamy. Kind of how it felt when Ethan ran his tongue over her swollen, wet pussy. The man was always intent on her pleasure. Just thinking about it, combined with the cherries and cake, made her nipples tighten.

Ethan groaned.

She opened one eye to see the vampire silently pleading with her from across the table. She slid her hand over the table and clasped fingers with him. The touch shivered over her skin.

"I felt that," he said. "The way you felt it. Really? That good?"

"I'm using my imagination, and thinking about you…with your head between my legs." She dipped into the cherry syrup and touched the fork to her lips, licking it off with a slow draw of her tongue.

Ethan sucked in his lower lip and eased his free hand down to his lap. Tuesday felt the rub of his palm across his cock as a visceral hum in her loins. The man's sexual energy was focused and targeted to his core. Acknowledging it started an aching throb at her clitoris. She stabbed another syrupy cherry onto the fork and this time held it between her lips and slowly crushed it. Cherry juice ran down her chin.

"I'd crawl under the table right now if there weren't

people sitting but five feet from us. But can you feel this?" Ethan's hand under the table must have squeezed his erection because Tuesday reacted with a gasp.

"Sweet bloody cherries, yes. You're so hard, vampire."

A sudden throat clearing beside them darted Tuesday's attention to the side. The man sitting at a table by himself, a small cup of espresso steaming before him, gave her a snide look down his nose.

The voyeur did not approve?

Tuesday pulled up Ethan's hand to trace the cherry juice on her chin. He then dipped that finger into her mouth and she sucked it. With a tender bite to the tip of his finger and a lash of her tongue, she was gifted with the exact right pressure to her clit that set her off. A deep and concentrated orgasm clasped her for a few seconds. Enough to lift her gasp to a vocal cry of "Oh!"

For his part, Ethan pulled his hand from her mouth and muffled his groan behind a napkin.

Tuesday leaned forward, panting and squeezing her thighs together to milk one last shock of vibrant sensation from the orgasm. Yes, right there. She bowed her head and said in a tight whisper, "That was so fucking good."

"I am suddenly a fan of rum-soaked cherries." He clasped her hand and they stood to leave. Ethan gave the voyeur a smirk.

And Tuesday said as they passed him, "Let them eat cake."

Hand in hand, they walked to Acquisitions headquarters, and entered through a nondescript door in an alleyway. The same door that Tuesday had walked out of days earlier and then had been bound to Ethan. Now they were bound in a different manner, and because of the choices they'd made to do so.

A dark hallway led to an elevator, which rose four flights. It was near midnight so the building was mostly quiet, though Ethan mentioned that there were always people in some department doing something at all hours of the day.

A small reception area let in moonlight across the single desk and curved walls. Tuesday stepped behind Ethan as he waited before a steel platform and some kind of electronic reading device that resembled the scanner a person walks through at the airport. He waited for green LEDs to blink, then grabbed her and rushed across the platform.

"You don't have access," he said as he punched in a digital code on a massive wood door before them. "But that sneaky move worked better than I expected."

"You've never snuck a girlfriend into your office before?"

"You're the first," he said as he opened the door and she walked through.

Though she had been in here briefly before, she'd not taken the time to look around because she'd been seriously in need of a bathroom break and had also been focusing on the sigil burning through the shackle rope Certainly Jones had placed on her.

Eerily quiet, and barely lit by pale moonlight, the dark room smelled like cedar. Tuesday slipped off her coat and let it drop to the floor as she walked up to the desk. Dim lighting blinked on and highlighted the hexagon structure of the room. An excellent shape for creating magic. The walls were solid, dark-stained wood, and the windows had a view of the city lights, yet she wouldn't be able to pinpoint a monument or tourist attraction for the life of her.

"A vampire's retreat," she decided. "Cool, calm and dark."

"I spend a lot of time behind this desk. Might as well make it comfortable."

"Doesn't look very comfy to me." She swung around the desk and sat on his chair, which— "Oh, mercy, I change that statement. Is this the most comfortable chair on the planet?" She wiggled on what felt like a living material that conformed to her shape and curves and… was that a sudden warmth? "Is it one of those massage chairs? Tell me it is, because I am so in to that."

Ethan reached under the desk and the chair suddenly began to vibrate and undulate.

"Oh, fuck yeah." She closed her eyes and put up her feet on the edge of the desktop. "Don't mind me. I'll fly to seventh heaven while you're doing whatever it is you have to do."

Standing beside the chair, Ethan opened the laptop on the desk and began clacking away on the keys. "Just want to make sure the holding room is cleared for tomorrow night. And that no unnecessary personnel are on sight. I've decided we're going to summon the demon with the familiar directly here to headquarters. It will work if we make the proper preparations. Looks like CJ is the only one scheduled to be in the building, save the tech guys, but they're on the first floor. I'm bringing in Cinder on this one. He's IT. He'll grant us access and make sure all wards are down."

"Mmm…" Tuesday let her head drift off the back of the chair and twisted to sit sideways, catching a particularly deep kneading motion at the base of her spine. "This chair could probably fuck me if I found the right position."

Ethan laughed. "You're a lot easier than I'd initially thought."

"Oh, come on, don't tell me you've never gotten off on the vibrations from this fabulous thing?"

"Can't say that I have. Though, what is it with you women and vibrations?"

"Hit us in the right spot and we will sing, baby, sing. You don't feel it?"

He frowned then. "No, I actually don't." Was that worry in his eyes? "Huh. You think our bond is wearing thin?"

"It's possible. I would guess it will last so long as my blood served you. But we can always refresh it." She slid a hand up Ethan's leg, aiming for the front, where his dark jeans did not conceal the erection. "Maybe I can make you hum a little tune, eh?"

"I won't stop you from trying. I have to verify the security locks are activated in a few sectors for tomorrow night..."

She squeezed his erection through the rough fabric and then unzipped him. The man always went commando and his penis jutted out as the zipper teeth separated. She wrapped a firm hand around the stick shift and began to drive, even while his attention was focused on the laptop screen. But he did move his hips to give her better access, and soon enough he closed the laptop and leaned against the desk.

Sliding forward on the wheeled office chair, Tuesday licked up from the base of his thick rod, slowly, following the pulsing vein to the sensitive foreskin below the crown. She took her time, making sure every bit of him received her tongue. His fingers slipped through her hair, clasping greedily, and he groaned and rocked his hips slowly.

He was right. She didn't feel every slow, lazy lick reciprocating on her pussy as she would expect because of their blood bond. Their connection had depleted. But that didn't make this any less exciting.

"I'm going to make this better than cherry cake," she said.

Ethan bent forward, pressing his hand over her crotch and finding her aching pinnacle with a firm touch. "I'll help."

The pressure of his fingers over her clit prompted her to answer with a careful nibble to the side of his mighty shaft. With a growl that must have birthed in his core, he bent his head over hers and muttered, "Take me in your mouth, Tuesday. Please."

The desperation in his tone would not allow her to tease at him, nor would her own desire to take him past her lips and feel the press of him against the back of her mouth. Cupping his testicles with her other hand, she fed on him greedily, slicking and lashing and sucking.

He slid his hand inside her leggings and slipped a finger between her folds, curling into her and gliding in deeply. She pressed up her hips, hilting him within her pussy and her mouth. Having lost direct contact with the vibrating chair, she could still feel subtle movement from it, and that coaxed her body to the high from which she wished to fall.

Ethan's fingers in her hair gripped and squeezed and his body began to tremor. Control was impossible. Surrender unthinkable. Meeting at a mutual peak and then plunging together was the only option. He swore, and came in her mouth. She, in turn, came in bucking thrusts against his hand.

Dropping to his knees before her, Ethan buried his face in her hair, his fingers caressing over her pussy and maintaining a firmness that extended her orgasm.

"Witch, you own me."

She liked the idea of owning him. Sexually. But no other way. He was a fierce, powerful vampire. The only kneeling she required of him was to satisfy her sexual needs.

"I'll share myself with you, lover. But let's never take ownership. Agreed?"

He nodded, then kissed her hard and deep, showing her an exquisite glimpse of the control he masterfully claimed as his own.

A knock at the door paused them both. Ethan hastily stood and zipped with a wince and a curse. "Sit up," he muttered as he approached the door.

Fluffing her hair and tugging down her shirt, Tuesday sat up on the chair and grabbed a pen, assuming… well, she wasn't sure what she was trying to reflect but the fake-secretary-looking-busy act seemed like a good move.

Ethan opened the door. "Cinder. I didn't think you were coming up. I don't need you until tomorrow night. I thought I made that clear in the text. Is there a problem?"

The tall, dark-haired man entered the room and Tuesday saw his red, ashy aura. But also…hmm—he was something beyond vampire, but she couldn't quite make out what that *else* could be. He eyed her a few seconds, sniffed, then smirked. What was that about?

"No problem," Cinder said. "Just wanted to ask you about the outer wards on the building and your phone was on forward."

"Right." Ethan took out his phone and tapped a few keys.

"If you're trying to pull a demon in," Cinder said, "you need the building to be open. But I'm not cool with letting down all the wards. The Archives could go crazy. All the captive beasts on the premises suddenly set free?"

"It would be for a brief period," Ethan assured him. "Is it possible to let them down only around the holding cell and then be on standby for immediate reinstatement?"

Cinder blew out a breath. He didn't look like any kind of tech guy Tuesday had ever met. Broad-shouldered and built like a bruiser, but oh, so pretty. Her sigil warmed. And that alerted her.

"Angel?" she suddenly said.

Cinder turned to her. "What?"

"I, uh…what are you?"

Cinder chuckled and swung to face her, crossing his arms high on his chest. "What are you?"

"I'm a witch. Your boss had me kidnapped from Boston, and flew me across the ocean while under the influence of a nasty but powerful drug to help him track the demon. Didn't you get the memo?"

The tech guy swung a look to Ethan, who shook his head. Then he offered his hand toward Tuesday, so she got up from the chair to shake it. And then she knew.

"Demon," she said. "But…you've fallen."

"Labatiel, the Flaming One, Angel of Punishment," he explained. A bit of pride in his tone, though. Expected of demons. "Used to be trapped under Paris until a sinkhole released me and I came to ground."

"Cool. Maybe. But…you're also vamp?"

He nodded. "It's a long story."

"I bet it is." Angel of Punishment, eh? That could prove an interesting history. "You got any suggestions for how to handle the demon we're going after tomorrow night? I mean, you two do hail from the same place."

"I don't know who you're after. The boss didn't enlighten me."

"It's need-to-know. Or it was," Ethan said with a glance to Tuesday. Oops. She'd said too much. But Ethan relented. "Demon's name is Gazariel."

Cinder hitched a clicking sound out the side of his mouth. "The Beautiful One. A primping idiot. That's who you're after? Why are you finding this so difficult? Just hold up a mirror and catch him while he's preening."

Tuesday giggled. "Oh, you men. Always thinking there's an easy button for everything."

"He's proving an evasive catch," Ethan said. "And the witch I thought could lure him to us is actually repelling him."

She did not miss Ethan's admonishing glance. She'd take it in retaliation for spilling the intel beans.

Cinder's gaze took her in none too kindly. "Then why is she still around?"

"She's, uh…" Tuesday could sense Ethan's sudden discomfort yet he hid it with an authoritative lift of his jaw. "Can you do it or not, Cinder? You'll have a day to figure this out. I'll need you to be on call to drop the wards only around the holding cell and then set them back up."

"The building wards will need to be briefly shut down as well. It's not as easy as flicking a switch. Dropping them is. But resetting them?" He shook his head. "That'll require a witch."

Tuesday stepped forward. "I, myself, happen to be a witch."

"I will only work with a witch who works for and has been approved by the Council. I can't do it, man," Cinder said to Ethan.

"I'll send CJ to assist you. That will work, yes?"

"The dark witch." Cinder exhaled heavily. "Fine. I've got to get things started. This is going to be a bitch." The vampire strode out, leaving the door open behind him. "You owe me, man!"

Tuesday looked to Ethan and said, "Now *he's* a Richard."

Chapter 19

Back at his place, Ethan wandered into the living room after kissing a sleeping Tuesday on the cheek. She had muttered something about needing to catch a few winks, had hit the bed as soon as they'd gotten back, and two minutes later she was out. The woman had a talent for dropping into a dead sleep.

Tugging off his shirt, he tucked it behind his head and slumped down on the sofa into a comfortable position. Then he took out his phone and checked texts and emails. He'd gotten an email marked urgent from CJ with intel about Anyx. The dark witch had looked her up in the Archives' vampire room. He'd checked *The Vampire Codex*, *the* book on all vampires—similar to the witches' *Book of All Spells*—and this was what he'd found:

Anyx—no known surname following marriage to Ethan Pierce in 1540 and subsequent divorce in 1600—has been observed to collect memento mori and death spells. 1720, she was stopped from using a plague hex on a village and was added to the Council's watch list. One incident in 1878 with a volatile organic poison resulted in the Archives seizing her eclectic collection from home in London, but other residences were not checked.

The vampire has remained under the radar but must always be kept on the watch list for occult fascination with bringing pain, suffering and death, or even possible experiments that could lead to mass genocide.

Known residences in Tampa, Florida, and Paris, France. Known former love affairs with Wolfgang Amadeus Mozart, Rasputin and Henri Telluir, a geophysicist of little renown. Current relationships unknown.

Ethan slapped the phone against his chest and muttered, "Anyx, what the hell have you gotten in to over the centuries?"

And had the book on vampires been updated recently? He'd thought it was a living book, always updating and rewriting the vampire history. Yet if Anyx was involved with Gazariel, the book had missed that. Unless Gazariel had lied to them about their relationship?

No, Ethan had seen the two in the restaurant. There was something going on between them.

As he'd told Tuesday, he'd witnessed Anyx's strange fascination for death early on and had extricated himself from a relationship that had no longer felt comfortable or safe for him. He and Anyx had lived as husband and wife for sixty years! And for the most part, they had loved and enjoyed one another's company. But they had spent a lot of time apart as Ethan served his tribe elders and fought in the Blood Wars. And Anyx, well, she'd traveled and tended her collection and kept it away from him until that one night he'd stumbled upon it.

Perhaps Gazariel was doing much the same after learning what a morbid and wicked vampiress he'd gotten involved with. Surely, for a demon who thrived on love and adoration, Anyx would present a challenge to his vanity.

It saddened him now to know that his ex-wife was so…strange. So dark and apparently evil. Was there a way to appeal to her? If she had been gifted the book with the Final Days code by The Beautiful One was there a chance Ethan could talk her into handing it over to him?

Judging from the report he doubted that would happen. She didn't seem mentally stable. So he had to set aside any lingering compassion he may have for the vampiress in order to help the greater good. And he could do that. He just…didn't want to know her reason why she had such a morbid fascination. He really didn't.

He texted CJ back with a request to recheck *The Vampire Codex* for updates, and for Anyx's Paris address. The report did not list it, but it should be entered in to a database somewhere in the Council's vast system. He'd send out a team to bring her in, but he didn't expect to find her. Something in his gut told him she had already received the gift. And that she may very well be trying to crack the code right now.

Heart sinking, Ethan clicked off his phone. He should be out there, looking for Anyx and Gazariel. But he had a solid plan for tomorrow, and it would work. He had to be patient.

There was one thing he could do. He paged through the dossier on the mission file on his phone and landed on the name of the muse who had created the book of names and sigils.

"Cassandra Stephens."

Stephans' location was currently unknown, but she had formerly lived in London and Berlin. Generally, phone numbers remained the same if the move was not a long distance. It was late, but he'd give it a try.

He dialed up the muse and as the phone rang he thought how odd it must be to know, as a muse, you were a human female—not immortal—who had been born to this realm and were connected to a specific fallen angel. And that angel's only goal was to find his muse and impregnate her in hopes of birthing a nephilim. Nephilim were monsters, and one had actually been born years ago. Cassandra Stephens and her Fallen One had helped to destroy the monstrosity. It was a long story, but Ethan could be thankful the woman was obviously kick-ass and determined not to let a label stop her from rising above her terrible fate.

After five rings, a sleepy voice answered. Ethan apologized for the late time. He told her who he was and who he worked for. "I don't know where you are, and I won't ask. But I need some information about the book of angel names and sigils you created."

"I…" A yawn was abruptly cut off. "Sorry about that. Uh, the book. It's been a while since I've had my hands on it. I thought it was with Raphael?"

"It's been stolen."

"Ah, shit. You need my help?"

"No, we've got things under control. But you wrote the book. Can you tell me how you created the code to enact the Final Days or even give me the code?"

"I'm sorry, Mister Pierce. I didn't think I was creating any such thing while writing the book. The code sort of magically formed and became the awful thing it is now. You know how this weird paranormal stuff works. Add in angelic magic and you've got some mysterious ineffable shit going on."

"So, not a clue what the code is?"

"I'm really sorry."

And if she hadn't created the code she certainly wouldn't have an idea if there was a way to stop it or call the whole thing off.

"I had to check."

"I understand," she said with another yawn. "Are you sure you don't need help? I can hop a flight and be… heh. I don't even know where you are."

"I'm in Paris, and I'm not sure what you could do to help. I've got a crew ready to take down the demon who has the book."

"I wish you much luck. But if the demon is no longer an angel, then you won't be able to attract him with his muse."

"I don't think he ever had a muse. He fell directly to Beneath."

"Then no, he wouldn't have a muse. If you've got a Sinistari blade lying around that could prove useful as a threat against the guy."

"Good to know. We may have one of those. Thanks, Cassandra."

Ethan hung up, and texted CJ to check the demon room for a Sinistari blade. He recalled Bron Everhart, the same retriever who had brought Tuesday to Paris and had taken such a blade in hand a few years ago on a mission to obtain the Purgatory Heart. Such a blade was formed from the halo of the fallen angel. Those specific angels fell beyond earth and to Beneath where they became Sinistari demons, those who hunted the Fallen Ones. An angel blade was supposed to be the only thing that could kill an angel, besides a halo. It might not have the same effect on Gazariel, but it could provide another good threat besides the reckoner. It wouldn't hurt to go in fully armed.

Prepping for tonight's adventure involved warding herself with the obsidian and a smoky quartz, both on leather cords hung around her neck. Tuesday had found a pair of spangled black leggings at the thrift shop the day she and Ethan had gone shopping. Perfect. On top, she wore a plain black T-shirt. Because when combined with her spangled fur coat, she certainly didn't want to overdo the sparkle.

On the other hand, some sparkly black eyeshadow was necessary. And she loved the matte violet lipstick. So did Ethan. It drew his hungry gaze, and that was all good.

She rarely drew wards on her skin, and wasn't going to put any on until she got to the headquarters and talked with Certainly Jones. If they were going to cast a spell together, they'd need to sync wards.

Blowing herself a kiss in the mirror, she checked for the alicorn, which she'd tucked at her right hip in the waistband of her leggings. And the athame she would carry in her coat pocket. Ritual weapons, not things she expected to use in defense. Maybe? She could poke an eye out with the alicorn, if necessary.

She strolled out by the bed and paused. Ethan paced before the window, back and forth from there to the record player. He didn't notice her, and his brow was furrowed. Of course, the man must have a million things going on in his brain right now. But he seemed different than his usual stoic, controlling boss-man self.

Padding over to him and waiting until he noticed her, when he did, she tilted her head. "Tell me why you chose this particular mission to step back into field-work," she asked. "Was it because the bait was so sexy and you couldn't resist spending time with her?"

His smirk softened his tension and his shoulders dropped. He reached out a hand and she clasped it, but he didn't tug her into an embrace. Instead, he turned to look out the window. They stood there, side by side, hand in hand, unable to pick out a star in the night sky, as the evening, while dark, was illuminated by millions of neon lights and streetlights.

"I needed to prove to myself that I wasn't washed up," he said quietly.

The confession surprised her. Coming from such a confident and strong man? He had it all together. Except when he was winging it without a plan. Okay, so he might need some practice to get back to where he once was with the fieldwork. But washed up?

"That's crazy. You've impressed me at every turn on this mission," she said.

"I missed capturing the demon. Twice," he said. "And I can't seem to quit fucking the bait. Does that sound like a professional retriever to you?"

She shrugged. "Not sure the qualifications for a retriever. I assume hexing the help isn't one of them, but it doesn't seem to be dragging you down."

He squeezed her hand. "I've become lax in my methods. My targeting and reconnaissance. I don't follow protocol—I make up my own. And—"

"And it's been a while, so give yourself a break, will you?"

"Any breaks I take may result in the world being smothered by myriad angel wings."

He did have a point there.

"You've got me by your side. That's got to count for something."

"It does. It really does."

"Then we're good to go? All confidence levels are high and alpha-charged?"

He turned, and with a sweep, lifted her by the legs and tossed her over his shoulder. Heading toward the doorway, he said, "Alpha-charged and ready to go."

Watching Ethan organize the players in this demon-hunting mission was like watching a commander order his troops. He exuded a control and knowledge that impressed Tuesday. And everyone knew exactly what their roles were.

Far from washed up. But that he'd told her as much meant he trusted her with such knowledge. And that was something she'd treasure. His confidence.

The familiar was already on the other side of the steel door in the clean room, inside the cage with his partner, having sex. Thomas had said he'd need half an hour to accomplish the task of getting sated, then the witch could go in and invoke the spell to capture Gazariel. And Cinder, the tech guy, would then take down the building wards to facilitate it all.

Certainly Jones, the witch who would perform the invoking, paced the hallway outside the main room, head down and arms crossed over his chest. Long dark hair spilled forward and covered half his face. A particularly bold tattoo right over his carotid clued Tuesday it was a ward against vampire bites. Smart witch.

Unless of course, the witch enjoyed a bite now and then.

She should have had Ethan bite her before they'd set out for this adventure. Might have come in handy to reinforce their blood bond. As it was, she decided it was a temporary thing that only lasted about twenty-four hours. It was fun while it had lasted.

The dark witch's pacing moved him past her.

"You don't think you should be in there so you know when the time is right?" Tuesday asked him.

He tapped his ear, and she noticed an earbud. "I've got audio. And trust me, that's as close as I need to be right now. That is one noisy woman the familiar brought along with him."

"Well, if you need any help?"

"You stay back and keep the wards on you. If we need your assistance, we'll ask."

She nodded and strolled back to the steel door to lean against it. Certainly had warded her to the nines against angels, demons, light magic and dark, as well. She felt as if a suit of armor sat on her shoulders. And it was only slim protection against Gazariel's influence should he breech the cage wards.

She'd felt those wards. They were strong. They should subdue the demon. With hope.

Glancing over her shoulder, she eyed Ethan. He was speaking to the reckoner, Savin Thorne, who had just arrived. The big man wore a bowler hat over his messy hair. A loose-fitting coat that looked cobbled from different fabrics, something a gypsy might wear, barely hung to his hips. And as he nodded and gestured with his hands while talking to Ethan, she noted the sigils, or possibly wards, drawn on the back of each of his hands. They hadn't been there when she'd met him yesterday. She hoped he wouldn't have to resort to actually sending the demon to Daemonia. Because without the curse lifted from her, that meant she would have to tag along.

No witch could survive in Daemonia for long. It would be a fate worse than any torture a vindictive witch hunter could mete out. She should have made it clear to Ethan that she was out if it came to that. But not like she could protest now. Such refusal would shut down the whole demon-summoning operation. Her presence was needed and it was not. Be here to sync all the magic and connect with the demon, yet don't get so close that she scared off the demon, or got sucked into his vortex of wicked magic.

This unexpected trip to Paris had become quite the adventure. Kidnapping aside, she was glad to be here. It gave her purpose. And often, when living for so long, there were days she wondered what good she was doing the world. And since her magic was dark, it was rare she felt she *did* serve the world goodness.

Once, she'd been a healer and had educated women. Why had she ever stopped? Oh, right. Lack of love did tend to change a person as the years grew long.

It had never mattered to her before, but lately she wanted to do good. To change. To rise up from the darkness she had caressed and made her own over the centuries and become someone worthy of giving and receiving goodness.

And love.

The thought startled her so much that she didn't hear Ethan call her name. Only when he gripped her wrist and bent to meet her eyes did she slip back into the present moment.

"You okay?" His gray irises were clear and focused. He may have felt washed up, but he was far from that. "I called your name twice and you're standing right here."

"Sorry. My mind was wandering. Yeah, I'm good." Or at least, she was trying to be. "What if the demon won't tell us where he put the book? Do we have a plan for bringing in the vampiress?"

"I have a containment crew on call to bring her in, but we're having a time locating her address in the database. I have hope, though."

"I hope your hope is effective. Because I thought you were using the reckoner as a threat."

"CJ has some magical thumbscrews to twist if Gazariel doesn't want to give us the information. We've done this before."

"The Beautiful One is not going to give up anything without a sacrifice from me."

"You don't know that."

"Yeah, I kind of do. He's an asshole."

"A Richard?"

"The number-one Richard of all Richards. He'll ask for my heart in exchange for the book, I know it."

"But that doesn't make sense. If he takes your heart, it'll return the curse to him."

"Maybe, maybe not. Maybe he can simply tug out

my heart and crush it and the curse along with it. But better he suffers and I die, than I live and he suffers."

"Let's not think like that. I'm going to protect you, Tuesday."

"I can take care of myself. I've some powerful magic. Probably more effective against the blood demon than your dark witch pacing over there like he's headed to his own funeral."

"The man has a wife and children. I'm asking a lot from him."

Yes, she recalled the feeling of overwhelming and true love she had gotten from CJ when she'd done a soul gaze on him. She wanted that kind of love. She really did.

"I still can't allow you to work the summons," Ethan said. "Gazariel will use your magic against us all."

"Not if the wards on the cage hold up. Let me go at him first. Break him down."

Ethan shook his head. "We're doing this my way. And besides, what if he's already given the book to Anyx? We're going to need him intact. And no magic you can throw at him will ever convince him to talk. You know that."

Tuesday nodded reluctantly. He was right.

"I expect to have a location on Anyx soon," he said. "I've got everything under control. This is what I do, Tuesday. Trust me."

"I do trust you. Completely."

"Thank you. Now, you stay back and out of the way. You've got all the wards on?"

"I'm loaded with them. You wouldn't be able to bite me if you wanted to."

"I can feel that repulsion. Which is why I haven't kissed you."

"And here I thought you were against PDAs."

"You can actually think that after our tryst in the alleyway? Or almost getting caught by Cinder in my office? What about in the restaurant?"

"I stand corrected. I see you're warded as well. The reckoner do that?" She tapped his throat.

"Yes." He stroked the lines drawn on his throat with a black felt-tip marker. She interpreted them as protective and closing, perhaps to keep him from speaking things the demon might try to trick out of him. "He suggested some additional protections to the ones I already have."

"Tell me one thing about the vampire chick you said you loved? The one who died by biting the witch."

"Huh?" Ethan glanced around to see if the other men were listening. They were not. "I don't understand."

"Did you promise to protect her always?"

"I, uh… Tuesday, you think I'm going to let you down?"

"No. I want to know if you let her down."

"That's cruel."

"It might be but… I need your truth, Ethan."

Ethan glanced to the men lingering in the hallway. None met his gaze. He lowered his voice and spoke near her ear. "I feel as though I let her down. But no, she chose that witch on the fly. I'm not sure I would have known he was a witch before she bit him, either. But I would have given my life to change it. To have been the one who took the bite and not her."

"You loved her that much?" Tuesday slid her hand along Ethan's cheek. Her heartbeats thudded. "More than your wife of sixty years? What about the chick who died from the blood transfusion?"

"Tuesday." He shook his head. "As I've told you, I've loved many."

Yes, and he'd loved a woman so much he would have died for her. And after knowing her but six months. Tuesday imagined such deep and abiding love happened only once in a man's life. Or a woman's. Yet he'd gone on to love others. And to experience heartbreak. And through it all, he survived. Perhaps Ethan's heart was capable of giving love to yet another?

She daren't dream. He would only be hurt if he fell in love with her. And he had been hurt by love more than enough times.

"You're a good man, Ethan." She kissed him quickly, then they turned as CJ spoke.

"The familiar is on target," the dark witch said. "Sated and open to bridge the demon. Ethan, notify Cinder to let down the wards. I'm going in. Everyone else follow, but stay back."

As Ethan called Cinder, they entered the clean room. The cage bars did not glow and the door was wide open. A naked woman gathered her clothing while a very naked Thomas lay sprawled on the center of the cage floor.

CJ approached the cage door. Standing aside to let the woman flee, he then gripped a bar in each hand and began to chant.

Tuesday helped the woman pull on her dress over her head. She nodded a quiet thanks, then looked to Ethan.

"You remember the way out?" he asked.

She shook her head.

"Thomas will be out shortly. Stand outside the door and wait for him. Thank you."

He held the door open and closed it behind her. Stepping up to stand beside the reckoner, Ethan crossed his arms and observed. Tuesday, back to the wall, kept a keen eye on the familiar in the cage, but also listened carefully to the Latin incantation CJ spoke. It was a standard demon-summoning spell with an adjustment to focus the reach within this realm. He battened it with protective sigils he drew in the air using a crystal wand. A white light trail followed in the wake of his movements. He traced a few of the spell tattoos on his left hand and then thrust his palm downward, facing it toward the familiar.

Thomas's body jerked and convulsed. Naked and sweating, he was open to allow a demon entity to inhabit his body only briefly before it apported into corporeal form. A spume of red smoke spiraled up from the familiar's pores, forming a tornado above him. The familiar opened his eyes, saw the red cloud and scrambled toward the cage door. As he fled, his body shifted, contorting and growing fur. A calico cat meowed and slipped out just as the cloud began to take human form.

Ethan rushed over and slammed the cage door shut, slipping a heavy bolt through a lock and activating the electronic security system with a few taps on the digital keyboard. The cage bars briefly glowed green then blinked out.

And within the cage formed the demon Gazariel, The Beautiful One. Long black hair spilled down his shoulders and to his elbows. Bare feet were marked with faint blue sigils. On his open palms glowed more blue markings.

He lifted his head, his red eyes glowing as he took in the cage and those standing around watching. On his cheek, Tuesday saw three long scratch marks. They bled black.

And when Gazariel's gaze met Tuesday's, he said, "You will suffer for this, my witch."

Chapter 20

The demon inside the cage stood tall, fists out at his sides. He wore black leather pants and no shirt. His abdomen was carved as if from stone and his muscles were many, forming him lean and imposing. Long streams of wavy coal hair hung over his broad shoulders and his red eyes glinted like rubies.

Slowly, the scratches on his cheek closed up, leaving but a spill of black blood trickling down his jaw.

With a hiss he released his wings, which spread to the cage bars without touching them. Black feathered wings that flashed like mirrors with each movement and seemed made of silk and sewn with silver threads. They were iridescent with all colors, much as a raven's wings.

Tuesday knew that angels rarely wore feathered wings, but demons often did. Had this angel's wings taken on a different form when he had fallen to Beneath and become demon? No matter. They were beautiful. He was beautiful.

And her sigil burned as if pleading with her to rush forth and touch those wings. To make contact with something that could both harm her and equally embrace her. The invitation felt so real.

She squeezed her hands, fingernails digging in to her palms to stop the urge.

The demon let out a guttural yell, retracting his wings when they touched the electrified bars. He swung about, his wings sending a rush of icy wind across the observers, lifting their hair and stirring up a bone-deep shiver that made Tuesday gasp.

Stomping a foot, Gazariel tested the steel cage floor. Thrusting out his hands, he sent demonic magic hurtling toward them, only to have it deflected by the wards. He took the brunt of that repulsed magic with a stagger backward and a screaming trill of swear words. He ended his tirade with a flip of his middle finger toward Tuesday, and a simple "Bitch."

Tuesday met CJ's eyes. The dark witch who had summoned the demon stepped back to stand beside her. "We'll leave him to the boss," he said quietly. "But stand on guard."

Always. Holding the alicorn in one hand and her athame in the other, she was prepared to fling some wicked magic toward the demon. Tuesday watched as Ethan questioned the captive.

"You'll get nothing from me that you could not get before," Gazariel announced. "How dare you steal me away from my very life?"

Tuesday had felt much the same upon waking inside this cage. But she would not sympathize with the demon. And yet, the compulsion to step forward and embrace him only grew stronger. This time a snap of the rubber band around her wrist was necessary.

The cat meowed and slunk toward the door. Tuesday leaned over to open it and the feline scrambled out.

"If you would have given me what I wanted during our first encounter I wouldn't have had to resort to such tactics." Ethan stood stoic before the cage, shoulders back and head lifted. A commander protecting his troops and interrogating the enemy. He wore wards drawn on the backs of his hands, beneath his chin and down his throat. But his true strength came from within; his courage and integrity. "You need only hand over the book, written by the muse Cassandra Stephens, which contains the code for the Final Days and I will release you. Simple as that."

Gazariel swiped a hand over his cheek, studied the black blood on his fingers, then gestured dismissively. "I don't have it."

"You are lying."

"I had it," the demon said with a sly red glance to Tuesday. "But now I do not."

"Then where is it?"

"In a safe place."

"Tell me where it is, and once I've retrieved it, you are free to go," Ethan stated. "Did you give it to Anyx?"

That caught the demon's attention. He gripped the cage bars, but released them as quickly with a hiss and a string of vile oaths that never would have been allowed Above. "I knew someone was watching us! Did you follow me, vampire? Why didn't you take me in hand that day when we were dining?"

"Did you give it to the vampiress?" Ethan repeated.

"Maybe." The demon rubbed his cheek again.

"You two had a lover's spat," Tuesday said, realizing now where the claw marks had come from. "Did she take the book from you and run?"

Gazariel flipped her off again. "Not worth my breath to converse with you lot of miscreants. I need something in exchange."

"How about your life?" Ethan offered. "You do know that if the Final Days is activated we will all die?"

Gazariel shrugged. "Assuming you remain in this realm. I, on the other hand, have made preparations to be located elsewhere."

"He doesn't have leave of this realm!" Tuesday blurted out. "He's as much a captive of the mortal realm as we all are."

Ethan cast her a castigating glare, which she took with a huff. She did not need a reprimand for providing him the facts.

"You know nothing about me, my witch," Gazariel growled through a tight jaw. He curled his wings forward, tucking them until the points crossed before his feet.

"I know everything about you, as you know everything about me," she said, and once again got *the look* from Ethan. She was supposed to stand back and keep quiet? She could not. Thrusting out an arm, she pointed the alicorn at the demon. "You are a vain and insignificant reject from Above, and then you were also rejected in Beneath and cast out to live in this realm. You, who couldn't bear to carry the curse of a loveless life so you put it on a helpless, dying woman. Some demon you are!"

Gazariel gripped the cage bars, and the action transferred mighty amounts of voltage through his system. He managed to hold on for much longer than Tuesday imagined any normal creature could, and as he did so, his eyes flashed brilliant crimson. Was he feeding off the electricity?

Ethan kicked a control button at the base of the cage, and the demon was propelled backward to collide with the bars at the back of the cage. Those bars hissed with smoke and sent the demon stumbling forward, so he almost landed on his knees, but he caught himself. Bent over, huffing, his wings slowly curled about him, enclosing him in a cocoon.

"Is she right?" Ethan asked. "Are you but a feeble reject from both Above and Beneath? Is it that your lover took off with the book, leaving you a simpering reject in her wake?"

"I don't have it. Not anymore. I was going to give it to her to—"

Tuesday filled in the words he probably couldn't bring himself to say—*to win her love*. Was the vampiress the one creature from whom Gazariel could not be loved?

"No." The demon stomped a foot. "I'm not going to utter a single word about that…bitch of a vampire." Gazariel lifted his head from the glinting cove of wings. His jaw was tight. He'd felt that pain from the cage bars, Tuesday knew. "Serve me your worst, Ethan Pierce."

"Very well." Ethan stepped back and gestured for Savin Thorne to step forward. The man tossed his hat aside, and shrugged up his shoulders, as if preparing to step into a boxing ring.

"Who is this mortal you've put before me?" Gazariel asked. "He may look imposing but I can feel no power within him."

The reckoner chuckled and rubbed his palms together before his face. When he spread his hands to face toward the cage, the wards on his palms took to flame. "I am Savin Thorne," he said to the demon. "I'm here to reckon you to Daemonia."

Ethan stepped aside to give the reckoner room to work. Tuesday stood just behind him. He could sense her in him. Because she was in him. And he didn't feel fear in her, but rather, indifference and a righteous anger. She hated this demon and wanted him gone. But he also knew they could not send him off to Daemonia until they'd gotten the information they needed from him. Nor could they actually send him away without also sending Tuesday along with him.

Thorne knew that as well.

The reckoner clapped his hands together over his head and began to chant something that sounded like a Polynesian tribal rite. It had a beat and a low, bellowing caw that sent chills up Ethan's spine.

Inside the cage the demon narrowed his gaze on the reckoner. With a shrewd sneer, he folded back his wings. He wasn't standing so tall and proud anymore. And it wasn't curiosity that bent him forward to better hear the reckoner's deep and loud voice. It had to be a nervous fear.

To Ethan's right stood CJ. The dark witch had crossed himself and touched some of the tattoos on his hand the moment the reckoner had started to chant. Ethan wasn't aware of any protections he needed against a reckoner. He'd worked with Savin twice before and had witnessed the man send a demon off to Daemonia in a cloud of black smoke. It had taken but ten minutes of chanting.

And they were nearing that mark now.

"All right!" the demon suddenly shouted, yet the reckoner kept up his wicked chant. "Make him cease and I will tell you where it is."

"Savin," Ethan said.

The reckoner silenced, closed his eyes and thrust his hands above his head again, but this time only touching together his forefingers, as if to pause something he could then continue when required. With a nod, he stepped back beside CJ.

Ethan stepped up to the cage. "Tell me."

Gazariel peered past him to Tuesday. "I will only tell my witch."

"That's not going to happen. She's not involved in this interrogation."

"I won't do anything to her. These damn wards have drained me already. And that bloody chanting. Ugh. I could almost see the gates to Daemonia. She knows she'll be safe. Yes?"

Behind him, Ethan felt Tuesday's nod more than saw it. He'd promised to protect her, and he did trust the efficacy of the wards in the room. And she was warded fully as well. He turned to look at her and without so much as a flinch, her confident posture conveyed to him that she was ready.

The woman was brave and strong. Of course she could handle this. Ethan nodded once, and Tuesday stepped forward.

Chapter 21

The leering look of satisfaction on Gazariel's face was slightly challenged by the fact that he was subdued, unable to reach through the bars and grab for Tuesday, as she knew he wished to do. So she walked up and stood but inches from those bars, and he did the same. She could feel him inside her. Feel his haughty vanity and his complex anger at the imprisonment.

And she well understood his pride in knowing that he had control over her, no matter the safeguards and wards. Because she would never have freedom so long as she wore his sigil.

And a larger part of her than she was comfortable with…wanted him. Close to her. Inside her. A part of her, as the sigil's burning caress promised.

"Where is it?" she asked, curling her fingers about the alicorn and athame. "Come on, it's late and I need to go home and wash my hair."

"Snark does not suit you, witch. I prefer those times when you are raging in your dark beauty, calling down the rains to chase away the dust storms, or sending out an army of gargoyles to defeat a band of marauders. Or what about that time you burned out a lecher's tongue for harming a child? You think I haven't watched you over the centuries?"

Behind her, Ethan cleared his throat. He wanted her to get on with it, but she couldn't force the demon when grandstanding was obviously his thing.

"I've never sensed your presence," she offered honestly. A creepy discomfort kept her from prompting for the details.

"I'm sure the sigil did. But you were focused. Honed to a precise and elegant weapon. And now look at you. Being led on a leash by an insignificant vampire and his band of not-so-merry men."

"The reckoner fucked with your sense of safety," she observed. "If sent to Daemonia you wouldn't last a day. And how long is a day in that place? Decades? Oh, the fun they'd have with such a pretty, spoiled Fallen brat such as you."

The demon reached to grab at her but recoiled when his fingers connected with the electrical field. "Bitch."

"Actually, it's witch. Get it right."

Gazariel chuckled. "I like your moxie, my witch. Despite your reliance on that silly plaything. An alicorn? Really? It's been tainted by vampire blood. It will no longer serve you in any significant manner."

She looked at the pearlescent twist of horn. It did seem a bit duller than when she'd first claimed it. But she wouldn't set it aside. That's what the demon wanted her to do.

Gazariel bowed his head toward her. "We might have made an interesting pair."

"Seriously? Nope. I prefer my men with balls."

The demon gripped his crotch defiantly, gnashing his teeth as he did so. "Words—"

"*Do* seem to bother you. But now let's get this done with, shall we? The sooner you tell me where the book is, the faster me and the band of merry men will let you go."

"You don't actually think they'll release me, do you? The reckoner stands greedily waiting. I can see the lust for revenge in his eyes."

"Revenge? You've done nothing to him."

"It is revenge for all of our kind. A secret he holds so tightly it keeps him from his true powers." The demon's eyes glinted as he met gazes with the reckoner.

"I was promised you would be released as soon as the book with the code is handed over," Tuesday said, not wanting to get into whatever issues the reckoner had with demons right now. "I won't allow them to go back on their word to me. I do have your word, yes, Ethan Pierce?" she said loudly.

"You do," Ethan said. "He gives us the location of the book. We retrieve it, verify it's intact. We let him go. Simple as that."

Gazariel considered it for a moment, his eyes flicking from red to the brilliant azure that must have lured thousands of women to their knees before him. So damn pretty.

But also a Richard.

And it was only with that thought Tuesday was able to keep it together and not attempt to reach for his chiseled abs.

"As the mean vampire guessed, I gave it to my girl-friend," he said quietly. Tuesday suspected none could hear but her, though the vampire should be able to with his heightened senses.

"She didn't love you," Tuesday said, trying out her earlier suspicion. "You thought by giving her the book you could win her love."

Gazariel lifted his chin imperiously.

"There was actually one creature in this realm who did not fall on her knees in adoration before you," she declared. "Must have been tough for a poseur like you."

"Enough!"

"Apparently, you were not enough for Anyx."

"I care little about that somber, death-obsessed vampiress. Besides, we broke up recently."

"Let me guess. Just before you were whisked away to this cage? I saw the claw marks," Tuesday said. "And you bleed black blood. No angel left in you, Beautiful One."

Gazariel's upper lip flinched.

"Why that book and that particular vampiress?"

"I had no idea, when first we met, that she had a disturbingly dark obsession."

"So I've been told." Tuesday kept herself from glancing Ethan's way. The vampiress did not sound like the sort any man could love. She must have some serious skills when it came to pleasuring them. "So you gave her a book with a code that could end the world as a sort of…love token?"

"I gave it to her days ago. She thanked me, but…she didn't say she loved me. Can you believe that?"

"Shocking," Tuesday said with all the snark exploding in that one utterance.

"I thought she would merely add it to her collection," Gazariel explained. "She collects death. Remnants from the *Titanic*. The leather straps from an electric chair that ended the lives of so many. A charm to give the bearer instant necrosis. Et cetera. So a code that could enact the end of the world? She was excited. It was the most powerful item she'd ever heard of. She was thrilled to have it. Little did I know she was using me to get what she wanted." He looked aside, and for a moment Tuesday almost saw regret cross his perfectly symmetrical face. "She's a bigger bitch than you are. Good riddance, I say."

"Along with the means to end the world? Gazariel, please."

He closed his eyes and sucked in a breath through his nose. "I do love it when you speak my name. It shivers through me like a teasing yet unrequited orgasm. Always promising yet never fulfilling."

Now she was ready to poke him in the eye with the alicorn, but Tuesday knew the wards worked on both sides of the cage bars.

"If you two are on the outs, then why the hell won't you give her up to us?" she asked. "Why not get the ultimate revenge against the one person who doesn't love you by sending us after her to claim the book?"

"Do *you* love me, Tuesday Knightsbridge?"

Pressing her lips together, Tuesday prevented an oath, but oh, did it tangle with her tongue for release. She needed to play nice with the demon, or they would never get anywhere with him. She pressed a palm over the sigil and said what she knew to be partially true, and what she hoped wasn't deeply true. "I do love you, Gazariel. You are beautiful. I adore you."

"Of course you do." Another deep inhale of satisfaction and he opened his eyes to beam a soft blue gaze upon her. She almost thought to see compassion in his irises. "I gave you freedom from death. And from love."

"Yeah, well... I would like to know love," she admitted.

"It is exquisite. I have it all the time. You are missing so much."

She tilted her head and couldn't stop the truth from spilling out. "I don't think what you believe to be love is really quite the thing. You are adored and worshipped. But that's not love. Love is...something different. It comes from the soul. It connects two people not out of desperation, or a worshipful lusting desire, but here." She beat her chest with a fist. "Deeply and to the bone. It is blood, bone and spirit."

The demon sniffed. "You think to know so much?"

"I know a lot, but certainly not everything. What I do know is that the manner in which I love you is not abiding or deep. It is only surface. You will only ever have surface love, Gazariel. And that makes you a sad, pitiful, impotent demon."

This time Gazariel's hand plunged through the cage bars, and even as he screamed at the pain of the wards burning his skin, he managed to grasp her throat.

Tuesday's body was pulled away from the weak attack, and she turned to shove Ethan away. "I'm fine. Just let me do this. I've got him. I do."

Ethan nodded. "You do. But I'm close."

Stepping back up to the bars, Tuesday waited for the demon to stop groaning and look up from his burned hand. The angry red skin smoldered, but they both watched as it healed, forming new, pale flesh and reshaping his broken fingers into long, elegant appendages.

"Admit you did a bad thing," she said to him. "Your ex-girlfriend has something that no one should be allowed to touch. And really? If she does manage to activate the code and brings down all the angels from Above, they'll smother you, too."

Shaking out his newly healed hand, Gazariel lifted his chin with a haughty thrust. "Assuming I remain on this mortal realm."

Tuesday crossed her arms, and stated flatly, "You can't go back to Beneath. Or even Above. You're stuck here." It was a guess, but she figured it was a good one.

Yet Gazariel looked down his nose at her. "It is as simple as going belowground. The angels won't fall through the earth. Not too far, anyway. Their wings will burn up the surface and the bodies of all those walking this earth. But Paris is a virtual maze of passages and tunnels beneath the manmade clutter."

Tuesday glanced to Ethan, who was hearing all of this. He didn't make a move or give her a sign that he understood what the demon was talking about.

"You think you'll be safe when your bitch of a girlfriend releases Above's angels as long as you're underground?"

"The catacombs are where Anyx said she intended to be when she set off the spell." Gazariel hung his head. "I thought she'd put it on the shelf next to her other collectibles."

"No, you didn't. You're not that much of an idiot."

The man sucked in his lower lip. The move reduced him to such a human thing. Truly, an impotent loveless creature. She was right; he had not known true, soul-deep love. And she knew that because she was exactly the same as him.

"Maybe you are an idiot," she said quietly. "Love dumb?"

"If you wish me to continue speaking to you so openly you should try a little kindness, my witch. I happen to know you and that vampire are currently engaged in a frenzied affair. Does he know the *other* way to break your curse? The one that doesn't involve my ripping out your heart?"

Tuesday closed her eyes and sensed that Ethan was listening, carefully. He didn't say anything. And she could not allow him to learn the truth.

"It's not something that's ever going to come to fruition," she said quietly. "And if I could rip out my heart and give it to you without dying, believe me, I would."

"I do tire of so much love some days."

"You've never been lovable a day in your pitiful life."

"I am an extremely lovable demon. Adored. Worshipped. Ugh. It can get tiresome, let me tell you."

"I wouldn't know."

"No, you would not." The demon glanced to Ethan. "But…you could."

Enough of the sly entendres about her love life.

"Come on. Where is Anyx and what sort of booby traps do we have to wend through to get to her?"

"She intends to enact the code under the full moon."

"That's tonight."

"I believe so. At the stroke of midnight." Gazariel rubbed his knuckles against his bare chest and blew on them. Casual. Just playing for time, now that he realized he might have the upper hand.

"Thorne," Ethan said from behind them.

The reckoner clapped his hands loudly and again set into his chant.

"Guess your time is up," Tuesday said, as calmly as she could manage. But really? She wasn't in any mood to get transported to Daemonia with this vain angel-turned-demon-turned-love-sick idiot.

"What do you want from me!" Gazariel shouted.

"Where is she?" Ethan demanded.

The reckoner's voice rose. The cage bars began to shudder.

"Fine! She's beneath the Temple of Reason."

Tuesday turned to face the men behind her, and as one they said, "Notre Dame."

Chapter 22

Outside in the hallway the crew gathered to discuss their next move. They needed to find Anyx STAT. Since she'd only had the book a few days, Ethan wondered if the vampiress had figured out the code. Gazariel hadn't known. They convened outside the clean room, leaving Gazariel inside the cage after he'd given them Anyx's address.

"Now what?" Savin asked.

"I'm routing the containment team to the address I just got for Anyx, but I suspect we won't find her there," Ethan said. "The demon is telling the truth. We need to go below Notre Dame."

CJ whistled. "Beneath holy ground?"

"This adventure gets more fun by the minute," Tuesday said with little sincerity.

"Isn't it old Roman remains below the church?" Savin asked.

"That's the public level," CJ explained. "There are tunnels beneath the church that snake down much deeper, perhaps five or six stories. We might have to do some spelunking."

"I know a guy who'll grant us access through the church. Want me to call him?" Savin asked.

"If you can get him here immediately," Ethan said.

Savin tugged out a cell phone. "I'll go along, but only if you need me. Or do you want me to hang around here? Babysit the demon?"

"We need to take Gazariel along," Tuesday said.

"No." Ethan shook his head. "We can't risk it."

"With a little blood magic the demon will lead us straight to her," she said.

"Like drawing a compass on his chest?"

"More complicated than that, but very doable. And CJ and I can shackle him and make him utterly incapable to do anything but walk and breathe."

Ethan looked to CJ. The dark witch nodded. "It's possible. If he's had sex with Anyx recently—and she drew his blood—we could work the spell. Remnants of her DNA would still be on or in him. But we'd have to combine our magics," he said to Tuesday.

"Not a problem. And if we bring along the reckoner he remains a threat to the demon to stay on his best behavior. But you're not going to send him to Daemonia as long as I'm wearing his sigil."

"Of course not," Savin offered.

"Tuesday, can I talk to you over here?" Ethan nodded down the hallway. "CJ, you and Savin prepare for our adventure."

"Will do," CJ said. "But first I've to head up to tech and make sure Cinder has the building wards back in place. Come on, Savin."

When the two men had left, Ethan took Tuesday by the arms and looked into her eyes for the longest time before he finally asked, "What's the other way to break the curse?"

"What?"

"I heard every word the two of you spoke. The demon said there was a way to break your curse without ripping out your heart."

She looked away from him, but he moved to the side and blocked her in by the wall, tipping up her chin and forcing her to meet the challenge in his eyes. "Tell me. You've known there was another way all along?"

"I've known since the moment the curse settled into me. He told me then. It's not something that will ever happen. And I will not tell you what it is, so to use one of your favorite lines, you don't get to tell me what I can and can't do." She shrugged out of his grasp and walked a few steps away. "You did promise to release Gazariel after we got the code. So the reckoner shouldn't even be an issue. I needn't worry about being tugged off to Daemonia. And I'm resigned to carry the curse within me for the rest of my days."

"Don't you want love, Tuesday? If there's a chance to break the curse in some other manner—"

"I said we will not discuss this anymore. Can you give me that?"

Ethan raked his fingers through his hair and gave her a nodding shrug. "I guess I have to. But will it interfere with the task we have before us?"

"Not at all. I swear it to you."

"Then you and CJ need to bespell the demon in whatever manner will help us, and we'll set him loose to lead us to Anyx. Do you have a means to stop the spell should she have already enacted it? Do you know how the code is activated?"

"I've not seen the book or the code. And I thought you were the man in charge. Don't you have information about how the code is activated?"

"It's a blood spell."

"How do you know?"

"That's what I was told."

"By who?"

"The one who ordered I retrieve the book," he said angrily.

"Who is?" Tuesday insisted.

Ethan looked away from her.

"Ethan? Who sent you on the quest for this book? Was it the Council? Because it doesn't feel right to me. You'd have more information if the Council—"

"It was a direct order from Raphael," he finally said.

"Raph— An actual—" Shivers traced Tuesday's nape. This was getting a bit too deep into angeldom and their mysterious ways for her comfort. "You got an order from an archangel?"

He squeezed the fingers of one hand before him and nodded. "Came to me a few days before you arrived with a demand we locate the thing."

"Why are you acting so weird about it? It's like you're embarrassed or—"

"I am not embarrassed. This is a need-to-know mission. And you don't—"

"Do not give me that excuse. I'm in this. Deep. And you couldn't have gotten this far without me. What's going on, Ethan? Do you often take orders from angels? How is Raphael involved?"

He gripped her by the shoulders as if to steady her, but he was actually finding his ground and forcing up calm when he wanted to walk away from her right now. His confession about not being up to snuff on fieldwork returned to his thoughts. Had he stepped into a mess too deep for even him to struggle out of?

"Raphael was keeping track of the book," Ethan said, "and…he misplaced it. That is confidential information. But you won't say anything, right?"

"Why would I? And to whom? I just think it's kind of weird that an angel allowed a demon to steal something so valuable from him." She tilted her head, and tried to read Ethan's gaze. "In fact, I find it nearly impossible that one so all-powerful could have had something taken from him without noticing. The only other option is that Raphael gave it up freely. And why would he do that?"

"I don't…" Ethan squeezed his eyelids shut. She was pressing him, guessing at scenarios that were turning out to be dreadfully true. And he'd never considered it, but had the archangel *purposefully* allowed Gazariel to steal the book?

"I think it's a test," Ethan finally said. "I don't know much, Tuesday. You have to believe that. I thought it was suspicious, too, after getting the command from Raphael to search for the book."

"But that could mean the angel might actually stand back and allow it all to happen. End-of-world stuff. Yeah?"

"I don't know about allowing things to go to completion," Ethan said. "I should hope not. But I don't know much about angels."

"Except that you take orders from any random angel that happens to request your services."

"He is an arch— Tuesday, we don't have time for this argument. Do you really want to do this now? Because it's not going to get us anywhere, and it will give Anyx more time to crack the code and enact the spell."

Frustration tightening her fists at her sides, Tuesday blew out a breath. Neither of them was helpless. They did have the power to stop this. Whatever *this* was.

"Fine. This whole adventure is fucked. Just like I knew it would be. But I'm with you. I promise. You got my back, I've got yours. Let's get to it. I can do blood magic, which is helpful if the code activation truly requires blood. And Gazariel is a blood demon. But I should go armed with supplies. Can I take a look around in the witch room and see what I can find?"

"I'll show you where it is." He held his hand out for her to take and she looked at it a moment. "I should have told you about Raphael from the start. But it wouldn't have changed things."

"I realize that. Maybe."

"I want things to be good between us, Tuesday. Don't block me out, please. We'll need to be strong and stand as one against whatever we next face. Can we do that?"

She slapped her hand into his firmly. "We can. And when this is over? I want to talk to that Richard of an archangel."

He pulled her to him. "When this is over we're going to talk about breaking your curse. For my sake."

"Why? Oh. Don't fall in love with me, Ethan. It won't end well for you."

And she strode off, but not before Ethan saw the tears forming at the corners of her eyes.

With CJ's permission, Ethan left Tuesday to ransack the Archives' witch room for whatever magical items she may need, then headed back to the clean room, where the demon was still caged.

He could not get the fact that Tuesday wasn't willing to tell him what could break her curse from his mind. Was it so much worse than having her heart ripped out? Nothing was worse than death.

The demon lifted his head as Ethan entered the room. Eying the base of the cage, Ethan verified that all the wards were lighting up the control panel. And he still wore the demonic wards on his hands. The wards on his throat would keep the demon from trying to trick useful information out of him.

The demon hooked his arms akimbo and inhaled deeply, expanding his chest. With a flip of hair over a shoulder, he asked, "You lied to her, didn't you?"

Ethan stepped up to meet the demon's blue gaze between the bars. "What do you think I lied about?"

"About releasing me."

"That wasn't a lie. Should we find the book, you're free to go. That is, if your girlfriend hasn't already tried to activate the code."

"My girlfriend? She was your wife first, vampire. You think I didn't know that? I could smell you on her. Wasn't sure what it was when I first fucked her, but since I've been in your presence?" The demon shuddered. "You are a part of her. Did you know about her weird and wicked obsession?"

"It's why she's no longer my wife. She's…troubled. And she needs to be contained."

Gazariel lifted an eyebrow. "Well then, it seems you've caged the wrong person. But isn't it like a man to want to imprison those females he can't understand?"

"You're a man, too."

"You think so? When I Fell I was neither one nor the other sex. Not much changed after becoming demon. And by giving Tuesday that hideous curse I found I could be either or. It's cute, the trick. Though I do prefer a dick to a clit. It's much more powerful, don't you think?"

"Apparently, you've never met Tuesday Knightsbridge. That's the most powerful clit I've ever met."

"Yes." Gazariel dragged his gaze up and down Ethan assessingly. "You love her. Poor fellow. You certainly won't survive through the night."

"You're an idiot. I've known her less than a week."

"Doesn't take more than a wink and a kiss to lose one's heart."

"You and I have chatted enough. The dark witches will be returning to bespell you. You'll lead us to Anyx."

The demon rolled his eyes. "I gave you her address."

"My team reports she's gone. The place was a shambles, as if she had no intention of returning."

"Bitch." The demon spat out a few words that Ethan assumed were demonic oaths. "She's really going to do it."

"Seems so."

"I need to get underground."

"We're all going underground in search of Anyx. But you have to do something for me."

"Something even more than being led around on

a leash for the shits and giggles of your merry men? What, pray tell, is that?"

"Promise me you'll take the curse from Tuesday. Give her the freedom to love that she deserves."

Gazariel lifted his hands and shrugged. "You really want me to rip out your girlfriend's heart? Okay, then."

"There's another way," Ethan insisted.

The demon approached the bars, and this time when he gripped them the electricity did not seem to bother him at all. Ethan again checked the steady LEDs to confirm the wards were activated.

"I've become conditioned to the pain," Gazariel said as he curled his fingers tightly about the bars and moved his face closer to Ethan's. His jaw was tense, but his expression remained calm. "You don't know what it is that will set my witch free from the curse, do you?"

"No."

"She wouldn't tell you? Because you did ask her about it. I know that much."

Much as he didn't want to admit his lacking trust with Tuesday to the demon, Ethan shook his head.

"It's not something I can give her, or even do for her," Gazariel said on a steady, deep tone. "You see, it's—"

"Ready to rock!" Savin and CJ wandered into the clean room. The reckoner punched a fight-ready fist into his palm. "Where's Tuesday?"

"I'm here!" The witch walked in and patted a leather bag she'd strapped across her chest. "Got all the accoutrements I'll need for a descent into the bowels of Paris to find a mad vampiress intent on destroying the world. And CJ has a bag of tricks as well." The dark witch patted his hip bag in proof. "Let's get the demon shackled and get on with this, yeah?"

Ethan glanced at Gazariel, who smirked at him as if to say "oh, well, now you'll never know the secret to freeing the witch from the curse."

"All right." Ethan stepped down from the platform. He'd learn the answer later, after they'd found Anyx. He would not set Gazariel free until he knew how to help Tuesday find love. "Can you bespell the demon without opening the cage doors and taking down the wards?"

"Of course." Certainly stepped forward, and with a hand held out for Tuesday, she clasped it and together the twosome began to work their magic.

Chapter 23

A witch generally avoided entering churches and cathedrals—for good reason—yet Tuesday was fascinated as she followed Ethan and CJ as they descended below Notre Dame two stories. Savin's contact had led them through the church basement, underground to a cold dark storage area, then had unlocked a vaulted door that had led into a cavernous blackness.

They'd quickly found a path. The walls were initially paneled with rotting wide boards, along which had been strung electrical cords—probably a good century old judging by the frayed cloth covering. As their footsteps tilted downward, the walls changed to limestone and the floors graduated from hard limestone to dirt.

Behind her, Savin and Gazariel brought up the tail. She didn't argue having the hulkingly handsome reckoner guarding her back. But the demon's presence tugged in her sigil.

By the seven sacred witches, why could she not simply tell Ethan how to break the curse? Revealing the truth wouldn't matter. It was not something he could do for her. And the way to break the curse was not something she could ever ask of another person. It simply wasn't done.

But giving him her truth suddenly felt important. If she told him, then she could move forward. Yeah?

"Bring Gazariel up front," Ethan called back.

As Savin shoved Gazariel past Tuesday, the demon waggled his tongue at her. The magic she and CJ had put on him kept him docile, and the blood compass they'd drawn on his chest would react to Anyx's presence. The demon didn't have to do a thing. They could read directions from the glowing diagram drawn in his own sticky black blood on his chest.

The crew waited, staring at Gazariel's chest, and were rewarded almost immediately with a flash of blue light.

"South," Ethan said, and he turned to lead them down a narrow aisle carved from limestone. Here and there an old section of wooden paneling and some ancient electrical wires were nailed to the wall. Chalk symbols marked by previous explorers were either signs of direction or made-up nonsense, maybe even cataphile gang symbols as Ethan suggested.

Parisian cataphiles were a fascinating subculture. Tuesday knew the crazy compulsion to explore the underside of Paris had existed for centuries. Actually, for as long as the city had existed. Daring cave spelunkers held underground parties and challenged themselves to find new, unexplored and extremely dangerous sections of the labyrinths. The catacombs spread all under Paris and in some areas as far down as seven stories.

When they'd been waiting for Savin's contact to find the right keys, Ethan had mentioned the legend of the vampiress who had been cursed by an angry lover in the eighteenth century. The lover had a witch bespell the vampiress frozen and put her in a glass coffin. She couldn't move her body, but she had remained conscious, always aware of what was going on around her. They placed the coffin somewhere in these very labyrinths. She had been found by a man who truly loved her decades ago. Needless to say, she'd gone mad during those centuries of suspended animation, and still struggled with sanity. It was a long and interesting story that Tuesday would have loved to hear more about.

While she wasn't much for spelunking, she wasn't afraid of the closed confines or the darkness. She had pulled on a white light upon entering and now vacillated whether or not to expend some magic to light up the ground with an illumination spell. There were patches of wet on the uneven limestone and dirt surface and she'd not worn shoes for hiking. Her boots had three-inch heels, and she could run in them, but forget navigating the bumpy surface with any skill. But she didn't know if they would find Anyx, and if so, how much magic she would require to stop the woman if she intended to activate the spell, so she holstered any nervous desire to use the magic for the time being and wobbled onward.

Gazariel walked ahead of them all, turning on occasion so Ethan could view the glowing map on his chest. The demon wasn't tied up, but CJ and Tuesday had put a heavy shackle on him. He was connected to her through the sigil, and much like the bonding spell CJ had cast on she and Ethan, Gazariel had to stay close, within the magic's range. And they'd wrangled as much of his demonic magic as possible. He was pouting, and every so often Tuesday felt the tug when she lollygagged behind.

If it wasn't a vampire leading her around Paris, it was a pouting demon tugging her deeper into the underground.

Gazariel actually deserved a good pout. Poor spoiled prince of vanity. Couldn't get the vampiress to love him so he had risked sacrificing the world to win that love?

Tuesday was able to stop herself from giving him a comforting hug, though.

They may need Gazariel to talk to Anyx. They may also have to use blood magic should the code already be activated. And that may require a lot of blood. From the same source. And they hadn't discussed exactly who that source would be.

By the blessed goddess, she prayed the vampiress had not the smarts to figure out the code from that book. A notebook in which some muse had scribbled down angel names and sigils? How irresponsible to put such to paper. On the other hand, that book had been in the care of an archangel. And now it was not. Superirresponsible. Didn't angels have their shit together enough to keep an eye on one very dangerous book?

Tuesday would give the asshole Raphael a piece of her mind. This whole experience was one big clusterfuck.

On the other hand, this adventure had introduced her to Ethan Pierce. And she wasn't going to begrudge that happy side effect.

The men leading their merry gang stopped walking. Ethan turned and looked to her and Savin, cupping a hand around his ear as a signal that they listen.

Gazariel stretched out an arm to indicate they should continue walking. "What are we—?" Savin hushed him.

Ethan glanced at the glowing sigil on the demon's chest and then nodded toward the end of the pathway, where the faintest glimmer of golden light flickered. The scent of flame mingled with the dusty dry limestone.

"Is it her?" Tuesday asked the demon.

Gazariel listened, swore, then nodded. He strode away from the front of the line.

"Onward," Ethan announced and took up the pace.

When he reached a T-turn, he stopped without going around the corner toward the light. Tuesday walked up to him and he slipped his hand into hers. "Listen," he said. They both listened to what the vampiress was saying just around the corner.

Tuesday didn't have to eavesdrop for long, or even understand the meaning of the words. The vampiress's tone and cadence made her heart drop in her chest. "She's chanting an invocation. She's cracked the code, Ethan. She's begun the spell."

"We need to move now." Ethan pulled a stake from his thigh holster, surprising Tuesday that he would wield such a thing. He nodded to CJ, who confirmed the command to move. "Get the demon up here."

Savin shoved Gazariel up toward the turn.

"What the hell do you want me to do?" Gazariel said in a tight whisper. "Did you see the scratches on my face? I'm not her favorite person at the moment."

"Talk her down. Get her to stop speaking the spell," Ethan said. "Or she dies."

"With that?" The demon snapped a finger against the stake Ethan held. "That's not going to scare her. She's been staked once before. Survived."

Savin gaped. Tuesday knew it was possible for a vampire to survive a staking if he left the stake in and allowed it to slowly work its way out of the body while it healed. Not a fast process, or, she imagined, painless.

"Then we'll use magic," CJ offered. "Get in there now, Gazariel. She's speaking the spell. We can't let her advance to a final declaration to open the very heavens Above."

The demon stood firm.

So Ethan tugged out a blade from a holster at his back hip and flashed it before Gazariel's face.

"Is that…?" Gazariel swallowed. "A Sinistari blade? Are you kidding me?"

"Does it look like I'm kidding?" Ethan asked.

With a sigh of resignation, the demon led the way into a vast chamber that was lit with dozens of black candles. Flames flickered wild crimson flashes on the stone floor and walls. A dais toward the back of the limestone chamber revealed Anyx standing with her back to them, her arms spread wide. Silver jewelry glinted in her hair and at her wrists and waist. She wore a black sheath and no shoes. All around her a circle of candles flickered. And a dark liquid glinted in the pentacle drawn within that circle.

"Blood," Tuesday said as she recognized the ceremony. Where she'd gotten so much blood—the chick was a vampire. Stupid to even wonder.

Ethan joined Gazariel, who stood stymied by the

scene. They didn't walk up to Anyx because a shallow trench about three feet wide and flowing with water dissected them from her.

Tuesday gestured to the flames flickering on the water. "A repulsion spell," she said to the men. "If you cross the water, even try to leap over it, you'll go up in flames."

"Defeat it," Ethan commanded her.

Not at all miffed that he'd sharply ordered her to do something, Tuesday spread her arms wide and chanted a suppression spell. There was no spell a vampiress could enact that she, a witch, could not counter.

Meanwhile Gazariel, nudged on by the threat of Ethan's blade, called, "Anyx! Come on, sweetie, let's not destroy the world today. I really like having humans around. Who's going to make my favorite filet mignon if they are all dead? And who's going to feed you, huh? Have you thought about that? You'll starve, bitch!"

The vampiress paused in her chanting, tilted her head, but did not turn to them. She was smart. If she paused the spell too long, it would dissipate.

A sweep of Tuesday's hand and the utterance *"Deflagro!"* snuffed the flames on the water. With an all-clear nod from her, Ethan jumped across, followed by Savin. Gazariel stayed put.

"So much power," Anyx called. "I must own it!" Now she turned, and with an elegant spread of her arms out from her sides and a curl of her fingers, she announced, *"Sarax conti expulsius!"*

The stone walls shuddered. Dust spumed from cracks, increasing the dry perfumed air. Ethan looked to Tuesday. She wasn't positive, but those could have been the final words to activate the spell. When the blood surrounding the vampiress began to bubble, then she was sure.

"That was it," she said.

"The code?" Ethan asked.

"Yeah, I'm not one-hundred-percent sure of the words, but I'm pretty sure they can be interpreted as 'open sesame, let the angels all fall down.' Get her out of that circle!" Tuesday turned and CJ already stood beside her. "We've got to penetrate her casting circle and strangle the spell."

Anyx shouted over her shoulder at Gazariel, "You were nothing more than a tool, you idiot demon!" And then she turned around completely. Elegant black hair, heavy like oil, spilled down her back. Eyes decorated with kohl glimmered with red. A visible red aura, much thicker than a vampire's usual aura, floated about her body. She was a part of the spell. It was her blood flowing in the water. Her scanning gaze stopped on the approaching vampire. "Ethan?"

Tuesday felt the intensity of the spell falter. The vampiress had to hold her focus to keep it going. If she was suddenly reunited with her ex? Fuck, she really didn't want to do this, but— "Go to her, Ethan!"

Stake held at the ready, Ethan approached the circle.

"It's really you? I've missed you, Ethan." Anyx took a step forward. Then, realizing she neared the edge of the circle, she stopped. Arms stretched out, she unfolded her fingers toward him. "Come to me. We can be together in the new world I am creating."

"Really?" Tuesday heard Gazariel mutter behind her.

"Anyx, you can't do this," Ethan said.

Tuesday and CJ quickly drew a circle on the limestone floor with black chalk before the flowing stream.

A channel cut through the rock from the stream to the dais, which was exactly what they needed. CJ flung out herbs and crushed troll hearts and recited a powerful cleansing spell.

Tuesday drew out the athame and looked at her wrist. Blood was needed.

"A whole freakin' lot of it," she muttered, feeling her heart fall to her gut. They needed as much blood as had already been spilled to counteract the spell.

This had become a no-return mission, and she was not happy about that. Because hey, she'd kind of thought that finding love would be a good thing. Like it was time to give it a go. And she'd found a man she wanted to risk that chance on.

Too late for regrets now. She wouldn't ask anyone else to do this. The magic in her veins was powerful and dark. Strong enough to subdue a spell a mere vampiress had cast.

Tuesday closed her eyes. "Fuck. Really?" The cut of the blade against her wrist did not yet pain her because she hadn't pressed deeply. If there was any other option, she wanted to hear it. Right now.

Five feet away from her, Anyx and Ethan had taken to arguing. He was trying to move her out of the casting circle but it continued to repulse him every time he tried to breach it with a stab of the wood stake.

"Gazariel!" Tuesday snapped her fingers. "Help him!"

With a heavy sigh, the demon leaped across the stream and started an argument with Anyx over her fickle ways. But when he mentioned her inability to come because she was a frigid bitch, she snarled and turned to face the dais again. One shout from the an-gered vampiress again ignited the flames in the stream. CJ hissed, as he was nearly burned, and then jumped inside the circle with Tuesday.

"We ready?" he asked her.

"I'll provide the blood," she said.

He looked at her then, knowing what the sacrifice would mean. They'd not discussed who would do this. Because it wasn't something a witch on a suicide mission would discuss. They'd wait until the last minute and hope upon hope it wouldn't be necessary.

"You sure?" CJ asked. "Maybe we should give Ethan a moment to see if he can get her out of the circle."

"Not going to happen. And we're all out of moments. We have to do this now." And as if on cue, the stone walls rumbled and the stream spat up fire. Tuesday pressed the athame tight over her wrist. "It's going to take a while to bleed out."

"No!"

Tuesday ignored Ethan's sudden shout. Bits of limestone began to rain from the cavern ceiling. It was now or never.

Tuesday drew the blade over her skin, but it didn't cut deeply because Ethan grabbed her by the shoulder and shoved her out of the circle. The vampire caught the athame as she dropped it. Tuesday landed hard on the stone floor. And she looked up to see Ethan draw the blade across his carotid. Blood spurted and he bowed over the circle as CJ directed.

"No!" she cried.

It was too late. She had been pushed outside the circle and Ethan's blood had conjured up a seal. She couldn't enter it if she tried.

Her lover dropped to the floor and stretched out his

hand to her. She could not touch him. What the hell was he doing?

She crawled up to the circle. "I wish you hadn't done this. I won't let you bleed out. I can't. There's enough blood, yes, Certainly?"

The dark witch shook his head. "We need so much."

Tuesday bowed her head. She would lose the one person she had just realized she cared about most. It wasn't fair. Ethan was already growing weak from blood loss. His eyelids shuttered. The hand he held extended, dropped limply onto the stone floor.

"Help me!" CJ called as he began the chant that would shut off the Final Days spell.

Though her heart had just broken and shattered, Tuesday nodded and crawled forward. Compelled to stop an evil that could harm so many more, she spread out her palms, embracing the circle and sending energy through her being. She matched CJ's tone with her own rhythmic chants.

Out the corner of her eye she saw the vampiress dash toward the entrance. Gazariel called to the reckoner to go after her and Savin did so.

And from behind her Gazariel suddenly let out an ear-shattering cry that harkened to the angels, who spoke in myriad tongues to mimic all the beasts on the planet.

Tuesday's chest suddenly burned as if the fire had leaped from the nearby stream to singe her. She struggled to concentrate, to focus her vibrations toward the circle and her dying lover. Ethan now barely supported himself. His blood streamed toward the fire. When it touched the flames, they flashed brilliant white and danced up the channel toward the dais.

The fire in her chest was unbearable. Tuesday screamed. The magic she put out suddenly left her in one final gushing effort. In the circle, CJ managed to capture that magic and directed it toward the dais, where the magic ball splashed into violet flames.

The limestone walls ceased shuddering.

CJ dropped to his knees over Ethan.

And Tuesday fell backward, yet landed in Gazariel's arms.

Chapter 24

The demon bowed over Tuesday, inspected her face and smoothed the hair away from her eyes. "The vampire did it," he said in amazement. "He broke the curse."

"The Final Days?" she murmured weakly.

"Well, that, too. I think. We won't know until we go topside and see if all the tourists are flambéed, eh? But, Tuesday, the curse you've carried for centuries—it's gone. Didn't you feel it? I certainly did."

She slapped a palm to her chest, where the sigil had burned so viciously she'd felt as though her insides would sizzle. "But…"

"A true love willing to die for you." Gazariel spoke the means to breaking the spell. "He sacrificed for you, witch. And I am also clean now. That damn curse is completely erased!"

"But that means… Ethan!" She shoved out of Gazariel's arms and scrambled toward the circle, where CJ now stood over the fallen vampire. The dark witch stepped out and jumped across the stream to inspect the dais.

The vampire was lying on his back, arms splayed, eyes wide, his mouth open and the blood continuing to pour from his carotid. Tuesday slapped her palm to the open wound. Blood spurted. She summoned a healing incantation, but it sputtered and merely sprinkled over Ethan's neck. She'd depleted her magic to stop the Final Days.

"CJ, help me! I have to stop the bleeding or he'll die."

The dark witch returned to the circle, which was no longer necessary to keep closed, and kneeled beside her. "I think he's already dead."

"No!" She took the dark witch's hand and pressed it over the wound on Ethan's neck. "Recite the blessing for a vampire's everlasting life."

They did so together while the demon stalked around them, observing. Such a blessing was a powerful invocation that a witch could perform for a vampire, granting him immortality that even a stake or beheading would find difficult to overcome. It was rarely used. And only the most powerful witches could summon such a thing.

After minutes of desperate chanting CJ tugged his hand away from Ethan's neck. "It's not working. We've both depleted our magic. If anything might work—he needs blood. That's a vampire's best hope for survival."

"Then he'll have it." Tuesday searched for the athame and found it tucked under Ethan's leg. Without a second thought, she drew it across her wrist and pressed it to Ethan's mouth. "Come on, Ethan! Don't leave me now!"

He didn't move, so she had to press her wrist tight against his mouth. He didn't swallow.

"Sit him upright," CJ directed Gazariel. "Help me!"

"I'm rather of the mind to get the hell out of here," the demon said.

Tuesday hissed at the demon. "I saved you from being consigned to Daemonia. You will help. Now!"

Begrudgingly, Gazariel helped CJ set Ethan upright so the blood would flow down his throat. It took a while, but after a few minutes Tuesday saw his Adam's apple pulse. He had swallowed. And she was growing distinctly weaker. She'd expelled so much magic that even a little blood loss was not going to keep her upright for long.

Her eyelids fluttered.

"You can't do this," CJ said. "We need another donor."

"You," Gazariel said to the dark witch.

CJ tapped a tattoo on his neck. "Can't. I'm warded against vamps. If he drinks my blood it'll kill him for sure."

"He's warded against demons, too," Gazariel said with a nod toward Ethan's throat.

"We need the vampiress. Go get her!" Tuesday commanded the demon.

"Seriously?"

Tuesday wanted to argue with the obstinate demon, but it was all she could do to keep her eyelids open and her focus on Ethan. He was swallowing now, and that was a good sign.

But with a flutter of her eyelids, she passed out.

Tuesday came to and the first thing she saw was her vampire lover embracing his ex-wife. He held Anyx's slender body to his chest and gripped her head to hold it aside as he supped at her neck. His hand caressed her breast where the thin black sheath had slid aside to expose the nipple, and she moaned in ecstasy. And Ethan increased his efforts, drinking from her. Taking from her. Enjoying her. Rubbing her nipple to give her pleasure.

That was not a life-saving moment. It was a graphic display of sexual desire.

Backing away on the limestone floor, Tuesday's back hit a wall. Someone grasped her hand and helped her to stand. "You okay?"

"No," she said to CJ. And she wasn't. Her head felt as if someone was stirring her brains with a spatula. And her chest might explode if she did not— "I need air. I have to get out of here. Now."

Turning, she crept out of the chamber in the direction they had come. No one followed her blood-drained wobbling pace. CJ would stay behind and keep an eye on Ethan. She hadn't recalled seeing either Gazariel or Savin in the chamber. Only the two ex-lovers entwined in a disgustingly sensual embrace.

Vampires did not have to hold their donors so…intimately. Taking blood could be functional and discreet. They couldn't have been closer if they had climbed inside one another. She didn't want to think about it. She wanted to erase that image from her brain.

Stumbling blindly forth, Tuesday entered a dark tunnel and summoned a glow of light on her palm. It sputtered. She was weak. She needed rest and to heal. To restore after the tremendous expulsion of magic and blood. She'd given Ethan her blood to save him.

But what had she saved him for? A grand reunion with his former wife.

Noticing the strong coppery smell from the old electrical wires that had greeted her upon descent into the catacombs, she knew the surface must be close and raced forward. And there by the old wood door that led into the bowels of the church above, stood Gazariel.

"I need to get out of here." She pushed past the demon, but he gripped her wrists. She did not bleed anymore and stopping movement now brought the woozy dizziness up again. Standing still was impossible. Her world wobbled. Or did she?

"You're weak, witch. You need rest."

"I will. But I need air now!" She faltered.

Gazariel lifted her into his arms and carried her up and through the ancient church basement. It was well into the morning hours, so the church was closed to tourists and their exit was not observed.

Finally, fresh cold air smacked Tuesday's face. It was still dark, yet the moon beamed across her face. As if blinded by a desert sun, Tuesday closed her eyes.

"Where should I take you?"

"Away from here," she murmured, then passed out.

Ethan emerged from below Notre Dame and staggered across the street from the church to sit on the sidewalk before a closed souvenir shop. Behind him CJ filed out and stretched his arms. The book containing the Final Days code was tucked in his waistband. Savin was carrying up Anyx—whom CJ had bound with magic, though she was nearly drained of blood not only from him but from the spell. She may or may not survive. He didn't care.

Tuesday and Gazariel had not been below when Ethan had finally ceased drinking from Anyx. He'd pulled away from her neck, swallowed the last hot gulp and had felt himself again. He'd touched death while lying in the circle. Hell, he must have briefly died. But Tuesday's blood had lifted him from that abyss. He'd felt it trickle down his throat as if a cool, clean elixir. And yet, he'd held back from taking too much from her. He hadn't been willing to take her life to save his own. Better to die than to take Tuesday along with him. She'd done nothing to deserve death. It had been he who had forced her into this nightmare.

When someone had dropped an unconscious Anyx before him, he'd dove in, knowing he could take enough blood from her—and not caring for the outcome. He'd fed on her viciously, yet the blood lust had spurred his desires. He hated that feeling, yet it had saved his life.

A heavy sweep of wings preceded the sudden appearance of Gazariel by his side. The demon kneeled beside Ethan, and gazed skyward. "Morning soon."

"Where is she?" Ethan could only manage to whisper the question. He was exhausted. He needed rest to fully recover.

"She wanted to get away from you."

Why would she…? And then he remembered seeing Tuesday shuffle across the chamber floor. The look in her eyes had not been of horror, but rather…betrayal. She'd watched him drink from Anyx. But she couldn't have believed that meant anything to him beyond sustenance.

Of course she had. He had seen it plainly in her tearing blue gaze.

"I took her to the airport," Gazariel said. "My witch is free of the curse. You broke the spell."

"I—I did?"

Gazariel chuckled. "She never did tell you what would do it, did she?"

He shook his head.

"It's something she has known since the day I placed the curse in her. A true love had to be willing to sacrifice his life for her. And…her true love did." The demon winked.

"True love? But I thought…" Ethan blinked, sorting out the few details he'd learned about Tuesday's dark curse. "If she couldn't have love, then how…?"

"Oh, someone could fall in love with her. Just, the moment the guy realized it, or she did, then all goes to Beneath. Apparently, her true love realized how much he did love her only in that moment before it would have went to hell. You pulled through by the skin of your teeth. Good going, vampire."

Gazariel stood. With a sweep of wings, he misted into black smoke and was gone.

Ethan closed his eyes. He was thankful Tuesday had been freed of the curse. And because of love?

"Yes." He did love her. And perhaps he had only realized it that moment he'd dove to push her out of the circle so she would not die to stop the curse.

And now?

"I need to get to the airport."

Chapter 25

CJ directed Savin to bring the vampiress to head-quarters, where she would be contained. The Council would decide what to do with a vampiress who would see fit to bring an end to the world.

He told the reckoner he'd be close behind, but needed to do something first. Rather, he needed to follow the whisper that had not ceased since he'd stepped out of the church. It was a disembodied voice that he suspected only he could hear. And it was close.

Wandering across the street and toward the gated garden behind the grand church, CJ slipped through the thick shrubbery and into the quiet privacy of a small yet groomed garden that saw many tourists during the day. Now he was alone. The whisper lured him toward a bench that faced the back of the church, before a view of the flying buttresses and the massive iron cross that tipped the church.

CJ did not recognize the man who sat on the bench. He was tall, appeared slender and was dressed in a smart brown-and-black pinstriped suit. His palm was propped on the top of a straight black cane, which looked more accessory than necessity. He didn't look at CJ; his stare seemed fixed on the cross atop the church.

"Give me the book," the stranger said.

And hearing the voice, which sounded like a mix of all the accents of the world, yet was clear and precise, and so *ethereal*, CJ knew who the creature was on the bench. Ethan had mentioned who had sent him on this mission.

CJ tugged the book from his waistband and clutched it tightly to his chest. "You didn't do such a good job holding onto it the first time."

"Give it."

"No."

The book flew into the angel Raphael's hands. And now he met CJ's gaze with eyes that were all colors and glowed with a depth that CJ thought surely he could fall into and never land. And that wasn't a romantic notion; it was a deep and abiding fear that tightened the skin all over his body and closed up his throat.

"I was having a little fun," the angel admitted. "We do things like that every now and a thousand years or so. Ta."

And with a massive swoop of wings that lifted the hair around CJ's face, the angel disappeared.

And CJ dropped to his knees, utterly relieved, pissed, and thankful to be alive.

* * *

This time, Tuesday crossed through security without once looking back. Determination held her head high. Her flight left in forty-five minutes. As she waited for a little boy ahead of her to put on his tennis shoes, she grabbed her coat from the conveyor belt and pulled it on. Slipping into her ankle boots, she frowned at the dusty dried mud from the catacombs on them. It was time to get the hell out of Paris.

With a toss of her hair over a shoulder, she wandered forward. Her gate was to the left, and she— All of a sudden, she stopped at the junction of the turn and stood there, allowing the world to swish by her on all sides as if sped up on a security tape.

Time seemed to stop and voices were muffled. Clothing brushed past her. The stifling inner air ceased to bother. Her heartbeats thudded to recall what Gazariel had said to her.

True love had broken the curse.

But if so, then how had he been capable of holding his ex-wife like that? Was she wrong to think that moment in the catacombs had meant something to Ethan? His love for her *had to* be true to break the spell. Or had it dissolved as quickly as his ex-wife's blood had entered his system?

She'd been starting to have fun with Ethan Pierce. And yes, she may have even begun to love him. Or at least, leave a hopeful door open that she'd recognize it if it was love.

But all for nothing, apparently.

And yet… "I really did fall in love." Her throat tightened. Tears threatened.

So when someone turned her around and pulled her

into an embrace to kiss her, Tuesday beat at the man's shoulder and kicked him on the shin in defense. When she saw it was Ethan, wincing as he bent up his injured leg, she gasped.

"Sorry," he said. "I shouldn't have surprised you like that. That was a Richard move. But I love you, Tuesday. You can't leave me. Not like this."

She slammed her arms across her chest and lifted her chin. "What about your wife?"

"You mean my ex-wife, who has been taken into custody to stand trial for reckless acts against humankind?"

"But I saw you." She squeezed a fist, hoping to staunch the tears, but they dropped down her cheeks. "You were holding her so tightly. Caressing her. I saw you stroke her…" She couldn't say it. It hurt too much to think of right now.

"I was taking her blood, Tuesday. And yes, I experienced a moment of sexual satisfaction. I'm a vampire. Drinking blood turns me on. But ultimately drinking Anyx's blood was a means to stay alive. Tuesday, please." He took her hands. "She means nothing to me."

"She's the one who saved your life."

"Not without your help. And your curse." He pressed his palm to her chest, right over her heart.

Tears spilled down Tuesday's cheeks as she struggled against throwing herself into his arms. "You've taken the curse from me. The sigil is gone."

"Gazariel said as much. It's true." He bowed his head to hers and tilted up her chin with a finger. "I love you, Tuesday. Truly. Deeply. Insanely. Not like the false, surface love you accused Gazariel of experiencing. I love you on a soul level. I can feel it in my blood, my bones and my spirit."

She gasped.

"And if you get on that plane and leave me I'm not sure what I'll do."

"You'd survive," she said simply. "We all do."

"But I don't want to survive without you. I know it's a lot to ask. And you have a home in Boston. But would you stay with me? Just a while longer? Please, Tuesday." His breath hushed against her ear. "I love you. I need you to believe me. I. Love. You."

The words felt true. They *were* true. Because if they were not, she would not recognize that right now. She'd still bear the curse and they might be standing in a desolate wasteland covered with the ashes of humans and angels alike.

The curse was gone. She could be loved. And…she was.

By the seven sacred witches, she really was.

"This is the second time I've come back to this airport intent on leaving."

"I don't think you're meant to leave." He smiled against her cheek then kissed it. "Not yet, anyway. Not until we've talked about us. You helped me to stop the Final Days. We've been through a lot. We've both literally walked through fire. Don't walk away from us now."

Us. Yeah, the word felt right. For now? For maybe a little longer. Together. Sharing their lives. She wanted to embrace that, to own it.

"I love you, too," she said. "I think I've known it for days."

She hugged him and tilted her head against his shoulder. She was tired and weak and, hell yes, she loved this man. Of course, he'd only been taking blood from

Anyx to survive. And his honesty about how it had felt meant a lot to her.

"Take me home," she said to him. "Your home."

Epilogue

A year later...

Tuesday dusted a long rosewood shelf lined with sea-shells of all shapes, sizes and colors. She could hear the ocean echo out at her, and wasn't at all surprised when a tiny giggle sounded from within the spiral of a nautilus shell. With a bounce to her step, she moved on to the next shelf, where a triton fashioned of more shells and some kind of metal that gleamed green was kept under glass.

This was the mermaid room in the Archives, and she'd been assigned to tidy it up today. And tomorrow. And for however long it took to clean the small and crowded room.

Certainly Jones had offered her the job after she'd decided to stay in Paris with Ethan a year ago. They'd

gone back to his place from the airport, talked and…
had a lot of hex. Blood-bone-spirit sex. Soul-deep stuff.
They were really in love. And that was something neither of them had felt in a long time.

They'd wanted to ride that feeling and follow it wherever it would lead them, so she'd made a quick trip home
to Boston, had rented out her property for an indefinite
period of time and packed up her clothes and magical
accoutrements. Now Ethan's place was a bit more un-
tidy and he'd had to relegate three quarters of his closet
to her wardrobe. And Stuart now answered to her com-
mands, as well as Ethan's.

And every morning Ethan either woke her with croissants and orange juice, or left them on the counter because he'd gone in to work and hadn't wanted to wake
her. She'd never felt happier.

With the curse completely gone it was now easy to
recognize love. Small things, such as the sun shining on
this snowy February morning, had lifted her smile and
given her a bounce to her step as she walked to work.
She had a purpose now, and a fantastic lover.

Life was about as fabulous as it could get.

Bending to inspect a glass container filled with some
kind of sparkling jewels, Tuesday realized the thin dia-
mond-shaped items with one curved edge were possibly
mermaid scales. Cool. She'd never in her lifetime met
a mermaid, and wasn't sure she wanted to. They were
supposed to be vicious.

When a man's hands suddenly covered her eyes from
behind, she sprang upright. She hadn't heard anyone
come in. And Certainly Jones, her boss, would never
do such a thing. So…

"Is it lunchtime already?" she asked with hope.

"I'm a little late." Ethan leaned in and kissed the side of her neck, sending a visceral shiver over her skin. "Had some business to deal with. Can we have a quickie?"

"Did you lock the door?"

"Always." His hand slipped around her waist and glided under her gray T-shirt that snarkily declared in block letters Don't Be A Richard.

Lunchtime sex had become a norm, and they were pretty sure no one was aware of their stolen liaisons. CJ would say something if he knew. That witch was a stickler about work ethic and protocol. So they were careful, but never quiet.

"I missed you," he said, turning her around to face him.

"It's been three hours since we drove here together from home."

"Three hours too long. I'm going to have to bite you again, and soon."

Their blood connection lasted about twenty-four to forty-eight hours. The shared sexual gratification that developed with a bite gave them the ability to hear one another's thoughts and to feel their emotions and sexual sensations. Love was a wondrous emotion that shimmered off Ethan like a warm summer sun. And yes, when they argued they could feel one another's anger, even fear, but that made the need to make up quicker. And they never quarreled much.

Tuesday tapped her neck. "Right here, big boy."

The vampire pierced her neck with his fangs, and while he did so, he slid down her leggings and she unzipped his fly. Behind her rose a nineteenth-century desk that he set her on as he licked at her blood.

Tuesday moaned as he slid his erection inside her and pumped slowly yet deeply. She enjoyed when they went at it fast and furious, but even more so when he prolonged every move, seeming to luxuriate in the depths of her.

"I've got another job you might be interested in," he said.

"For Acquisitions?" She had helped him with one case regarding retrieving a grimoire from a crone a few months ago. All it had required was some sweet talk and a commitment to drinking the bitch under the table. Tuesday would never touch moss liqueur again. Oh, the hangover! "Does it involve another washed-up crone?"

"Faeries."

"Why me?"

He shrugged and licked her neck to seal the wound. He thrust inside her still. "It's a magic thing. Faeries are trafficking in humans, accept without the usual changeling to replace the stolen baby."

"And why, exactly, does Acquisitions need to get involved? What do you need to acquire, Monsieur Director? And would you tell me if an angel were using us as pawns in his stupid game of playing with the inhabitants of the mortal realm again?"

"I would tell you, and Raphael has not been seen or heard of since his selfish ploy. Did I tell you the book with the Final Days code suddenly appeared on a shelf in the angel room a few weeks after our adventure?"

She gripped his ass, pulling him deep into her. "You did not. But good to know. I hope it's chained, warded and bespelled to Kingdom Come. Mmm, lover, pull out and slip your cock over my clit. Yes. Like that." She bowed forward, putting her forehead to his shoulder.

"The faery thing will be fun for us," he said. "Maybe?"

She knew that tone. He was diving in to adventure once again. For a man who had worked a desk job for so long, he'd been taking on more jobs himself. And fieldwork suited him. As it did her.

"I do like trying new things," she said. Grinding her body against his erection, she mined the humming orgasm that whispered up to her core. "You think we'll ever get back to America?"

"Do you want to return?"

"It does carry memory of a lot of good times."

"Like witch hunts and torture?"

"Yes, Richard, just like that. You know me too well."

He hilted himself inside her, and that was all it took to fly. Tuesday's head fell back and she pulled her lover down to bite through her shirt at her breast. He didn't break skin. They'd save that for later.

"I'd like to keep the witch in Paris for a while," he said as he watched her face move through the joy and elation of orgasm. "Deal?"

She pulled herself back up to stare into his eyes. "You do have a lot to offer a witch who has been without love for centuries. Deal."

* * * * *

Jane Godman writes in a variety of romance genres, including paranormal, gothic and romantic suspense. Jane lives in England and loves to travel to European cities that are steeped in history and romance— Venice, Dubrovnik and Vienna are among her favorites. Jane is married to a lovely man and is mom to two grown-up children.

Visit the Author Profile page
at Harlequin.com for more titles.

AWAKENING THE SHIFTER

Jane Godman

This book is dedicated to my friends, Gill, Karen
and Andrea. I won't embarrass them
by saying how long we've known each other...
but it's been a long time!

Chapter 1

This was where Khan felt alive. The only place he knew for sure he existed. The heavy, thumping beat of the drums pounded in time with his heartbeat. The screams of the crowd pulsed along his nerve endings. Exhilaration fizzed through his bloodstream, sending his energy levels into overdrive.

In front of an audience of thousands, or in this case, tens of thousands, with millions more watching on TV or live streaming…this was the only place his life had any purpose.

He didn't move. Head bowed, arms outstretched. Fire and fury exploded around him, but Khan waited. Pumped up the expectation beyond fever pitch and kept it hanging. Teased and tormented until the yelling and pleading from his fans became a fervor in his blood.

When he finally raised his head, he felt his own vigor

pulse through the audience. The devil horn sign was repeated over and over as far as the eye could see. Two fingers at the side of the head. The sign of the beast. *Our sign.* Nothing matched this…except maybe sex. The two experiences were similar, with the need for release becoming overwhelming. The climax came when he delivered his performance, poured himself into his spectators, gave them everything he had.

Dense smoke rolled like fog from the stage and, within it, colored strobe lights danced in time with the drumbeat. Giant LED screens at the rear of the stage projected alternating images of fire, close-ups of snarling animals and the band's logo, a stylized symbol resembling three entwined number sixes. At the side of the stage, explosions went off at random intervals, shooting orange flames high into the night sky.

The other members of Beast were unleashing a storm around him. Behind his vast, gleaming circle of drums, Diablo exuded raw, brooding vitality. His chest was bare and his tattooed biceps bulged as he hammered out a manic beat, his blue-black hair flopping forward to hide his face.

At the front of the stage, red-haired Torque, on lead guitar, was all burning drama and flickering movement. The air around him glowed with life, and he matched the sweeping arc of his hand on his guitar to the explosions at the side of the stage. In contrast, Dev, on rhythm guitar, held his body statue still, the movement of his flying fingers the only sign of life. His white-blond hair and pale skin added to the illusion that he was carved from ice. Slightly to the left of center, just behind Dev, Finglas was lost in his bass guitar, a faraway expression on his face.

"Unforgettable." Khan felt the stadium still as he elongated the word, starting on a whisper and ending on a screech. He knew the power of his own voice, knew what people said. *Is Khan the best rock singer ever? Does he have the greatest vocal range of all time? Or is he just a showman?*

Khan didn't give a damn about speculation and comparisons. Tonight, in Los Angeles—and at the simultaneous concerts in Manchester, England, and in Sydney, Australia—as long as they were talking about him, that was all that mattered.

"Unforgettable" was their bestselling track from the album of the same name. As he launched into the number and the crowd sang along, Khan gave them what they expected. Throwing back his red-gold mane of hair, he swaggered, swayed and jumped around the stage in skintight leopard print pants and a flowing white shirt slashed to the waist. His voice ranged from husky purring to wild yelping, with acrobatics to match.

He ended the song in one of his favorite ways. Approaching Diablo, Khan howled out the final chorus while dry humping the drum kit. It was always a crowd pleaser. It was less popular with Diablo, whose expression became even more tempestuous. Ged Taverner, Beast's manager, frequently warned Khan that he would one day push Diablo too far.

"When I'm asked to identify your body, Tiger Boy, there'll be a drumstick through the center of your eye."

Acknowledging the adulation of the crowd, Khan returned to the front of the stage. Before he could speak, he was conscious of a change in the atmosphere. A curious hush fell over the packed stadium, something Khan had never known. He wasn't sure he liked it. Silence? Where was the validation in that?

A slender figure swept onto the stage. Sarangerel Tsedev, known as Sarange, was unmistakable. One of the few people in the world who, like Khan, needed only one name. Even if that hadn't been so, her place on the stage was assured, her ability to silence thousands well established.

Although she was one of the most famous singer-songwriters in the world, Sarange was also the organizer of this concert. The Animals Alive Foundation was her nonprofit organization. Tonight was about raising awareness of endangered species. She had driven forward this vision, persuading the biggest names in the entertainment industry to come along with her. All across the globe people were watching this spectacle unfold and donating millions. The final tally was likely to be billions. Against all the odds, she had succeeded in uniting the world in a common cause.

It had always been the plan that Sarange would join Khan for the official Animals Alive anthem. This was the finale, the culmination of all her hard work. What was striking about this encounter was that it was the first time two of the biggest names in the music scene had met in person.

Khan had seen Sarange on screen many times, of course. He had heard her described as one of the most beautiful women in the world, and that accolade had piqued his interest. Yes, she was stunning. He had acknowledged it and promptly forgotten about her. Now, as Beast played the first few bars and she walked toward him, he realized she was a whole lot more than stunning.

She wore a simple full-length white shift dress. High-necked at the front, swooping almost to the cleft of her buttocks at the back, slit to the thigh on both sides. The evening breeze molded the lightweight material to her body as she walked, highlighting the perfection of her figure. Her waist-length hair was iron straight, its blue-black sheen emphasized by the strobe lighting. As Sarange drew closer and raised her microphone, singing the first few lines of the song she had written—a love song to the creatures of the planet—he caught his first glimpse of eyes that were like chips of blue ice.

Forcing himself to focus, he circled her, growling out his response. The audience went ballistic. Could they feel it? Sense what he had experienced the moment she walked into view?

Khan knew what was happening, knew what the legends said. It was like a mantra imprinted into every shifter's psyche.

When you find your one true love, you will mate for life.

He had heard the stories about how a shifter instantly knew its mate. How the sudden hit of attraction and lust was like nothing he, or she, had ever encountered before. It was said to be irresistible, an injection of pure, molten heat straight into the bloodstream.

Yes, he'd heard other shifters talk about that feeling. He'd just never believed it. Until now. Until he'd seen Sarange. Breathed her in. Felt her touch his soul.

And now he was in deep trouble. For so many reasons. The thoughts tumbled over themselves as he continued to perform on autopilot. As far as the world was concerned, he was Khan, charismatic lead singer of the hugely successful rock band Beast. And that's exactly who he was. Who his *human* was.

But, like all shifters, Khan had two equal sides to his psyche. They existed in harmony, the traits of one complementing the other. He was a weretiger. Half human, half tiger, he had the ability to shift seamlessly from one form to the other. Because of the life he had chosen when he met Ged—if "met" was the best word to use to describe the encounter—he spent most of his time in human form, but that didn't mean his inner tiger had been subdued. Those instincts were as powerful as ever. For Khan, as for all shifters who chose to live among mortals, day-to-day living was a constant balancing act, a striving to maintain anonymity.

Rock star by day, tiger by night. He was the mightiest of the big cats, with teeth, claws and a personality to match, but that was his deepest, darkest secret. He wasn't about to reveal it to anyone, particularly not Sarange, darling of the paparazzi. It didn't matter how much she made the blood in his veins sizzle, or how much she triggered a zipper-straining reaction farther south. It didn't even matter that she had her own, equally compelling secret.

Because, as soon as he saw her, he knew. Sarange's secret was the same as Khan's. She was a shifter, too. Khan had scented her before he saw her. That gorgeous face and stunning body hid the soul of a werewolf. That knowledge made everything Khan was feeling right now so far beyond screwed up he thought he might just be going crazy.

He was a tiger. She was a wolf. Cats and dogs? They were natural enemies. Put them together and the claws came out and the fur flew. Even if Khan had been able

to do what the legends said—settle down, take a mate—
it would never be her.

The tales about the unbreakable bond between true
mates hadn't foreseen this particular problem. They
dealt only in success stories. Happily-ever-afters. It was
always possible Khan's dilemma had never arisen until
now. He needed answers. Having found a mate he didn't
want, a shifter couldn't walk away—could he? Once the
bonds were forged, could they be broken?

He was about to find out.

There had never been any question about who the
headline act would be. Never any doubt about who
would sing the Animals Alive anthem as the concert
closed. Beast was the hottest rock band in the world.
Although Sarange hadn't been to any of their concerts,
or met them in person, she intended to tap into that
raw power.

Even if the lead singer was a total jerk.

She had watched enough footage of the band over
recent weeks to reach a simple conclusion. Khan was
a strutting, narcissistic show-off. She knew better than
anyone that that was the perfect qualification for a rock
star. Unfortunately, there was enough evidence to prove
he was exactly the same offstage. She'd been hoping to
enlist Beast's continued help after the concert. It made
sense. *Beast.* It had the potential to be the perfect part-
nership. Their name combined with hers, their pulling
power, the two contrasting audiences…between them,
they could have taken awareness of the plight of endangered species to a whole new level. Having watched
interviews with Khan and done her research into his
lifestyle, she'd changed her mind. Promiscuous, arro-

gant, conceited, he just about summed up everything she disliked in a man...in a *person*. Khan described himself as "the guy who dived head-on into hedonism." Yeah. He was a jerk.

As she walked out onstage, she gave herself a firm reminder. This was for the Animals Alive Foundation, the non-profit organization she had founded. Its mission was to maintain the environments of endangered species through fundraising and education. All she had to do was get through one song. Five minutes out of her life to get the attention of Beast's followers. She didn't have to like this guy to sing with him. Performing was what she did best. She achieved a melting expression as she sang the first lines of the anthem that meant so much to her.

Sarange was used to crowds, but this was an emotional high like nothing she had ever experienced. This was the culmination of over two years of hard work. Of being told it would never happen. Big fund-raising gigs were last century. Austerity measures meant there was no spare cash. People, not animals—that was the way nonprofit worked these days.

Kicking open slammed doors. Pulling down barriers with her bare hands. It was one of her strengths, but it had been hard. Fighting the establishment one interview and rally at a time. *If we don't care for animals, how can we care for each other? When they are extinct, your regrets will be worthless.* Sound bites. Slogans. Pins. Banners. Every album she made, every photo shoot, every gig...like a general rallying her troops, she used each as another opportunity to get more people on her side.

But the feeling that tore through her as she reached Khan had nothing to do with the triumph or relief of this night. It had nothing to do with viewing figures or pledges. It was about *him*. Something crackled in the air between them and around them. It was electrifying, thrilling and scaring her at the same time.

The film footage she had watched hadn't done Khan justice. He was startlingly handsome. Tall, with a lithe, muscular grace, his features almost perfect. He had high, carved cheekbones, a straight nose and breathtaking amber eyes. Almost perfect because his mouth was too full and sensual for perfection. But those eyes…they were mesmerizing. Set under slanting brows, they reminded her of a cat's in the way they drew her in and refused to let her go. As he closed the gap between them, he was staring at her with an expression she couldn't fathom. He could have been playing a part for the audience, but, if he was, he was good. Frighteningly good. Because she was instantly swept away by the hunger in his gaze.

This song wasn't supposed to be sexy, for God's sake. But the way Khan was standing behind her, not touching her, but almost touching her, his body moving in sinful time to the music…nothing had ever affected her this way. It was as if he was an illegal high and she was dragged into addiction after her first hit.

As they sang the last verse, Sarange was barely aware of the other acts who had performed throughout the course of the evening joining them on the stage. This night would go down in history. It would be remembered as the night she had alerted the world to her cause. And in her own life it was the night everything would change because she had met Khan.

When the song ended and the sound of Khan's voice died away, she felt bereft. He still hadn't touched her.

Not once had he placed a hand upon her. She closed her eyes, willing him to do it now. To wrap his arms around her waist as he stood behind her on the stage. To let her feel the warmth of his body as they swayed in time to the music.

She opened her eyes to see a close-up of her face projected onto the giant screen at the rear of the stage. To the watching millions, the look of enchantment in her eyes had to do with the concert. Only Sarange knew the truth. She wondered if Khan had guessed. He was the reason for her rapture. Turning her head, she sought his gaze for confirmation.

She didn't get it. Khan had already left the stage.

Because of the number of acts performing in the stadium, there hadn't been enough dressing rooms for everyone, and Beast had been forced to share. They had arrived in Los Angeles that morning at the end of a three-month tour. Now that the concert was over, their tour bus would be taking them to New York, where the band was based. Predictably, the roads around the stadium were blocked. Their security team had advised them to remain in the dressing room, and they faced a lengthy wait before they could depart.

It was always the same when they were together for any length of time. At least on the bus there were sleeping compartments where they could escape each other's company. Now there were five massive egos competing for space in a small room.

"This sounds like the start of a bad shifter joke," Dev said.

Diablo scowled at him from under lowered brows. "What does?"

"Us, all crammed into this room. You know. A tiger, a dragon, a black panther, a snow leopard and a wolf…" Apparently sensing he had lost his audience, Dev shrugged and lapsed into silence.

The atmosphere had reached the point where sizzling tension was about to become boiling animosity, when Sarange burst through the door and jabbed a finger into Khan's chest. "You arrogant jerk!"

Khan, who was stretched full-length on the only sofa in the room, opened his eyes as she leaned over him. Although her presence made his pulse soar, he managed to hide the effect she had on his emotions.

"I'm an arrogant jerk who is trying to get some rest." He closed his eyes again.

"How dare you walk off that stage like it didn't matter? Like you had someplace more important to be?"

Khan sighed and uncurled his limbs. Stretching, he got to his feet and looked down at her. Her hands were on her hips, and her lips were drawn back. Werewolves generally steered clear of confronting him. The hierarchy that existed in the animal world also applied to shifters. Tigers outranked wolves. It was a simple matter of superior size, strength, razor-sharp claws and lethal teeth. Even so, Sarange was displaying clear signs of wolf rage. Snapping and snarling. Normally he found it so unattractive. On her it was hot as hell.

"I thought I was a volunteer out there on that stage." Khan kept his voice light, knowing how much it would annoy her. He needed to infuriate her further if he was going to push her away. "Pardon me for not realizing I signed up to the slavery option."

Her indrawn breath was so harsh it sounded like a growl. He had to grip his hands hard at his sides to stop himself from shoving her up against the wall right there and then before hauling up the hem of that too-sexy dress.

"I think this is our cue to leave." Torque jerked a thumb in the direction of the door.

"Really?" Dev looked from Sarange's furious expression to Khan's watchful one. "Looks like this could get interesting."

"No need to go, guys." Khan tossed the words over his shoulder without breaking eye contact with Sarange. "Our visitor isn't staying."

He saw Torque wince at his dismissive tone. That distaste was the effect Khan wanted to have on Sarange. He needed to drive her away. Right away. Make her view him with hatred and contempt. If he couldn't make this aching, burning longing go away, he could at least make sure nothing ever came of it.

Although she was looking at him with scorn, Sarange wasn't going anywhere. She had come here with a purpose, and with classic wolf tenacity, she was going to see it through. His bandmates had clearly recognized her intention and, following Torque's lead, were heading for the door. Khan couldn't even call them on it. Couldn't question their loyalty. Over the years, his relationship with them had become the closest thing he had to friendship. But he was a tiger. A big cat loner. Powerful, sensual, selfish and controlling. His need to dominate the group was far greater than his human need to be liked.

As soon as the door closed behind them, Sarange was back on the attack. Like a beautiful wolf gnawing on a bone. "I was warned about you. Narcissist. Playboy. Jerk. That's what I was told. I don't know why I thought you'd be different."

"Nor do I."

A strangled sound of fury issued from her throat. "You are the most infuriating man I've ever met."

He laughed. "This is nothing. I can get a lot worse."

She drew a breath. "You made a commitment to this concert. You were the headline act. When you walked out on the finale, you gave a message to the audience that it didn't matter—"

He flapped a hand at her. "I get it. Let it go, wolf girl."

Her brow furrowed. "Wolf girl? What the hell is that supposed to mean?"

Khan stared down at her, incredulity jolting him out of his attempted nonchalance. She appeared genuinely confused. What the hell reason could she have to pretend *not* to be a werewolf? Was it possible Sarange didn't know she was a shifter? He'd never heard of that happening before, couldn't believe it was conceivable. Yet she was looking at him as though he was crazy.

Maybe that was the explanation. He might just be crazy after all. Had he gotten this all wrong? Could it be that she *wasn't* a werewolf? He dismissed that thought instantly. Khan's shifter instincts were pure and true. Beneath the expensive perfume she wore, the scent of Sarange's skin made his nostrils flare. She smelled of female wolf. Of lichens and berries, frost and pine. Of dark, sharp evergreens and ice-hard ground. It was an aroma that should have been alien to his inner cat. Instead, it was making his mouth water.

He wanted to taste her so much it hurt. And Sarange felt it, too. It was there in the depths of those unusual light eyes, in the flare of her nostrils, the way her nipples tightened and pressed against the thin cloth of her dress and in the warm, honeyed scent of her arousal. In the way her breathing came hard and fast as she faced him with a mixture of confusion and passion clouding her features.

Sarange moved first, wrapping her arms tight around Khan's neck and pulling his lips down to hers. She kissed him hard and hungry, claiming his lips as anger and lust powered through them both. Khan was helpless. No matter how hard he tried to resist, his need for her was too strong. His large hands seized her toned buttocks through the cloth of her dress, squeezing hard as he pulled her tight against him.

It was more conflict than kiss as Sarange squirmed desperately in his hold, her hands clawing at his shoulders. Their mouths clashed, tongues fighting, caressing, battling for supremacy. Khan was instantly rock hard, harder than he'd ever been. As he pressed his erection into the soft curve of her belly, Sarange moaned and broke free.

A dozen conflicting thoughts chased around in Khan's head as, breathing hard, they glared at each other.

Tigers and wolves...cats and dogs. How can she not know?

Make her leave.

Beg her to stay.

Kiss her again. This time make it last forever.

Just as he lifted a hand to slide it behind her head and draw her back to him, Sarange stalked out of the room.

Chapter 2

Sarange didn't know what she was feeling. So many emotions were competing for dominance inside her she couldn't begin to single out or categorize any individual one. Generally, her temperament was even. She didn't have mood swings. Yet after one brief encounter with Khan, her senses were swaying like a barometer needle in changing weather.

It was a relief to reach her dressing room without encountering anyone who wanted to talk to her. As the concert had approached, the demands on her time had increased. In the past few weeks, she had barely had a minute to call her own. Tonight had been a whirlwind of questions, requests and suggestions, all of which appeared to require her personal intervention.

Sarange had endless patience. It was part of her makeup. Her birth parents, whoever they were, must have bequeathed it to her with their genes. But right now she didn't want to cope with someone else's problems. Even for the sake of Animals Alive, the organization that had been her life's work for so long. The thought caused her a pang of guilt, and she managed to quell it. Just for once, she was going to put duty aside. She was going to spend a little time alone analyzing what had just happened to her.

How had she managed to let the most arrogant, infuriating man she had ever met get to her? *And by "get to me" I mean turn me on so much I almost burst into flames*. Just the thought of how Khan made her feel had her breath catching in her throat and a renewed thrill of desire pulsing through her body.

What is wrong with me? She closed the door behind her and leaned against it, releasing a long sigh. Despite his devastating looks, Khan was not her type. She didn't like overtly dominant men. Sarange had no desire to settle down. Now and then, she speculated about the reason. Did she have abandonment issues linked to her strange past? By ensuring she was the stronger partner in any relationship, was she making sure she couldn't be hurt? Although it made a strange kind of sense, she didn't feel it was a valid explanation for her choices. Perhaps she was just cold-hearted? It wasn't something that affected her strongly enough to probe deeply.

Now she thought about it, her brief relationships had all been with men who conformed to a certain category. *Undemanding* was the first word that came to mind. Did she deliberately choose partners who wouldn't challenge her? It wasn't a question she had considered until now, and she didn't like it. Didn't want to start psychoanalyzing herself just because Khan had strutted onto her horizon. *So what if, up to now, I've chosen sweet, considerate guys? The sort any woman would have no problem taking home to meet Mom and Dad?*

Not that Sarange had a mom and dad. She had an uncle and aunt who did the same job. She tried to picture taking Khan home to meet Bek and Gerel Tsedev. The thought made her choke back a laugh. It was never going to happen, but the image was amusing.

It wasn't just his arrogance that triggered a warning about Khan. It was the way he stripped away her control, and did it with such relish. *Wolf girl.* That was what he had called her. What had he meant by it? One thing was for sure, it wasn't a compliment. The tone of his voice had been scathing, while the look in his eyes had scalded her. She assumed he meant she liked to be in charge. He had judged her on first impressions, likening her to the leader of a pack. It was a curious analogy, but their encounter had hardly been conventional. If she hadn't walked out when she did, heaven alone knew what would have happened next. She had a feeling it would have led to passion beyond her wildest imagination followed by a world of regret.

Hadn't she been equally guilty of basing her opinion of Khan on sensational reporting and the antagonistic, thrilling clash from which she had just walked away? She pushed herself off from the door and made her way to the refrigerator. Snagging a bottle of water, she drained half its contents in a few quick gulps.

This violent attraction she felt toward Khan, this uncertainty and angst about her feelings, the burning restlessness that made her want to turn right back around and finish what they'd started…it was all new to her. New and frightening. She didn't like feeling this way.

Sarange's life was neat and tidy. She liked it best when everyone knew what they were supposed to be doing and no one deviated from the script. This felt wild and unrehearsed. Khan had thrown her so far out of her routine she couldn't see a way back. And the scary thing was, she wasn't sure she wanted to.

Her whole body was still trembling with a combination of excitement and outrage. Curiously, she felt as though the electricity coursing through her veins was there to stay. How could that be so? The answer was simple. It couldn't. Put a little distance between her and Khan and she could forget him, get back to normal. It wasn't as if he could have any sort of lasting effect on her life. Was it?

A knock on the door startled her into spilling water down the front of her dress. Instantly, she wondered if it was Khan, and her feelings went to war over the possibility. Excitement trilled through her at the thought of opening the door and seeing him again. At the same time, anger flooded through her. There could be only one reason why he would follow her. He must be confident she would fall into his arms again.

And won't you? She hated this. Hated the way her body was pulling her in two different directions. Because she had no idea what she would do if she opened that door and Khan was standing on the other side of it. There was a strong possibility she would launch herself at him, but whether the outcome was a kiss or a punch remained to be seen.

With a hand that shook slightly, she turned the handle and opened the door. Her initial reaction told her everything she needed to know about her feelings. The man who stood there was most definitely not Khan.

Shorter, slighter, with dark hair and sharp features, his smile oozing charm. It wasn't his fault Sarange wanted to slam the door in his face because he wasn't the person she longed to see. Her heart gave an uncomfortable downward lurch. She had a wretched feeling it was a signal. A warning that no one else would ever be good enough. From now on, the only person she would open a door to with a willing smile would be Khan.

This was straying into the realms of the absurd. This man, whoever he was, had begun to regard her with a slightly bemused expression. "Your manager said this would be okay. I'm Gurban Radin, owner of Real Planet Productions. We spoke on the phone last week."

Forcing herself to concentrate, she dredged up a memory of the conversation. "Of course." She held out her hand and he shook it enthusiastically. "Come in, Mr. Radin."

"Just Radin, please." He stepped into the dressing room. "I wanted to stop by and congratulate you on the success of tonight's concert. After what I've just seen, I'm even more keen for us to work together on the project we discussed."

Sarange nodded. "I'm looking forward to making the documentary with your company. Obviously, returning to my home country of Mongolia will be exciting for me. Even more important than that will be the focus on the plight of the blue wolves. They are one of the most endangered species on the planet."

Radin paced the small room excitedly. "I don't know if you're aware of it…if you've had time to check yet?" He held up his cell phone. "But the response to your duet with Khan has been phenomenal. Social media is going wild. The electricity between the two of you was incredible."

"We are performers. That's what we do." Sarange hoped her voice didn't sound too cold, but at the same time, she wanted to dampen some of his enthusiasm. And maybe some of her own. She also had no idea what her performance with Khan had to do with the wildlife documentary she was supposed to be making.

"Exactly." Radin's eyes shone with zealous light. "We need to use that, and also capitalize on the public enthusiasm."

"How do you propose to do that?" Sarange had a feeling she wasn't going to like the answer.

"By getting Khan to make the blue wolf documentary with you."

Being a rock star meant living on his nerves. The life was high-energy, high-profile and high-stress. Khan was permanently in the public eye and on someone else's agenda. He had known how it would be when Ged helped him escape from captivity. This was the life Ged had offered him, and he had embraced it with gratitude. Khan was good at it—the best—but it didn't always suit his big-cat temperament. His inner tiger craved solitude and supremacy. Juggling the two sides of his persona wasn't easy, and he had been looking forward to this time after Beast's tour as a chance to unwind before they started work on their new album. It hadn't happened.

It had been weeks since the Animals Alive concert, and the intervening time had taken the madness of his fame to a whole new level. The entire concert had fired the public imagination, but his duet with Sarange had been the highlight. The chemistry between them had been tangible to those watching. Rumors of a romance between the bad boy of rock and the world's most glamorous singer had persisted ever since. They couldn't look at each other that way and *not* be in love; that was the argument that pervaded every website, magazine and TV program.

Always the subject of paparazzi attention—the press was desperate to catch him out in bad behavior…and they often succeeded—Khan had been unable to move out of his New York apartment. Ged had advised him to lie low.

"Something else will come up in a day or two to attract their attention, and this will all be forgotten."

It hadn't happened. *Kha-range*—Khan wanted to put his foot through the TV screen the first time he heard *that* celebrity fusion name—had become a media obsession. Hotels and restaurants, keen to boost business, fanned the flames by hinting at sightings and bookings. Engagements, weddings, a secret baby, breakups…the whole range of stories had hit the headlines in the last few weeks.

And the job offers had rolled in. The moneymen, seeing the opportunities in a collaboration between Khan and Sarange, had come up with an eye-watering range of ideas. Films, TV specials, a record deal, interviews, photo shoots, advertising, even a book.

Khan had lost count of the number of times he had said no. Today was different. Today he would get to say the word to Sarange herself.

"No." He tilted his chair back so he could rest his shoulders against the wall. At the same time, he placed his feet on the glossy glass surface of the meeting table.

The gesture was calculated to annoy Sarange. From the way her light blue gaze grew even icier as it dropped to his scuffed biker boots, he guessed he'd succeeded.

"I don't think you've quite grasped the concept." Gurban Radin, the guy who was in charge of the production company, leaned forward earnestly, resting his clasped hands on the table. "What we're proposing is unlike anything that's ever been done before. Two major stars being filmed as they travel together to a remote region of Mongolia to see the blue wolves in their natural habitat—"

"What part of 'no' didn't you understand?" Khan had no problem being rude to this guy. He hadn't asked for this meeting. He'd started out polite, but now they were taking up his valuable rehearsal time, and they still weren't listening to him.

"The Animals Alive Foundation would benefit from your contribution." Ged's eyes held a play-nice warning. Khan saw that look on his manager's face on a regular basis. Sometimes he felt a pang of pity for Ged. He worked so hard to keep Khan, his most famous client, out of trouble. He didn't always succeed.

"I'll write a check. Name your price." Khan yawned. "The answer is still no."

He could see Sarange fighting to keep her temper under control. He could read her emotions, even though he didn't want to feel that connection to her. Part of the reason he had agreed to this meeting had been to test his resolve. The last few weeks had been torture. Every minute of every day, his body craved her. It wasn't like going cold turkey on an addiction. It wasn't getting easier as time went by. He didn't have any periods when he didn't hunger for his fix. If this was the rest of his life, he was screwed.

He really shouldn't be here. Keeping away from her would have been the wisest move, but the rest of the world was conspiring against him. Even Ged was giving him some powerful reasons why he should consider this latest offer. In the end, Khan had taken a break from precious rehearsal time so he could look at Sarange and see how she was coping with the whole fated-mates, enforced separation situation. He hoped she was doing better than he was. And he wondered if she'd gotten a handle on her inner wolf yet. Because that whole denial thing was seriously weird.

Now that he was up close to her, he could see she was suffering. His gaze lingered on her face, drinking her in. Today her hair was drawn back in a thick braid that hung to her waist and she wore a crisp white shirt. Her jeans were tucked into soft leather boots. Even in casual clothing she managed to look like a Mongolian princess. Her face was heart-shaped, with flat high cheekbones tapering to a pointed chin. A broad, arrogant nose and full mouth added to the regal look. The only giveaway to her werewolf heritage was her eyes. Set under thick, soaring dark brows, they were twin chips of blue ice. Khan could see pain and confusion in their depths. Unlike him, he could tell Sarange still had no idea why she was hurting.

Life could be hard, and Khan knew from experience that went double for shifters. He experienced a brief, dangerous pang of sympathy for Sarange. Someone should sit her down and explain how these things worked. Not him. No way was Khan going there. But he wanted to take away that lost, hurt look in her eyes and replace it with the cynicism she would need to develop if she was going to survive as a werewolf in the human world. Maybe Ged could talk to her. The guy who had dedicated his life to rescuing damaged shifters had the experience and the skill.

"Are we done here?" Khan placed his hands on the table, indicating he intended to leave. Because he couldn't put his body under this strain for much longer. There was only so much torment he could endure. And fighting the need to drag Sarange into his arms was just about the worst torture he had known. Coming from Khan, a weretiger who had endured capture, imprisonment and near death, that was quite an admission.

"Wait." Sarange's voice was quiet, almost pleading. When she raised her eyes to his, it was as though there was no one else in the room. "Just hear me out. Please?"

In spite of the voice in his head urging him to get right away from her and do it fast, Khan sank back into his seat. There was a tiny flare of gratitude in her eyes. And, in that instant, he was lost. He understood how medieval knights of old felt when they performed heroic deeds to prove their worth. Climbing beanstalks, defeating dragons—although the only dragon he knew was Torque, and he was generally harmless—and breaking magic spells. She wasn't going to ask him to do any of those things. But he knew she was going to test his resolve.

"After to the red wolves, the blue wolves of Mongolia are the most endangered in the world. This pack has been gradually decreasing over the years so that now there are fewer than a hundred left." Her voice was low, passionate. It was obvious how much this cause meant to her. "I agreed to travel to the region to make a documentary to raise awareness of their plight. Now the production company—" her eyes flickered to Radin "—have said they will withdraw the funding…unless you and I make the film together."

"Why would they do that?" Even as Khan asked the question, he knew the answer.

"Isn't it obvious?" Sarange gave a bitter little laugh. "They'll draw a huge audience because of the recent public interest in us." She said the word "us" the way Khan thought it. Within bitter quotation marks. "It all comes down to money."

Radin spoke up quickly. "We will, of course, be making a substantial contribution to the Animals Alive Foundation."

Sarange ignored him. "Even if this film gets made, it may be too late for the blue wolves. The prediction is that they will be extinct within five years. But if we can raise awareness, begin a breeding program…who knows? There may just be a chance we can save them."

"Why not make the film yourself using Animals Alive Foundation funds?"

"We couldn't allow that." Radin's voice was smooth. "My company owns the rights to the documentary. How it is made is our decision."

The sensation of being trapped was beginning to prickle along Khan's spine. They thought they had him. Conscience, publicity, environmentalism, guilt…they thought they'd pressed all the right buttons and gotten him where they wanted him. Even Ged, his *friend* Ged, was expecting him to agree.

Well, to hell with this. Swinging up from his seat, Khan stalked out of the room without saying another word.

Chapter 3

"Can I show you something?"

Sarange was so angry she wanted to barge past the man who spoke. She wanted to do a lot more than that. She wanted to eradicate anything to do with Khan from her life. If only it was that easy. Ever since she'd met him, it was as if he'd taken control of her thoughts as well as her body. For weeks now, she had been functioning only in relation to him. He was the first thing she thought of on waking, and the last image in her head at night. He occupied her whole attention in between, and then she dreamed of him while she slept. Her entire being burned with longing for this man. A man she had met once. A man she intensely disliked. It was the wildest, scariest, most wonderful feeling she had ever known.

Coming here today, knowing she would be seeing

him again, had made her feel like a school kid with a crush. For days, she had been battling the butterflies in her stomach and the clamminess of her palms.

Will he remember the kiss? Does he wish it had ended differently? She had repeatedly tried to force her thoughts onto the most important thing. *Can I persuade him to change his mind about collaborating?*

When Khan had first walked into this meeting room, the roller coaster of her emotions was almost too much to bear. She had nearly convinced herself that her imagination was playing powerful tricks on her. She couldn't possibly have fallen as fast and as hard for Khan as her body was telling her she had. The guy was an overbearing, conceited jackass. No woman in her right mind could find him attractive. Okay, his face and body were incredible...*oh, heaven help me, I've been taken in by his pretty face and mouthwatering biceps.*

Sarange had been at the pinnacle of fame for over a decade. If good looks and muscles were what she wanted, she could have taken her pick. And, now and then, that was what she had done. Brief, pleasant relationships that had ended without regret or recrimination. But what she felt for Khan? This wildness? She had no idea what it was. All she knew for sure was she had to fight it. If she didn't, it would take over her life.

This issue with Radin and the documentary was a complication she could do without. Over the years, the Animals Alive Foundation had grown beyond her own desire to protect the endangered species about which she cared. Sarange's driving passion had become a global nonprofit organization, her primary function. Recently, her singing and songwriting had taken second place to her role as a wildlife ambassador.

Even so, she couldn't explain why she was so drawn to the plight of the blue wolf pack. *What the hell is wrong with me?* First there was this restless longing for Khan. Now she wanted to storm in and help a subspecies of wolf that was probably doomed anyway. There were bigger challenges facing the animal world. Ones that would attract far greater attention. Elephants, pandas, tigers...*fight the sexy fights.* It was no good. She didn't understand why, but the blue wolves called to her. Sarange would do what she could to save them.

It was her desire to protect the blue wolves that had brought her face-to-face with Khan again. She tried to tell herself that was why she had flown from Los Angeles to New York for this meeting. It wasn't out of any overwhelming desire to see him. And he had just rejected her. Again. She had created a situation in which he could storm out on her like a moody teenager...

She drew a deep breath and forced her focus back into the room and onto Ged Taverner. As he rose from his chair, Ged kept unfolding until his big, muscular body towered over her. As she looked up at him, it occurred to Sarange that she could have felt intimidated. Although her bodyguard was standing by the door, this guy looked like he could wrestle a bear with one arm tied behind his back. Instead, Ged radiated a curiously protective aura.

What was he saying? He wanted to show her something?

"I'm sorry. I don't have time..."

"This won't take long." He placed a hand under her elbow, his touch gentle but firm. The sensation of being swept along by forces beyond her control took over again. What was it about these people? Ever since she had encountered Khan, her life hadn't been her own. Did that extend to his whole entourage?

They left the meeting room and Ged led her to the elevator. As he gestured for her bodyguard to wait, Sarange tried another protest. "I've wasted enough time traveling to New York for a meeting that has proved pointless. I can't see any reason to hang around."

"Five minutes." She capitulated, nodding to the guard to meet her at the car. Ged smiled as he pressed the button for the basement. "Thank you."

After exiting the elevator, they followed a short corridor. "Although the members of the band come from all over the world, once Beast became famous, they all moved here to New York. We tried a number of different recording studios before we settled on this one."

"If they come from all over the world, how did they get together?" Sarange didn't want to be intrigued by Beast. Didn't want anything to do with the world's greatest rock band and its purring, strutting, infuriating frontman, but Ged's words interested her in spite of herself.

"I brought them together." Why did she sense a huge story lay behind that simple statement? In spite of their dynamic personalities, Beast didn't give much away about their private lives. Biographical details about the band members were scarce. In the past, Sarange had curled her lip at what she believed was a publicity ploy. The enigmatic tough guys of rock. She wondered for the first time what they were hiding.

Ged held open a door, motioning for her to precede him. When Sarange stepped inside, she was in a recording booth. From behind a clear glass panel, she could see a small, circular stage. Khan was seated on a stool in its center. He had drawn his wild mane of red-gold hair back with a simple elastic band, and his head was bowed as he clutched a microphone to his chest. His whole attitude was despairing.

Sarange turned to regard Ged. This didn't feel comfortable. It felt a lot like she was intruding on Khan's privacy.

"I've known him to spend hours perfecting a single note." Ged's voice was quiet as he looked over her head at the lone figure on the other side of the soundproof glass. "This side of Khan doesn't fit with his public image. The stage persona, the guy who'd laugh in the devil's face? That takes a hell of a lot of hard work."

He flicked a switch as he spoke and Khan's voice filled the booth. The song wasn't one of Beast's. It was an old love song, with a sweet melody, haunting in its intensity. Khan didn't apply any of his usual vocal fireworks to this performance. Alone, unaware of his audience, and with no backing music, he closed his eyes, pouring his heart into the song.

As she listened, tears burned the back of Sarange's eyelids. What *was* it about this man? Where had this invisible thread that pulled her to him come from? And how the hell was she going to sever it? She didn't know whether to be glad or sorry that Ged had shown her Khan had another side to him. Would it have been easier to walk away believing he was shallow and self-absorbed? Khan had given her no choice. She had to walk away. It was never going to be easy.

Ged waited until Khan had finished singing before he spoke. "His vocal range is unique. Khan can sing opera just as easily as rock."

As if to demonstrate, Khan started to sing again. The

same ballad with a slightly different emphasis. There was something rawer in the emotion this time. God, he could tell a story with that voice! The last version had made her think of unrequited love. This one was a whole lot hotter. It conjured up visions of steamy sex and crumpled sheets...and it made her whole body burn.

"Who is he?" She tilted her head back to look at Ged. The question, coming out of nowhere, surprised her.

Ged didn't falter. "He is Khan." Ged said it as though it clarified everything. And maybe it did. Khan was one of a kind, defying explanation. "This campaign you have with the blue wolves, is that because of your own heritage?"

"I certainly have an interest in their plight because I was born in Mongolia, but that's not the only reason I want to help." She still wasn't sure why she felt so fiercely about this pack of wolves. Her homeland, heritage, Mongolian folklore...none of those things could quite account for the intensity of emotion this cause aroused in her.

"You must know that's not what I meant."

Sarange frowned. "What else could you possibly mean?"

Ged's expression was unfathomable. It reminded her of the look in Khan's eyes when he had called her "wolf girl" just before she initiated that devastating kiss. *What is it with these people and wolves?* Was it to do with the name Beast? Were they looking to use wolves for some sort of gimmick? Ged was staring at her as if she was an alien being. As if he couldn't make up his mind what to do about her.

Enough was enough. Whatever his problem was, she really didn't have time to spend analyzing it. On balance, she decided she was glad Ged had shown her this other side of Khan. Although her pride was still stinging, it helped to know he wasn't the one-dimensional jerk of first appearances.

She turned toward the door. "You're Khan's friend. Why does he hate me?"

Ged took a last look at the lone figure. "Khan doesn't really do friendship. And it's not you he hates—" he flicked the switch, and the booth went silent "—it's himself."

Beast had won Best Band at the Rock the World Awards for the last two years. This year, when they burst onto the stage to receive the award for the third time, Khan looked out at the sea of faces in the vast audience with a feeling close to apathy. The great and good of the music industry were gathered under one roof to honor their own, but there was only one person he wanted to see. He already knew Sarange wasn't there. If she'd been there, he'd have felt her.

They were in her town, yet she'd stayed away. It was her message to Khan. He knew she felt this invisible, unbreakable thread as powerfully as he did. By not attending this prestigious ceremony, she was showing him she was stronger than he was. She didn't need to see him. Didn't need the buzz that came from his nearness. This was what he'd wanted, yet the despair he felt was like a giant rock sitting on his chest. How could he miss what had never been his? All he knew was there was an aching hole in his life that could only be filled by Sarange. How was he ever going to learn to deal with this constant gnawing pain?

Beast was closing the award ceremony with a number from its new album. It was time to don his rock star persona and do what he did best…drive this crowd wild. Doing it when his heart had just been ripped out and his limbs felt like lead? That would be a new experience.

The way the band played together had always been creative and intuitive. Each member was individually talented, but when they came together they became so much more. Maybe it came down to what they'd all been through before they got together. Their music did the talking because their emotions had been shredded. From Khan's raw yipping, screeching tones, through Diablo's wild drumming to Finglas's haunting bass lines, their unique sound pulsed with primal energy.

Physically they complemented each other perfectly as well. Each member of the band had his unique, onstage personality. Khan was all strutting, purring egomania. Diablo was solitary, stealthy and quick tempered. There was Torque with his quick-fire restlessness and Dev, in contrast, who remained cool and aloof. Finglas was the newest addition to the band. The young Irish werewolf had replaced Nate Zilar, the long-standing bass guitarist, and was just finding his place among the big personalities. Finglas often appeared detached, but he could raise as much hell as Khan when the mood took him. As a cast of characters, the band came together with a power that couldn't be manufactured. Beasts in the true sense of the word, they were one of a kind.

Behind them, giant LED screens played recordings of their signature three-sixes logo, roaring flames and the snarling jaws of wild animals. The cheering audience enthusiastically demonstrated the horned sign of the beast by pointing their fingers at the sides of their heads. The number ended on a wild note when Khan climbed to the top of the lighting installation at the rear of the stage, hanging perilously by one hand as he howled out the final verse.

He sprang back onto the stage, landing in a crouch at Torque's feet.

"And that, my friend, is how to bring the house down," Torque said, as they walked off the stage. "I thought it might be literally. That set didn't look very stable."

Khan shrugged. "Remember Moscow?"

Dev caught up to them. "How could we forget? Although I blame Ged for booking us into a theater with balconies. He must have known you'd climb into them."

"How was I to know that building was unsafe?" Khan scowled.

Torque draped an arm around each of their shoulders. "Those were the days. Collapsing balconies. Irate Russians. Hot women. Cold vodka."

"Talking of which—" Dev steered them toward the bar at the back of the vast auditorium "—Ged is waiting for us. Best behavior, guys. The press is out in force tonight, always looking for the money shot of Khan in a compromising position."

Khan cursed under his breath. He wasn't in the mood for socializing, and he was never in the mood to have his behavior regulated. Over time, he had learned to strike a balance between his human and tiger personalities. On occasions like this, he drew on his human need for company, suppressing his cat desire for solitude. And there were usually compensations. On a night like tonight, he could generally find an outlet for his wild sexual appetite. The problem was, his body had decided it had found his mate, meaning his desire for sex with anyone other than Sarange had deserted him. It was a highly inconvenient side effect to an already out of control situation.

Until now, Khan's sexual instincts had mirrored those of a tiger in the wild. He supposed humans would call it promiscuity. Tigers would call it common sense. Find a female, have sex with her as often as possible within a short time frame until she was carrying his cubs, then move on to the next female. It was a simple rule for big cats in nature to ensure fertilization. As a human, of course, Khan was meticulous about using protection to ensure that didn't happen. Thankfully, his inner tiger didn't take over completely.

Monogamy wasn't part of the tiger social structure, but despite his inner cat, Khan wasn't all wild animal. He didn't get to be that lucky. Being a shifter, he got to live within a set of expectations that applied to all shifters. Ones that said he needed a mate. It seemed there was no right of appeal. Even though there were so many things wrong in this case. The mate the Fates had selected for him was the wrong species. She didn't know she was a shifter. *And don't get me started on who I am...*

Khan bit back a smile. Monogamy without a partner? Wasn't that called celibacy? That should keep Ged happy. At least there would be no sensational kiss-and-tell stories tomorrow morning.

"Come and join me, Tiger Boy." As if in answer to his thoughts, Ged appeared at Khan's side. He was carrying a bottle of brandy and two glasses. It was always serious when Ged got the brandy bottle out.

By some miracle, they found a quiet corner table and Ged sloshed brandy into the glasses. Around them, celebrities were getting drunker and noisier. Finglas was locked in an embrace with one member of a girl band, while her bandmate wrapped her arms around his waist from behind.

"That guy is after your reputation as the bad boy of Beast." Ged tilted his glass toward Finglas.

"The way I feel right now he's welcome to it." Khan leaned back in his seat, draining his glass in one gulp.

"Does this newfound apathy have anything to do with Sarange?"

Khan stared at his manager, the man who had rescued him from a cage and given him his life back. For long, unblinking seconds he said nothing. Then he sighed. If Ged wanted information from him, he would get it. He might as well cut out the part where he tried to resist.

"You've heard some crazy shifter stories in your lifetime, Ged. Shall I tell you a new one? One that takes screwed up to a whole new level?" He dropped his voice, glancing around to make sure they were the only ones who could hear. "How about I tell you the story of a tiger who fell for a wolf? If that wasn't bad enough, it gets even crazier. It turns out she didn't know she was a wolf."

Khan reached for the brandy, planning to pour himself another glass. To hell with it. He drank long and hard straight from the bottle, wiping the neck on the tail of his designer shirt when he finished. "I know."

Khan's eyes narrowed. "You know what?"

"I've met Sarange. I know she's a werewolf." Ged took the brandy from Khan and tilted the bottle to his own lips. "And I agree with your assessment. She has no idea what she is."

Khan slumped down in his seat. "Has that ever happened before?" If anyone was going to know the answer to that question, it would be Ged.

"Not that I'm aware. Violet, Nate's wife, lost her memory for a while." Violet was a werewolf who had joined them on tour recently. When she and Nate got married, he had left the band. "Part of that memory loss meant she forgot how to shift. That was temporary, but this is different. Sarange seems unaware that she has *ever* been a werewolf."

"What I don't understand is how she can be a shifter yet not want to shift. It's the most powerful urge we have. Right up there with breathing and sex."

Ged had been about to take another drink, but he lowered the bottle. "Judging by some of the situations I've had to bail you out of over the years, I'd say sex is the strongest urge *you* have."

Khan stretched his long legs in front of him. "I'm a cat. We enjoy the hunt."

"Yet you're not hunting tonight?" Ged raised a brow.

Before Khan could tell him to butt out, the music was lowered and the sound turned up on the big screens that were located on each wall. "You might want to listen to this, guys." Torque came to lean against the wall next to them.

The screens were all showing the same news story. The announcer's voice filled the room. "We're returning to our main story. Earlier this evening a group of four men broke into the Los Angeles home of singer, songwriter and animal rights activist Sarange—"

Khan was on his feet in an instant, his heart rate kicking up to explosive new levels. "What the…?"

"—although the men fled when the singer's bodyguards came to her aid, Sarange sustained minor injuries in the attack. It is believed the intention was kidnapping—"

Khan didn't hear any more. He couldn't think straight. Someone had tried to abduct Sarange. She had been hurt. His mate had been in danger and he hadn't been there to protect her.

Ged's hand was firm on his shoulder. "Go to her."

Chapter 4

How many different ways was she supposed to answer the same question? Tiredness and frustration were getting to Sarange now. It was beginning to feel like she was the suspect as the detective waited with his notebook open and his pen poised.

"I've already told you, Detective Kidd." Sarange thought she did a pretty good job of keeping the annoyance out of her voice. "They came into my bedroom through the balcony."

He tapped his pen against his teeth. It was a mannerism he'd already used a few times. If it continued, he might find himself eating that pen before too much longer. "See, that's where I'm struggling." He shook his head, and Sarange decided he'd modeled his mannerisms on various TV cops he'd seen. "You're saying that four men climbed up the front of the house and in through the balcony to this suite in broad daylight without being seen and without triggering the alarm system?"

"That's exactly what I'm saying."

Sarange had decided not to go to the Rock the World Awards. She hadn't declined, she had just decided she wouldn't turn up. Even though it was one of the biggest nights in the music world's calendar, she wasn't going to put herself through the humiliation of seeing Khan again. She might spend every private minute fighting the cravings, but she didn't have to do it publicly. She couldn't trust her emotions around him, and no way was he going to get another chance to humiliate her.

Even if he didn't reject her this time, what did she anticipate would happen between them? A one-night stand? She shivered at the thought. Spontaneity, stepping outside the boundaries, seizing the moment…they were all alien to Sarange's nature. She played by the rules. That, and the fact that she lived her life in the full glare of the public eye, were probably the reasons she'd never hooked up with a stranger. *I don't do wild.* An image of Khan came into her mind, bringing with it a surge of longing to break free of her self-imposed constraints. Although she thought she knew her own mind, her treacherous body kept giving the idea of a one-night stand an enthusiastic thumbs-up.

Her resolve had held firm. Vowing to avoid social media, she had spent the day in her office, doing her best to focus on Animals Alive paperwork. The attempt had been futile. The white-hot desire and almost insane longing for Khan weren't going away, no matter how hard she tried to push them aside. Knowing he was in the same town made it so much worse. It was as if an endless recording that could not be turned off was playing inside her head. Khan had entered her soul like a mind-altering drug, meaning she was no longer responsible for her actions.

Eventually, she had succumbed and checked her cell phone. Almost with a will of their own, her fingers found images and recordings of Beast arriving at their hotel. And there was Khan. Her heart melted at the sight of him. Glittering, feral, predatory. With his usual grace, he bounded from the limousine ahead of his bandmates. The sunlight turned his hair to burnished copper as he acknowledged the shouts of the crowd with a wave.

Who was she fooling? Of course she was going to the awards ceremony. There was no way she could stay away from him. That invisible thread that drew them together was pulling her to him harder and stronger than ever. It had been as she was in her dressing room, trying to decide what to wear, that the men had burst in from the balcony.

Sarange could understand Detective Kidd's confusion. It matched her own. Her luxurious home was secure. She lived in a gated community. She had three live-in bodyguards. Her security system was the best, and most up-to-date, that money could buy. There was no way four men should have been able to get close to her house, let alone inside her personal suite. She should not have a sprained ankle and a bruised cheek because she had fought them as they tried to drag her back out onto the balcony. It was only because she had her cell phone in her hand, with its personal attack alarm enabled, that she had been able to summon Marco, her head of security.

Her bodyguards had rushed into the room while calling the police. With remarkable agility, the intruders
had vaulted back over the balcony wall and scattered
through the grounds before they could be caught.

"I didn't imagine them." She was tired now. Yet
surely she should feel more traumatized by her experience? Instead, her overriding emotion was dis-
appointment that she wouldn't get to see Khan. "My
bodyguards saw them, too."

The detective consulted his notes. "And these men
made no attempt to hide their faces?"

"That's right. I've already given your colleague a
description." Sarange resisted the temptation to sigh.

"Tall, muscular, medium brown hair, amber eyes,
sharp features." His eyes probed her face. "That's your
description...of all of them?"

"Yes." They had been through this. Several times.
She knew how weird it sounded. "They could have been
quadruplets."

Before he could say anything else, she heard a commotion. It sounded like it was downstairs, possibly in
the entrance hall. Disturbances didn't happen in her
house. In her life. She paid people to make sure of it.
Now, twice in one day, her ordered existence was being
tilted off course. But this time, she knew the reason.
She could feel it...*him*. Khan was close by. She had no
idea *how* she knew he was the source of the fire and
fury taking place elsewhere in her home. She just did.
This connection they had transcended normal rules.

Detective Kidd turned his head to look at the uni-
formed officer who was standing by the door. "Find
out what's going on."

Before the police officer could move, Khan strode

through the door, instantly filling her bedroom with his presence. Those hypnotic eyes, golden and fiery, fixed on Sarange as though there was no one else present. "They tried to stop me seeing you."

Sarange's head of security burst into the room behind Khan. His shirt was torn and a scratch on his face oozed blood. "I'm sorry. He was like a wild animal..."

"It's okay, Marco." And it was. Suddenly, it was as though she had been wrapped in a protective blanket. Without words, Khan had managed to do what the police and her bodyguards couldn't. Just by being there, he had reassured her that she was safe.

"Call me if you need anything." With obvious reluctance, Marco left the room.

Khan was about to cross to the bed when he appeared to notice Detective Kidd and his companion for the first time. "Why are these people here?"

"The detective wants to ask me some more questions."

"I think not." No one could do arrogant like Khan. As he turned that feline gaze on Detective Kidd, the words of protest died on the police officer's lips. Moving to the door, Khan held it open.

"There is something very strange about this incident. If you think of anything else, give me a call." Tossing a look of dislike in Khan's direction, the detective and his colleague left.

Sarange barely had an instant to wonder why Khan had come here. After taking so much trouble to show her he didn't want anything to do with her, why was he in her bedroom right now? And why was he gazing at her with *that* look in his eyes? Within a second or two of the door closing, he had crossed the room and dropped on one knee beside the bed, catching hold of her hand and raising it to his lips.

"I wasn't here to protect you. I will never forgive myself for that." The antagonism was gone. His voice throbbed with genuine regret.

This should be weird. That was her first response to his words. She should run a mile from a man who spoke to her that way. She definitely shouldn't tangle her hands in his hair, or utter a sound that was midway between a laugh and a sob. This shouldn't feel like the best thing ever to happen to her. Yet, as she touched Khan, she could feel strength and heat flowing from him and into her body.

This is real. Whatever it is, this is happening.

"Who were they?" Khan lifted his head. "Did you know the men who broke in here?"

Sarange shook her head. "I've never seen them before. They didn't speak to me, so I don't know what they wanted. They were trying to drag me out of the house when I raised the alarm. Marco and my other bodyguards burst in. They called the police, but the intruders had already gone."

Khan raised a hand, his touch featherlight as he traced the bruise on her cheek. "They hurt you."

"Because I fought them."

There was a flash of fire in the depths of his eyes. She glimpsed something in him then, something raw and animal. It called to an answering part of her own character. A part she hadn't known existed until now.

"You are safe now. I'm here." His smile was pure insolence and undiluted mischief. "You no longer have to rely on second-rate protection."

"I get a rock star for a bodyguard?"

He got to his feet, and she looked up at him. He was breathtaking. "You get Khan." The words should have been conceited. Instead they comforted and scared her. Was it possible to feel those conflicting emotions at the same time? It seemed Khan could make her feel the impossible.

Khan pulled a chair over to the side of the bed and sat in it. Resting his feet on the mattress, he leaned back with his arms folded across his chest. Sarange turned on her side, drinking in the beauty of his profile. "You can't stay there all night."

"How else will I make sure you are safe?"

It was on the tip of her tongue to suggest he could join her, but she stopped short of saying the words. This wasn't a fling, or even the start of a brief relationship. This was beyond anything she had ever known. There was magic between them, but there were barriers as well. She still had no idea what this attraction was about. She suspected Khan knew and was fighting forces that went way beyond her comprehension.

She spent the night content to drift in and out of sleep, enjoying the deep contentment his presence brought. Strange snippets of dreams gripped her as slumber pulled her deeper into its embrace. Four men who all looked alike. Blue Fire. Great Tiger. Golden Eagle. The words meant nothing and everything. Each time she stirred and opened her eyes, Khan was there, watching over her.

Her life had just changed forever, and she didn't know whether fear or excitement was her strongest emotion. She only knew she had never felt either with such intensity.

* * *

Sleeping was one of Khan's favorite activities. Fortunately, he could do it pretty much anywhere. When he was on stage, he expended huge amounts of energy, and afterward his inner tiger took over to restore his energy. While on tour, he had been known to spend half the day sleeping. It wasn't considered unusual among his bandmates. Diablo and Dev were also werecats. No one flinched when Finglas bowed down before the full moon, Torque took to the skies or Ged disappeared into the forest for hours. There was mutual respect among the group for the diverse traits of the individual members.

So sleeping in a chair at Sarange's bedside shouldn't be a problem for him. Physically, it wasn't. He could curl his long limbs into a comfortable position and, catlike, be asleep in seconds. Even though they hadn't spoken about her attackers and their motivation, the possibility that they might return was at the back of Khan's mind. He wasn't afraid of that. They wouldn't sneak up on him while he slumbered. Khan didn't know who these people were, but he could go from sleeping to waking in an instant. The slightest sound, movement, scent, even a shift in the air would alert him to danger. His every sense would power up and be ready to take on the enemy. His fingers curled into the shape of claws as he looked forward to the prospect of confronting them.

No, it wasn't the physical practicalities of sleeping in a chair that bothered him. It was the problem of being so close to Sarange and not touching her. He had crossed a line tonight. Resistance had become acceptance. He had been fighting his attraction to her so hard that he had ignored another part of his role as a mate…protection. Alongside the admission that he had a duty to care for her, some of the barriers he had worked so hard to erect had come tumbling down. He couldn't remain antagonistic toward her when he needed to be at her side 24/7. He didn't know what the future had in store, but the present held a new rapport. Khan could snarl about the quirk of fate that had brought them here, but he was honest enough to admit he liked it. A little too much.

Although why watching Sarange sleep should bring him so much pleasure, he had no idea. She lay curled on her side in the huge bed, with one hand under her uninjured cheek. Her braid hung like a glossy rope over her shoulder, and the bedclothes had slipped down to reveal her pink pajama top. Her features were relaxed, her long lashes shadowing her cheeks, her lips slightly parted. And, alongside the fire in his blood, something softer bloomed within him.

He'd had enough torture. There was only so much nobility one person could stand. Slipping off his shoes, he leaned over Sarange and pulled the comforter up to her shoulders before lying down next to her. He was fully dressed. She was beneath the bedclothes. Resisting temptation would be a new experience, but he was prepared to try it.

Holding his breath in an attempt not to disturb Sarange, he settled his weight, turning on his side and mirroring her position. This was the problem with being a solitary being living among social creatures. Khan was used to doing what made him feel good without considering others. He stopped short of breaking the law and tried not to hurt anyone—either physically or emotionally—in the process. Even so, he had a lot in common with the ultimate hedonists who had colonized this human world. Like a domestic cat, Khan sought his pleasures, took them and only considered others as a means of getting what he wanted.

Right now his perfect pleasure was lying next to him…but he wasn't going to take her. His life had changed the moment he saw Sarange. The fabric of who he was comprised a unique pattern, woven by his experiences. It was ever-changing with old colors and textures fading and disappearing and new ones emerging. Even Khan had no idea how long he had been alive, or where his life had begun. Held in captivity in China, he had been in his tiger form when he was captured. The darkness, despair, hunger and weakness of his imprisonment had lasted many lifetimes. His captors had used silver to weaken him, but they couldn't kill him. He was unique, and that frustrated them. Now and then, he suspected his captors might have been werewolves, but he had no idea why they wanted him. A weretiger against a group of werewolves? It should have been no contest. That had been his last coherent memory of his capture until he was rescued by Ged.

Kept in a cage barely larger than a large dog kennel, deprived of natural light and half-starved, Khan had been close to death when Ged, acting on a story passed on by one of his informants, found him.

Ged was an enigma, even to his closest friends. A werebear of giant proportions, in his human form he poured his considerable talents into the day job. How he balanced managing one of the most successful rock bands in the world with his other persona was a mystery. Ged helped shifters who were injured, damaged or at risk of harm. Khan knew very little about his rescue work, only that Ged was the founder of an international team. *Like the Red Cross for shifters.*

Ged had always hoped that, once Khan was restored to full health and the trauma of his captivity had receded, his memory would return. It never had. There were snippets now and then. Of stalking deer along thicketed watercourses. Of vast, arid deserts. Of peering into shoreline bracken. Of crawling through a latticework of tangled low shrubs, emerging into willow and poplar forests. Nothing of himself, of who he was. *Who is Khan?* He had no idea.

Yet lying here, breathing in time with Sarange's rhythm, inhaling her sweet scent, he felt something stir inside him. Barely enough to call a memory, different to the bonds that bound him to her physically and emotionally. Certainty. That was what it felt like. A confidence that this woman was part of who he was. That pattern in the fabric of his life? The vibrant threads Khan didn't recognize had been woven by a different hand. *Hers.*

He didn't know how that could be so when Sarange believed herself to be human. She had no memory of herself as a shifter, let alone a shifter whose life had intersected his own. They both appeared to have a remembrance short circuit. Now that they had met, was it possible they would trigger each other's memories?

On that optimistic note, Khan draped an arm over her waist and rubbed his cheek against the silken mass of her hair. Sarange murmured in her sleep and he smiled as he closed his eyes. This was the only pleasure he needed.

Sarange came awake abruptly, unsure what had alerted her to danger. Moonlight streamed in through the light drapes as her eyes searched the darkened corners of the room, seeking confirmation of what she already knew. Someone was in the room. No, not some-*one*, there was more than one person, standing just inside the balcony doors. Before she could do anything, the strong arm around her waist tightened its grip and a hand moved up to cover her mouth. Her first instinct was to struggle, but then she remembered.

Khan. He was signaling for her to stay silent. Sarange gave a slight nod to show she understood and he moved his hand away. Although his touch reassured her, she couldn't help being concerned. If the same men had returned, it would be four against one. Surely it would be better if she used her cell phone alarm and got security up here?

With a stealth that amazed her, Khan slid from the bed. Noiseless and unerring, he made his way across the room. His night vision must be incredible. A crash and a cry signaled that he had reached the intruders.

Sarange weighed her options. She could lie still and speculate about what was happening. Or she could find a way to go to Khan's aid. Switching on the lamp at the side of the bed, she froze in horror at the scene unfolding in her luxurious bedroom.

The four men who had tried to abduct her earlier were back. Even as fear kicked in and her heart rate soared, she took a moment to notice all over again the weirdness of their similarity to each other. She had fought them; she knew they weren't in disguise. They didn't just look alike. They were identical. Were they quadruplets? Clones? She swallowed hard. Was it possible that they weren't human?

Unsure where that last thought had come from, she

snaked out a hand for the cell phone on her bedside table. Khan was going to need help after all.

"Don't call security." Khan's voice was like a whiplash. He was half-turned away from her, but he must have seen the movement out of the corner of his eye. "I've got this."

One of the men was already bleeding hard from a cut across his cheek. Did Khan have a knife? Sarange couldn't see anything in his hand. She remembered when Khan had burst into the house earlier. Marco had tried to stop him from seeing her and had suffered scratches to his face as a result. The wound on this intruder's face was too deep to have been caused by fingernails...

She slid from the bed, trying to scour the room for something she could use as a weapon while also keeping her eyes on Khan. The four men began to circle Khan, their manner predatory. She didn't like the matching smiles on their faces. It looked too much like they were snarling.

One of the men lunged and Khan was on him in a blur of movement, fighting like a wild animal. He didn't adopt a conventional style. Feet, fists, teeth and nails all went into the attack. His opponent went down fast under the onslaught.

The other intruders joined in, leaping on Khan. As incredible as it seemed, he kept going without pause. Swinging, slashing, powering into them. It was like watching a giant beast taking on a group of lesser creatures.

But something was happening. As if acting on an unseen signal, the four men were changing. It was swift and subtle. One second their human bodies were being tossed around by Khan as they attempted to bring him down onto the expensive cream-and-rose rug. The next, their facial features had elongated. In place of a nose, they each had a snout. Instead of a mouth, they had huge jaws with sharp snapping teeth. Their limbs stretched, becoming lithe and muscular. As they shook off the remains of their clothing, Sarange saw thick brown fur covering their bodies. A new scent pervaded the air. Like animal fur and carrion, it reminded her that she wasn't dreaming.

Wolves? Sarange shook her head in an attempt to clear it. These were no ordinary wolves. *There are four werewolves in my bedroom.*

As if in confirmation of that thought, one of them threw back his head and gave a single, triumphant howl.

Even as she tried to process why four werewolves had come for her and tried to abduct her, Sarange's thoughts were on Khan. This took the danger to a whole new level. He might have been able to fight four men— although that must have taken some kind of superhuman strength—but this? Four sets of lethal canines trying to rip out his throat? Four sets of claws aimed at his belly?

Khan didn't seem concerned. On the contrary, he was smiling as he faced the werewolf pack.

And...oh, my goodness. This can't be happening.

Yet somehow she knew it was going to happen. The transformation was over in the blink of an eye. Khan's clothing burst apart. Beneath the remaining shreds there was brilliant orange fur slashed across with diagonal stripes, each as thick, black and straight as a hand-drawn charcoal line. In his place, a giant tiger reared on its hind legs, lips drawn back in a snarl that revealed white fangs almost as wide as Sarange's wrist.

The attitude of the werewolves changed in an instant from aggression to fear. Whimpering, they abased themselves, pressing their bellies into the floor and flattening their ears.

Khan dropped onto all fours. Even by the dim light provided by the moon and the lamp, Sarange could see the ripple of pure muscle beneath his thick pelt. *And why am I noticing his muscles when there is a tiger in my bedroom? A tiger in place of the man who had his arm around me minutes ago?*

The sound that filled the room was a soft, echoing rumble of pure menace. Originating in the depths of the tiger's deep chest, it shook every part of Sarange's body, even though she knew it wasn't intended for her.

How do I know that? How do I know he's not going to turn on me once he's finished with those werewolves?

The answer was simple. He was Khan. And he was hers.

At the sound of the tiger's growl, the wolves scrambled into action. Heading for the open doors, they couldn't scramble over the balcony rail fast enough. Khan followed them, his movements deceptive. That big body appeared to barely expend any energy, but he covered the space between him and the werewolves in double time, staying just behind them.

As Khan sprang from the balcony, Sarange ran to see what was going on. From her vantage point, she watched as the security lights below, triggered by movement, came on. The alarm remained silent, and she guessed the intruders must have disabled it and the security cameras before they broke in.

Below her, the elegant patio resembled a scene from a movie, as four werewolves crouched behind deck furniture to avoid the prowling tiger. Eventually, they broke free and headed across the lawn toward the pool. Khan was after them in a bound. The last view Sarange had was when he caught up with them on the extreme edge of her property.

With a shaky exhale, she turned on the lights and sat on the bed, waiting for his return. Because he would return. And when he did, he had some explaining to do.

Chapter 5

Khan knew the werewolves wouldn't be able to outrun him. He'd never come across another shifter that could match him for speed. The problem was, once the werewolves leaped over the perimeter wall surrounding Sarange's property, they did exactly what he expected them to. They split up and ran in four different directions.

Wolf instincts. He could never understand it. They would sacrifice one for the sake of the pack.

Khan's inner tiger was prompting him to kill, but his human senses were urging caution. He could catch one of the werewolves, but forcing the guy to shift back and start talking? That needed privacy and time. And a tiger in the heart of Beverly Hills didn't have the luxury of either of those things. He faced a choice. Risk bringing chaos and carnage into the heart of the human world, or let the werewolves go.

The two halves of his psyche went to war. While his tiger was pushing him to hunt and kill, his human was arguing for restraint. Because he was in tiger form, it would be easy to go with the voice of his inner animal. His tiger instincts were strong, but he fought them. Reluctantly. Now was not the time. This was definitely not the place.

The werewolves had been given a powerful warning. They knew what they were dealing with. They would be back—tenacity was one of wolves' strongest traits—but Khan would be ready for them.

With a feeling of resignation—a tiger always knew when to give up the hunt—he turned back toward Sarange's house. He should shift back before he was seen. That way, his only problem would be that he was a naked man in the heart of Beverly Hills. That, and the fact that he needed to talk to Sarange about what she had just witnessed. He had hoped to ease her in gently to his shifter status. The werewolves had taken that opportunity away from him.

Shifting back, he kept to the shadows. Even in his human form, he retained elements of his inner cat. They showed through in his strength, speed and agility. When he had fought the four men back in Sarange's bedroom, there was no hesitation. He had known he could take them on and beat them. Just as he knew now he could scale the wall surrounding her house. Nimble as his inner cat, he pulled himself up and over the wall, dropping into a crouch on the other side.

Khan's eyes scoured the darkened yard, his keen vision easily picking out the security cameras. Sarange had live-in security, but no one had been roused by the arrival of four intruders. The werewolves had somehow bypassed her security system. His protective instincts went into overdrive again, his hands curling into the shape of tiger claws. *If I hadn't been here...*

He forced his breathing back to a regular rhythm. He had been here. He *would* be here. But they still didn't know what the werewolves wanted from her. All they knew for sure was this wasn't a robbery. This was about Sarange.

Using the ornate shrubs and flowers as cover, he made his way across the yard. Stepping onto a patio table, he climbed from there onto the balcony. Swinging himself over the rail, he looked around for something to cover his nakedness. He couldn't see anything. Maybe that was because his gaze was immediately captured by an ice-blue stare.

Arms folded across her chest, Sarange was standing in the doorway, blocking his entrance to the room. "You can start talking now."

"I was hoping to shower first. Maybe find some clothes."

"You turned into a *tiger*." He wasn't sure whether the wobble in her voice was caused by anger or shock. It didn't matter. She kept going, coming toward him until he was pressed up against the balcony rail and she had to tilt her chin to look up at him. "I need to know what's going on."

He caught hold of her upper arms, and as soon as he touched her, she collapsed into his arms. The feel of her body against his drove every other thought out of Khan's mind, and a harsh groan of surrender was dragged from him. His whole body was entranced by her. His eyelids half closed as if weighted and he lowered his head, compelled by a force beyond his control to graze Sarange's lips with his.

I don't want to control this.

The instant his mouth touched hers, their ragged breathing united in a single rhythm. Sarange melted into him, nuzzling his lips with her own. He clutched her tighter to his wildly beating heart, deepening a kiss that left Khan reeling. Achingly tender, it should have been unique. So why the hell did it feel so familiar?

His body was on fire, his arousal in danger of reaching epic proportions. Khan needed to regain control of the situation. But he was naked, with a beautiful woman in his arms. Restraint, never easy for him, was getting harder by the second.

"I'm hungry." He murmured the words into her hair.

"I can tell." She glanced down at his erection. In the moonlight, he could see a blush staining her cheekbones.

Khan groaned as temptation almost got the better of him. He pressed his forehead to hers. "No, I really am hungry. For food. Shifting affects me that way."

"Shifting?" She wrinkled her brow. "Is that what you call it when you change?"

"Yes. I'm a shape-shifter."

She was silent for a moment. When she raised her eyes to his, the anger was gone. He wasn't sure he could name the emotions that replaced it. There was a healthy dose of understandable confusion, but he thought he could see acceptance. Of what, he wasn't sure. His shifter self? Or of *them*?

"Take a shower. The security guards have spare uniforms. I'll see if I can find something to fit you.

Although—" there was that blush again "—you are very big. Then we'll go down to the kitchen. You can talk while you eat."

Khan had already eaten the remains of a cold chicken, a quiche and a bowl of potato salad. He had washed this feast down with a half quart of milk. Now he was prowling the kitchen, opening cupboards and regarding Sarange with a look of dismay. "No cookies?"

"I don't really eat sweet things."

"Let me guess." He pointed to the chicken carcass. "You'd rather eat the meat than the salad. You like your steak rare. No one ever quite cooks it bloody enough for you, am I right?"

She blinked at him, the hairs on the back of her neck prickling slightly. On one level, it didn't matter how she liked her steak. On another, it was scary that Khan could somehow get inside her head and know that much detail about her.

"Is your special tiger sense telling you that?" *What else is it telling you? Is it telling you who those men—those* werewolves—*are, and what they want with me?*

Khan came to sit on a stool next to her at the counter. "I'm not sure I have a special sense. Maybe it was a lucky guess."

She shook her head. "You're going to have to do better than that."

"I know."

He gazed into space, gathering his thoughts, and she took a moment to study him. The sweatpants and T-shirt she had found were stretched tight over his bulging muscles, and his hair was still damp from the shower. Now that she knew what she was looking for, she could see the tiger in the man. It was there in the tawny tint of his hair, the broad, arrogant nose, the fiery gold eyes. In the lines of his body, she could see the coiled strength of the mighty beast, the long, lithe sinews and the powerful muscles. Most of all, she could see it in his mannerisms. Khan *was* a cat. He was the ultimate rebel. His movements were all stealth and grace.

He was breathtaking, and yet…he was the opposite of everything she had believed she wanted in a man. In the past, she had never admired flashy good looks and strength. She'd have run a mile from a promiscuous narcissist like Khan. So why did it feel like everything, her whole life, her next breath—*who I am*—was wrapped up in this man?

Was that why she had accepted his shape-shifting, if not with ease, at least with composure? Although her mind was still struggling to make sense of what she had seen, she had felt no real surprise or skepticism. Instead there had been a sense of "So *that's* what this is all about."

Yet a man to whom she was attracted—more, this was so much more than straightforward attraction—had changed into a tiger before her eyes. She should be cowering in a corner at least. Probably there should be screaming involved. Sitting next to him, gazing at him as if her whole world hinged on his next breath, was possibly not the most sensible approach to how this night was unfolding.

Sarange had a feeling she had waved goodbye to sensibility around the time she first set eyes on Khan.

"I'm not an expert on the history of shape-shifters." When he turned back to face her, the smile in his eyes undid her. Took everything she was and unraveled it.

Sarangerel Tsedev came apart and became…just his. "You would need to talk to Ged if you want an in-depth analysis."

"I want to know about you. Anyone else can wait. Start by explaining what you meant when you said you are a shape-shifter."

"It means I can take on the physical form of an animal while maintaining my human consciousness." He regarded her warily, as though unsure of her reaction.

"Can you do it any time you want?"

Khan nodded.

"But you control it? It doesn't just happen without warning?"

Another nod.

"Can you become any animal you choose?"

"No, I'm a weretiger. My DNA is part human, part tiger." There was a note of pride in his voice. "With an extra shifter-something thrown in for good measure."

"Were you born this way?" She had so many questions, but no uncertainty. He was telling the truth. Even if she hadn't seen the evidence for herself, she would know it.

He pulled in a long, slow breath. "Most shifters are born with their abilities. Rarely, they are converts. That means they are turned by a bite. It can happen in conflict. If a shifter leaves a victim close to death but still alive, that person will himself become a shifter."

"Like the horror stories of werewolves?" Sarange thought of the movies that had scared her when she first came to America. Although nothing could have prepared her for the scene that had played out in her bedroom a few hours ago.

"Exactly. It's a big responsibility. But shifters living

in the human world are peaceful. Conflict is rare. The other way a human can convert is voluntarily."

"Really?" Sarange couldn't imagine a situation in which that would happen. "Do you guys hold recruitment drives?"

He laughed. "No. When a human falls in love with a shifter, he, or she, might choose to take the bite of his mate." *Ah.* A little bit of electricity crackled through the air briefly. "But I believe I was born a shifter."

"You believe it? That sounds like you don't know."

"I don't." He was on his feet again. Restless, noiseless, stealthy. Opening the blinds to peer out at the darkened yard. Rearranging the utensils on the rack. Taking the knives from the block and testing their sharpness against his thumb. "I don't know anything about my early life."

Sarange slid from her perch on the high stool and went to him. Standing close, she reached up a hand and ran it through the thick mass of his almost-dry hair.

Khan ducked his head, pushing back against her touch, a smile curving his lips. "I know what you're doing."

"You do?" She hadn't thought about what she was doing. Had just acted on impulse to try and soothe him.

"You're stroking me."

"So I am." She continued the movement, pushing her fingers through his hair, watching in fascination as he visibly relaxed.

"Just so you know—" his voice was almost a purr "—catnip doesn't work."

She laughed. "I'm glad you told me." She looked into those incredible eyes. "Can you talk about it?"

He hunched a shoulder in a half shrug. "There isn't

much to talk about. I was rescued from captivity by Ged about ten years ago. I can't remember anything before that. I don't even know exactly how I came to be captured."

As he spoke, every part of his body tensed once more. She could hear the pain in his words, felt each one being dragged out of him. "I know Ged is you manager, but what else does he do?"

Without knowing it, she had found the right question. At the mention of his manager's name, Khan relaxed. "Did you ever read the stories of the Scarlet Pimpernel?"

Sarange wasn't sure where this was going, but she nodded. "He was the fictional hero who rescued French aristocrats before they could be sent to the guillotine. He pretended to be a bumbling Englishman, but in reality, he was a quick-thinking escape artist."

"Ged is the shifter version of the Scarlet Pimpernel," Khan said. "By day he is long-suffering rock star manager Ged Taverner. By night he is a werebear who rescues shifters from danger."

Sarange shook her head in an attempt to clear it. "This night keeps getting stranger." There were still so many questions that needed answers. She decided to start with the obvious. "Those men who came into the house earlier? They were also shifters. Do you know who they are?"

"No. They are werewolves, but I've never seen them before. I didn't manage to catch up with them to find out why they were here, but they'll be back. It's the wolf way. Tenacity is in their blood. Once they have a mission, they won't give up." His eyes scanned her face as though seeking a response.

What do you want from me, Khan? I know nothing about werewolves, but you're looking at me as though I have the answer. I don't even know the question.

"And now that they know what they're up against, they'll reinforce the pack."

Sarange cast a scared look over her shoulder. "What shall we do? They'll tear my human security guards apart."

Khan stretched his arms above his head. "Right now? We'll get some sleep. They'll need time to regroup. Wolves don't do anything spontaneously." His smile managed to reassure her and heat her blood at the same time. "Tomorrow we'll bring in a few reinforcements of our own."

While Sarange slept, Khan walked the house and grounds, learning the layout. Getting to know his territory. He had napped briefly, but he was conscious of danger nearby, threatening his mate.

Tigers don't mate for life.

It was an insistent little voice in his head, warning him to keep his distance. He didn't need any more warnings. This whole situation couldn't get any more screwed up. He was a shifter who couldn't remember anything prior to his rescue ten years ago. Sarange didn't even know she was a shifter. To make things worse, they were from different species. Just about as opposite as two beings could get. Unfortunately, no one had told their raging hormones about the obstacles. The instincts drawing them together were stronger than anything driving them apart. *As if we were free to mate and be together for life.* The thought caught him hard in the chest, knocking the breath from the lungs. It wasn't a good idea to indulge in *if only*. And at some point, he was going to have to tell Sarange that. How the hell he was going to begin *that* conversation, he had no idea.

Tigers don't mate for life, but shifters do.

That was the problem. Now that they'd found each other, he had a feeling there would never be anyone else. For either of them. How do you tell a werewolf, who doesn't know she's a werewolf, that she can't mate with a tiger? Those cute internet pictures of domestic cats and dogs snuggling up together? Not the same thing as lifelong mates. Lions and hyenas? Leopards and jackals? Tigers and wolves? It didn't happen.

Oh, hell. I need Ged here. This is a halfway-down-the-second-bottle conversation.

Luckily, Ged was on his way. When it came to reinforcements, there was only one group of people Khan trusted. Beast members bickered their way around the world. Their competing egos didn't allow for true friendship. Khan knew he was a big part of why that was true. Put a tiger at the center of any group and the grandest of the big cats was always going to stake his leadership claim. Khan shook his head. The idea that he would ever back down and let anyone else take his place was so ridiculous it wasn't worth considering.

There were other big, alpha male personalities in the band. The next fight was always only a snarl away. The peacekeepers—Ged and Torque—had their work cut out, particularly when Khan and Diablo clashed. But when it mattered? Khan would trust his bandmates with his life.

"Let me get this straight." Ged was used to getting "bail me out" calls from Khan at any hour of the day or night. Even so, his voice had been a sleepy rumble.

"We were due to fly back to New York at noon. Now you want us to change our plans. Instead of working on the new album, we're going to move into Sarange's house and take an extended vacation while we do body-guard duty."

"There are plenty of recording studios in Los Angeles," Khan had said. "We don't have to stop working."

Just as Khan had known he would, Ged had agreed. Because that was how it worked. No questions, no explanations, no protests. His friends—because that was the closest word he could find to describe what they were—would have his back. And when the time came, Khan would do the same for them. When Ged brought Beast together, they had been a collection of lost and damaged souls. Each of them had a horrific story to tell. Joining the band had been their rehabilitation. Maybe it was their redemption.

As Khan walked through the grounds in the early morning light, the foul werewolf stench of the intruders lingered. It was strange how that worked. Khan hated the smell of werewolves. Even in their human form, he could barely stand to be in the same room with them. He had built up a sort of immunity to the scent of his bandmate Finglas. He could tolerate his aroma, without liking it. Almost as if the guy wore an obnoxious cologne. So why was it that Sarange smelled like the sweetest thing in the world? She was a werewolf. Khan should detest her scent. Instead, he couldn't get enough of her. He wanted to nuzzle her, sniff her skin, lick her all over...

He looked up at the balcony that led to her room, picturing her asleep in that big, ridiculously opulent bed. He couldn't help the leap of joy his heart gave every time he thought of her. Dogs and cats. Had there ever been a time in the past? Could the first time be now?

Those werewolves had come after Sarange for a reason. Why now? What was going on in her life right now that meant four werewolves wanted to abduct her? Diablo would sneer at Khan's first thought.

"The world does not revolve around you, Tiger Boy." It was Diablo's favorite phrase.

Diablo was wrong, of course. And Khan delighted in telling him so. "Try telling the world that."

Right now, when he was examining what was happening to Sarange, Khan's entry into her life was one thing that could have triggered the werewolf attack. Why? He had no idea. He was simply considering the possibilities.

The only other things he could think of were the Animals Alive campaign and Sarange's determination to save the blue wolves. Again, when it came to trying to establish a link between either of those things and the intruders, Khan came up with a big, fat nothing.

He was tired of thinking. It was still early. The world wasn't fully awake. There was only one place he wanted to be. Up close to Sarange. Pressed so tight against her even a sliver of light couldn't get between them. That sounded like a plan. Breaking into a loping run, he retraced his steps back to the house.

Chapter 6

Sarange had given orders to her housekeeper, Henry, about rooms and food, and requested that Marco liaise with the manager of the gated community about the tour bus. People always assumed that she was a loner, but that wasn't her choice. Sarange liked having others around her. Being alone was just the way her life had worked out.

Having Beast around? That was going to take some getting used to. It was like her cool, luxurious home had been turned into a snow globe. Shaken up, it was now a blur of noise and color. In addition to Khan, there were now five other big, muscular men taking up every corner of her space. They had been there half a day and she was already tripping over guitars, boots, jackets, empty take-out boxes and beer bottles. They didn't seek each other out to have a conversation. They yelled from one end of the house to the other. And they spoke in a strange shorthand only they understood. One minute they were snickering at jokes no one else was part of. The next, they were exploding with rage over an imagined slight.

"We are an acquired taste." Torque, the lead guitarist, smiled at her with sympathy in his unusual eyes. Just when she thought they were dull and gray, they appeared to change color, reminding her of opals as they shimmered with iridescent light.

"After what's happened over the last few days, I'm happy to acquire it."

It was true. She'd take noise and mess if they brought her safety…and Khan. Although she still wasn't sure what benefits Beast brought over a team of security guards. Khan had admitted that Ged was a shifter. Did that mean…? She cast a sidelong glance in Torque's direction. If he was a shifter, she couldn't figure him out. What was his alter ego? Something with quicksilver movements and lightning reflexes.

"Dragon."

"Pardon?"

"That's what you were wondering, isn't it? I'm a weredragon." Torque grinned at her dumbfounded expression. "But don't worry, I promise not to burn your house down."

She was still wondering if he was joking when Khan called the band together in the sitting room, outlining why they were there. He turned to Finglas. "Have you heard anything about these guys?"

Finglas gave a long-suffering sigh. "You say that as though I hang out in werewolf bars, or I have wolf informants." Khan frowned and Finglas held up a hand in a gesture of peace. "No, I don't know anything about these guys. But werewolves who are prepared to draw attention to themselves by going on the attack? That's not normal." He turned to Sarange. "And they all looked alike?"

"Identical. Their hair was a medium brown color, their eyes were light—sort of a golden brown—and they all had the same features. I got a good look at them. Both times."

"And they're not a pack you know?"

Sarange frowned at the strangeness of the question. A pack she knew? Just how many werewolves did he think she was familiar with? Being a lycanthrope himself, Finglas possibly thought everyone had shape-shifter acquaintances. Before she could answer, Khan took the conversation in a different direction.

"These guys didn't come here to rob or kill Sarange. They were trying to abduct her. Someone wants her. I brought you here to protect her, but I need to find out who that someone is."

"That's a dangerous move." Ged's deep, calm voice held a warning note. "If you want information, it means when they come back we have to keep at least one of them alive. Even then, getting a werewolf to betray his leader won't be easy. A wolf's loyalty is second only to its stubbornness."

"Ahem. Wolf in the room." Finglas quirked a brow in Sarange's direction. "Two wolves, actually."

Okay, this was getting seriously weird. She decided it was time to call him on the implication that she was a werewolf. "What do you mean by that?"

Finglas regarded her with something that looked a

lot like amazement. Before he could speak, Ged's placid voice intervened. "Can we get back to the logistics?"

Ged's apologetic smile to Sarange took the heat out of the way he'd redirected the conversation away from her question. She supposed he was right. Keeping them out of danger was more important than her vague feeling of unease about Finglas's strange comments. Finglas was a werewolf. Maybe they were all eccentric. How would she know? He was the first one she had met.

"The werewolves have been here twice. Both times in a group of four. That's a small pack, but they were expecting to come up against only human bodyguards. Now they know there's a tiger waiting for them. They'll rethink their strategy, but they won't be deterred."

"They should be." Khan's lip curled.

Ged shook his head. "You know that's not the werewolf way. They will be wary of facing a tiger, but they won't back down. Werewolves will see their task through to the end. They will sacrifice a few foot soldiers for the sake of the mission."

"You mean they'll be happy to throw a few werewolves to Khan as a distraction while the others focus on Sarange?" Torque said.

"Exactly." Khan's golden gaze was fierce as he looked around the room at his bandmates. "I'm relying on you to make sure they don't get as far as Sarange."

Diablo yawned. "We can take a few werewolves."

The feeling that she had stepped into an alternate reality was growing stronger by the second. Her ordered world had become a place of danger and she had no idea how or why it had happened. Now her elegant sitting room was filled with shifters who were calmly discussing how to kill werewolves. *But let's not forget the im-*

*portance of keeping at least one alive. You know, just so
we can find out who is behind this plot to abduct me...*

Could she have somehow, in the last few days, drifted into a nightmare from which she hadn't woken? That was how this felt. That curious dream-state feeling that everything was the same, yet *different*. That she had changed. That dreaming Sarange and waking Sarange inhabited the same body at the same time, but had separate experiences. All the time, there was something important that was being hidden from both parts of her psyche.

Right now she needed time to breathe and think... and she needed the answer to one very important question.

"I need to talk to you." From Sarange's troubled expression, Khan could guess what this was about. *Damn.* He should have known Finglas would say something. It was his own fault for not warning the others in advance.

She left the room and he waited until the door closed behind her. "This is going to sound strange, but she doesn't know she's a werewolf."

Finglas choked on the soda he had been drinking. "You're joking, right?"

Khan sighed. "No. She genuinely has no idea."

"We all know what trauma feels like. It affects every shifter in a different way. Until we know Sarange's story, we can't understand what made her this way." Ged placed a hand on Khan's shoulder. "Just go easy on her. Take it slow."

Khan's smile was rueful. "You think I can't do sensitive?"

"I think you're a tiger."

He found Sarange in her bedroom, pacing the length of the patterned rug. She paused when he entered the room, turning to face him, and he got the feeling she wanted to throw herself into his arms. It was more than a feeling. It was a certainty, based on a memory deep in his heart and his muscles. He even braced himself for the impact of her weight against him.

But she held back. "What's going on? Why does Finglas think I'm a werewolf?"

Because you are. He took her hands in his, feeling the quiver that ran through her body, and drew her down to sit next to him on the bed. "I guess he's wondering why you are being pursued by werewolves."

"That's a mighty big leap. I'm not in denial about the existence of werewolves. I saw them with my own eyes. But what you're suggesting doesn't make sense. Werewolves are after me, so I must be one myself?"

"It makes more sense to a shifter."

She leaned her head against his shoulder, seeming to take comfort from his nearness, and the depth of his responsibility to her hit Khan full force. It was a new sensation for him. New, but not unknown. How did that work? He wasn't sure, he only knew it was tied into his complex feelings for this woman. He was a loner. He walked away from caring, but he would never walk away from Sarange.

After a few minutes, she raised her head. Those unusual eyes were so ice-chip light, they should have appeared cold. Instead, they conveyed a strength of emotion that swept him up and dragged him under. "You can protect me physically, but I need the truth from you."

"What do you want to know?"

"When we first met, you called me 'wolf girl.' Did *you* think I was a werewolf?"

Go easy on her. Take it slow. Ged's words hadn't allowed for an out-and-out question. "Yes."

Her eyelids fluttered closed and he caught her tight against him. To hell with cats and dogs. If there was ever only one moment in his life that mattered, this was it. Holding Sarange in his arms as if he would never let her go. Showing her with his strength and his body how much he needed her. Encircling her. Keeping her warm and safe until the trembling in her limbs subsided.

"Why? What made you think that?" The whispered words left his heart raw and bleeding.

"Shifters know other shifters. We recognize each other."

"Could you be wrong?"

"There's always that chance."

She tilted her face up to look at him, her eyes widening. "You don't think you're wrong."

He didn't respond. Instead, he lay on the bed, drawing her down to lie next to him. "Tell me about your early life."

Sarange nestled into his side. "I don't talk about it when I give interviews because it sounds too much like a fairy tale. I was found by a shaman when I was a few days old, wrapped in a reindeer hide, miles from civilization."

"A shaman? Is that a wise man?"

"In this case a wise woman, a shamanka. In Mongolia, shamanism is widely practiced and known as Tengerism. The shaman are the intermediaries between the visible world and the hidden realm of the spirits. The shamanka who found me was a member of a nomadic tribe. She had left her people briefly to be alone and commune with the spirits."

Khan couldn't see her face, but he could hear the warmth in her voice.

"Her name, the closest you can get in Western words, was Golden Wing. I called her Grandmother. My childhood was spent as part of the tribe, traveling the snow-packed tundra, caring for the reindeer, goats and sheep."

"That's a long way from LA."

She laughed. "When I reached my teens, Golden Wing announced one day that she had family in California. Although emigration from Mongolia had become more common, and my grandmother had insisted on educating me, America was like a distant dream. But it was a dream that came true. While I was here, my American family recognized my singing ability and I auditioned for a TV talent show. The rest, as they say, is history."

"And your grandmother?"

Sarange was silent for a moment. "Golden Wing died not long after I came to America. I was heartbroken that I wasn't with her at the end. I'll always wonder if she knew she was ill and perhaps sent me here to start a new life. The relatives I was staying with adopted me. They were her relatives, not mine, of course. I have no idea who my birth family is." She seemed to shake off the introspective mood. "It doesn't matter. My aunt and uncle Tsedev are my *real* family."

"Have you been back to Mongolia?" She was right, it did sound a lot like a fairy tale.

"Only once. It felt different. Like I was going back as a tourist instead of as little Sarangerel, the girl who rose at dawn and milked the goats."

If she was a werewolf, she'd have been little Sarangerel, the girl who rose at dawn to *eat* the goats. Khan decided not to break the mood by mentioning that. "You should take a backpack. Do it the hard way."

She leaned her chin on his chest. "Like you would?" Her eyes were teasing. "Mr. Hedonism?"

He lifted her so she lay on top of him, wrapping his arms tight around her waist as she squirmed in his hold. Letting her feel the aching length of his erection against the softness of her stomach. One slender thigh slipped between his, and she stilled, sensing the change in his mood.

A tiny gasp escaped her. "This is the reason you haven't made love to me."

Khan tangled his hand in her hair, tilting her head to his. "There are many reasons. None of them have anything to do with not wanting you."

Her lower lip trembled. "No matter how much you want me, you can't change who we are. If you're correct about me, I'm the last person in the world you should want. I'm not even the right species."

Khan muttered a curse, sliding a hand behind her head and bringing her lips down to his. "Who cares about right when wrong feels like it was meant to be?"

As soon as Khan kissed her, moving his big, warm hands beneath her T-shirt and up her spine, arousal slammed into Sarange with all the force of a freight train. It was a need unlike anything she had ever known, so powerful it should have scared her. Instead, it excited her. Made her picture experiences beyond her previous imaginings. That was what Khan had done to her. Flung her past the outer limits of her curiosity.

The images that filled her head were so incredibly explicit that it was hard to believe she had never been intimate with this man. It was as if she knew, in erotic detail, how it would be between them. As though her body and mind were working together with perfect sensual timing. Her nipples tightened and her sex heated as her inner muscles clenched in expectation.

When Khan lifted his head to study her face, his golden eyes were glazed with lust and uncertainty. "This affinity between us… I've never felt anything like it before."

Sarange liked that she wasn't the only one feeling thrown off balance. His eyes burned into her, telling her everything she needed to know about his need for her. Her world had been tilted wildly off course, but clinging to Khan was what she wanted. His touch, his warmth, his kisses, they were the only things that made any sense. Emotion blossomed deep within her. Certainty came in its wake. This feeling. This knowledge that Khan was everything, that being with him was her whole life…it was a bone-deep commitment, stronger than a vow.

Passion was an electrical current in the air between them, in and around their bodies. Sarange raised her hands above her head, allowing Khan to pull her T-shirt over her head. "That's because your soul already knows me." The words resonated through them both. She had the strangest feeling of them lighting up time and space like a string of fairy lights illuminating a path to bring them together.

When he kissed her again, the connection tingled all over her body as if a spell was cast with each touch.

Pulling him closer, she tasted his lips, his mouth and his tongue, wanting more each time.

As he removed her bra she squirmed, pressing her legs tight together to relieve the ache between them. Khan's hands roamed over her exposed flesh as his mouth swooped down on her nipple. It ignited a fire through her bloodstream.

"I want to make you feel so many things." His voice was hoarse as his lips moved to her other breast. He turned her so she lay on her back as his hands moved swiftly to undo her jeans. "So many different ways I want to make you scream." Her jeans were thrown to the floor with her underwear quickly following. "Would you like that, Sarange? Do you want me to make you scream?" He laughed as he lowered his head and nipped the sensitive flesh of her breast again. "Or howl?"

Even though the idea that she could be a werewolf hadn't fully taken hold in her mind, that single word made her surge against him. Still fully clothed, Khan inched down the bed.

"Open your legs for me."

Slowly, Sarange parted her knees. Khan moved into place between them, spreading her thighs farther apart with his broad shoulders. His fingers slid up and down her crease, opening her to his gaze.

"So pretty. Pink and wet. Just perfect" He lapped her center in a single lick. The slightly rough texture of his tongue was delicious, making her gasp and shudder.

Khan circled her opening with the tip of his tongue. "I already knew how you'd taste. The sweetest flavor in the world." He plunged deep and she cried out, grasping his hair in both hands.

Replacing his tongue with two fingers, he moved

his mouth up to concentrate on her clit. With his other hand, he circled one hard nipple with a fingertip before squeezing the tight flesh in time with the thrust of his fingers.

Incoherent sounds escaped Sarange's lips as she clutched his hair tighter, shaking and thrusting her hips toward his mouth. Her inner muscles gripped him hard and her thighs began to tremble as her body sought its release. Khan nipped at her nub with his teeth as his fingers curled up, finding the sweet spot inside her and triggering spasms of pleasure that rippled out of control. The fire in her blood flared to new heights and her whole body began to vibrate.

"Khan…"

Her hands moved to his shoulders, clawing at his smooth flesh as every muscle tightened with shards of diamond-bright pleasure. And as she arched off the bed, the sound that left her lips *was* a lot like a howl. The climax that roared through her was the most exquisite torture she had ever experienced. And it went on and on as Khan kept his mouth on her, licking in time with the shudders that shook her, slowing gradually until she reached a standstill.

He moved to lie next to her, smoothing her hair back from her face.

Sarange sighed. "That was…"

"Amazing?" His grin was pure Khan. "Felt that way for me, too."

The look in his eyes started a slow burn deep in her core all over again. "Do you have a condom?" she asked.

"I'll be right back." He slid from the bed, going to where his luggage—delivered by his bandmates earlier—was stacked near the closet.

When he returned, he shrugged quickly out of his clothes. Sarange's breath caught in her throat. Khan was always magnificent, and she had glimpsed him naked when he returned from his pursuit of the wolves, but now...

She raised her arms to him. "Come to me, my tiger."

Khan lay on the bed next to Sarange. *Come to me, my tiger.* He wouldn't have believed it was possible to want her more. Yet, as soon as she uttered those words, they thrilled through him, spiking his desire even higher. As if they had a meaning beyond what she said. A code that spoke directly to his nerve endings. When Khan kissed her, it started out soft and persuasive. He parted her lips with his tongue, entering her mouth with gentle licks. When Sarange returned his caress, the slow start was soon transformed into plunging thrusts as their tongues met and twirled together.

"I need to touch you." Sarange's eyelids drooped as she studied him. "All over."

Her fingertips left surface-of-the-sun heat trails as they danced over the muscled ridges of his abdomen. Tracing up his biceps, over his shoulders, and around his back, she dropped around to run her hands over his taut ass. His muscles tightened and trembled as though shot through with electricity. The anticipation of her touch hadn't come close to the reality. His mind was shutting down, handing him over completely to sensation.

Returning to the front of his body, Sarange reached for his straining cock and ran a finger lightly around the head. Khan hissed. It was the only sound he was capable of making.

She moved her mouth to his collarbone, nipping

lightly, seeming to know that was his most sensitive place. Encircling his shaft, she gripped the base before slowly stroking his length.

"Feels good." Khan managed to get the words out through gritted teeth.

"That's what I want. I want to make you feel good." Her eyes were on his face, watching his reaction to her touch.

How could he explain that "good" didn't come close to explaining how she made him feel? That everything else faded into nothingness in contrast to this? Even being on stage, the one thing in his life that had felt real and true, became meaningless compared to Sarange.

Her hand on him was too much, and he placed his own fingers over hers, stilling her movements.

"Condom," he explained hoarsely, glad he was still capable of rational thought.

When the protection was in place, he moved in position between her thighs. He studied Sarange's face, exulting in how she looked in that moment, eyes half-closed, cheeks flushed, lips parted. He rubbed himself against her, up and down, and her head fell back.

"Look at me." His words were slurred with desire.

Sarange lifted her head, giving him back the eye contact he needed. For an instant, he held her there. Their gazes caught and locked as if a pause button had been pressed on time and space.

Then Khan lowered his eyes and watched the point where their bodies met as he pushed into her. The sensations powering through him were extraordinary. Forget the legends. Nothing had prepared him for this. It was a bond like no other.

"Sarange." He threw his head back, feeling his connection to her in every part of him. Mind, body and soul.

Sarange was trembling all over. Her hands tightly grasped his upper arms, her teeth gripped her lower lip and her breath was coming in shallow gasps.

He paused, regarding her with concern. "Is this okay?"

"Don't stop." She lifted her hips, urging him to continue. "Please…"

He inched inside her a little more, halfway into her. He could feel her stretching to take him. His neck and shoulder muscles strained with the effort of holding back from pounding hard and fast. The feeling of driving slowly into tight heat was too delicious to rush. It was like a warm memory and he wanted to savor every second.

As his feelings threatened to overcome him, he took a couple of deep breaths. Looking back at where their bodies joined, he pushed forward once more. Sarange arched her back, surging up to meet him.

"You're so big."

With a final thrust, Khan seated himself all the way to the hilt. "Too big?" He growled…because growling seemed to be all he was capable of doing.

She tossed her head from side to side on the pillow. "Just perfect."

He tried to go slow, starting out by pumping in and out, adding a roll to his hips that had Sarange grinding her pelvis against him. But slow wouldn't quench the fire that was raging out of control between them. It was as though this need had been burning his whole life. He picked up the pace, thrusting deep, feeling her body clench around him.

Pulling his hips back, he drew his shaft through the tight grip of her inner muscles, paused a beat, then thrust hard once more. Sarange shook wildly. Her vaginal walls clasped him and her eyelids fluttered closed. He felt the moment her orgasm gripped her, held her suspended in time before tipping her over into violent, whole-body shaking pleasure.

Khan continued to thrust into her, taking her harder, using the aftershocks of her climax to increase her pleasure.

"Khan…" In that second, as he stared at her, something more than their gazes locked and something beyond their bodies connected. Two more deep, hard penetrations and fire streaked along his spine. He came so hard it felt like his heart was exploding. At the same time, a tightness inside him unfurled. The darkness that had been part of him for a very long time just got lighter.

He purred his pleasure deep in his throat, holding on to Sarange like he was never going to let her go. As he waited for the world to stop spinning, he wondered if he ever *could* find the strength to release her. Because finding Sarange had been like finding a missing part of himself. The image wasn't yet complete, but every second he spent with her added a tiny piece to the overall picture that was Khan.

Chapter 7

Sarange didn't recognize this version of herself. Letting another person into her life and her heart was a new experience, one that contrasted with everything that had gone before. She didn't know why the fear of loss was so strong inside her. Maybe it was because of her abandonment as a baby, although she questioned if that could be true. All she knew for sure was that she had always backed off from intimacy. It was a simple formula, one that had worked well until now. If she didn't let anyone get close, she couldn't get hurt.

There were other reasons why this was out of character. She had a house full of guests. That brought responsibility. Sarange was good at duty, organization, order. Yet she had abandoned all those things to lie in Khan's arms. Wrapped in their own world, here in her room, in her bed. The rest of the world had faded away. And she was *enjoying* it.

She didn't care that those people downstairs—his bandmates, her staff—would think of her as a horrible hostess. That they would raise their brows and exchange knowing glances about her and Khan. All that mattered was his chest beneath her cheek, his fingertips tracing her spine and the occasional rumble of his laughter when they spoke. They didn't speak much.

In between talking and touching, there was plenty of time for thinking, but her mind seemed to have been infused with the same soporific effects as her body. Her adrenaline levels should have been sky high. Right about now she should have been running for the hills, or calling the police. Not only did she have four werewolves on her tail, she also had a weretiger in her bed. And he was trying to convince her that she was a werewolf herself.

Surely the last thing she should be doing right now was indulging in delicious, toe-curling, sheet-ripping sex with the aforementioned big cat? The thought made her bite back a smile. What had Khan said? Right and wrong didn't matter when it was meant to be. It was crazy, but true. The wildest, most impossible series of events had brought her into his arms. Yet, in this instant, within the protective mantle of Khan's embrace was where she belonged.

Being with him seemed to have unleashed an inner self she hadn't known existed. There was a wild side to her that she didn't recognize, but it was one she definitely liked. And it was as if a cache of hidden memories was waiting just out of reach. *But why would I have hidden memories?* Unlike Khan, Sarange knew who she was. She remembered everything about her life.

This sense of not knowing herself, this new duality, bothered her more than the idea that she might be a werewolf. Or were the two things entwined? Was it possible that the perception of being two people was because she *was*? Without knowing it, could she be the person she had always known…and a werewolf?

Surely, I would know? I don't feel any burning desire to howl at the moon. I have never met anyone and longed to rip out their throat. I don't even like red meat…

And yet there was the affinity she felt to the blue wolves. It was overwhelming. From the first time she had heard about them, their plight touched her more than any other animal she had heard of. She even dreamed of them. Sarange was an animal rights campaigner. It was her life. Yet that remote wolf pack had called to something deep within her.

She sat up abruptly, hugging her knees up to her chin. "The blue wolves."

Khan frowned. Lazily, he tugged the comforter around his waist as he moved into a reclining position against the headboard. "You think that's who these werewolves are?"

"No." Sarange was thinking out loud, trying to clear her head of a jumble of thoughts that were only half-formed. "The blue wolves are a small pack, a subspecies of the Mongolian gray wolves. They are unusual because of their blue eyes. True wolves shouldn't have blue eyes. It's thought to be a genetic mutation unique to this pack." She turned her head to look at him. "There is no longer one single idea of what it means to have traditional Mongolian coloring, but in my tribe when I was growing up, I was considered unusual because of my blue eyes."

"You have blue eyes. So do they. It's a tenuous link at best."

"I agree…if that was all. But it's more about what I feel. Here." She pressed a fist to her chest. "When I heard that the blue wolves were in danger of dying out, it became an obsession with me to do something to save them. I've always felt strongly about helping endangered animals, probably because of Golden Wing and the tradition in which she raised me. Shamanism is animalistic. Her belief was that, in the spirit community, all beings are equal. Humans are not greater than other creatures."

"Who told you that the blue wolves were at risk?" Sarange had noticed that expression in Khan's eyes before. It was his tiger look. He appeared lazy and unconcerned, but there was razor-sharp concentration in those golden depths.

"My aunt Gerel. I think she has some shaman tendencies, although, having embraced a Western lifestyle, she keeps them hidden. When I was approached by Radin to make a wildlife documentary in Mongolia, naturally I wanted it to be about the blue wolves. You met him when we discussed the documentary. He owns Real Planet, the production company that came up with the original proposal. Radin is the creative brain behind the operation. As I told you, he changed his mind and wanted you and me to work on the program together when the rumors started about our relationship. Getting us together was a money spinner."

"It seems to me we need to find out more about the blue wolves."

"We need to speak to my uncle Bek." Although the man who had adopted her when Golden Wing died had lived in America for most of his adult life, he was an expert on the history and culture of his home country. "Right now."

Khan's hand on her wrist stopped her from jumping up there and then. When Sarange raised a questioning brow, he nodded toward the open balcony door. The light was already fading. "The werewolves will come back under the cover of darkness."

"If I'm a werewolf, I should be able to fight alongside you." Sarange's expression was stubborn as she faced Khan. Wolf determination was etched in every line of her body. It shook him all over again that she could have reached adulthood not knowing who she was.

They had eaten dinner with the rest of the band. Ignoring Marco's objections, Sarange had given her human security team the night off. Khan didn't want any witnesses to what was about to happen. Now he was organizing where everyone should be in readiness for the inevitable werewolf attack. The only problem was Sarange. She had decided she didn't want to return to her bedroom and wait there while Khan and his bandmates confronted the intruders.

"That argument is flawed on so many levels." He tried not to sound patronizing. This was her house. She was the person in danger. He didn't want to take the decision-making away from her. Okay, that wasn't true. He *did* want to take over. He wanted to wrap her up and keep her safe from harm. Forever. But he already knew Sarange well enough to be aware that a display of alpha-maleness from him wouldn't go down well with her. "You've only just discovered you may be a werewolf. You aren't even half convinced it's true. Suppose it is. You have no idea how to shift into your wolf form, do you?"

She drew herself up to her full height, opening her mouth as she appeared about to voice a protest. Under his probing gaze, she subsided. "No."

"Take the whole thing to the extreme. Imagine what would happen if you did face a pack of experienced werewolf fighters alongside an experienced group of shifters. Even supposing at the last minute you discovered your own ability to shift, do you believe you would also find a hidden talent for fighting to the death at the same time?"

Sarange huffed out a breath. "Well, when you put it like that…"

He gripped her shoulders, drawing her closer. "I know how hard it is for you to hand this over to others."

"Do you? How is that?" Her gaze scanned his face, and there was a tremor of fear in her voice. "It's true, but how do you understand me so well, Khan? And how do I know you like I know myself?"

He wasn't sure telling her what he knew would be helpful. After a brief debate with himself, he decided *not* telling her would be unfair. "There is a belief in shifter legend that there is one mate for each of us. That we are fated to meet that person and be together for life."

"You think that's what has happened to us?" Her brow wrinkled. "But how could that be true of us? You are a weretiger. If you're right about me, I'm a werewolf. I may be new to your world, but I'm guessing that puts us at opposite ends of your shifter spectrum. We can't be together forever. We may not be at elephant and mice incompatibility levels, but we're not far from it."

Khan started to laugh. "Elephants and mice?"

"You're picturing it, aren't you?"

Sarange was trying to keep her voice stern, but he could see the smile in her eyes.

"Admit it. It would be quite a love story," he said.

She allowed a chuckle to escape, but shook her head. "I need you to focus your cat attention span back on us. What you said about mates would explain the attraction we feel. It wouldn't explain the other things."

She was right, of course. He knew what she was going to say, but he couldn't give her any answers. He could probably throw a whole load of more questions back at her.

"When I touch you, it's electric. But why do I feel like it's happened a hundred times before? When I look at you, my pulse races. But why do I feel like you're the missing part of me I never knew I'd lost? My lips say the words. *We shouldn't be together. You're a tiger. I'm a wolf*...apparently. But my heart doesn't listen, because my soul knows different."

What she was saying resonated deep inside him. Khan didn't want to leave her and go into a fight. His mind and body were still reeling from the effects of their lovemaking, of a connection that had taken them beyond anything physical. He had known the moment he first saw Sarange that they had a unique bond, but sex had elevated it to a whole new level. And she was right. There was a mysterious sense of *knowing*. Could they have been together before in another life? He was a shifter. He had to open his mind to the mysteries of the universe, but that idea took some getting used to. And there were other problems to deal with right now. Problems that had teeth, claws and came in a pack.

He pressed his lips to her temple. "I don't know. All I know is I feel the same. And maybe when these werewolves come back, we'll get some answers." He tilted her chin up so he could scan her face. "Promise me you'll stay here. That way I can focus on them without worrying about your safety."

She nodded. "How lucky was I that you came into my life at just the right time? When these werewolves appeared and attacked me, I had you here to protect me."

"Or we could look at it another way." Her brow furrowed in confusion as he voiced the thought that had been troubling him. "Just after I came into your life, a group of werewolves turned up and tried to abduct you. Was it a lucky chance that I arrived in time to take care of you? Or was I the trigger for their attack?"

Sarange might have agreed to stay in her room, but Khan hadn't said anything about not watching the action. From her balcony, she had a good view of most of the grounds at the rear of the house. If the werewolves wanted her, this was the way they would have to approach her suite.

When she had bought this property, it felt like a dream come true. And yet…part of her still missed the wide-open spaces and freedom of her childhood. A land where everything, as far as the eye could see, was untouched. Living in a gated community with bodyguards, alarms and security cameras often felt alien and restrictive. It closed her down from friendships and even acquaintances. Sarange liked people—*is that because I'm a werewolf, a pack animal?*—and being a celebrity could be a lonely life. She had her aunt and uncle, of course. They were more than her family, they were her link with Mongolia and her past life.

For the first time, she wondered how much of her fairy-tale life had happened by chance. Could Golden Wing have foreseen this future for her? Even arranged it? The thought was foolish. How could a lone shamanka, all those thousands of miles away, have so much influence that she could shape the future? Sarange was growing fanciful, her mind making connections that didn't exist. There were enough strange things happening without the need to invent more.

In the moonlight below her, Khan was a shadowy figure prowling the darkened yard. The security lights, triggered to activate at the first sign of movement, had been disabled. She knew the other members of Beast were deployed at strategic points around the gardens.

"Let the werewolves get in, surround them, trap them." Khan's instructions had been delivered in a cold, precise voice. There was no trace of the frivolous rock star. He had been a general directing his troops. How did she know he had done that before? *Because I was there.*

More than a military leader directing his men, he was a tiger ordering his dragon, wolf, bear, panther and leopard. The knowledge of who they were was still sinking in. It was surreal. This was Beast, one of the best known bands in the world. Now she knew why they protected their privacy so fiercely, why biographical details about them were so bland. They were hell raisers, but no one knew much about where they went after they partied hard. All that legendary raw energy they brought to a performance? Sarange was seeing for herself, up close, where it came from. On stage, they were five uncaged animals. The effect was eye-watering.

It was a still night, and sound traveled. She could hear traffic in the distance, and a faint breeze rustled the trees. Her hearing had always been good. Did that mean…? *Oh, dear Lord, can I please stop taking every thought back to whether I'm a werewolf?*

Her annoyance spiked and took a sudden nosedive as a new sound caught her attention. Faint, stealthy, unmistakable. Someone—more than one someone—was climbing the outer wall. Her gaze went to Khan as he dropped to a crouch in the shadows below the balcony.

Sarange's eyes strained to count the figures making their way over the manicured lawn. Definitely eight. Possibly ten. Already in wolf form. *Too many.* There were only six people protecting her. Khan had underestimated the opposition.

As the werewolves neared the balcony, the yard beneath her erupted into life. The lack of light meant it was like watching a flickering black-and-white movie, but she could see enough. In addition to the tiger just below her vantage point, she watched two other big cats burst from the shelter of the ornate trees at the far side of the yard. She registered that the muscular black panther who aligned himself with Khan must be Diablo. Silent as a ghost, Dev, now in the form of a huge snow leopard, sharp and white in contrast to the shadows around him, moved into place at Khan's other side.

She couldn't focus on the trio of big cats for long. Not when, from the opposite corner of the house, Torque strode into view, still in human form. Raising his hands, he unleashed a series of explosions in his path. As he walked, he grew in size until he towered over the werewolves and big cats. Even in the darkness, Sarange could see his eyes were bright red, the color filling the entire surface. The pupils had become vertical black slits. He blinked, his top and bottom lids moving in reptilian manner to meet each other.

As Torque broke into a run, the clothes tore from his body. His arm and leg muscles thickened, and he dropped onto all fours, enormous claws the size of a mechanical digger churning up the lawn. Giant wings unfurled, and a spiked tail flicked out before he opened his mouth to shoot a stream of blue-white flame in the direction of the werewolves. Transfixed, Sarange watched as Torque, the most mild-mannered band member, became a fearsome, beautiful dragon. He rose and hovered, his wings spanning most of the house.

Maybe six will be enough. The thought had barely formed when Finglas, a lithe werewolf, and Ged, a huge, majestic bear, appeared. They closed off any avenue of escape. Khan's plan had worked. The werewolves were surrounded.

Some deep-seated instinct told Sarange the werewolves would not retreat. Even when faced with such fearsome opponents, they had a mission, and they would see it through. She could understand that tenacity. It was part of her own makeup.

The moonlit scene quickly became all action. The three big cats bounded forward in one fluid movement of bared teeth and lethal claws. The werewolves, caught unawares, attempted to scatter across the lawn. They weren't fast enough and Khan, Diablo and Dev each caught a werewolf in his mouth or between his paws.

Sarange had expected to be horrified by the brutality of their attack. Maybe it was the unreality of the shadowy scene. Possibly it was because it happened mercifully fast. Blood appeared black as it sprayed up from the throats of the captured werewolves. Movement ceased. The big cats flung the lifeless bodies aside and moved on. She watched it, if not with indifference, with acceptance. With a sense that this was how it had to be. This was the shifter world. It was brutal, but necessary.

Throwing off one of the smaller werewolves as it leaped onto his back, Finglas sank his teeth into the attacker's belly. His victory howl was muted. No need to alert the neighbors.

Surprisingly graceful for such a large animal, Ged bounded into the center of the action, throwing himself into the fray. Landing on the back of one of the startled werewolves, the mighty bear used its lethal claws to tear a chunk of flesh from its victim's neck. The whole time, Torque hovered over the scene, shooting jets of fire at any werewolves who were not directly involved in the fight.

The werewolves rallied. Targeting Khan as though sensing he was in charge, two of them brought him crashing to the ground. With a roar of fury, the huge tiger rose on his hind legs, attempting to shake them off. A swift white streak came to his aid as Dev hurled himself on one of the werewolves, sinking his teeth into its neck and prying it loose from its hold on Khan. Diablo hooked his claws into the other attacker and seconds later the werewolf lay twitching on the patio below where Sarange was standing.

The fight didn't last long. As she watched the conflict unfold, Sarange wondered how she had ever thought the werewolves would win. They were hopelessly out-classed by the superior fighting powers of their opponents. Before long, her beautiful yard was littered with discarded werewolf bodies. It was carnage.

Dropping into a crouch with his teeth bared, Khan patrolled the area. *Keep one of them alive.* That was what he had said. They needed to be able to question one of the werewolves.

Obedient to his leader's command, Finglas dropped one of the werewolves at Khan's feet. Although injured, the werewolf snarled at the huge tiger standing over him. Sarange felt a flicker of unexpected emotion. Was it respect? A sense of pride that a werewolf would dare show defiance to a big cat? It was a fleeting sensation. That werewolf had been sent to abduct her. She might admire his courage, but she couldn't feel any sympathy for him.

Khan subdued the werewolf by placing one huge paw on its back. The fight was over. He shifted back and signaled for his companions to do the same. Six naked men gathered around the injured werewolf.

"Ged and I will take this guy inside and persuade him to shift back."

Even in the moonlight, Sarange could see the way Khan's lips drew back in a snarl to show his gleaming teeth.

"Then I want to talk to him. The rest of you need to clean up out here. Don't leave any trace."

"Do you think we might be able to get dressed before we start?" Dev's cool tones brought a hint of normality to the surreal situation.

Khan gave a snort of laughter. "I guess I can permit that."

Sarange pressed her hands to her cheeks as she stepped back inside the bedroom. The fact that she'd just been watching six magnificent naked men without embarrassment probably wasn't the strangest aspect of this situation. It was simply a measure of how much her life had changed.

Chapter 8

"Are you okay?" Khan moved closer to Sarange, speaking quietly so only she could hear.

"I'm fine." Although she tried to sound convincing, her teeth were doing their best to chatter and her eyes seemed to be open too wide. Surely it was understandable? It wasn't every day there was a bloodstained werewolf lying on the expensive marble tiles of her kitchen floor. "What are you going to do with him?"

Khan glanced down at the werewolf. "He's going to tell us who he's working for."

The werewolf whimpered and flattened his ears, abasing himself on the floor. His show of defiance was over. Sarange knew about animal behavior. He was getting as low as he could in an attempt to show Khan he was no longer a threat.

"What if he doesn't shift back?" If the werewolf

stayed in his animal form, it would be an effective way of not answering questions.

"He will." Khan's expression was grim. And determined.

He and Ged wore sweatpants. The other members of the band had also slipped on the same garments and boots or sneakers before returning to the yard for the cleanup operation. Sarange didn't want to inquire too closely about what that would entail. Memories of horror stories and movies came back to her. Could werewolves truly be considered dead without silver bullets or knives? Wasn't beheading or fire necessary? It was probably best if she kept her attention right here in the kitchen and didn't speculate on what might be going on outside.

Using the toes of one bare foot, Khan rolled the werewolf over onto his back. He lay still, regarding Khan with wary eyes. Crouching, Khan gripped the shifter's throat. "You have thirty seconds to shift back, my friend, or I'll rip off your balls and make you wear them as a necklace."

Sarange gulped. This wasn't the laid-back Khan she had gotten to know. She didn't know if the werewolf believed him...but she did.

"I'd do as he says." Leaning over Khan's shoulder, Ged spoke directly to the werewolf. "I've seen him do it. Wearing your own balls? Not the look any guy wants to go for."

The words weren't needed. The werewolf had shifted back into human form before Ged finished speaking.

"Wise choice." Khan got to his feet. "Now talk. Who do you work for?"

The man rubbed his throat and sat up slowly. It was

easy to see his thought processes as he looked at the two large men standing over him and appeared to measure the distance between them and the door. He clearly decided quickly that escape was out of the question.

"I don't know his full name." His voice came out as a croak.

"I'll get him some water and something to cover himself." Sarange went to the fridge to get a bottle of water. When she handed it to the werewolf, he gulped down half its contents in one long swallow.

As she left the room to go to the nearby bathroom in search of a towel, Khan was speaking again. "Okay, we'll go along with the story that you don't know the name of your leader. For now. Where are you from?"

Sarange returned moments later and handed the towel to the werewolf who wrapped it around his waist. He looked bewildered. "I don't understand."

"It's a simple question." Khan's voice was impatient. "Do you come from Los Angeles, or are you from somewhere else?"

Sarange could see why he was asking the question. The werewolf had what she thought of as traditional Mongolian features. Although those stereotypes were becoming outdated as the world changed, she herself was an example of what her own people would consider a typical Mongolian. This man's eyes were a curious light green color and hers were blue, but his appearance was otherwise similar to her own. One thing was certain. He was not one of the four men who had broken into her house on the previous night.

"I am from Ulaanbaatar." Clearly terrified, the young werewolf cast another longing glance in the direction of the door.

"It's the capital city of Mongolia," Sarange said in answer to Khan's raised brows.

"You're a very long way from home." Khan's impatience appeared to be fading. Sarange was glad. This werewolf was barely more than a teenager. Quivering all over, with deep scratch marks to his side and back, he was pathetic rather than threatening. "You'd better tell us how you came to be here. Start by telling us your name."

"I am Jirandai. Known as Jiran. Although I'm a werewolf, I lead a normal, human life in my home country. I am a student at the National University of Mongolia and I came to America on an exchange visit. I have been studying at Berkeley for the last three months."

An uncomfortable prickle ran up Sarange's spine. "Who is your professor at Berkeley?"

Jiran turned his attention to her. "Bek Tsedev."

"Why does this matter?" Khan asked. His eyes probed her face. The connection between them was so strong that she could tell he already knew it *did* matter. Knew Jiran's response to her question had thrown her off balance.

"Bek Tsedev is my uncle, the man who adopted me when I came to America. He is a professor in the Department of East Asian Languages and Cultures at University of California, Berkeley."

"Did you know this?" Khan swung back to face Jiran so rapidly that the young werewolf scurried backward across the floor, only stopping when his back collided with a cabinet. "Were you aware of the connection?"

"No! I swear…" He covered his face with his hands. "I don't know how it happened. I don't understand any of this."

Ged placed a hand on Khan's arm. "Let me try."

He knelt on the tiles beside the cowering werewolf. "How did you meet the other werewolves who came here tonight?"

Sarange was surprised at the gentleness in the big man's voice. It had an immediate soothing effect on Jiran, who turned toward Ged in relief. "I went to a nightclub last night with a group of friends. We were approached by a man who talked as though he knew us. We tried to explain that he was mistaken. Then we realized he knew our secret—" Jiran drew in a shuddering breath "—he knew we were werewolves."

"How did he know that?" Ged asked.

Jiran shook his head. "I don't know how he could. Even at home in Mongolia, my friends and I have always been careful about our anonymity. Our pack is small and we don't draw attention to ourselves. Here in America, none of us had even shifted. But this man, Bora, seemed to know everything about us. And it was like—" he shook his head "—it didn't matter. It was okay that he knew all about us. I think he must have given us something powerful to drink."

"Were you drinking a lot?" Ged's voice remained calm and quiet. Sarange sensed he was sympathetic toward the young man, who was clearly confused and frightened.

"I didn't think so at the time, but I can't think of any other explanation for how I felt then or why I can't clearly recall what happened." Jiran shivered. "Because the next thing I remember, we were here. I lost a whole twenty-four hours. Then my friends and I were caught up in a fight with you and I don't know how, or why."

Ged got to his feet and Khan drew him to one side. "Do you believe that?" Khan's voice was skeptical.

"I think I do." Ged studied the forlorn figure on the floor. "If he's lying, he's good."

"I believe him." Sarange didn't know why, but the young werewolf's story tugged at her heart. Her intuition told her his story was real. "Do you think he was drugged?"

"Either that or hypnotized," Ged said. "Possibly bewitched."

Khan still appeared unconvinced, although Sarange could see he was wavering. She had a sudden awareness of a powerful difference between them. He didn't have the same sort of empathy she did. It wasn't because he was hard or cold, it was simply his tiger DNA. He wasn't a pack animal. Reading others wasn't a strong part of her experience. *So what does that say about me? Does it mean I* am *a pack animal?* That wasn't the important part of her flash of insight. What mattered was that she and Khan complemented each other. They had focused on the tiger-wolf, cat-dog thing as though it was bad. As though it should drive them apart. Yes, they were opposites. *But we complete each other. Together, we are whole.*

There was only time for that brief thought before she turned back to Jiran and his plight.

Ged, of course, was part bear. He routinely distinguished between threatening and nonthreatening behavior in other animals. His driving traits were intelligence, empathy and the desire to protect. Khan seemed to relax when he knew Ged was prepared to trust what Jiran was telling him.

"This Bora, was he one of the werewolves who was with you tonight?" Khan asked.

"No." Jiran shook his head. "I only saw him in the nightclub. I didn't see him again after that."

"How did you get from San Francisco to Los Angeles?"

"I don't know." The young werewolf became distressed again. "All I know was I was in that club talking to Bora, and then I was here in the middle of a fight."

"Did you know the other werewolves who were here?" Khan ran a hand through his hair. "Other than your friends?"

"No, but there were a few minutes just before we shifted when I was able to get a look at them in human form. There were four of them. They were older than us and they looked exactly alike." Jiran choked back a sob. "And my friends…now they're all dead, aren't they?"

That was one of the hardest things to accept. From what Jiran was saying, a group of innocent young men had been sent by someone—*Who? Why?*—to their deaths tonight. Sarange could feel her own sorrow reflected back at her from Khan and Ged. They had done the killing, but they would never have deliberately harmed those innocent young men.

"Who is your pack?" She placed a hand on Jiran's shoulder as she spoke and he regarded her with wide, troubled eyes. Why did she need to know? How did she know it mattered?

"Although I am a gray werewolf, my mother was a blue werewolf—" he ducked his head in a gesture of submission "—and I bow to you, blue werewolf leader."

Khan and Sarange discussed the possibility that they could be recognized. Theirs were two of the most famous faces in the world. They had also recently been subject to intense media speculation about their relationship. In the end, they wore beanies and oversize shades and checked in separately for the flight from Los Angeles to San Francisco. Sarange disguised her slender figure beneath baggy sweatpants and a man's sweater. Khan still thought she was the hottest thing he had ever seen.

Sarange had relaxed once she knew Beast would be guarding her house. They also decided that Jiran should remain in Ged's care for the time being.

"We don't know what this guy, Bora, will do when he finds out how the attack went down. Once he knows Jiran survived and can identify him..." Khan had left the sentence hanging.

"I'm not sure I could identify him. The conversation I had with him is a blur." Some of Jiran's composure had been restored after he took a shower and Finglas, the smallest member of the band, had lent him some clothes.

"He may not know that." Khan's words had driven the color from the young werewolf's face.

Now Khan gripped Sarange's hand as they exited the airport building and made their way to the rental car complex. She had been quiet ever since Jiran's strange vow of allegiance to her as the blue werewolf leader. She also looked tired. It was close to dawn and they hadn't slept. Once they had made the decision to come to San Francisco, Ged booked them onto the next available flight.

"What makes you so sure your uncle will have the answers to your questions?"

Even though her eyes were hidden by her shades, he could tell she had been lost in thought. "I don't know.

Not for sure. But Bek was in touch with Golden Wing before she died, so he's the only person who knows anything about my early life. And he's an expert on Mongolian history and culture."

"What about your aunt?"

Sarange smiled. "My aunt Gerel is the sweetest, kindest woman you will ever meet. She often reminds me of Golden Wing. Perhaps she would know about my link to the blue wolves, but I think she is sometimes a little afraid of her shaman powers. Her health is poor. That's why I don't want to descend on them unexpectedly at their house. I'd rather visit my uncle at the university to ask my questions, then go see my aunt for a social call."

"So the plan is to check into a hotel and get a few hours' sleep before we drive out to Berkeley?"

Sarange rolled her shoulders wearily. "That sounds like the best plan ever. And maybe when we wake up it will all have been a dream."

"Not all of it." His voice was husky as he gazed down at her.

Her fingers gripped his tighter. "Except us. I will never wish that away."

After they'd completed the rental car formalities, the drive into the city passed in an early morning blur. Khan took the wheel while Sarange used her cell phone to check them into a discreet hotel she had used before. They both knew the score. Anywhere they went, they took a chance on being recognized. This was the life they had chosen. Complaining about it would be hypocritical. But there were times when anonymity was needed, and there were things they could do to minimize the chances of being identified.

When they reached the hotel, Khan drove straight into the underground parking lot. From there, they took an elevator directly to reception, where the clerk had their room key ready for them.

"My kind of place," Khan said as they took a second elevator up to the second floor.

"In case anyone asks, we are Mr. and Mrs. Wolf."

He grinned. "Is that an invitation for me to unleash the beast within?"

Although she laughed as she stepped into the room, when she removed the shades her expression was serious. "I'd rather you held me."

Khan dropped their bags to the floor. "I can do that... For as long as you want me to."

How about forever? The thought was unprompted, but, for the first time, it wasn't unwelcome. He wished he could explore it. Wished there wasn't this strangeness pressing down on them. A man called Bora had sent a group of young men to Sarange's house a few hours ago alongside the four werewolves who had tried to abduct her the previous night. Apart from Jiran, all of those werewolves had died. Either Bora thought his werewolves would succeed in capturing Sarange, or he knew they would die. Both thoughts were too horrible to contemplate. Could he have knowingly sent them to their deaths? Had the mysterious Bora used Beast as a murder weapon? And why?

Sarange moved into the circle of his arms, pressing her cheek to his chest. They stood that way for long, still minutes until he felt her breathing settle into the same rhythm as his. Her heartbeat slowed. He sensed her relaxing. There was nothing about the situation they were in that was okay. Except this. In the midst of madness, they had found each other, and there was a world of rightness about that. He didn't understand it, but he was happy to accept it. More than happy. She was the best thing that had ever happened to him. Even though he knew nothing about a huge chunk of his life, he knew that.

Sarange raised her head. "I have no idea what's going on."

"Nor have I. For now, let's concentrate on getting some sleep." He kissed the top of her head. "Then we'll go in search of answers."

This dream was the most vivid Sarange had ever had. The night sky was lit with sacred fire. Chanting voices rose and fell in time with the steady drumming of fingertips on taut animal skin. The blue-eyed watchers stood on the snowy peaks, observing the human ritual. Sarange felt their approval. Their spirits touched hers. Human, wolf, tiger, shifter. In that instant, it mattered not. They were as one.

The shamanka's voice rose above the others, high-pitched and nasal, as she raised their joined hands aloft for all to see. Sarange held her breath. This was the moment. She turned to the man at her side, saw the love in his eyes, felt the acceptance of their people. They were united...

A flash of movement on the periphery of her dreaming vision caught her attention as the golden eyes of the gray wolf gleamed. He was gone almost as soon as she locked her gaze on his, but his presence unsettled her. The shamanka continued to chant while the tribe sang and drummed and the blue wolves looked on, but the gray wolf's presence had interrupted the spirits. It was an omen.

Sarange woke, shivering at the intensity of the emotions the dream had provoked in her. It was as if she had been watching a movie. No, it was more than that. *It was as if I was there.*

She sat up, checking the clock on the table next to the bed. Even though it felt like she had slept for hours, it was still only noon. A warm hand closed over her wrist and she turned to look into Khan's sleepy gold eyes.

"Something is troubling you."

She settled back down, lying on her side so her face was only inches from his. "Just a dream."

He cupped her cheek with one hand, pressing his lips to the pulse at the base of her throat. "Tell me."

"It was very vivid. Some sort of tribal celebration. I think, from the dream I just had, that it was to do with a marriage. The spirits came together to celebrate. Wolves, humans—" she laughed "—there was even a tiger in the background somewhere. Although I suspect anyone trying to interpret my dreams wouldn't have far to look for the source of *that* part of it."

Khan smiled. "Can I help it if I'm unforgettable... even when you're asleep?"

Even though she returned the smile, the remembered sense of unease returned. "There was something there in the background. A feeling of menace. The dream was clear enough for me to see the source. It was a gray wolf, lurking in the shadows, watching the celebration."

"Is it possible you dreamed about a gray wolf because of what Jiran said?"

"It's not only possible, it's likely. But that doesn't alter the feeling of the dream. Until the gray wolf appeared, the spirits were aligned and the portents were positive." She felt that shiver again, like a cold hand running gleeful fingers down her spine. "The gray wolf unbalanced that, and turned it into a nightmare."

Khan pulled her closer. "That's all it was. And, considering everything that's been happening to you, I'm surprised it wasn't a whole lot worse."

"Maybe it would have been…if you weren't here."

One of his hands slid down her back to her bottom while the other curled around the nape of her neck. "Sarange." His voice was barely a whisper against her hair. "You are so beautiful you take my breath away."

He traced the seam of her lips with his, coaxing them to part. When his tongue met hers, everything but the feel, taste and scent of Khan vanished. Need coursed through her as his tongue danced with hers in sweet, languorous passes and deep thrusts. Only breaking the kiss for seconds, they stripped away the few clothes they had worn to sleep in.

Using the heel of her hand on his shoulder, Sarange pushed Khan onto his back, skating gentle kisses down his abdomen. He huffed out her name on a breath.

"Shh." She looked up at him with a smile. "I'm busy."

Flicking out her tongue, she licked her way down the length of his erection.

"Damn." Khan pressed his head into the pillow, arching his back and jerking his hips upward.

Placing her lips to his tip, she kissed all the way around the sensitive head of his cock. Taking his groan as a sign of approval, she curled her fingers around the base of his shaft, sliding her hand up and down, while engulfing him in her mouth. Khan muttered a curse as he tangled his fingers in her hair.

Plunging down hard, she took him deep, letting him strike the back of her throat. Khan pumped his hips in time with her movements. Reaching for her hips, he swung her lower body around until it was in line with his face.

Once she was in the position he wanted, Khan parted her folds with his fingers. Opening her to his gaze, he buried his face in her sex, thrusting his tongue into her, over and over. He set her on fire, driving her into a frenzy within seconds. Sarange moaned, bobbing her head up and down faster over his straining erection. When her legs started to tremble, Khan grabbed her by the waist and tipped her onto her back.

"Need to be inside you when you come." He scrabbled on the floor for the jeans he had abandoned earlier.

Locating a condom in his pocket, he had it on in record time. Sarange reached up, cupping a hand to the back of his head and pulling him down into a kiss. Every touch heated her blood until she was lost in him. Lost *to* him. Their tongues met as his hands moved down her sides and over her hips, lifting her to him. She raised her pelvis and opened her legs, unable to wait another second.

Khan lined himself up with her entrance and drove right in. Sarange gasped, her back arching at an extreme angle, pressing her body tight to his. From hip to shoulder, there wasn't a part of them that wasn't touching. Yet she needed more. Needed to press closer, to claim him. To mark him as hers. Trailing openmouthed kisses along his jaw and neck, she dug her nails into his shoulders and writhed against him. Craving more, even though it was already too much.

As soon as she drew a breath, Khan moved. "I love

how you tighten around me." He lifted himself with his elbows on either side of her head, watching her face as he pushed into her. "Love the feel of those hot muscles taking me deeper."

Sarange tried to say his name, but the only sound that left her lips was a strangled cry. The noise seemed to spur Khan to move faster and harder. Slamming into her, never letting up on the delicious, relentless thrusts, he gripped her chin, keeping his gaze fixed on hers.

"Let me hear that sweet sound again, Sarange. Show me how it feels when I'm inside you."

Desperately, she cried out his name and raked her nails down his back.

"I need to come, Sarange, but not without you. Never without you."

"Together." She managed to gasp out the word as the first spasms hit.

Pleasure exploded, sending a million tiny shards through her nerve endings as her body stiffened beneath him.

"Always—" Khan pounded harder, his pelvis hitting her clit with each movement, pushing her further over the edge. "Always together from now on."

Her orgasm crashed through her at full force, taking away the ability to even scream, and she clung to him, shuddering wildly. Khan dropped his head to her shoulder, pumping in short, shallow thrusts as she felt him jerk and tremble with his own release.

Chapter 9

"Always together from now on?" Sarange stood on the tips of her toes to press a kiss to Khan's lips.

Her long plait was still damp from the shower and she smelled delicious. Soapy clean and fresh with her own unique underlying scent. She was seriously testing his ability to concentrate.

"Pardon?"

"That was what you said." She blushed. "When we were having sex. You said, 'always together from now on.' That's quite an ambition. I know it's a fantasy, but it's quite unrealistic to expect that we could always climax together..."

Khan caught hold of her waist. "Is that what you thought I meant?"

Her brow furrowed. "What else could you mean?"

He dropped a kiss on the end of her nose. "If we stay

here and discuss it, we might not catch your uncle at the end of his classes."

Sarange pulled on her hat and shades. "I suppose you think you just neatly sidestepped that conversation."

He laughed. "I have enough experience of wolves to know I didn't."

"Now you're being cryptic." She followed him out of the room. "Wolves may have taken up a big part of our time lately, but what do they have to do with it?"

He waited until they were alone in the elevator before he answered, "You, my beautiful werewolf, are as tenacious as your brothers and sisters in the wild. Which means I'm sure you will bring the subject up again."

She appeared to give the matter some thought. "We don't know for certain than I *am* a werewolf."

"I think we do."

Sarange sighed. "If that's the case, why don't I feel something when you say I'm a werewolf?" They passed through the hotel reception and made their way to the underground parking lot. When they were in the car, she elaborated. "I have no wolf feelings at all. No desire to shift. No idea how to do it if I did. There is no part of me that feels wolf-like."

"I wonder if you ever did? Is it possible you once knew you were a werewolf, but like the werewolves who came to your house last night, you've been hypnotized, drugged or bewitched into some kind of memory loss?"

"That's a scary thought." Sarange slumped down in her seat, watching the buildings pass by. "I don't understand why anyone would want to do that to me. And for a plot like that to be successful, it would need the collusion of my family. If I was born a werewolf, Golden

Wing must have known. When she found me, I was too young to hide who I was from her."

"We're heading to the right place." Khan rested a hand on her knee. "Let's hope your uncle can answer some of your questions."

Sarange didn't look reassured. "I was already in my teens when I came to America. Bek may be able to tell us about Mongolia and what he knows about the blue wolves, but I'm not sure how much information Golden Wing gave him about me and my early years."

Khan could sense her frustration. It matched something inside him. The feeling that part of his life was missing and that no amount of pushing or pulling either inside himself or externally was going to get it back. There was always that sense of incompleteness. Too many what-ifs and whys. At least Khan knew *what* he was even if he didn't have all the details of his story. Sarange didn't even have that. It was no good other people telling her. She would have to find her inner wolf for herself.

They drove in silence through slow-moving traffic, reaching the Department of East Asian Studies at Berkeley just over half an hour later. Sarange smiled as she indicated an ancient yellow Citroën. "Bek is still here. That's his car."

Khan found a parking space close by. "Sarange, have you ever considered using some of your millions to buy your uncle a better car?"

She laughed. "I have offered. Many times. He won't hear of it. Don't let Bek hear you criticize his beloved Chinggis."

Sarange clearly knew her way. Leading Khan from the parking lot into the building, she removed her shades before approaching the clerk at the reception desk. The woman smiled as she recognized her. "It's nice to see you again, Ms. Tsedev. The professor was just talking about you the other day. He's still in his office. Go on up."

"Do you come here regularly?" Khan asked as they mounted the stairs.

"Not as often as I'd like. If I can get away, I try to come and see my aunt and uncle." They reached the second floor and turned a corner onto a corridor. "Since Bek spends so much time here, I have to pry him away from his desk if I want to take him for lunch."

She knocked once on a door and, hearing a voice from within, entered. The man seated behind the desk looked up with a hint of impatience. The expression vanished when he saw who his visitor was. A broad smile lit up his features and he rose to his feet, enfolding Sarange in a hug.

"Now, this is a good way to end a bad day."

"You wouldn't have bad days if you didn't work so hard." Sarange's voice was affectionate, and Khan stood back, content to observe the exchange.

Bek shook his head. "Nothing to do with work. This is about a group of missing exchange students."

Sarange cast a brief glance in Khan's direction. Should they tell Bek what they knew? Jiran would be returning, but the other werewolves who had gone to her house were all dead. She decided to wait and see how the visit went. Introducing the subject of werewolves to her gentle, but conventional, uncle would not be easy.

"Are you going to introduce me?" Bek's question put an end to any immediate thoughts of the Bora problem.

Sarange reached out a hand. "This is Khan."

Bek smiled. "A very distinguished name."

"Of course." Sarange frowned. "Why didn't I make the connection?"

Khan looked from one to the other with a touch of bemusement. "You've lost me."

Bek pointed to a picture on the wall. It was a portrait Khan had seen before. This was a copy of an original that had clearly been painted centuries earlier. It depicted a black-eyed, white-robed man with a scant gray beard. The image was compelling. The painter had managed to convey great energy in that seemingly blank stare.

"You share your name with a Mongolian hero. His personal name was Temujjn, but he was given the title Chinggis Khan, the closest translation of which is 'Supreme Ruler.' You may have heard the western pronunciation of his title... Genghis."

"Like everyone else, I have of him," Khan said. The dark gaze of the man in the picture caught and held him. "But I didn't know he was considered a hero. I thought he was a bloodthirsty despot."

"Chinggis Khan was the founder of our nation," Bek said. "A mighty warrior who led his army to carve out an empire stretching from the Caspian to the Pacific. But you are right. Historians calculate that he was responsible for the deaths of about forty million people during the Mongol conquests."

"Golden Wing used to tell me stories of Chinggis Khan's birth," Sarange said. "About how he was descended from the wolves."

Bek nodded. "The wolf plays an important role in Mongolian culture. Wolves are respected for their power, stealth and tenacity. Because the Mongols are traditionally herders and hunters, we have great respect for the wolf as a powerful and skilled hunter. It is believed that Chinggis Khan was the spiritual descendant of a very particular wolf."

His words stirred memories to life inside Khan like a stick causing the embers of a dying fire to flare. "The blue wolf."

How did he know that? He knew nothing of Mongolia or the blue wolves, yet something came to life within him at the words. Something powerful and primal. It was almost a memory. How could he have known Chinggis Khan was supposed to have been descended from the blue wolves? Sarange had talked about the wolf pack many times and he had felt no connection to them. Yet the link to Mongolia's great leader triggered a pull, a certainty, inside him. It was like the words he had just spoken were drawn from deep inside his very soul.

"It was the union of the wolf and the tiger." Sarange looked around her as though seeking the source of the words she had just uttered. As though they couldn't have come from her own lips. Khan knew how she felt. It was as if they were both under the same spell.

Bek looked surprised. "Although it is now suggested that the importance of wolves in Mongolian history and culture has been overplayed, that is a little known fact about the starting point of the legend. There is a story about how, almost a thousand years ago, a great Caspian tiger came to the aid of Chinua, the female leader of the blue werewolves, to defeat a rival gray werewolf pack. Their romance led to the birth of a great shapeshifter dynasty. Although Chinggis Khan was human, it is believed that theirs was the family from which the great leader was descended."

"A tiger and a wolf?" It was the union his heart craved, but Khan couldn't contain his skepticism. "Even in a legend, that's asking for a stretch of the imagination."

Bek smiled. "It is one of the greatest love stories ever told, enduring throughout the centuries until the tiger was taken from the wolf by enemies who wished to destroy their dynasty. Chinua vowed to search for her lover forever, but her body grew weak and faded away. Her spirit is said to roam our great country, seeking her lost love. Since then, the conflict between the blue and gray werewolves has raged unchecked. Now it is said that the gray werewolves are on the rise and a sure sign that the blue werewolves are losing the fight is the fact that the wild blue wolves are dying out."

"I don't understand." Sarange frowned. "These are just legends. But even if they were true, how could something that was happening in the werewolf sphere affect the natural world?"

"There is an affinity between the blue werewolves and their wild counterparts."

"Perhaps a Caspian tiger will come again to save them?" Khan kept his tone light, signaling his continuing incredulity. He hadn't come here to listen to a fairy tale.

"The Caspian tiger is extinct. Although we speak of folklore, I do not believe, even in the world of shapeshifters, that it is possible for a long-dead creature to rise again." Bek roused himself from the sadness that had gripped him as he spoke of the ancient legend. "But you didn't come here to listen to old stories of my homeland." He gestured to a large, well-worn sofa and indicated the coffeemaker.

Khan and Sarange sat down, but declined the offer of refreshments. "I hope my aunt Gerel is well? I'm looking forward to visiting her when we leave here."

Bek nodded. "You know she is always happy to see you."

He pulled forward the chair from behind his desk and sat opposite them, tenting his fingers beneath his chin. Khan decided he wouldn't want to be a troublesome student on Bek's program. The mild-mannered professor had a quiet, perceptive stare that indicated he knew they weren't here for a social call. He was biding his time, waiting for them to tell them the real reason for the visit.

"There have been some strange events taking place in my life." Sarange had obviously decided to get straight to the point. "Things that may be linked to my childhood in Mongolia. I wondered how much Golden Wing told you about me before she died."

Bek was silent for long moments. "We didn't know Golden Wing well before she sent you to us. She was distantly related to Gerel. When she wrote to Gerel asking if you could visit, it was the first time we had heard from her in many years. Although we came to live in America when we first married, the pull of shamanism was still strong for us. Golden Wing said she wanted you to experience a world beyond the tribe, even beyond Mongolia. She said the spirits told her you were destined for greatness."

"I never knew that." Sarange looked and sounded surprised.

"So Golden Wing knew Sarange would become famous?" Khan said. "Do you think that's why she wanted to send her to America? To give her the opportunity to appear on the TV talent show?"

"No." Bek infused the word with a meaning Khan couldn't grasp. "Golden Wing was a powerful shamanka. Her ability to reach the spirits was possibly the strongest of any ever known. There were some within the shamanic tradition who questioned why she didn't take her healing arts and teachings to a wider audience. But she chose to live simply within a nomadic tribe. Her message that Sarange would achieve greatness was not about fame or fortune. Those things would have been meaningless to Golden Wing."

"So what did it mean?" Sarange asked.

Bek shrugged. "I have no more idea now than I did then. Gerel and I agreed to your visit to please Golden Wing." He smiled. "But once you were here, we didn't need any incentive other than the pleasure of your company. Gerel's health has never been good and we couldn't have children of our own. When Golden Wing died, we didn't adopt you out of duty or pity. We did it because we loved you."

Sarange's eyes were filled with tears. "I know that. I have been very blessed. I don't know what happened to my birth parents, but I found love...first with Golden Wing and then with you and my aunt Gerel."

Bek leaned forward and clasped her hand warmly. "I'm glad we showed you how much you mean to us."

"Could the greatness in Sarange's destiny be about the work she does to save endangered animals?" Khan asked.

Sarange's brow cleared. "That must be what Golden Wing intended. By sending me here to you, she set in motion a chain of events that meant I would have the money and influence to do something to help animals that are at risk of extinction. No matter what I do, it's never enough to save them all, but that must be the greatness my grandmother talked of. The spirits intended for me to do this."

"It's hard to know what else she could have meant." Although Bek smiled, Khan had a curious feeling that he remained unconvinced. "But you said strange things had been going on. That worries me. What has been happening?"

Sarange reached out a hand and placed it in Khan's. There were two men in the room, one of whom she had known and loved for many years. Yet her instinct had been to reach for Khan. His heart gave a glad little bound at the message of trust behind the gesture.

"This is going to sound very odd—"

"Sarange, this has been one of the strangest weeks of my life." Bek ran a hand through his thick black hair. "It started with a visit from a man who attempted to persuade me to drop everything and give a talk to a political party in Mongolia. He was most persistent, offering a large donation to the faculty and an all-expenses-paid vacation for me and Gerel after I had delivered the talk. Even though I explained that this was the busiest part of the semester, he was most reluctant to let it go." There was a faint look of distaste on Bek's face. "Even if I had been able to get away, I would not have accepted his invitation."

"Why?" Khan was diverted by Bek's obvious hostility toward the idea.

"The Chanco Party is a relatively new, but increasingly powerful, political movement in Mongolia. Let's just say I disagree with every policy they have," Bek said. "Moving on to the rest of my week, I am now dealing with the problem of a group of five missing exchange students. What I'm trying to say is, I don't think anything you can say will add to the strangeness."

"I'm not so sure." That odd, uncomfortable feeling of certainty gripped Khan again. "What was the name of the man who wanted you to drop everything and go to Mongolia?"

"Bora."

Bek was still shaking his head in disbelief as they exited the building and crossed the parking lot. "Humans transforming into animals is an integral shamanic belief. I grew up hearing stories of werewolves and other shape-shifters. But this story is incredible. The world I live in today is not the one of my childhood. I can't believe those missing students are werewolves."

"Sadly, for four of them, we have to say they *were* werewolves," Sarange said. The sense of horror and incredulity still lingered when she thought about it. "Only Jiran survived."

"And the man called Bora was behind this?" They had reached Bek's car, and he halted beside it. "He recruited, or tricked, these students, into going to your house? Why would he do that?"

"I have a horrible feeling it was to test our strength." Khan put forward the first theory he had.

Sarange shivered, wrapping her arms around her body as though protecting herself from a chill. "You mean he sent those young men to their deaths simply so he could find out how strong you and your friends were?"

His second theory wasn't any better. "Or he was showing us just how evil he can be."

She raised a hand to her lips. "Do you think he was observing the fight?"

Khan nodded. "I'm sure of it."

"That's horrible. He watched them die in some sort of experiment."

"Why would this man want to get me to go to Mongolia?" Bek asked. "I have no influence over these students beyond what happens on the program. I'm not a werewolf." He gave a shaky laugh. "I can't quite believe I just said those words out loud. The talk he wanted me to deliver was routine, the sort of thing I do regularly. I don't understand my place in his plans."

"It's possible he didn't know how much the exchange students had confided in you. He clearly knew you were an expert in shamanism. Maybe he wanted you out of the way. Sending you to Mongolia was one way of achieving that." Khan paused. "Or he wanted to use you to influence Sarange. If he had you in his power, she would be more likely to do what he wanted."

Bek looked dubious. "A visit to another country wouldn't have happened fast. Even if I'd been able to reschedule classes and leave within a few days, it wouldn't have been soon enough."

"I've got a feeling we'll be hearing more from the mysterious Bora, so we may discover more about his motives soon." Khan moved toward the rental car. "We'll meet you at your house."

Sarange settled into the passenger seat. "Do you think Bora knows we're here?" She cast a glance over her shoulder, unable to shake the fear that a malignant presence was pursuing them. "That he could be watching us?"

Khan had been about to start the engine, but he paused. Turning his body toward her, he placed his hands on her shoulders, drawing her to him. "If he is, he'll soon find out he made a mistake. I told you I'm going to keep you safe. That hasn't changed."

Sarange gave a sigh as she nestled her cheek into the curve of his neck. His touch instantly soothed her. "I believe you. I just wish I understood *why* you have to keep me safe. Why does someone I don't know want to harm me?"

Khan kissed her before releasing her. "We will find out what this is all about. I promise you."

Bek and Gerel lived in a small, cozy house overlooking Muir Beach. Bek had called ahead, and when they arrived, Gerel was waiting on the doorstep to greet them. Sarange always experienced a rush of affection for the woman who had been like a mother to her since she was fourteen, but it was stronger than ever this time. As she embraced Gerel, concern hit her hard. Her aunt looked even more frail than usual. It was as if her health had rapidly declined since Sarange last saw her.

Gerel was tiny and she had to tilt her head right back to look up at Khan. "You are not what I expected."

His lips curved into an amused smile. "Can I take it from that statement that you are not a fan of rock music, Mrs. Tsedev?"

Sarange had never seen Gerel become flustered. Usually she was the most serene person Sarange knew. Now, as she twisted her hands together and studied the top step, her expression was agitated. "I meant you are not the sort of person I expected Sarange to become involved with."

Bek stepped out from the house and slid a hand under his wife's elbow. "You are not making this any better, my love." His voice was mildly amused. "But I don't suppose Khan will be offended."

Khan laughed. "Far from it. I'm not the sort of person *I'd* expect Sarange to get involved with—" he lowered his voice as he followed Sarange into the house "—but my reasons for saying that might surprise you."

"Now is not the time to mention your tiger tendencies." Sarange's warning whisper was for his ears alone.

"Don't worry. I won't disgrace you by showing my stripes while we're having dinner."

She shook her head at him, half amused and half outraged at his audacity. How boring her life had been before Khan swaggered into it! Even though the past few days had been a blur of danger, this time spent with him had been a precious gift. She hadn't changed how she saw herself, but he had made her see another side to her being. The problem was… Khan was the other side to her. *He is the other half of me. The tiger to my wolf.*

It was not the best time for such a momentous revelation. She was finally prepared to open her mind and heart to the idea that she was a werewolf. But now she was taking a step further. She was also accepting that, just like that legendary leader of the blue werewolves, she needed a tiger to complete her. There was a reason why opposites attracted. It was that Khan brought with him all the things Sarange lacked.

She shone a spotlight on herself. And she saw a wolf. She liked order, hated when her routine was disrupted. Bek and Gerel were her only family, but they meant everything to her. If she gave her friendship, it was a precious gift, not lightly bestowed. She was fiercely loyal to the few friends she had. Khan had called her stubborn. She smiled. A dog with a bone? Once she got her teeth into something, she refused to let it go.

Sarange liked rules. She liked to know where she was meant to be and what she was supposed to do when she got there. She had a reputation for being the least demanding person in the music industry. The ultimate professional. *Or am I just obedient?* Doing the right thing because, in a pack, there was no place for a maverick.

She glanced across at where Khan was standing in her aunt and uncle's kitchen, admiring the view while Gerel fixed him a drink. The ultimate maverick. He had brought chaos into her ordered life. Brought all the things Sarange would have said she hated. Spontaneity. Disruption. Defiance. Rules? To Khan they existed only to be flouted. Authority? It was there to be challenged. In Khan's world, other people bowed down before him. He did nothing to please them. He was bold, loud and beautiful. A tiger who already owned more of her wolf heart than she cared to admit.

"Put the drinks on hold, Gerel." Khan turned away from the window, his eyes flashing a golden warning. "We've got company."

Chapter 10

The yard at the rear of the house sloped down and had an ocean view. The light had almost gone, but the prospect of the neat garden with the distant water beyond was stunning. Khan, whose eyesight was as good in the darkness as it was in the daylight, had been admiring this through the full-length window when his keen gaze caught the first movement.

"Bek, I'm guessing most of your visitors use the front door?" He kept his eyes fixed on the shrubs, where he had seen the activity. There it was again, so slight only a tiger would catch it.

"Yes." There was a nervous quiver in the older man's voice. "Shall I call the police?"

"No. Get Sarange and Gerel upstairs. I'll take care of this."

"But—"

"Do as he says, Bek." Gerel's voice was surprisingly calm as she interrupted her husband's protest. "We can trust Khan."

Khan didn't have time to examine the strangeness of her words. He was too intent on what was going on beyond the window. Over to his left. There were four. This opponent liked that number. So did Khan. Four posed no problem for his inner tiger.

Unfortunately, he reckoned there were another four over to his right.

"What's going on?" Sarange was standing just behind him.

He frowned but kept his gaze on the darkened yard. "You are supposed to be upstairs."

"I decided to try being rebellious for once in my life."

"It doesn't work that way." He risked a glance over his shoulder and caught a flash of understanding from her blue eyes. "I do the rebelling. You're the one who holds me back."

He looked back at the yard and Sarange moved closer, resting her chin on his shoulder. He felt her sigh reverberate through him. "You feel it as well? We are opposite halves of the same whole? That's how we work."

"I feel it. I sure as hell don't understand it."

"You don't need to understand it. If you accept it, you know you need me here next to you. Completing you."

He flicked another glance her way. "I don't want you in danger."

"I'm not. I'm getting you out of it."

"Stop being such a stubborn she-wolf."

She laughed. "Only if you stop being such an overbearing alpha tiger."

Even in the face of a looming threat, the exchange

felt easy. Like they had teased each other the same way
a hundred times. And wasn't it time to face up to the
truth? To admit that they *had* done these things that
felt so familiar. He didn't know enough about how the
cosmos worked, but he was a shape-shifter. He wasn't
going to question the intricacies and mysteries of the
universe. Somehow, some way, he had known Sarange
before. She had played an important role in his life.
More than that. Without knowing it, she held the key
to who he was.

Now was possibly a bad time for soul searching. No
matter how many intruders were out there in the shadows, his mate was in danger and Khan would defend
her with his life. And that vow worked both ways. He
sensed a new determination in Sarange. A change had
taken place, and with it there had come a new steadfast-
ness and courage. Hiding away wasn't an option. She
was going to face her adversaries no matter where the
confrontation might lead her.

Just the way she always did.

"Stay close to me." He had no real expectation that
she would listen to him. His instincts told him she
would go her own way. They also told him to trust her.
Sarange wasn't weak and helpless. She wasn't a tiger,
but the bravery and vitality that flowed through her
veins were strong enough to move mountains.

"Khan." Her breath brushed his cheek and he turned
his head. "I may not know what is going on, but I know
one thing with absolute certainty. You are talking to
the person who taught you everything you know about
werewolf warfare."

Was that true? No matter what he thought, Sarange
believed it and it was too late now to do anything other

than trust her judgment. The shadows on the edge of the garden were closing in. Men were emerging from the shrubs. Their enemies were encircling them.

Khan slid the window open just wide enough so that he could step through the gap. The breeze carried the first chill of nightfall and the salty tang of the ocean. Sarange pressed close up behind him.

"Werewolves." Her voice was barely a whisper. "I can smell them."

"You're getting good at this." He drew her with him to one side of the small deck area, crouching low as he scanned the yard. "You're almost a shifter."

"Now I just have to find a way to shift."

"Do you think you can do it?" As he looked her way, her face was a pale blur in the darkness.

"There's only one way to find out."

As she shrugged out of her clothes, the night air caressed Sarange's skin, leaving shivery pinpricks in its wake. *I want this.* The thought surprised her with its passion. She had hidden behind her cool, professional persona for so long. Now the desire to reach inside herself and find her inner wolf was overwhelming in its intensity. *Let's get on with it.* The real Sarange had been hidden for too long. It was time to release her. To meet her. Again.

There was just one problem. Shifting. What was it? How did it happen? Before she had met Khan, it was something that happened in books and movies. It was fiction. Like fairies and phantoms. She had never paid any attention to the logistics, because it wasn't something she would need. *Why the hell didn't I take notes in those horror movies instead of covering my face with my hands?*

"There is more magic than science in being a shifter." Khan's voice was softly persuasive, almost as if he could read her mind. "You need to think your way into your inner wolf. She's there, deep inside you. You have to find a way to set her free."

I have a wolf inside me. The thought should have been scary. Instead, it was curiously liberating, as though everything finally made sense. *She* made sense. Instead of skimming the surface of who she was, she was shining a light into the darkest recesses of her soul. It was something she had never wanted to do. She had never wanted to inquire too closely into the darkest corners of her psyche. What if she didn't like what she found? What if, instead of order and calm, she found chaos? Now she was seeking a part of herself that was wild. She wanted to set the untamed part of herself free. Wanted to know what it would be like to break free from the restraints of her human self and find the animal within. Sarange the wolf. She was looking forward to unleashing her.

Deep inside her body, something stirred. In a part of herself she had shut off and never examined, a surge of something unexpected and primal made her utter a soft cry. She stifled it instantly, pressing a hand to her chest and breathing hard.

"Do you feel her?" Khan kept his voice low. Sarange nodded, unable to speak as the feelings continued to surge and grow. "Let it happen. Let your inner wolf take over."

Let it happen? She couldn't stop it. That newly discovered part of herself was in control now. Her inner wolf was taking over. Sarange curled tightly into a ball. A moan—a sound close to a howl—left her lips as she gave herself up to the feeling of shifting. The first sensation was of her body tightening as her limbs stretched and changed shape. *There is no pain.* The thought was clear and sharp, taking her by surprise. Her jaw lengthened and her features altered. Her canines grew into fangs, her fingernails sharpened and became claws. Shifting was the right word. It was over quickly. It was part of who she was. Sarange the human wasn't gone. For now, she was the one who was hidden. There was no conflict in the exchange. She was both human and wolf. They were equal. Both valued. Both unique.

She liked Sarange the wolf. The feel of thick fur covering her body was like being wrapped in silver-colored velvet. Her wolf stance was confident, the lines of her body lithe and strong. Her movements were effortlessly fluid. Teeth, claws and muscles were in perfect condition. This wolf knew how to take care of herself, knew how to take the lead. She was in charge...and even Khan knew it. As he removed his clothes and shifted into his tiger form, she could see it in his eyes. Respect, recognition and joy combined.

Sarange didn't know the details of their story, but she knew enough. Khan had once walked at her side. With every step, he had shouldered her burdens and listened to her problems. He had been her mate, her friend and her protector. But Sarange had been his leader. He had bowed his head to her along with her werewolf pack.

The werewolves moving toward them out of the darkness were not her pack. Having shifted, she felt her senses become supercharged. Her heightened awareness of smell and her sensitive hearing brought every tiny movement to her. She sniffed the air and tilted her head, knowing that Khan would be relying on his own dominant sense—his sight—to fill in what she couldn't see.

His restless head movement was the signal they both recognized. Moving side by side, they left the deck and launched into a surprise attack. The night breeze whipped against Sarange's face, bringing the aroma of the night to life. This wasn't her homeland, but some of the elements of her world were here. She relished the dank scent of earth and the feel of wet grass beneath her paws. The moon hung three-quarters full over the ocean and she took a moment to appreciate its magical beauty.

The memories came flooding back. Similar fights, always at Khan's side. Invading werewolf packs that wanted to destroy her dynasty, to bring her down as leader. Stories abounded about the tiger and the wolf, but even the legends couldn't do them justice. *We are an invincible team.* Bound by a mystical bond, they were stronger together than the sum of their parts.

Sarange crouched low, baring her teeth in readiness for the attack as the snarls and howls of the invading werewolves rent the night air. It seemed they already knew who they were facing. Blue Wolf. Great Tiger. A legend born centuries ago beneath an Asian sky was coming back to life…and these attackers didn't want to be caught up in its might.

Khan launched into the attack. He fought like a demon. With a furious snarl, he lunged at the nearest werewolf. They rolled together across the grass. It was an uneven fight. Khan's huge claws ripped into the tender skin of the werewolf's abdomen, causing the creature to yelp as sharp talons sliced through fur and flesh. When he had finished with him, Khan flung his opponent across the yard.

Lightning fast, Khan lunged, throwing himself on top of another intruder. The werewolf tried to fight back. It was a futile attempt. Khan pushed down hard on the werewolf's rib cage. The sound of bones crunching under pressure was sickening. The werewolf drew back its teeth and a howl of rage echoed through the night sky.

Khan gave a warning growl. It was a message. Back off. He would allow the injured werewolf to live if it stayed out of the rest of the fight. The werewolf snarled a defiant response.

Under that ancient sky, the blue wolf and the great tiger had learned not to give second chances. Lowering his snout, Khan bared his giant canines. Using his teeth like knives to tear into the exposed flesh of the werewolf's throat, he ripped into muscle. Blood flew in a dark arc. Another of their enemies was down.

Sarange experienced a surge of energy. A bloody battle wasn't something she relished, but she wasn't afraid of it. The recollection of past conflicts came back to her and she moved toward the werewolves. One of them made a break toward the low wall that bordered the property and she set off in pursuit. *You came here to intimidate me. Let's see how that works out for you.*

The werewolf's agonized whine sliced through the air as Sarange caught up to him and her long talons dug into his side. He thrashed about, in an attempt to throw her off. Sarange swiped at him, slashing down his face. Blood spewed out of the werewolf's open mouth. A ripple of triumph swept through Sarange as she saw fear flicker in the depths of her opponent's eyes. She used it to her advantage, gouging again.

With a surge of strength, the other werewolf pulled himself up on his hind legs, drawing Sarange with him in a deadly embrace. Teeth snapped and claws slashed as they writhed together, both determined to gain the upper hand. Fighting to keep his fangs from closing on her neck, Sarange let out a yelp of agony as sharp claws caught the soft flesh of her belly.

On the periphery of her vision, she was aware of Khan catching an attacker in midair. There was a sickening snap as his teeth closed on its neck. He cast the werewolf's body aside like a limp rag doll and moved on to the next.

Spurred on by his success, Sarange raised a paw and swiped it once again across her opponent's face. Blood welled in a line down the center of his snout, spraying across both their faces. Seizing her chance, Sarange drove the other werewolf to the ground, pinning him down on his back.

Canines bared, she struck fast, tearing deep into the flesh of his throat. The warm coppery flavor of his blood flooded her mouth. Her human wanted to recoil, but her wolf was in charge. The werewolf beneath her struggled and thrashed. Sarange followed her instincts. Shaking her head violently, she heard the crack of his neck breaking. When she lifted her head, her jaw dripped blood and the other werewolf lay lifeless at her feet.

Bounding to Khan's side, she worked with him. They harried the remaining opponents, confusing them until they didn't know where the next snap of teeth or swipe of claws was coming from. Khan caught a retreating werewolf by the hind leg and dragged it across the grass before sinking his giant fangs into its neck. Another werewolf landed on Sarange's back and she shook it off with a furious growl. Before she could wrestle it to the ground, the animal took off and cleared the wall in a single leap. She weighed whether to follow and decided against it. This was not the raw wilderness of Mongolia. A werewolf fight in the streets of San Francisco? It was unlikely to go unnoticed and she didn't want to be part of the ensuing news story.

She moved back to stand beside Khan, reaching up to rest her muzzle on his broad shoulder. Feeling the thick expanse of his fur and his powerful tiger muscles sent a renewed thrill through her body. She tilted her head back, seeking the low-slung moon. A soft, triumphant cry left her lips.

I have found you at last, my tiger.

"I may only know about these things from legends and movies, but I believe a werewolf can only truly be killed by beheading?" Bek used the flashlight he carried to illuminate the scene of carnage that had once been his elegant yard. He looked pale but was quite calm considering what he had just witnessed from his bedroom window. "And that a silver sword must be used?"

Khan had shifted back and pulled on the jeans he had discarded before he shifted. "That's right. The bodies of these werewolves have been brutalized, but they are not truly dead. To leave them this way would be the ultimate cruelty. Their injuries will condemn them to a half life. They will be unable to resume their place in either the human or the shifter worlds."

"What do you propose we do with them?"

Khan ran a hand through his hair. It was a good question. There was an unwritten shifter code. Fight with honor. Die with dignity. No trace of conflict must remain for the forces of human law and order to find. There was also a responsibility to the enemy. He and Sarange owed these werewolves a shifter's death. There was just one problem. He didn't have access to the means to provide it.

Sarange reappeared, having showered away the blood from her skin and hair. She had changed into sweatpants, T-shirt and sneakers. Khan guessed she must keep spare clothing here at her aunt and uncle's house. Gerel was at her side. Khan wasn't sure how Sarange's quiet, gentle aunt was going to cope with the sight of the broken and bloody werewolf bodies littering her lawn.

Gerel surveyed the scene silently for a few moments. "I guess you're going to need a silver sword?" She might have been asking if he wanted cream in his coffee.

"Um—" Khan didn't often find himself at a loss for words, but this was one of those rare occasions "—that would be useful."

"I'll be right back." Gerel returned to the house.

Bek watched her with an expression of disbelief. "I have no idea what that's all about."

Sarange placed her hand on Khan's shoulder and rose on the tips of her toes to kiss him. "I have wolf blood on me," he warned.

"Wouldn't be the first time I've kissed you bloody." Her voice was husky.

"You remember that?" He studied her face in the light that spilled out from the window. She had been amazing in that fight. Stylish, graceful...deadly.

Sarange shook her head. "Not properly. Not fully formed memories. I just know we were together in the past."

He nodded, returning the gentle pressure of her lips. "We have some gaps in our relationship timeline."

Gerel interrupted any further conversation. She stepped through the open window, carrying a gleaming silver sword.

Bek swallowed so hard Khan heard the click in his throat from several feet away. "Where did you get that?"

Gerel's smile was gentle. "I keep it in the loft." She handed the sword to Khan.

"Are you able to hold that?" Bek asked. "Isn't silver poison to a shifter?"

"I'm unique. I don't know how, or why, but I can't be killed by silver…which means I can't be killed." He looked at the sword in his hand. "This stuff is a toxin to me. It leaves me weak, but it doesn't overpower me the way it does with other shifters." He smiled at Gerel. "I see you have bound the handle of this in leather. That greatly reduces the impact."

She nodded. "That's what I'd heard. How about you dispose of these bodies? Burying them in the woods is going to take some time. Bek, you will need to get a couple of spades from the garage and some of the tarp we use when we go camping. Wrap the bodies in it before you put them in the trailer. I don't want to have to clean up blood." She smiled. "While the three of you get my yard back to normal, I'll organize dinner. We can talk while we eat."

Even Khan, who had just met her, was shocked at the transformation from kindly, middle-aged lady, to werewolf disposal expert. Sarange and Bek appeared frozen in shock. Gerel hummed quietly to herself as she went back into the house.

Khan approached the first werewolf body. "I'm glad there isn't any other property close by."

"Why?" Bek looked like a man who had to rouse himself from a trance to ask the question.

"This is not something we want to risk the neighbors catching sight of." Khan gripped the leather-bound handle of the sword with both hands and raised it above his head.

"I'll go and get the things we need from the garage." Bek scurried away before Khan brought the blade down on the werewolf's neck.

It was messy and unpleasant, but Khan knew the task was a duty. He was a loner. He didn't get involved in other people's fights or politics, whether human or shifter. But he knew the basics of his kind. On the whole, shifters lived peaceful, anonymous lives. It hadn't always been so. This was a point they had reached over time. Centuries ago, bitter fighting within and between different shifter species had threatened to spill over and disturb the peace of the human domain. Tearing down the veil that existed between worlds couldn't be allowed.

To humans, shifters should only exist in legend. Along with other creatures of the otherworld—vampires, phantoms, dryads, elves…to name a few—interactions between werewolves and mortals must be prevented.

When the worlds did collide, there was an obligation to protect humanity from the truth of what lay beyond the veil. Since his rescue from captivity, Khan had been involved in a few shifter skirmishes, none of which had necessitated this sort of cleanup operation. Even so, as he strode around the yard in the moonlight with Sarange at his side, performing the final act of kindness on the broken werewolf bodies, he knew he had done this many times before.

"We fought many battles for our homeland." He was breathing hard when he lowered the sword for the final time.

"They were determined to take it from us." Her voice had a dreamy quality to it as though she was with him, but talking about something just beyond him.

"Who were *they*, Sarange? The gray werewolves?"

When she spoke, he picked up on her frustration. "I don't know all of it. Not yet. When I do, we'll know why they have come after us again. Then we will be able to crush them once more."

Her voice resonated through him. Strong and decisive. Khan would follow wherever she chose to lead. But for now, he decided they needed to take some immediate action. "Let's get these bodies into the woods and start digging. I'm dirty, smelly and hungry…and I want to know why your aunt had a silver sword hidden in the loft."

Chapter 11

The thought hit at the same time that Khan carried the last werewolf body to the edge of the grave. What if an overly vigilant paparazzo had managed to find their location? The fans who longed for pictures of Sarange and Khan together would be stunned if they could see them now. If a long-distance lens captured images of what they were doing among the redwoods... The image caused Sarange to utter a snort of laughter.

Khan glanced up from his task. By the light of Bek's powerful flashlight, his torso was shiny with sweat and streaked with dirt. "Is something wrong?"

"I was picturing tomorrow's headlines if there happened to be a photographer hidden in the trees."

He grinned. "Kha-range? Celebrity wolf killers?"

Bek shuffled his feet impatiently. "You two might find this situation amusing, but I'd prefer to get on with it and get out of here."

"A few more spadesful of earth should do it." Khan's strength was phenomenal. After digging a deep pit, he had hauled the tarp-wrapped remains of the werewolves into it. Now the grave was almost completely filled in.

Once he had finished, Sarange stepped back and surveyed the burial site. "We need to cover the grave with branches and leaves."

Bek had driven toward Muir Woods. Instead of following the tourist trails, they had carried the werewolf bodies into the dense, lesser used parts of the forest. Once Khan was satisfied they were deep enough in the woods, they had chosen this site. It was unlikely even the hardiest hiker would stray this far from the park trails, but Sarange wanted to make sure the grave remained hidden.

Once they had disguised the area to Sarange's satisfaction, they made their way back to Bek's car with its attached trailer. "The tarp protected the trailer from bloodstains, but we can clean and disinfect it properly later," Khan said as he climbed into the back seat.

They completed the return journey in silence. As Bek pulled into the drive, he turned to look at Sarange. "When you said there had been some strange events taking place in your life, perhaps I should have asked you to elaborate. Although nothing could have prepared me for the reality of what you were talking about."

"I would not place you and Gerel in danger for anything." Her voice trembled with emotion.

Bek placed a hand on her knee. "This is your home. Where else would you come when you need help?"

Where else indeed? As she covered his hand gratefully with her own, she had a crystal-clear image of a sky so dark it was like velvet scattered with diamond stars. Of pristine lakes; empty, rolling steppes and majestic mountains. Of Khan at her side and her pack running with them. The blue werewolves of shifter legend were the nomadic people of her past. *Where else would I go? Maybe to my home. To the land that is now called Mongolia.*

Inside the house, the delicious aroma of Gerel's home-cooked chili greeted them. Sarange led Khan up the stairs in the direction of the room that was still "her" bedroom. It was the room she slept in when she stayed here. Warm, cozy, filled with the remnants of her past. She felt comfortable here in the place that had been her sanctuary for so many years.

Gerel had carried their bags up here and laid clean clothes on the bed for Khan. He examined them in surprise. "Did your aunt iron these?"

"Probably." Sarange smiled. "Gerel is a homemaker in the true sense of the word. It matters to her that the people around her feel comfortable."

"She clearly doesn't know I spend most of my time on tour with a group of other men. I usually pick my clothes up off the floor. That's if Diablo hasn't kicked them halfway down the bus in a temper."

"I know enough about your relationship with Diablo to guess that happens when you provoke him." Sarange held open the bathroom door. "Everything you need is in here. I'll wait for you downstairs."

His eyes flashed gold fire, scorching her skin with a blaze of passion. "You're not joining me?"

"As tempting as that offer is, I wasn't the one doing the dirty work…and I need to talk to my aunt and uncle." It was true, but she wasn't sure where she would start. How was she going to explain something she didn't understand herself?

Khan's expression softened. "They are good people and they love you. Just tell them what you know."

Her brow furrowed so hard it hurt. "What do I know? Every time I think I see something in my past—*our* past—it feels like I get sand thrown in my eyes all over again."

"They may be able to help you see things more clearly."

Sarange wasn't hopeful, but she left him to shower and went back downstairs feeling vaguely embarrassed. It was as though she had let Bek and Gerel down by being caught out in a teenage misdemeanor. How did she begin to tell the two people she loved most in the world about an undiscovered past, a secret identity, about which she was only just learning? Bringing a bloody werewolf battle into the backyard of their quiet home was hardly on the same level as teenage misbehavior like staying out past her curfew, or trying a sneaky cigarette.

It seemed harder because this was the closest thing she had to a home. Her own luxurious house in Los Angeles was part of her celebrity persona, but this was where she felt at ease. Settling into a chair at the scrubbed pine table, she felt as if she had never been away. When Gerel placed a basket of her home-baked corn bread in the center of the table, Sarange surprised her aunt, and herself, by bursting into tears.

I'm supposed to be some mighty werewolf leader? I can't even smell my aunt's home-cooking without crying.

It was some time, and several tissues, before she was able to speak. "I don't know what's happening to me."

"This is your destiny." Gerel drew Sarange's head onto her shoulder the way she used to when she was younger and she needed her aunt's soothing presence. "This is the greatness of which Golden Wing spoke."

"You don't mind that I'm a werewolf?"

Gerel laughed. "I have been waiting for this day for a very long time."

"You have?" Bek selected a bottle of his favorite wine from the rack. Bringing it, a corkscrew and glasses to the table, he joined them. "Was there any point at which you considered enlightening me about that? Or about the sword you had tucked away in the loft?"

Gerel patted his hand. "You knew when you married me that I had the same powers as all the women in my family. I have the ability to enter the spirit realm."

"Are you a shamanka?" Sarange asked. She had always suspected her aunt had the same powers as Golden Wing, perhaps in a lesser degree. It was a relief to hear her finally admit it.

"I do not practice shamanism day to day. When we left Mongolia, I left that part of my life behind me," Gerel said. "But I can communicate with the spirits. I have some influence over the natural world."

"Did you know I was a werewolf?" It hurt Sarange to ask the question. Until Khan had entered her life she had trusted Gerel and Bek more than anyone. If she discovered now that Gerel had kept such a momentous secret from her, the knowledge would tilt her life even farther off course.

Her whole world had already been tipped upside down. Losing sight of what mattered to her, what grounded her... No, she couldn't bear that as well. Gerel's next words left her light-headed with relief.

"I would never have kept such an important piece of your story from you." Gerel drew a breath as she took hold of Sarange's hand. "But I would be lying if I didn't confess that I always knew there was something different about you. Something more than the talent that carried you to the top of your profession."

"The stubbornness and inability to let go of an argument didn't give you a clue that she's a wolf?" Khan entered the kitchen and slid into the seat next to Sarange, his teasing smile taking the sting out of the words.

His presence instantly warmed her. In the midst of all this chaos, there was *him*. And as crazy as it seemed, she would happily take everything that was thrown at her in return for Khan. For how he made her feel. She had been half alive before she met him, believing she was content and secure in the life she had. One look at Khan had blown that myth apart. It scared her now that she might have continued on that steady course and never have discovered these feelings. Might never have known this restless, burning hunger. This pure, perfect peace.

What frightened her even more was the thought of what the future held for them. Khan had no memory of his past before his captivity. Sarange, thrust into a new reality over which she had no control, had snippets of memories that lacked detail. The only certainty was that their past lives were somehow entwined. They needed to unravel the mystery of their shared story if they were to vanquish this faceless enemy who was so determined to destroy them. But what would they uncover? Once this fight was over, would the past set them free? And what sort of future, if any, would that freedom grant them? Because, although he had only been in her life a short time—*he has been* back *in my life a short time*—a future without Khan was one she didn't want to contemplate.

Gerel served dinner and Sarange was amazed at how hungry she was. "Does shifting always make you feel as though you are half starved?" she asked after she had demolished her second bowl of chili.

Khan, who was embarking on his third helping, nodded. "It's the same for every shifter I know. Changing into your animal form, and back again, seems easy, but it uses a huge amount of energy."

Gerel nodded. "You are replenishing the physical strength your transformation has used with food. But shifting also requires a great deal of psychic energy. You must take care of your entire being."

"How do I do that?" Sarange asked. "I'm still in shock about this whole thing. I don't understand how I can be a werewolf, how Jiran can have believed I was the leader of the blue werewolves, and how I can remember being a leader of an ancient dynasty with Khan at my side. Am I remembering my werewolf self?" She frowned. "It doesn't seem that way."

"You are trying too hard to force your memories," Gerel said. "Relax, and they will come to you. Behind the reality we see, there is a web of life. It is a network of invisible links that connect the spirits and living things, the past and the present. The truth is simple. The blue wolf is your guardian, Sarange, the animal with which you most closely identify. But you are not a wolf. You are a shifter—part wolf, part human. Both parts of your being are equal."

"So I am not the leader of the actual blue wolves? The wild animals who are now endangered?" It seemed strange to be asking her aunt these questions. To accept that Gerel, the quiet, unassuming woman who had devoted so much of her life to bringing up Sarange, suddenly seemed different. She had an inner glow, a new energy. Her strength seemed to be returning by the minute. A wave of emotion washed over Sarange. In that instant, Gerel reminded her more than ever of Golden Wing.

"No, but their plight may be linked to what is happening with you." Gerel frowned. "If you are the leader of the blue werewolves, there is a bond between you and the wild wolves. When you are in danger it will impact them."

Sarange reached for the glass of wine that Bek had poured and swallowed some of the rich ruby liquid. "How can I be leader? I write songs and campaign for animals." She leaned her head against Khan's upper arm.

"This is about the past as well as the present," Gerel said. "Time is like a silken thread. It can be stretched to its fullest length, or it can be twisted back on itself. When that happens, past and present can touch and the strands of time can cross. Sometimes it can happen briefly and we get that strange feeling of déjà vu. Sometimes it goes on for longer and we hear stories of reincarnation."

"Is that what has happened to Khan and me? Are we reincarnated souls who loved each other in the past?" Saying it out loud no longer felt strange. It made sense. It was their story. Their truth.

Khan took hold of her hand, twining his fingers with hers. "I think we already know the answer to that question."

She was amazed at the depth of emotion in his voice. His golden gaze locked on hers, drawing her in. Giving her a glimpse of his soul. The tenderness was intoxicating. This was Khan. Bold, strutting, loud, arrogant. A tiger in every sense. Except with her. With Sarange he wasn't afraid to show this side of himself. And every time she looked into his eyes she was drawn deeper into enchantment.

"But we don't know all of it." She could hear the frustration in her own voice. "It's like a puzzle with half the pieces missing."

"This all kicked off when we met. It feels like someone doesn't want us to be together." Khan looked at Gerel for confirmation and she nodded. "Around the time we met, we had the offer from Radin to go to Mongolia and make his documentary about the blue wolves."

Sarange quirked a smile at him. "I seem to remember you were less than enthusiastic about that suggestion."

Khan had a range of smiles. From the one that made fans swoon to the one that was just for Sarange and melted her heart. This one held a mix of mischief and sheepishness. "That was when I was still fighting how attracted I was to you."

"Fighting it by pretending you hated me?" She couldn't resist trying to make him squirm just a little bit.

She should have known better. Khan didn't do squirming. The smile intensified, heating every part of her. He raised her hand to his lips, pressing a kiss into the center of her palm. "I don't like losing, but this one time? It felt good."

"It seems like going to Mongolia to make that documentary might be a good idea." Bek's words brought their focus back to the problems facing them. "It would take you to the heart of the blue wolf territory. Perhaps that's what you need to jolt your memories."

Khan raised a brow at Sarange. "What do you think?"

She nodded. "It's a good idea. The plans went on hold when you refused to take part. Radin was determined. At first, he just wanted me to make the documentary, but then he changed focus and insisted he wanted us both."

"I think we should pay Radin a visit in the morning."

"So tired." Sarange's gaze slid toward the bed as she closed the bedroom door behind them.

"Really?" Khan placed a hand on either side of her waist, pulling her toward him. "Because I had a few plans…and all of them require you to be conscious."

Warmth blossomed in the lightness of her eyes. "I guess I could be persuaded to stay awake a little longer."

Khan was close to exhaustion himself, but as soon as he got close to Sarange his body fired up with a new energy. All he wanted to do was hold her. To let his hands roam over her curves, to hear the soft sounds she made when he touched her. He flipped the long braid back from her shoulder and trailed his thumb along her collarbone, delighting in the way her breathing instantly hitched up a notch.

She wanted him as much as he wanted her. He could see it in her eyes every time he looked her way. With the slightest touch, they both went up in flames. Just the way the shifter legends predicted it would be. She was his mate. This was how it would always be for them. He would always want to kiss those perfect lips, to tear her clothes from her body, to run his tongue over every inch of her skin, to make her scream his name as she came so hard she saw stars.

He trailed a line of kisses along the graceful curve of her neck, the contact lighting white fires throughout his nerve endings.

"Khan." Sarange shivered as she murmured his name. He loved the way her body instantly responded to him. Her eyelids fluttered closed as her hands reached for his shoulders. Her nipples were already diamond hard against the thin cotton of her tank top.

Tipping her chin back, he kissed her. Slow and gentle. The sound she made was midway between a gasp and a murmur. Quiet and pleading. Her hands moved to the hem of his T-shirt, pushing it up over his torso. Khan raised his arms above his head, assisting her, and the garment was quickly flung aside. Featherlight, Sarange's fingertips traced the muscles of his abdomen and he sucked in a breath. That instant response worked both ways. Her touch was like a brand, leaving fiery tendrils in its wake.

Khan began to move, not breaking contact with Sarange. When he reached the bed, he pulled her down with him. She moved to straddle his hips and Khan gripped the round globes of her ass, rocking his pelvis against hers.

After lifting her tank top over her head, he covered her breasts with his hands. They were perfect, warm, soft and full against his palms. Bringing her closer to him, he drew one nipple into his mouth. Sarange cried out, her fingers sliding into his hair. Flicking his tongue over the hard nub, Khan watched her face as she arched her back, tiny gasps escaping her lips.

He flipped her over onto her back, bending his head

to lavish attention over each breast in turn until she was moaning and writhing under him. When she reached out a hand for the button on his jeans, he caught hold of her fingertips.

"Not yet. After the evening we've just had, you need to relax. Let me make you feel good." He watched her face as he spoke. "I'm going to make you come. That's what you need right now."

Sarange murmured his name as he moved down her body, kissing the space between her breasts, then across her rib cage, before sliding down the elasticized waist of her sweatpants. He kissed the skin he exposed as he removed her sweatpants and underwear. Parting her thighs, he bent his head and ran his tongue along the glistening length of her slit.

"So wet for me already."

He could feel tension in every line of her body. Even through her arousal, he could sense the damage done by the extraordinary events of the last few hours, and he was determined to erase them. Using gentle strokes of his fingers and tongue, he explored her, teasing and tantalizing her. Almost immediately she was digging her nails into his shoulders, rocking her hips against him and pleading for more. Khan had wanted this to be slow, but she was at the brink so fast he could already feel her muscles stiffening.

He slid two fingers deep inside her as he massaged her clit with his tongue, driving her over the edge. Sarange shattered, her body shaking hard as she turned her head and smothered her cry with the pillow. Khan withdrew his fingers and kissed his way up her stomach. When he moved back up to kiss her lips again, she held him like she was never going to let him go. Which suited Khan just fine, since his own arousal had reached volcanic proportions.

The kiss heated up so fast Sarange gasped. Khan removed the remaining items of his clothing and returned to press close against her. Sarange's warm sex pressed against his rock-hard cock, inflaming him further. He skimmed his hands over her hips, lifting her tight to him, letting her feel him press into her.

"Condom." The word came out on a gasp as she squirmed against him.

"We can use one if you want, but we don't need to." She met his gaze, her brow furrowing in confusion. "Now that we know for sure that you are a werewolf, you have the same cycle as a female wolf. You are only fertile during the mating season. All that remains is for you to trust me when I tell you I'm clean."

He wasn't sure how she would take that piece of information. Was now a good time to mention it, or was it a mood killer? She was still and silent for a moment, then the flare of passion in her eyes intensified.

"I want to feel you inside me with nothing between us…my tiger."

Khan growled as he parted her knees and sank deep into her. Sarange writhed under him, scoring his back with her long nails, rocking her hips as she matched his thrusts. At the same time, she murmured his name over and over, encouraging him.

Nothing had ever felt like this; he knew it with a certainty that made his mind go blank. This connection between them was so right, so natural. Everything about Sarange—her smell, her taste, her skin, her lips—had been designed to fit him. Chemistry, trust, bonding. He guessed it was all true. Mate-sex really was the best sex.

He rolled them over, lifting her on top of him. Sarange straddled him again with her knees either side of his hips. Her long braid flopped forward and her breasts bounced teasingly close to his face. Gripping her waist, he drove his hips up in time with her movements. She tipped her head back, her expression one of pure concentration as she focused on riding him.

"Khan." Her tongue flicked out and his eyes were drawn to the sheen it left on her plump lower lip. "I'm going to…"

"Yes." He lifted her almost all the way off him, bringing her down hard and fast onto his cock, rocking his pelvis against hers. "Come for me, Sarange. Come with me."

Her whole body went rigid as she called out his name. He turned her onto her back again, driving into her deeper and tighter until they both cried out at the intensity of the sensation. Shuddering, Sarange clung to him as her climax stormed through her.

With her internal muscles clenching around him, Khan arched into her with long strokes. His vision went dark as he followed her into the abyss. There was only Sarange, his mate, this moment, this pleasure, this intensity. He gave himself up to it before collapsing beside her, holding her close, and fighting to regain his breath.

After several long, silent minutes, Khan drew the comforter over them. "Sleep."

Sarange's eyes were already closed as she nestled closer to him. "Despite everything that's happened, with your arms around me, I think I can."

Chapter 12

The following morning, Khan called Ged, who told him everything had been quiet at Sarange's house since they had left. That information appeared to confirm Khan's suspicions that Bora was watching Sarange. If she was the target, there was no need to attack her Beverly Hills home when she wasn't there. The thought chilled him. *Step out of the shadows and fight me.*

When Sarange called her manager, she was greeted as though she had dropped off the face of the earth instead of having been out of touch for a day. Grimacing at Khan, she did her best to explain her absence without going into detail.

"I'm on my way to see Radin. Khan has decided to do the documentary on the blue wolves." Since their faceless enemy wanted them in Mongolia, they had decided to call his bluff.

She ended the call sometime later. It was incredible how much her life had changed in such a short time. In the past, a call with her manager would have her making notes, firing questions, giving instructions. Now she wanted to hurry the conversation along so she could end the call and get back to what was important. The whole time the single thought *I'm a werewolf* persisted, pushing everything else to the back of her mind.

Almost everything. There was just the little matter of the vicious werewolves on her tail…and the man at her side. Both dominated her thoughts, but for very different reasons.

They had left Bek and Gerel's house before it was light, not even pausing to grab a cup of coffee before setting off. Khan had decided to drive rather than fly, reasoning that, if Bora was watching them, it would be harder for him to track their whereabouts. Now, almost six hours later, having stopped for breakfast on the way, they were approaching Los Angeles.

"When Ged freed you from captivity, where exactly were you being held?" Sarange studied the noble lines of Khan's profile as she asked the question.

"China." She could feel the tension coming off him in waves. "In the Xinjiang region."

Sarange knew of Xinjiang, China's largest province. Situated in the northwest of the country, it was a vast region of deserts and mountains that bordered her own homeland, Mongolia.

"Is that where you are from?"

"I don't know where I'm from." Although Khan's voice was devoid of emotion, she sensed how much it hurt him to talk of his past.

She was reluctant to push him further, but she knew

the mystery of their shared past could hold the key to what was happening to them right now. Through her work with Animals Alive, she had learned about tigers in the wild. The ultimate symbol of an endangered species, the raw beauty of the tiger was captivating, its story tragic. She trawled through her memory for some understanding of the remaining habitat of the tiger. Khan, of course, was not really a tiger. He was a shifter. Just as with her and a wolf, there were similarities, but also differences between him and the wild animal.

"When you shift, you look like a cross between a Siberian and a Bengal tiger, but you are bigger than either of them."

Khan hunched a shoulder. "Since I don't know my parents, I can't ask them about that." He flicked a glance at her, the look in his eyes softening. "I'm sorry. I don't know how to talk about myself because I don't know who I am. I call myself a Bengal, but you're right. I don't look a hundred percent like any tiger alive today."

Sarange frowned. "Do you think you could be a tiger who is no longer alive?"

"I felt pretty much alive last night…and again in the shower this morning." He quirked a brow in her direction and Sarange felt a blush heat her cheeks.

The memory of his hands on her body, of his tongue exploring every hidden part of her, of him inside her, made her squirm with renewed desire. "You know that's not what I meant." She forced herself to concentrate on the conversation instead of on the way he could take her to heights of pleasure she had never even dreamed of. "There are some species of tiger that are already extinct. If you have been alive for a very long time, your animal self may be one of those."

Khan's lips turned down in an expression of distaste. "I'm not sure I like the idea of being extinct."

She decided on one more probe. "Is Khan your real name, or is that something else you don't know?"

"When Ged found me—when he dragged me from the cage where I'd been imprisoned—I was close to death." His voice when he said the words stirred something in her, a pain so sharp it made her want to cry out. Instead, she gripped the sides of the seat hard and let him continue. "I could barely speak, but I said one word. *Khan*." He shrugged. "Ged assumed it was my name and that's what I've been called ever since."

"Although Khan is a common name across the world now, it was originally Mongolian," Sarange said. "It means 'leader' or 'ruler.'"

"In that case, it was a useful name for the lead singer of a group of misfit shifters." Khan's reluctance to continue the conversation was evident.

They completed the remainder of the journey in silence. Real Planet Productions was located in a large gleaming office block in West Hollywood. Occupying an entire floor, Radin's small but successful production company was gaining recognition as the creative force behind several powerful wildlife films and documentaries.

Sarange looked up at the facade of the building with the sun reflecting off the windows. "If Bora is following us, aren't we exposing Radin to danger? Should we warn him?"

"If Bora turns up, we'll deal with him." Khan paused at the entrance to the building, catching hold of Sarange's forearm and halting her before she walked inside. He surveyed the revolving door for a moment or two before taking her hand and walking in at her side.

Sarange had called ahead and spoken to Radin's personal assistant. She and Khan had discussed the potential hazards involved in the move. On the one hand, by making an appointment, they were giving the enemy a heads-up about their whereabouts. On the other, they needed to be sure that Radin would be available to see them. In the end, they had decided that arranging to see Radin was the best option. The mysterious Bora seemed to know their every move anyway. One phone call wasn't going to make any difference to whether he had a welcome party waiting at Radin's office or not.

Now they were here and it appeared to be a regular working day in a prestigious office block. There was no pack of snarling werewolves awaiting them in the black marble and mirrored lobby. They were able to take the elevator to the tenth floor without being accosted. Once there, they were greeted by Radin's personal assistant, Maria, a coolly efficient young woman who pretended not to notice that the story the world had been waiting for was standing in her reception area. Khan and Sarange were holding hands right in front of her.

"Radin had an unexpected visitor, but he asked me to let you know he won't keep you waiting more than a few minutes." She gestured to the office just behind her desk. "Can I get you anything to drink?"

They both declined and went to stand near the window, looking out at an uninspiring view of similar buildings.

"We will get through this. Together." Khan's voice was low enough so that only Sarange could hear. It felt like there had been other times when they had stood this way, just the two of them, facing a very different view. And he had made the same promise.

"But then they took you from me."

"Pardon?"

She shook her head, unsure where the words had come from, experiencing a sensation of utter desolation. It felt as if Khan had been torn from her side by hostile hands. Was that what had happened to them? Back in the mists of time? She thought of the shifter love story Bek had told. Of how, against the odds, the Caspian tiger and Chinua, the leader of the blue werewolves, had come together and created their own unique dynasty. When he was taken from her the blue werewolf had vowed to search for him forever, but her body had grown weak and finally faded away.

Had Chinua been reborn? The thought was like a thunderbolt of realization. More than that. It was one of certainty. Sarange tilted her head back, gazing up at Khan as she saw it all. Or most of it. The day she found Sarange, Golden Wing had left her tribe for a reason. But it was not the one she claimed. The shamanka had not gone to commune with nature in solitude. She had gone in search of the werewolf child she knew she would find on the vast, frozen tundra. And, having discovered Sarange, she had taken her back to the tribe and raised her as a human child. *Without ever telling me who I was.*

Why was that? Why had Golden Wing allowed her to grow up never knowing the truth about herself? Not only that she was a werewolf, but that she was the reincarnation of the great blue wolf leader of Mongolian legend? There were so many unanswered questions chasing around in Sarange's mind. How had her were-wolf instincts remained subdued for so long? Why had Golden Wing insisted on sending her to America when her destiny was clearly tied up in her home country of Mongolia? Why was *this* time in her life the tipping point for so many momentous changes?

"You are a Caspian tiger." In her work with Animals Alive Foundation, she had heard of the largest tigers ever known. There was an ambitious conservation plan under way to bring them back to their natural Central Asia habitat.

"You sound very sure." Khan cast a glance over at the desk where Maria had her head bent over some papers.

"Not just any Caspian tiger. You are *the* Caspian tiger." Emotion made Sarange's voice husky. "My Caspian tiger."

He stared down at her, realization and acceptance dawning in the golden depths of his eyes. "And you are my blue wolf. My Chinua."

Tears pricked the back of her eyelids. "Do you remember?"

"Some of it. Enough to know it's true." He ran a hand through his hair. "As crazy as it sounds, I remember us."

She laughed. "So do I. A little. It's still blurred, like I'm looking at it through cracked glass, but—" she lifted a hand and touched his cheek "—my God, Khan. The story Bek described as one of the greatest love stories ever told...that was us, wasn't it?"

Before he could reply, there was a shout and a crash from Radin's office. Without pausing, Khan leaped across the reception desk and flung open the door. Sarange was just behind him. The sight that met her eyes as she entered the office brought them both to an instant halt.

Radin was lying on the floor, apparently unconscious. The room looked as though a struggle had recently taken place. Papers spilled from the desk onto the floor, and a chair had been tipped over. There was no one else in the room.

"How did he get out of here?" Khan barked out the question to Maria while Sarange dropped to her knees beside Radin, checking his pulse.

"I don't know." Maria's face was white as she looked at her boss. "This is the only door."

Radin opened his eyes, blinking at Sarange and wincing as he lifted a hand to the back of his head. "What the hell...? He hit me with my own award." His hand shook as he pointed to a bronze statuette lying on the floor. He sat up slowly, his gaze wandering around the room before fixing on the desk. "And my laptop is gone."

"Gone where?" Khan was standing by the open door, his expression thunderous. "I still don't see how he—whoever he is—got away."

Sarange sat back on her heels, her head spinning. She guessed she already knew the answer to her next question, but she felt obliged to ask it anyway. "Who was in here with you?"

"A guy I've been working with on an outline for a new film. Today was the first time we've met."

"And his name is Bora." Khan's face was grim as he spoke.

"How did you know?" Radin frowned, whether in surprise at Khan's words or in pain, Sarange couldn't be sure.

"Call it a lucky guess."

* * *

At Khan's insistence, they moved fast. "I'm supposed to be recording a new album," he said, overriding Radin's protests about scheduling. "We do this now, or we don't do it at all."

Radin, having waved aside Sarange's suggestion that he should seek medical help, was seated at his desk, his fingers tented beneath his chin as he studied them. "What made you change your mind?"

Khan flapped a dismissive hand. "Let's get down to business. Sarange and I will be on our way to Mongolia later today. You can email us the details of when and where your team will meet us. Unless the documentary is no longer an option now that you've lost your laptop?"

Radin bristled slightly. "Everything is backed up. It's an inconvenience, nothing more."

Khan couldn't get rid of the twitchy feeling that something was wrong. He almost laughed out loud. Something was already very wrong. His instincts were telling him that something *more* was wrong. It must be Bora's lingering scent, or the knowledge that his enemy had been close.

He prowled the room, his gaze going to the full-length window and the street below. How the hell had Bora gotten out of here after he attacked Radin?

"And you'd never met this guy before today?" He swung back around to face Radin.

"I already told you that." Radin was starting to sound slightly irritable. "Twice."

"To be fair—" Sarange's calm voice cut across the exchange "—Radin has just been hit across the head."

Her gaze locked on Khan's. It had been quite a day already. There had been the revelation that they were the legendary lovers of Mongolian wolf-lore, then the realization that Bora had been in the building—just feet away—and had somehow eluded them. Khan wasn't good at appreciating the feelings of others, but he could read the message in Sarange's eyes. She wanted him to go easy on Radin. He supposed it was only fair. The guy was human, injured and shaken.

With a sigh, he took the seat next to Sarange on the opposite side of the desk to Radin. His protective instincts were on high alert, pushing everything else to the back of his mind. His focus was Sarange. Always Sarange. But he didn't like Radin. There was nothing he could pinpoint about the other man to justify that feeling. It was possibly based on a certain warmth he detected in Radin's eyes when they rested on Sarange, a widening of his smile when he looked at her. His expression was… Khan struggled to find the right word. Awed? She was one of the most famous women on the planet, for God's sake. Millions of people looked at her that way.

"What was on your laptop?" Sarange asked.

"Everything. My whole life." Radin gave a snort of laughter. "But I back my work up, so, although the guy who took it has details of everything I've done, I have copies."

"Why would he want to steal your work?" Sarange frowned. "I'm sorry if this sounds ignorant, but has he taken anything of value?"

"Yes. He's taken my original ideas, and those of my clients." Radin shuffled one of the piles of papers on his desk as though attempting to get them back into some sort of order.

"We all know that's not what this is about." Khan had

hidden his impatience for long enough. "This is about the documentary you want to make with Sarange. I take it all the details were stored on your laptop?"

Radin nodded. "Everything was finalized. Location, script ideas, timings. We have an experienced wildlife camera crew who have worked with wolf packs in other parts of the world. We were ready to go when, or should I say *if* you were?"

"You must have been confident I'd change my mind," Khan said.

His intention had been to make Radin squirm, but, although the other man appeared to have trouble maintaining eye contact, he didn't back down. "I'd worked hard on the planning. If you weren't going to do it, I was going to get someone else."

Radin was lying. It was coming off him in waves. He wanted Sarange for this because of her Mongolian heritage and because of who she was. She would light up the screen with her beauty and she was an animal ambassador. Her passion for endangered species would shine through. Put her in his documentary and Radin was guaranteed a success. Then he'd seen her and Khan together onstage and the dollar signs had appeared before his eyes. He wanted to use the chemistry between them and the rumors about their relationship to make money from his venture. On one level, Khan admired his astuteness. On another, he remembered that this was supposed to be about a species of wolf that was threatened with extinction. *What the hell happened to ethics?*

So what if this guy was a little sleazy? The end result was the same. He and Sarange were going to Mongolia anyway. They believed that the answers to what was happening lay there, just as they felt that the blue wolves were at the heart of the issue. Sarange would get her documentary. The profile of the blue wolves would be raised. And Radin? It was possible he had turned up with his documentary suggestion at the wrong time. That it was all a coincidence. Khan didn't believe any of that. He had every confidence that Bora, Radin and the blue wolves were all tied in to what they would find in Mongolia.

But what he couldn't define, or begin to express, was the feeling that had gripped him ever since Sarange said those words. *You are* the *Caspian tiger. My Caspian tiger.* He knew she was right. Before his captivity, he had been the Great Tiger of Mongolian legend. He had fought, lived and loved at Sarange's side. So why was there a feeling of dread in his heart at the thought of returning to Mongolia? What had happened in his past to make him view a return to that land with trepidation?

It didn't matter. This was about Sarange and he would walk through the gates of hell for her.

Sarange was experiencing the strangest feeling. It was as if the tiredness induced by the long journey was going into reverse as they got closer to the Mongolian capital of Ulaanbaatar. At the same time, the curious tingling feeling of unseen eyes watching her was increasing. Flying from Los Angeles to Beijing felt like it had taken forever. Now, after a lengthy layover, they were almost there. Just her, Khan…and Jiran.

"Take me with you."

They had returned to her house, and as she had been throwing clothes into a backpack, Jiran's plea had made her pause.

"This will not be a vacation." She had tried to let him

down gently. He still appeared to be in shock. It was hardly surprising. Having come here to study, he had been thrust into a nightmare. "If you want to go home to Mongolia, I can arrange that."

"No." He shook his head. "I want to help find the man who killed my friends. I want justice…and I can be your guide."

She had considered that, eventually taking the suggestion to Khan. "It's all very well being the Blue Wolf and Great Tiger of ancient lore, but Mongolia is a vast, empty country. I don't know where to begin the search for our past. Maybe having a guide wouldn't be a bad thing."

"I agree, but I'd prefer someone other than a traumatized boy."

"You and I have the teeth, claws and muscles. Jiran may be from a rival gray werewolf pack, but he knows the Altai Mountains. That's the only area where blue wolves still survive. It is also the place where legend says Chinua had her stronghold in a time before the land was called Mongolia." She had placed a hand on his arm. "Let Jiran do this. It will restore his lost confidence."

His golden eyes had looked beyond her words and into her soul. "This is about more than restoring his pride, isn't it, my *koke gal*?"

The words shook her. "That's what you used to call me. *Koke gal*. Blue fire." She didn't know how she understood his meaning, since she wasn't sure what language he was speaking. Although it resembled modern day Mongolian, the dialect was different.

"Flashes of this language keep coming to me. It's driving me crazy because I only get snippets of it now and then, never a whole sentence or anything I can make sense of. Just odd words. But that one I'm sure of. Blue fire." Khan shook his head as though trying to clear it. "How did you know what it meant?"

"Bek has ancient texts on the wall of his study, and your words reminded me of those. But the main reason I knew what you were saying was that I have heard those words from you before. Many times and in another life."

That was why Jiran was with them now. Because of the blue fire in Sarange's veins. That extra sense that told her they needed him. Never mind why. The part of her that was Chinua knew they would require the young gray werewolf's help. Perhaps it would be when they reached the Altai Mountains. The formidable, beautiful range extended through China, Mongolia, Russia and Kazakhstan, the jagged mountain ridges deriving their name from the word *altan*, meaning "golden."

Once they landed, the interior of the airport was like any other. It was only when they stepped outside that Sarange was reminded that she had made the dramatic transition from Los Angeles to Mongolia. Cabdrivers immediately clamored for their business, but Jiran led them toward the bus station.

"Anyone with a vehicle can provide a cab service in Mongolia. There's a good chance we'll get ripped off."

Sarange was about to point out that money didn't matter. So what if a Mongolian cabdriver cashed in on their journey? She could afford to pay more than the going rate. Then she realized how that sounded. It made her appear like the worst kind of spoiled celebrity. She remembered Khan's comments about seeing her country as a backpacker and decided that was the way to enjoy it. And possibly the best way to stay under Bora's radar.

The bus was full and Sarange was squashed tight up against Khan for the duration of the journey. It wasn't a hardship. He placed an arm around her to keep her safe and she leaned in close to the hard muscles of his chest. They passed a variety of methods of transport including different vehicles, carts, yaks and the occasional camel.

"Can you feel it?" He murmured the words into her hair.

"Yes." She tilted her head back to look up at him. "We are being watched."

He looked over the top of her head, his gaze roaming around the crowded space. The other passengers were mostly tourists. Although they were a mix of ages, they were predominantly backpackers. A few signaled their relative affluence with suitcases.

"Can't see anyone here who fits the profile," Khan sighed. "It's a pity we don't know what the profile is."

"Jiran does," Sarange reminded him. "He has met Bora."

"Another good reason to bring him along." He leaned closer to Jiran. "Do you see anyone here who looks like the guy who approached you in the nightclub?"

Jiran's complexion paled as his gaze skittered around the vehicle. "No. Absolutely not."

Sarange shivered slightly, pressing closer to Khan. "Invisible eyes on us?"

A soft growl started somewhere deep in his chest. "I don't care whether he's invisible or not. If Bora thinks he can intimidate me, he can think again."

Chapter 13

As they exited the bus, Khan studied the slightly depressing Soviet-style architecture all around him. It came as a shock. It was an enormous, pulsating city with wild traffic, sinful nightlife and a bohemian culture. It was chaotic, ever-changing, yet traditional, hinting at adventure and excitement. This was not the Mongolia he had been expecting.

Sarange and Jiran competed to explain that the concrete ugliness of Ulaanbaatar's buildings wasn't typical of the whole country.

"Once we leave the city, it is all open space," Jiran said.

"There are vast deserts, rolling sand dunes, mountains and parklands…this is the most beautiful country in the world. Right now all I want to do is get clean and sleep. I don't care if we are supposed to be doing this on a budget." Sarange's face wore an expression that wasn't going to tolerate any argument. "I want a suite with a huge bed and a bath big enough to swim in." She pointed across the square where they were standing to a large building with flags waving above its impressive entrance. "That place will do."

Beast had played a series of gigs in Moscow about eighteen months earlier, and the lobby of the Mongolia Palace reminded Khan of the grandeur of the Russian hotels the band had stayed in. Since Sarange was hugely famous in her own country, her face featuring on billboards around the capital city, she resorted to her beanie-and-shades disguise once more while Khan checked them in.

"Once I've caught up on some sleep, I'm going to visit my family," Jiran said as he left them to make his way to his own room. He bowed his head to Sarange. "If that's okay?"

It surprised Khan that Jiran had slipped so easily into a subservient role with Sarange. He didn't know much about wolf hierarchy, but he knew enough. In the wild, the alpha male ruled his pack with the alpha female at his side. But Sarange and Jiran were from different shifter packs, groups that had traditionally been at war. He was male and she was female. It made no sense for Jiran to bow down to her.

Sarange nodded. "Just be careful. I think Bora already knows we are here."

That was another thing that bothered Khan. *Another thing?* There were so many competing claims on his attention it was getting hard to focus. And his DNA was half cat. Concentration wasn't his shifter strong point.

It was just as well his human senses were supercharged when it came to looking out for Sarange.

"*Bora.* That means gray, doesn't it?"

Both Sarange and Jiran regarded him in surprise. "No," Sarange said. "In Mongolian we say *saaral* for gray."

"Now you would. But in the past it was *bora.*" Snippets of that ancient language kept returning to him and he was sure of it. "If your animal guardian is the gray wolf and Sarange's is the blue wolf, shouldn't you be enemies? In fact——" Khan kept his gaze fixed on Jiran's face "——if Bora is linked to the gray werewolves, shouldn't your allegiance be to him?"

Jiran paled. "You don't believe that, do you?" His pleading eyes traveled from Khan's face to Sarange's. "Bora tried to kill me...he killed my friends..."

Sarange placed a hand on his arm. "I trust you."

He visibly relaxed. "Thank you." Casting a scared look in Khan's direction, he scurried away.

"Is that wise?" As Sarange inserted the key card into the door of their room, Khan watched Jiran's retreating figure.

"Right now I'm going with my instincts. I haven't seen or felt anything from him to make me think he's double-crossing us." She stepped into the room and shrugged off her backpack with a sigh of relief. "But if he tries, I'll know how to deal with him."

He closed the door, leaning against it and drawing her to him. "I remember now. You can be a scary werewolf leader."

"Only when I need to." Her smile made his heart lighter. "You know what I want to do now?"

"You already said. Bathe, then sleep."

"Even before that." She ran her hands up his arms, her touch, even through his clothing, making his flesh tingle. "I'm still coming to terms with all this. You and me. The past. Being a werewolf. Being in charge. I want to get out of the city. Find somewhere we can be alone. Somewhere I can shift and run free." The smile became mischievous. "Let's take my wolf for a test drive."

Khan laughed. "That's the most un-wolflike thing I've ever heard you say."

Sarange grabbed his hand, pulling him back out the door toward the elevator. "I know a tiger who's a bad influence."

The Zaisan Memorial was a huge structure set high on a hill south of the city. "If we head in that direction, there are surrounding hills nearby where we can be alone," Sarange explained, using the towering monument as a guide.

As darkness fell, the busy capital city was coming alive. Bars, clubs and restaurants were teeming with people all determined to enjoy themselves. Khan's shifter shared their urges, but with a different purpose. His inner tiger cried out for freedom.

Ever since his release from captivity, he had suppressed his shifter instincts, pouring his energy into the band. He had focused on Khan the rock star, preferring to forget Khan the tiger. Not knowing who he was, how he had ended up in that tiny cage, emaciated, humiliated, disconnected from either human or shifter reality...he hadn't wanted to think about that time. It still hurt him to recall it now.

But his mind-set had recently undergone a change, and he didn't have far to look for the reason. She was right here at his side, holding his hand, her long stride matching his. Everything about her matching him. He hadn't wanted Sarange in his life, had fought strenuously to keep her out. Nevertheless, she was here. And now that she was in it, his life was different. The past had caught up with him and he was glad.

He didn't know it all. He had no idea where he had been born. His childhood, family, all those details about what had shaped him…they still remained a mystery. But he knew he had loved Sarange, or Chinua, as she had been at that time. At some point in his life, the impossible had happened. The tiger had fallen in love with the wolf. And side by side they had created their great dynasty.

"I would never have willingly left you, my *koke gal*." The fierceness of the emotion that seized him as he said the words almost brought him to his knees.

"I know. That's why I searched for you." Her grip tightened on his hand, her fingers fitting the spaces between his perfectly. *Completing me.* "I couldn't live without you."

There was no self-pity in the words, no drama. It was a simple statement of fact. One Khan understood absolutely. Before the great Chinggis Khan united the warring tribes and founded the Mongol Empire, Chinua had been one of the most powerful leaders in the region. Her enemies had tried, and failed, to destroy her by force. They had resorted to the only thing that could damage her. They had taken away her reason for living.

Khan had been Chinua's mate, her love, her constant companion. When they captured Khan, Chinua's reign had been ended. She had been devastated. Her personal decline had been followed by a deterioration in her clan.

The mighty werewolf leader ceased to function without her tiger. And Khan knew it was the same for him. He had never known how long he was imprisoned. Years? Decades? He had no sense of the passage of time in that hell. Now he knew it had been centuries. Almost ten of them. A thousand years of pining for Sarange.

"Why now?" he asked. "After all this time, why has fate brought us back together now?" Khan couldn't believe it was all coincidence. Ten years ago, Ged had been given information that led him to Khan. He had found him and brought him back from the brink of death. Not only that, he had given him a new life as a rock star. In a parallel story, Chinua, her body and spirit destroyed by the search for her lost love, had been reborn as Sarange. Who also happened to be a famous singer…

"Maybe we had to meet again now because we are needed."

The thought chilled Khan. He wasn't sure he was ready to be needed. He could accept that his past self had been a responsible warrior who had stood shoulder to shoulder with the woman he loved and fought for what he believed. But now he lived a different life. His jokes about hedonism were partly true. He didn't want to be shaken out of his comfort zone. It was a self-preservation mechanism. The thought of captivity filled him with dread. *I don't know if I could do it again.*

Sarange looked up at him, her face an accurate reflection of his own thoughts. "Does that frighten you?"

He considered lying to her, being the strutting alpha male the world saw on stage. But this was Sarange. She deserved better than the act he gave everyone else. "Yes."

Her mouth tightened into a line. "It terrifies me."

He halted his stride, catching hold of both her hands so she swung around to face him. "No matter how much it scares me, I will never let you down. You are my *koke gal*. My blue fire. Almost a thousand years have passed since I first held you in my arms, but you mean as much to me now as you did then. We will do this side by side, the way we always did."

"The way we always did." She nodded, her expression changing, becoming determined. "I could always count on you, my tiger."

They skirted the monument that was a tourist destination in daylight, heading instead for the surrounding forest. As they progressed deeper into the trees, Khan was reminded of the enchanted forests in a child's fairy tale. This one beckoned them deeper into its darkness. Its pulsing heart called to them and he could sense Sarange's restlessness growing to match his own. The moon was high and bright. A wolf moon. It illuminated the groves. Coils of vaporous mist lingered, writhing around their ankles like the smoke effects of a Beast concert, sensual and illusory. Most of the time a haunting silence hung over the ground. Nothing stirred. Now and then, the flute-like piping of a lingering songbird rent the silence high above them.

Mahogany brown tree trunks soared heavenward like ancient sentinels guarding the path. Khan's sharp eyes saw gems of amber clinging to their crusty exteriors. His sharp ears picked up the metallic, tinkling sound of a stream and he caught a glimpse of its bright silver ribbon through the lace of leaves.

Once they were deep enough into this nighttime paradise, Sarange turned to face him. "This is where I want to shift."

At the words, he felt something stir in the space between them. Something dark and irresistible. The weight of his past, of everything he'd denied for so long, was there in the icy blue of Sarange's eyes, and Khan's tiger leaped in response. She overloaded his senses and it was intoxicating. He could feel his shifter self rippling in the depths of his muscles, and simmering in his bloodstream. The call of his tiger was beating in time with his heart.

They stripped off their clothes and left them at the base of a tree. Khan reached out his hands and Sarange took them. She gazed into his eyes as he shifted. It was quick, quiet and natural. His human features changed, his golden eyes widened, his powerful body elongated as his muscles grew. Within seconds, the man was gone and Khan's tiger was before her. He knew he was a magnificent animal, standing almost eight feet tall on his hind legs. He dropped onto all fours and Sarange ran a hand through the thick orange fur of his neck. Khan rubbed his whiskery cheek against her thigh, maintaining eye contact. Waiting.

Slowly, Sarange lowered her head, studying the forest floor. He could tell what she was thinking. She was new to this. She wanted to savor it. Last time it had been a necessity, this time...she wanted to think about it. He could see the moment when she surrendered to the emotions coursing through her and gave herself up to her wolf. It was the most perfect, natural shift from human to animal, a harmonious exchange between the two beings who resided within her. She was a shifter, she felt the power of her other self surging through her veins.

Dropping onto all fours beside Khan, Sarange's wolf threw back her head and gave a single, triumphant howl.

Side by side, the tiger and the wolf ran through the forest, moving in time with each other. Khan was conscious of his power and speed compared to her lighter, slenderer frame. He was protective of her, shortening his long strides to match hers, pausing if he thought she was tiring. High on a ridge overlooking the river, they paused, their body language warm and loving. She rubbed her face along his neck and he growled long and low in appreciation.

They moved together and apart, challenging and inviting, in a timeless dance of mating. When they came together for the final time, she rolled onto her back, trusting him completely, a wolf presenting her unprotected belly to a tiger. He stood over her, baring his teeth as if he was about to rip out her tender throat. Two creatures who should never come together except in anger, tied by bonds of tenderness. When he released her, the female scampered to her feet, running from him toward the forest once more. With his long stride, he easily caught up to her and they ran together again, shifting back as they reached the cover of the trees.

Khan pushed Sarange up against the trunk of a tree, holding her naked body in place with his own. He was fire and she was ice, but when they came together, the ice infused the fire with a gentler passion that melted them both. The taste of him was seductive and potent, reminding her of their past and sending a hit of euphoria straight to her sex. Hunger, pure, clamoring and fiery, invaded her body.

After their run through the forest, she needed him

right there and then. She plowed her hands into the thick, dark gold mass of his hair, her fingers tugging on the silken strands, pulling him closer as she took his tongue into her mouth, relishing the taste and feel of him.

A shudder tore through her as his big, warm hands stroked her bare back. His touch sent so many sensations, swift and brutal, rushing through her, striking at her core, making her gasp with instant longing.

Cold air prickled over her heated flesh as the breeze caught her. It added a momentary relief from the red-hot flames burning her flesh.

Khan's hand tugged on her braid as the fingers of the other reached upward, cupping one breast. Sarange sucked in a desperate breath at the heat of his hand burning her. It was like he was imprinting himself into her bloodstream. Her body was a riot of sensation and she didn't know where one feeling ended and the next one began. All that mattered was Khan, his touch and those brilliant gold eyes blazing into her.

He bent his head and the sharp edge of his teeth grazed sweet ecstasy along the sensitive skin of her collarbone. It was just the right side of too much.

"I need you." She barely recognized her own voice. "Always."

His fingers moved to her nipple, tightening as his teeth nipped a path lower. Capturing the hard, sensitive bud between his thumb and finger, he rolled it, making her senses reel out of control with pleasure.

Her arousal spiked until her clit was throbbing with erotic pain. Gripping his hair tighter, she drew his lips back to hers. His tongue licked, his teeth nipped, his lips devoured. Sarange was left breathless and moaning as she arched closer to him.

She stared up at him, at the strong, harshly carved features, and her heart short-circuited. There was so much strength and hunger in his expression. His eyes appeared neon bright in the moonlight. Intense and glowing with hunger. His expression was tight with lust, his lips even more full than usual from their kisses. But there was more than desire on his face. Mates loved. They had loved. Loved each other with an intensity that had destroyed them.

Khan returned to take her lips once more and she felt the world fall away. She lost everything in the pleasure of his touch and the deep, probing intensity of his kiss. Her nails dug into his arm as a soft moan left her lips. She wanted him now, under the moon that called to her inner wolf.

She wanted to unleash this big, powerful male here alongside her memories of him. Here in the outdoors. Wanted them both panting and wild. Wanted to make up for the years apart, the times she had wandered this land alone, searching for him, wishing, wanting, aching...unable to function without his touch.

Pushed hard against the tree trunk, she could read Khan's thoughts. Knew with breathless certainty, as his gaze caught and held hers, that he wanted the same thing.

"Sweet Sarange." His voice rumbled through her, stirring her emotions into a frenzy. With him her strength dissolved. With him she could allow herself to feel, to be vulnerable.

His hand flattened on her stomach, sliding lower, his fingers trailing a heated path of desire in their wake as he cupped her sex. With a soft cry, Sarange lifted herself on the tips of her toes, pressing closer into his probing fingers. It was too much. His touch scorched her. She almost exploded with pleasure as he rubbed against the swollen nub of her clitoris.

"You smell perfect." His teeth raked along her jawline. "You smell like mine."

His words exerted as much power over her as his touch.

"You are so beautiful." His hands returned to cup her breasts, his fingers tormenting her nipples into even harder peaks. "All those years. I thought I'd forgotten, but I couldn't erase your memory from my mind. I thought you were a dream. Now I know you were a memory."

Her heart almost broke at the words and the look in his eyes as he stared down at the rapid rise and fall of her breasts. Then her mind went blank as Khan wrapped his lips around one agonizingly tender tip.

The white-hot feel of his mouth tugging on her nipple sent a lightning bolt of pleasure through her. Her back arched away from the tree trunk and she gave a strangled cry of rapture.

Moving down her body, he pressed a series of kisses from her breasts, down her stomach, across her abdomen and along both hipbones.

The world was spinning out of control. As she tilted her head back, Sarange could see the stars whirling across the velvet darkness. The harsh trunk of the tree pressed into the flesh of her back, hurting her while the pine needles stung her bare feet. Cold damp air prickled over her bare flesh. None of it mattered. Her only sensations were caught up in the man kneeling at her feet. His fingers parting her legs, his lips pressing kisses on her inner thighs, his hot, hungry tongue stroking along her seam.

She arched toward him, her fingers gripping his shoulders, nails biting into his flesh as he licked and sucked, tipping her over the edge into an abyss of trembling arousal. Distantly, she was aware of the half snarl, half growl that left Khan's lips the instant before they covered her throbbing folds and he sucked her swollen clit into his mouth.

His tongue flickered back and forth over the tortured little nub while his fingers probed her tight entrance. Sarange was shaking so hard she could barely stand. Pleasure tore through her, leaving her weak and trembling with the need to climax.

"Khan…" She was close to screaming as he pressed two fingers inside her, stretching her flesh as he caressed her. Calloused fingers worked deep inside, stroking her inner muscles until she was writhing and close to sobbing.

The first vibrations were building inside her, tightening her muscles, sending her nerve endings into a frenzy. Khan continued to lick and suck, driving his fingers in and out of her, slow and steady, then fast and hard, then slowing the pace again. Sarange's breathing was so erratic she couldn't even beg him for more.

Then the explosion hit, breaking over her with such fury she couldn't do anything except cling to Khan and ride the waves of a climax so intense she thought it might break her in two. Khan kept going, that masterful tongue and those skillful fingers driving her onward, until every last shred of pleasure had been wrung out of her and she hung limp in his arms.

When she finally lifted her head, she was breathing hard. Khan's lips were tender on hers and she raised her hands, holding them on either side of his face for a moment or two.

Watching him as he stood naked before her in the moonlight was one of the most erotic things she had ever done. Coming up close to her, Khan swung her around so she was facing the tree. Grasping her wrists, he pinned them above her head, holding them in place against the trunk with one of his hands. His feet moved her legs apart as he pressed up behind her, fitting his body to hers. His chest hair rasped the smooth flesh of her back. The front of his thighs were hard and strong as they pushed up against the back of hers, his pelvis thrust tight into her buttocks.

And then…he was pushing his cock into her still spasming vagina with long, slow, deliberate thrusts. His teeth gripped her shoulder, and his free hand grasped her waist. He rocked his hips, sending heated darts of pain-pleasure ricocheting through her. Sarange cried out, tilting her head back. She was on fire, inside and out. Her overstimulated internal muscles drew him in, every stroke of his rock-hard shaft over her sensitive flesh taking her to new heights.

"I'm coming again." She could hear the note of disbelief in her own voice as she pushed back against his thrusts, keeping time with the demands of his rhythm.

It was too much, not enough. Too fast, yet she needed him to speed up. Too hard, but she wanted him deeper. His pelvis slammed into her as her muscles clamped onto his cock. Khan's powerful pounding filled her, stroked her until she came apart again. This time she clenched around him, heightening every feeling. Ecstasy stormed through her as her second orgasm hit and she bucked and writhed against him.

She felt Khan's thrusts increase as the first wave tore through her. He growled and his bite pierced her shoulder. The pain intensified the aftershocks, sending her wild with renewed delight. Deep inside her, she felt him pulse and jerk.

His head lowered onto her shoulder as his whole body stiffened. She felt him join her in an ecstasy as deep, dark and exquisite as the night that surrounded them.

"This." It seemed like hours had gone by instead of minutes when Khan withdrew from her and turned her to face him, cradling her in his arms. "This is everything. You. The night. The forest."

Sarange nodded against his chest. "But we have to fight for it."

The growl rose from somewhere so deep within him she thought it must have started in his soul. "Always. But we will win." His arms tightened around her. "I don't care who stands in our way."

She tipped her head back to look at him. "Maybe before we do any fighting we should try to remember where we left our clothes?"

Chapter 14

"There is someone I think you should meet." Jiran eyed Khan warily as he said the words. It was his standard expression when he looked Khan's way.

Khan wasn't in the best of moods. He didn't like mornings, although the quality of the breakfast buffet had gone a long way to restoring his equanimity. They were leaving Ulaanbaatar later that day for the Altai Mountain region and Sarange wanted to pay a visit to the political offices of the Chanco Party first. Bora's suggestion that Bek should travel to Mongolia to give a talk at the headquarters of the political group might have been an excuse to get Sarange's uncle here. The Chanco Party might have no links to the gray werewolves.

An internet search had elaborated on what Bek had told them. The Chanco Party was a relatively new political force. Rising remarkably rapidly, predictions were that members would do well in the country's forthcoming elections. The trajectory of their increase in popularity was stunning. There were rumors of vote rigging, even voter intimidation, which was dismissed by the Chanco Party leadership as jealousy from their opposition.

Sarange's plan was to go to their headquarters and politely request a meeting. Khan was more in favor of kicking doors down and a confrontation. They had been debating the options in the hotel dining room when Jiran joined them.

"Who do you think we should meet?" Khan hoped Jiran wasn't about to invite a group of autograph hunters along.

"My father," Jiran said. "Like me, he is a werewolf, one of the gray werewolf pack." Khan was about to refuse, but Jiran's next words made him pause. "He knows something about the Chanco Party."

"Do we have time for this?" Khan asked Sarange. He half hoped she would respond in the negative. Action, not conversation, was what he wanted.

"Why not?" She smiled at Jiran. "Can your father come here this morning?"

He nodded eagerly. "He is waiting in the coffee shop across the road. I will go and get him." He gave them an apologetic look. "My father doesn't use a cell phone."

Khan watched him go. "Still sure you trust him?"

"Still giving him the benefit of the doubt." She frowned. "We have nothing to link Bora to the Chanco Party except the offer to Bek. It's very tenuous."

"Without that we have nothing." Khan tossed back

the last of his coffee. "For now, let's see where tenuous takes us."

When Jiran returned, he was accompanied by a man who was an older version of himself. "This is my father, Houlun. He speaks English."

Khan indicated the empty seats at their table, and the two men joined them. They didn't talk until a waiter had served coffee.

"I take it Jiran has told you what brought us here?" Sarange said.

Houlun's expression was serious. "I was shocked to learn of what had happened in California. How this man named Bora manipulated a group of young werewolves into fighting the way he did. I am a werewolf. I'm used to the way our lives can become violent. Although I mourn for his friends, I'm glad Jiran survived. But if Bora is the man I think he is, his actions are predictable. At least, they are to one who knows the motives of the Chanco Party."

Khan sat up straighter. "You think you know who Bora is?"

"Possibly. Maybe I should start by explaining my involvement with the Chanco Party?" He looked from Sarange to Khan and they both nodded. "The tribal loyalties of the Mongol werewolves go back into the mists of time. Among the werewolf community here, there is a saying that the gray wolf cannot thrive while the blue wolf lives. The Chanco Party is the modern day, political face of the gray werewolves. Although they present themselves as human—and they have attracted many human followers with their policies—they are remnants of the gray werewolf tribe. And one of their aims is to wipe out any remaining trace of the blue werewolves, who are a minority group."

"Does that mean this is a cultural thing?" Sarange asked. "The Chanco Party is hiding behind its true policy, one of genocide against the blue werewolves?"

Houlun nodded. "As the Chanco Party has risen in prominence, attacks on blue werewolves by gray werewolves have been increasing throughout the country. And because blue wolves in the wild are the guardians of the blue werewolves, they are dying out."

"You are a gray werewolf." Khan fixed his gaze on Houlun. "Why are you telling us this?"

"Because what is happening is wrong." The other man's quiet dignity was convincing. "Just because I belong to a different group doesn't mean I believe in persecuting a minority. Not all gray werewolves agree with what the Chanco Party is doing." His voice became quieter. "And my wife, Jiran's mother, was a blue werewolf."

"You said you had some involvement with the Chanco Party?" Sarange said.

"To my shame, I have to admit that I was once a member." Houlun lowered his gaze as he sipped his coffee. "They are very good at recruiting gray werewolves with promises of improved lifestyles. It was only once I was on the inside that I realized what they were covering up. I left when I knew how deep the viciousness and corruption went. That was several years ago. Things have gotten worse since then."

"Tell them the rest," Jiran urged.

"I have friends who are still members of the party. They tell me the leadership is excited about something big happening. Something that will take down the blue werewolves forever." Houlun cast an apologetic glance in Sarange's direction. "They say it will make the destruction of Chinua and her tiger mate look like nothing. The gray werewolves still see that as their glorious victory."

Khan clenched his fist tight against his thigh. "And this man, Bora, is he a member of the Chanco Party?"

"If he is the man I'm thinking of, he uses many disguises and different names," Houlun said. "But I think I have heard him referred to as Bora."

"Can you recall any of his other aliases?" Khan asked.

"No." Houlun shook his head regretfully. "I'm sorry."

"We're going to the offices of the Chanco Party this morning," Sarange said. "Will you come with us?"

Houlun looked alarmed. "I would not advise it. They will know you are a blue werewolf."

"What will they do? Kill me in broad daylight?" Sarange's words were joking, but Khan felt the anger begin to rise deep within him at the suggestion. That was what these people wanted. They wanted to kill her. The thought made it difficult for him to focus on anything beyond his rage.

"I cannot stress how dangerous these people are." Houlun persisted in his attempt to dissuade her. "Especially to you."

"Then they won't be expecting me to come calling, will they?"

Houlun turned his attention to Khan. "You should talk her out of this."

"Have you heard the stories of Chinua, the blue werewolf leader?" Khan asked.

Houlun looked slightly confused. "Yes."

Khan indicated Sarange. "You're looking at her. And you should know that nobody talks her out of anything."

The Chanco Party headquarters were housed in a nondescript office building. It made Sarange think of government offices with lengthy queues and filling out of forms. Houlun had overcome his reluctance and agreed to accompany them. He seemed determined to protect her from any harm that might be awaiting her inside. Such concern from a man she had only just met—a *gray werewolf* she had only just met—touched her. Perhaps there was hope for peace between the warring werewolf factions after all.

Sarange had abandoned her disguise. She wanted the leadership of the Chanco Party to know she was in Mongolia and she was coming for them. Khan had also tucked his shades into his top pocket. When they entered the building, a bored-looking receptionist looked up at their approach. Her eyes widened as she studied them. Two of the most famous celebrities in the world had just strolled in and interrupted her mundane day.

"I'd like to see the person in charge." Sarange spoke in Mongolian, while giving the woman the benefit of her front-of-camera smile.

"I'm not sure…" The receptionist regained a little of her composure. "Do you have an appointment?"

"No, and I'm only in town for a few hours. I'd appreciate half an hour of his, or her, time."

"Um…if you'll take a seat, I'll see what I can do." The receptionist indicated a group of plastic chairs. Houlun and Jiran obediently sat, while Khan and Sarange remained standing. The woman behind the desk picked up the phone and began speaking urgently into it.

"What's she saying?" Khan asked.

"Exactly what you'd expect. She's trying to explain to the person she's calling that Sarange—yes, *the* Sarange—has just walked in here with a famous rock star. She can't remember your name, but she's describing you." Sarange bit back a smile. "It seems whoever she is talking to is a Beast fan. Although I'm not sure he, or she, believes her."

Khan did an impatient circuit of the lobby. When he returned, he jerked his head in the direction of a poster at the side of the reception desk. "My grip on your language isn't great, but it looks to me like the Chanco Party is planning a celebration."

Sarange read the details. "They're holding a gala dinner here next week." She grimaced. "I guess you wouldn't want to be the blue werewolf who accidentally gate-crashed *that* occasion."

A few minutes later a tall, thin man emerged from an office to the right of the reception desk. Sarange's newfound instincts kicked in. Yes, he was a gray werewolf. He was frowning impatiently, until he saw Sarange and Khan. Then the frown melted away and became an expression of incredulity.

"I am Damdid Gandi, Secretary of the Chanco Party. We weren't expecting you."

Sarange introduced her companions. "Do you speak English? Khan doesn't speak Mongolian." They had already established that her words weren't strictly true. As Khan's memory was gradually returning, it became clear he did speak a form of Mongolian. Unfortunately, it was outdated and he found it difficult to follow the modern dialect.

Damdid nodded, switching languages easily. "I spent

a year studying in London. Please, come through to my office."

They followed him into a large room that was furnished in a more comfortable style than the lobby. Damdid spent a minute or two organizing chairs for everyone. Sarange got the impression he was using the distraction to collect his thoughts.

"This is an unexpected honor." Unexpected, yes. Honor? Sarange wasn't so sure a gray werewolf would voluntarily describe her presence in quite that way. She decided she didn't like Damdid Gandi. It had nothing to do with the fact that he was a gray werewolf and everything to do with the fact that he was an unpleasant man. Both her wolf and human senses were telling her that clearly. She didn't need Houlun's prior information to tell her Damdid was a bully who would prey on the weak…or on a downtrodden minority. Her wolf instincts were onto it immediately. *Not an alpha, but wouldn't you love to be one, Mr. Gandi?* "We weren't expecting this visit."

"I wasn't planning on making it." She kept her voice light and conversational. "But I am passing through Ulaanbaatar on my way to the Altai Mountains. Having heard about the work you do, I thought there was an opportunity for us to collaborate."

"You did?"

Damdid's polite mask slipped for an instant. She saw incredulity and something more in his expression. She didn't like the something more. It was feral and nasty.

"We all know the ancient legends about the feud between the blue wolves and the gray wolves. We also know how damaging those stories can be to modern day allegiances in our country." She waited for some acknowledgment and Damdid inclined his head. "You may have heard of my work with the Animals Alive nonprofit organization? I'm here in Mongolia to make a documentary about the threat to the blue wolf pack. It's heartbreaking to think that one of our iconic creatures faces extinction."

"I'm not sure how this affects the Chanco Party."

She noticed how Damdid's face hardened. Her work with the blue wolves was directly contrary to the aims of his party. If the guardians of the blue werewolves died out, the werewolves themselves would be damaged beyond repair.

"I'm offering you a public relations opportunity." *One I'm fairly sure you won't take.* Sarange's only reason for coming here today had been to look someone from this organization in the eye and find out if her suspicions were true. Were they linked to Bora? Every instinct told her they were. Anything she said was just an excuse for getting through the door. "If the Chanco Party works with me on my efforts to save the blue wolves, you can redress some of the bad publicity you've been getting."

Damdid bristled. "I'm not sure what you mean."

She was tired of the game. "I'll be blunt with you, Mr. Gandi. There are rumors that your party is responsible for inciting violence toward those who are perceived to be ancestors of the blue werewolves—"

Damdid made a sudden movement, and Khan was out of his seat like lightning. "Stay where you are."

"You can't come in here and threaten me." Damdid's complexion took on a sickly hue.

Khan placed both hands on the desk, leaning forward so his face was inches from the other man's. "Just did."

Damdid gave a shaky laugh. "Try telling the world out there your story about werewolves."

"I don't need to," Sarange said. "And nor do you. You have a public face and you maintain it well. But within this room, we all know the truth. We know what the Chanco Party is about. You have one policy…the annihilation of the blue werewolves and anyone descended from them."

His smile resembled a snarl. "Since we are being honest, let me assure you we will succeed."

"Who is Bora?" Khan asked.

"Your worst nightmare."

The words had only just left Damdid's lips when Khan lifted him by the front of his shirt and hurled him across the room. Damdid hit the wall opposite his desk with a thud and slid down it. He was still shaking his head in shock when Khan's fist connected with his face.

"Don't even think about shifting unless you want your evil gray throat ripped out."

Damdid stared up at him with dazed eyes.

"You think Bora is a nightmare? Give him a message from me. Tell him there's a Caspian tiger after him and there's no place he can hide where I won't find him."

Since the alternative would have meant spending forty-eight hours on the road, they had decided to fly from Ulaanbaatar to Ölgii in the extreme west of the country. Houlun drove them to the airport.

"I wish I could come with you." Jiran's father shook his head regretfully. "But I have to work and my employers have no idea that I am a werewolf."

Khan laughed. "I can imagine the news that you need time for werewolf duties might come as a bombshell.

Anyway, we need you here to watch what's going on at the Chanco Party headquarters. Let Jiran know if you notice anything suspicious."

Jiran snorted. "How will that happen? He refuses to use a cell phone. And even if he did, we are unlikely to get a signal in the mountains."

"When you do get a signal, you can call me on my landline." Houlun's voice held a mild rebuke. "I'll watch the headquarters for any new developments."

Sarange kissed his cheek, making him blush. "Thank you."

The three-hour flight on a small plane tested Khan's patience more than the longer flight from Los Angeles to Beijing. Being confined in one place didn't suit him. He needed to be able to get up and walk around. The larger aircraft had given him that freedom. This felt—his mind shied away from the comparison, but he forced it onward—this felt like captivity.

Sarange placed her hand over his and he saw understanding in her eyes. "It breaks my heart that there are more tigers in captivity than in the wild."

He shrugged. "Hopefully their experience of imprisonment will not be the same as mine. And many places are doing valuable conservation work. The blue wolves are not the only ones in danger of becoming extinct."

No matter how many chances she gave him, he couldn't talk to her about it. About the living hell of it. About the pain and degradation of being the mightiest beast of them all, yet brought so low. Of how the hardest part had been believing he would never see her again.

"I don't understand why they didn't kill you." Tears shimmered briefly in her eyes as she said the words. "When they first captured you, it would have been so much easier to murder you then than to keep you alive for all those years."

"I've thought about it. A lot. And the only reason I can come up with for them to keep me alive is that they couldn't find a way to kill me. Silver can't do it."

Sarange frowned. "How is that possible? I'll admit my knowledge is limited, but I thought all shifters could be killed with silver swords or bullets."

There was a time, not so long ago, when he wished his captors had killed him. Now, looking into the clear blue depths of her eyes, he was glad they hadn't. He still couldn't think of that time with anything other than pain, but he had come through it. He was here again with Sarange, doing what he was meant to do. Caring for her, protecting her, fighting at her side. Was it wrong to wish for some time to just enjoy being with her?

As if she read his mind, Sarange stretched. "When all this is over, we should take a vacation."

"Did you have somewhere in mind?"

"Somewhere warm, just you and me—" a smile curved her lips "—where clothes are optional."

A growl left his lips as he pressed them to her ear. A little shiver ran through her as he spoke. "When we're alone, you can always dispense with the clothes."

When the plane landed at Ölgii, they disembarked at the tiny airport in the mountains and he stretched his long limbs in relief. Breathing in the pristine air, he looked around him at the stunning landscape, framed by high peaks. They were in a beautiful, remote part of the world to which very few foreigners ever ventured. They were met by a guide from the ger camp where they would be staying. His name was Surkh, and as he loaded their belongings into his jeep, he explained that

Radin's film crew had been in touch. They would be arriving in a day or two.

"What is a ger camp?" Khan asked as the jeep commenced a bone-rattling journey along an uneven track.

It was Jiran who answered. "A ger is a traditional tent used as a dwelling by nomads in the steppes of Central Asia. It's portable, round and covered with animal skins or felt."

"So I'll be sleeping in a tent in the mountains?" Khan studied the snow-covered peaks with dismay.

Sarange laughed. "Many ger camps are quite luxurious."

"Let's hope ours is one of the many." The chill wind was already whipping through his clothing.

The jeep journey took almost as long as the flight, and by the time they arrived at the camp, Khan was tired and hungry. The scenery they had traveled through was incredible. They had passed through several river valleys and seen hollows with semidesert landscapes, Alpine peaks, narrow river canyons and broad valleys. They had caught glimpses of deep limestone gorges, open steppes, as well as lakes, wild rivers and waterfalls. The mountains above them rose as high as forty-five hundred meters and were covered with permanent snow, glaciers and vast tracts of forest.

It was already dark when they descended from the jeep and Surkh's wife, Merkid, gestured for them to accompany her into the largest of the gers. There, an authentic meal of boiled sheep's head had been set out on a table. Once they had eaten, they were shown to their luxurious ger tents. Khan's spirits rose when he learned that the camp was equipped with flushing lavatories and showers with hot and cold water. The camp also had cell phone accessibility, but Surkh explained that the signal could be problematic.

"I don't care." Khan pulled Sarange down onto the bed next to him. "I could live here forever."

"No adoring crowds?" Her voice was teasing.

"You can be my audience." He started to unbutton her blouse.

"You would miss the limelight."

He shook his head. "Not when I have you."

There wasn't a door to the ger, but a bell at the entrance was the signal that someone wanted to enter. Khan muttered a curse when it rang. "I was going to say 'and no interruptions...'"

Sarange smiled as she rebuttoned her blouse. When she went to the entrance, Surkh was waiting just outside. He pointed to the nearby mountain ridge. "Blue wolves."

Putting on warm clothing, Khan and Sarange stepped outside. Maybe it was the utter isolation of the location, the vast darkness of the sky above them and the sheer number of stars scattered across it. Or perhaps it was the story he knew had unfolded here. The curious, yet enduring, love story between two creatures who were such complete opposites. *Our story.* Whatever the reason, Khan felt a shiver run down his spine. At the same time, from the ridge above the ger camp, a howl echoed into the night. Long, low and mournful, the single voice was soon joined by others.

"It is strange." Surkh turned his head in the direction of the sound. "The blue wolves do not usually venture this close to the camp."

Sarange translated his words for Khan.

"How does he know they are blue wolves?" Khan asked.

"Their cry is not the same as that of the gray wolves." Sarange answered his question herself. Her expression was confused as though she was unsure how she knew that information.

Surkh spoke again.

"He said it is almost as if they are offering a greeting." Khan saw a single, shining tear slide down Sarange's cheek as she stepped forward into the clearing beyond the camp and faced the ridge. "And that's exactly why they're here. We have waited a long time for this reunion."

Khan stood back, trusting her instincts, even though a tremor of fear ran through him when he realized what she was doing. After a few minutes, he noticed a change in the howling. It was hard to pinpoint the difference. *Wolf-song.* That was the only way he could describe it. They were celebrating. Singing without words. Offering their own unique music.

Then, out of the darkness, they came. Silvery shapes, gliding out of the shadows. They moved toward Sarange like blue-eyed ghosts.

Khan held his breath. Could he close the distance between them in time if the wolves became aggressive? There was no sign of hostility as they approached in a triangular formation, one large male in the lead, others following, fanning out into a larger group at the rear. Wolf hierarchy. Pack dynamics always came first.

The lead wolf reached Sarange and they gazed at each other for a moment or two. Then the wolf nudged her hand with his nose. It was the trigger to release Sarange from an apparent trance. She dropped to her knees and wrapped her arms around the animal's neck.

Across the distance that separated them, Khan heard her sobs as the other wolves surrounded her and she hugged each of them in turn.

Chapter 15

Sarange had always felt an affinity with animals that was beyond anything she had with other people. Believing it came from her upbringing and Golden Wing's own connection with the natural world, she had embraced it. As her fame and fortune grew, she had used her influence to speak out as a force for good. Becoming an ambassador for the creatures she loved had been a beacon in her life. Until she met Khan, it had been her passion.

Because she was high-profile, she had been fortunate enough to have many moving and exciting encounters with animals. Radin wasn't the first person to see the potential of putting her in front of the camera. She was charismatic, beautiful and passionate about wildlife. Her biggest problem was the number of projects she had to turn down.

Orangutans in Indonesia, elephants in Nepal, gorillas in Uganda…they had been just a few of the memorable moments, but nothing had prepared her for how she would feel when she encountered the blue wolves.

She had been raised to believe that humans and animals shared a common spiritual plain. Golden Wing had explained that humans identified strongly with certain animals—their guardians—and that the attraction was mutual. During life's important moments, it was possible that those animals would present themselves as guides or comforters.

But Sarange's meeting with the blue wolves was so much more than anything that had happened to her before, or anything that Golden Wing had spoken of. The closest thing she could compare it to was coming home.

When she heard that first wolf howl, it had resonated deep within her, calling to her personally. She knew how that made her sound like the ultimate narcissist. A celebrity who turned up in the wilds of nowhere and believed the wolves spoke just to her? But it was true. This pack of blue wolves had come to greet *her*. That was the only reason they were here.

And when they touched her, nudged and nuzzled her, let her hug them…it was the most incredibly moving moment. Both parts of her psyche—human and wolf—felt the surge of emotion equally. It was so much more than the feelings she had experienced in the past from the trust of a wild animal. This was about *her* animals, her pack. They were hers and she belonged to them. Past and present collided in that instant. Rolling around on the hard ground together, they reinforced those bonds and it was wonderful.

Tears of pure joy ran down her cheeks. These majestic and beautiful animals were part of her. Her feelings about their plight became clearer now. She loved all animals, but this was more. Her family was endangered. For them she would take the fight higher and further. She would stop at nothing to ensure their survival.

With a final few nose bumps, the wolves faded back into the darkness. Sarange remained kneeling, sitting back on her heels. The intensity of the moment took time to fade. She knew now that no matter where she was in the world, that connection would feel as strong as if she were right here with the wolves, burying her hands in their thick fur and rolling on the ground with them. She had discovered a part of her life that had its meaning imprinted into her soul.

Wolf. It's who I am. She would wear that badge with pride from now on.

She was aware of a movement at her side and turned her head to see Khan kneeling beside her. His eyes were filled with wonder. "That was incredible."

She nodded, not sure she could trust her voice.

"It's cold out here."

Sarange had barely noticed the icy temperatures, but his words drew her attention to the iron-hard ground beneath her knees and the chill wind cutting through her clothing. "Shall we go inside?"

He rose and slid a hand under her elbow, helping her up. For a moment or two, she leaned against him, looking up at the star-splattered sky. "So many life-changing moments within a month. It all started when I walked out on that stage and saw you."

His smile took some of the chill out of the air. "What can I say? I do my best to be out of the ordinary."

Khan's arm was warm and strong around her as they

walked back to the ger. Once or twice, Sarange glanced back at the ridge. She couldn't see anything in the darkness, but she knew they were there. Her family was watching over her.

The following day they set out early, hiking deep into the interior of the mountainous region with Surkh as their guide. He explained that the area was considered sacred to the local population.

"There are rock carvings, standing stones, burial mounds and Kazakh cemeteries right across this area. And, of course, there are the remains of the fortress that was said to have belonged to the mighty Chinua."

Sarange halted abruptly, her heart suddenly developing an extra beat. "Can you take us there? To the place where Chinua lived?"

Surkh pursed his lips. "It is many miles from here."

"That's where we want to go."

Something in her voice must have convinced him, because he nodded and changed direction, striding out toward a steep incline that took her breath away. They made their way across steep ravines and into deep valleys with towering ice peaks in the distance.

"Is this the territory of the blue wolves?" Sarange asked as she walked alongside Surkh.

"Yes. Many rare and threatened animals live in this region including the snow leopard, ibex, lynx, wolf and bear. The gray wolves are more common at lower altitudes, and the blue wolves live here among the peaks. They used to roam right across the Altai region, but their numbers have dwindled and they are now found in smaller packs."

"So the gray wolves and blue wolves don't compete for the same habitat?" Sarange asked.

"That used to be the case. But as the gray wolf habitat has been threatened by man, the two species have been forced to fight for territory. The blue wolves, having a smaller population, are usually the ones to suffer in a confrontation."

It seemed that nature reflected the shifter world. The gray wolves dominated in both realms, while their blue counterparts were suppressed. Yet there had been a time when both packs were equal, even when the blue werewolves had dominated. And the change had come when Chinua had been defeated. When Khan had been taken from her. Now they were planning…what? To do the same thing again? She cast a glance in Khan's direction. No, that was not going to happen. She would fight that with every fiber of her being. Besides, the first werewolf attack had been an attempt to abduct her. Bora had other plans for her. The thought worried her and aroused her fighting instincts at the same time.

Surkh had brought food and they halted, sitting on a rocky incline to eat sausages, yak cheese and noodles. They washed this feast down with hot sweet tea. Jiran explained that he had been to this region before on climbing expeditions.

"I have climbed Mount Khuiten, one of the highest peaks of the Altai Mountains. It borders Russia, China and Kazakhstan."

Surkh regarded him with new respect. "That is a difficult climb. You look like a gray werewolf, but you must have other skills." It was the first time he had given any sign that he knew they were anything other than human.

Jiran blushed. "My mother was a blue werewolf. I am proud of both sides of my heritage."

When they set off again, the terrain became more difficult and a mist descended, making it hard to see more than a few feet in front of them. At the thought of having to turn around and make the return journey, Sarange was beginning to regret her request to come and see the fortress. She had no memory of this place, and all that was left of the fortress was likely to be ruins. What was the point of traveling all this way to look at something that would be meaningless? Just as dejection was taking over, Surkh halted.

"There."

She followed the direction of Surkh's pointing finger. And gazed into her own past.

Standing high above them, the fortress rose out of a spur of craggy brown rock, appearing to float on a bed of cloud. The vast, multitiered citadel clung to the mountain ridge like a sleeping snake. Its walls gleamed white, and its roof tiles had survived the test of the centuries, retaining their bright red color.

"Oh." Instinctively, Sarange reached for Khan's hand, and he was at her side immediately. His powerful torso pressed against her shoulder and she could sense his own emotion as he gazed at the beautiful image before them. "Can we go up there?"

Surkh looked up at the sky. "If we do, we will not get back to the ger camp before nightfall."

"We'll risk it." Khan was already heading toward the fortress, taking Sarange with him. "Jiran, are you okay with this?"

The young werewolf had been gazing openmouthed at the spectacle before him, but he nodded in response.

"My mother told me stories about this place. I never believed it was real."

It took them another half hour of climbing before they reached the entrance to the fortress. There was an eerie feel to the place as they walked through huge double gates that hung open as though they were waiting for them.

Perhaps they are.

The thought was like a voice spoken out loud in Sarange's ear.

"How has it been so well preserved?" she asked Surkh.

"It is not perfect," he warned. "The exterior is impressive, but once we get inside, you will see that time has caused damage."

As they entered the building, she saw immediately what he meant. It was a shell. The exterior walls had survived the test of time, but the interior had crumbled. It didn't matter. Her memory supplied the missing images. She knew that the circular area in which they stood had once been the great hall.

"We gathered here each evening." Her voice was dreamy as she said the words, her mind filled with pictures. She could see her followers. The brave blue werewolf warriors, their female mates and the cubs playing in the center of the hall. She could hear the laughter and the chatter, smell the food and the scented rushes on the floor.

"The hunters would bring the kill to the kitchen." Khan pointed to his right. "Over there. There was always plenty to eat."

Sarange smiled. "Even for you, my tiger."

Jiran and Surkh stood back and watched them as

they walked through the ruins, reminiscing about the rooms and galleries that had once occupied the space. It felt like she'd been here yesterday. At the same time, it felt like they were intruding on someone else's reality. As they stepped into the section that had been their bedchamber, Sarange felt light-headed with a combination of joy and grief.

"We thought we had forever." The words were squeezed out through throat muscles that were too tight.

"We did, until they took it from us." Khan's features were as harsh as the jagged mountain peaks.

A shout from Jiran brought them back to the present. "Men. Dozens of them." The young werewolf pointed over the battlement into the valley. "Coming this way."

"What shall we do?" Sarange looked around. "We're trapped here. There is no way of getting out and no-where to hide."

"We'll stay and face them." Khan took her hand. "This is our territory."

The four of them walked out to the great gates. Khan and Sarange stood slightly ahead of Jiran and Surkh as they anticipated the appearance of the men. They didn't have long to wait. Within a few minutes, the men Jiran had seen from the battlements were approaching the gates. All of them wore the traditional dress of the nomadic Tuvan people of the region. As a group, they halted a few feet before the gates.

One of the men stepped forward. "We wish to speak to your leader."

Khan made a movement to restrain Sarange, but she stepped forward. "I am the leader you seek."

The man studied her for a moment before dropping

on one knee and bowing his head. "When we knew that Chinua was risen, we came to offer our allegiance."

When Sarange moved forward to greet him, she saw his eyes were as blue as her own. All the men surrounding him had the same blue fire in their eyes. Her heart expanded with pride. Her werewolf army had found her.

Galba, the man who had led the werewolf army to them, told them that a shamanka had visited each of the blue werewolf tribes in the area to inform them that Chinua had returned and that she needed their help to defeat the gray werewolves.

"What was this shamanka's name?" Sarange asked.

Galba looked puzzled. "I don't remember if she told me. Does it matter?"

"I suppose not."

Khan could tell from Sarange's expression that it did matter, but he didn't get an opportunity to ask her why.

They made their way back to the ger camp together with the werewolves. Luckily, since the blue werewolves were nomadic, they had brought their horses and equipment with them, including tents. Surkh was relieved that he wouldn't have to find accommodation for all these people as well as the camera crew who would be arriving the next day. When he tentatively raised the subject of food, Galba assured him they would fend for themselves. The nomads would set up their own camp close to a mountain stream and hunt for their own food. It was what they always did.

"Radin's team may get more than they expected if the gray werewolves arrive and there is a werewolf fight in the middle of their filming schedule," Khan said.

"I'm sure you could use your tiger powers of persuasion to get them to part with any footage we didn't want made public."

He was pleased to see Sarange's spirits had been restored. When they had walked around the fortress, he had felt her sadness and understood its cause. Although it was many centuries ago, it had been their home. They had lived, loved and laughed there. Yes, they had fought constant battles to keep their place in the world, but it had been a happy one. Seeing it now, an empty shell, was a reminder that what they once had was in the past.

Reincarnation. The word had a hollow ring to it. Could past lives ever truly be recaptured? Almost a thousand years had passed since they last stood at those battlements. The view was unchanged and the feelings remained as strong as ever, but so many lifetimes had gone by. A great warrior, born of the dynasty they had created, had shaped this country. They were the same people, yet so very different, marked by the passage of time and the experiences they had endured. Khan's spirit had been broken by his captivity, Sarange's by their separation. They were together now, but the wounds inflicted on both of them ran soul deep. Once this nightmare was over, could they recover? Heal the injuries so that only scars and memories remained?

Even if that was the case, for Khan there was still another question. One that refused to go away. *Who am I?* When he was asked that question in his rock star life, his first response was always a swaggering *"I am Khan."* But who was Khan? What was his reality? He had uncovered part of his story. Now he wanted it all.

He watched Sarange as she walked with Galba, discussing the forthcoming fight with the gray werewolves. *I want it all.* She was what he wanted. The certainty gripped his heart like a vise, triggering an emotion so strong it made him gasp. It was like sunlight breaking through cloud. He wanted his mate, his love, his life. At his side, in his bed, forever. He wanted to see her smile first thing every morning and last thing every night. That militant light in her eyes when she disagreed with him? He wanted that to be a permanent fixture in his life. He wanted them to have the little things. Although fighting monsters was one way to bond, he wanted walks on the beach, nights at the movies, pizza and beer. Ordinary...but not ordinary because she would be there.

He knew Sarange felt the same way. He saw it in her eyes when she looked at him, felt it in her body's response when he touched her. It was always there, electrifying the air between them. *How can I offer her all of me when I don't know who I am?* She wouldn't care. He knew that. *But I care. I won't give her a lie.* And that was what it would be. Until he had his full story, he was pretending to be whole. The thought stripped away his newfound happiness and confidence. Almost sent his mind hurtling back into that hellhole where he had been imprisoned.

Almost. Just at the right moment, Sarange turned her head and looked his way. The blue fire he loved so much shone from her eyes, restoring his balance. *I won't lose this. Won't lose her.* A thousand years of hell was worth it for that one smile.

So I don't know who I am. He added finding his identity to the list of impossible tasks facing them.

Radin's camera crew arrived at noon the next day. The team of three was led by an experienced wildlife photographer called Jenny Monroe. She explained that many of the shots they took would not require Sarange or Khan to be present.

"The final documentary needs your voices, obviously, but that will be done back in the studio. The wildlife shots here will be captured by the team, and could take weeks—" she grinned at Khan's look of horror "—which we appreciate that you can't commit to."

Khan gave an exaggerated sigh. "My manager would kiss your hands and feet in appreciation if he heard that. He's already tearing his hair out that I've interrupted the making of a new album to be here."

"I promise not to keep you on location any longer than necessary," Jenny said. "Radin has been honest about what he wants. The two of you together on screen as much as possible in the blue wolf habitat. That's what will bring in the money."

Sarange grimaced and Jenny shrugged an apology. "Look at it as a way of raising awareness of the plight of these animals. If we can get some shots of you with the blue wolves in the background, great. If not, we'll see what we can do in the editing."

If the camera crew noticed the presence of dozens of nomads just beyond the confines of the ger camp, they didn't mention it. Possibly they believed this was a normal situation, or that the region was more densely populated than it had first appeared. The only comment Jenny made was that it looked like they would have to travel to find the blue wolves, since they were unlikely to come this close to so many people.

"They will come," Sarange said.

Jenny gave her a pitying look. "Don't count on it. I've been doing this job a long time, and wolves are one of the hardest animals to film. There are legends that paint them as aggressors, but the reality is that they're naturally cautious around humans. There is fear on both sides. We have to start by building up respect and trust. That's one of the reasons this shoot may take some time."

"You will have no problem getting your pictures." Sarange maintained her serene expression. "And you will not have to edit me into them."

Khan could tell Jenny thought she was dealing with an eccentric, or possibly egotistical, celebrity. He decided not to enlighten her. It would be more entertaining to watch her reaction when the truth unfolded.

It happened just as he expected. The sky was the color of indigo velvet and the first stars had made their appearance when the alpha wolf gave a single, mournful howl from the ridge.

"What the hell is that?" Jenny dashed out of her ger, her face ashen.

"It's a greeting." Sarange pulled on her sweater as she walked past the edge of the camp and into the open. "One that is older than time."

Khan beckoned for Jenny and her team to follow him. They stood back, observing, as Sarange waited. Before long, the huge alpha male came into view, his coat gleaming in the moonlight. High on the ridge, his pack continued to howl, filling the night with their wolf song.

The silver-gray male reared up on his hind legs to at least seven feet. Towering above Sarange, he paused before placing his huge paws on her shoulders.

"We should do something." Jenny's voice shook with

nerves. "He'll tear her apart. Doesn't anyone have a gun? A tranquilizer dart won't work fast enough."

"Watch." Khan kept his own eyes on Sarange, still fascinated by her relationship with the wild wolves.

The huge wolf brought his face down to Sarange's, rubbing his muzzle along her jawline. Jenny stifled a cry as he opened his mouth, revealing canines like daggers. Sarange tilted her head back and the wolf gently licked her cheek.

"Did he just…?" Jenny turned to look at Khan, her jaw dropping in shock.

"He kissed her," Khan confirmed. "And here come the others. They wish to pay their respects as well."

As Sarange wrapped her arms around the alpha wolf's neck, the rest of the pack came into view. The hierarchy was evident as the wolves approached Sarange in order of rank. Starting with the alpha female, they greeted her with nose bumps and wolf kisses until each of the adults had paid homage to her. Then the cubs were finally allowed to rush forward as a group and frolic around her feet. Laughing, she returned the embraces of the adults, played with the youngsters and spoke to them in a half language only she and they appeared to understand.

"Can you start recording this?" Jenny spoke quietly to one of the mesmerized camera team. She turned to Khan. "Tell me this isn't staged. Those are wild wolves, right? They're not from a sanctuary, or someone's private zoo?"

"This is one of the endangered wild blue wolf packs that roam this area. They have had no interaction with humans that we know of. Surkh tells me they had never ventured close to the ger camp until two nights ago when Sarange arrived. If anyone else tries to go near them, they take to the hills."

"What is she? Some kind of wolf whisperer?" Jenny looked across at where Sarange had almost disappeared under a mass of worshipful wolf bodies.

Khan laughed. "Still worried you may not get enough footage of Sarange with the wolves?"

"What about you?" Jenny asked. "Can we get you in there as well?"

Khan grimaced. How was he going to explain this to her? He could hardly tell the truth. That where he was standing now was just about as close as he could get without sending the wolves skittering away in fear. If he tried to get any nearer, even Sarange's presence wouldn't be enough to soothe their nerves. *Put a tiger among the wolves? I don't think so.*

"That's where you will have to get creative with your editing."

Chapter 16

Sarange called Khan, Jiran and Galba together at dawn a few days later. "The blue wolves are restless. I think it means the gray werewolves are close."

"My concern is the camera crew," Khan said. "Surkh and Merkid practice shamanism. I'm not saying they will take a werewolf battle in their stride, but they understand the mysteries of the universe. Three foreigners caught up in the middle of an ancient blood feud? I'm not sure I want that on my conscience."

"We need to distract them." Sarange felt a surge of confidence. The part of herself that was Chinua thrived on this sort of situation. The legendary general leading her troops. She bit back a smile. There was no trace of the pampered A-lister. "Galba, I need your men to reconnoiter the area. Find out where the gray werewolves are. When we have that information, we'll send the camera crew on a false trail. Tell them a blue wolf pack has been sighted somewhere in the opposite direction and make sure they're gone overnight." She turned to Jiran. "You can be their guide."

He had been listening with an expression of eager anticipation. Now his mouth turned down at the corners. "I want to take part in the fight. I owe Bora."

Sarange placed a hand on his arm. "I need you to do this, Jiran. Although the camera team members are vulnerable, they're also dangerous. If they get caught up in the fight, they could be killed or injured, but if they witness a werewolf fight, or even worse, get a recording, they'll endanger every shifter living in the human world."

Jiran hunched his shoulders. "If it means that much to you…"

"It does."

His expression lightened, reminding her of a schoolboy given a reprieve after being caught in a misdemeanor. "Maybe I should go with Galba's men when they survey the area?"

"That sounds like an excellent plan."

There was a slight swagger to Jiran's walk as he followed Galba to the nomad camp. Sarange was aware of Khan's eyes on her face, of the amused expression in their golden depths. "You never had any intention of letting that boy fight, did you?"

"I hoped to avoid it," she confessed. "But, like you, I was never quite sure where his loyalties lay."

"Now?" A smile quirked his lips as he continued to gaze at her.

"Oh, now I have no doubt he's on our side. Which is why I'm not prepared to expose him to any danger."

He placed his hands on her hips, drawing her to him. "You are a formidable woman, do you know that?"

"I think you may be confusing me with someone you once knew. Name of Chinua."

He rested his forehead against hers. "I remember her. A wolf on the battlefield and a tiger in the bedroom."

She choked back a laugh. "You are shameless."

"Is that a challenge? Because when it comes to shameless, I can take this to a whole other level."

"I believe you." She sighed. "And your shamelessness is deeply tempting, but we have work to do."

"Work?" He frowned. "No one told me about that."

"Jenny wants footage of us both together. A bit like a wedding photo shoot without the party." She paused, biting her lip. "I didn't mean…"

"Sarange, I think a thousand-year-old engagement gives you the right to talk about marriage without worrying that I'll take to the hills." He looked amused.

"But you're Khan." As soon as she said the words, she regretted them. She wasn't even sure what she meant. Yes, he was Khan. *Her* Khan. Her beloved tiger. He wasn't the person the fans saw. The arrogant, whirlwind rock star was an act. She knew that better than anyone.

He was the same man she had loved all those years ago, but he was different because of what had been done to him. She could see how deep the hurt and insecurity went. And it cut her like a knife. *They did that to him because of me.* Took his majestic tiger spirit and tore it to shreds. She didn't know if it was the same men who were coming for them now, or their ancestors. She didn't care. If Bora had been Chinua's enemy, they had an ancient score to settle. If he was new to this fight? Well, he was going to regret the day he got involved.

"Yes, I'm Khan." The pain in his eyes almost cut her in two. "I only wish I knew what that meant."

She took his face between her hands, tracing his beloved features with her fingertips. "It means you're mine." She felt him relax beneath her touch. Grasping her wrist, he turned her hand so he could press a kiss into the center of her palm. "You know what else it means?"

His smile melted her. Just turned her into a helpless puddle of longing. "Tell me."

"It means, no matter how hard you try, you're not going to get out of doing some work this morning."

"We are outnumbered." Galba's expression was troubled. "My scouts tell me the gray werewolves are coming in great numbers from the southeast."

"You know what we need to do." Khan spoke in an undertone to Sarange. She would reach this conclusion herself, but time was running out and he wanted to help her along.

"I do?" Her expression was puzzled as she turned her head to look at him.

"Think about what lies east of here."

He could see her considering and discarding different options. Then the frown lifted from her brow and she nodded. "Of course." She straightened her shoulders. "Galba, get your men ready. We're going to the fortress."

The werewolf regarded her with even greater respect. "Chinua's fortress? From there, we cannot fail." He bowed low before leaving them.

"What about me?" Jiran asked. "Is the plan still for me to distract the photographers?"

"Yes," Sarange said. "If you don't, they're going to think it's mighty strange when Khan and I disappear with the entire nomad tribe."

"Have you been in touch with Houlun?" Khan asked. "I can't help wondering what's going on at Chanco headquarters while the gray werewolves are on the march."

"I spoke to my father earlier today. He said everything seems quiet in Ulaanbaatar, except for the preparations for the big celebration."

"Let's see if we can't spoil the gala by defeating their army when they reach the fortress," Khan said.

"There's no time to lose." Jiran became businesslike. "I'll take the camera crew in the opposite direction of the fortress." He went away and a few minutes later they heard him calling to Jenny that he knew where the largest pack of blue wolves could be seen.

"There is hope for that boy yet," Khan said.

"Yes, Grandpa." Sarange's smile was mischievous.

He groaned. "You're right. I sound like someone's grandfather. Or a stern father, at the very least." She hesitated and he frowned. "What is it?"

"I wondered…"

He ducked his head to look more closely at her face and was surprised to see tears in her eyes.

"Did we have children? If we did, why don't I remember that?"

"I don't recall either. I wonder if the fact that neither of us remembers means that we didn't." He drew a breath, preparing to talk about the thing that hurt him most. Every time he thought about leaving her, his heart splintered and his mind scattered into a thousand fragments making rational thoughts impossible. Determinedly, he held them together. "And maybe, if we'd had a family, you—Chinua—would have kept going, for them, instead of searching for me?"

The tears spilled over, streaking her cheeks, but Sarange appeared not to notice them. "If we didn't have children, how did we build a dynasty? Chinggis Khan was supposed to have been descended from the blue werewolf pack we established."

He held her close, cradling her against his chest. "That's just it. He was descended from the blue wolves. There is no mention of a tiger in his family tree."

She stood very still for a few moments. When she raised her head, the tears were gone but her face was pale. "Are you trying to tell me we couldn't have a child because we are different species? We can be mates, but we can't have children? Just like in the natural world, dogs and cats don't have hybrid offspring?"

This was not the conversation he wanted them to have just before they went into battle. But they had always been honest with each other and he wasn't going to change that now. He took her chin between his thumb and forefinger, tilting her face up to his. "I honestly don't know the answer to that. But we are shifters. We have human genes. And I guess there's only one way we're going to find out the answer to this question."

"You mean…?" She gulped back another sob. "We try?"

"Yes, I mean we try. But first we have to go and kill some bad guys." *And I have to figure out where the hell I came from.*

As Sarange went to gather a few items of warm clothing together, Khan speculated on that conversation. Of course he wanted children with her. He wanted everything with her. But he was fearful that he might have felt the same way a thousand years ago, with no outcome. Could Sarange be right? Her cats and dogs comparison was a clumsy one, but it was true. This wasn't a question for even the most skilled human doctor. It would rock the scientific world to its core and blow the anonymity of every shifter in the world wide open. It wasn't even a problem he was going to take to Ged, the shifter oracle. Right now it was one he was going to put to the back of his mind while he focused on the immediate problem of keeping Sarange safe.

Galba and his men were ready and waiting. Sarange explained that her childhood had been spent with a different nomadic group. Her tribe had been reindeer herders in the northernmost part of the country. Here in the Altai region, the Tuvan nomads used horses to navigate the difficult terrain. Now Galba was insisting that she should ride his horse.

"You are the leader. It is not fitting that I should ride while you walk."

To please him, Sarange acquiesced to his request. It meant the long hike to the fortress was a boring one for Khan. The horses, obviously used to their werewolf masters, were skittish around him. Khan had come across this issue once before. Ged was always careful about photo shoots. Generally, shifters tried to avoid causing distress to animals. Horses were particularly sensitive to the genes of a shifter.

On one occasion, an overenthusiastic photographer had decided to introduce an equine theme into a magazine cover without warning Ged in advance. The result could have been carnage. The poor horses with their highly developed awareness, not only of the presence of big cats, a werewolf, a bear and a dragon, but also of the mysticism of the shifter world, had reared and plunged in terror. The situation had only been resolved when Beast left the scene immediately.

These horses, more accustomed to the presence of shifters, were not exhibiting the same signs of distress. Nevertheless, it had been evident the first time he met Galba that they were not comfortable if Khan got too close. For that reason, he was staying in sight of, but slightly apart from, the group.

His boredom was relieved slightly by the sight of a golden eagle soaring overhead. With its giant wings outstretched, it hovered briefly over the group before circling away toward the higher peaks. Within minutes, the bird had returned to hang in the air over their group once again. It repeated this pattern over and over until Khan might almost have believed they were being followed by a bird of prey.

Despite the warm clothing provided by Surkh, several hours of hiking through strong winds blowing fast and cold through the valleys and down the ravines, disturbing the freshly fallen snow and taking the icy edge off the glaciers, had Khan shivering when they arrived at the fortress.

"Oh, my tiger." Sarange held out her arms as she dismounted. "Come here and let me warm you up."

"At least I didn't get overpowered by the eagle." He stepped into her embrace, enjoying the sensation of her rubbing her hands up and down his arms.

"What eagle?"

"The one that followed us most of the way." At least his teeth seemed to have stopped chattering. "You can't have missed it. It was so big it blocked out most of the sky."

Sarange looked bemused. "I didn't see an eagle. Galba, did you notice an eagle following us?"

Galba shrugged. "No." *A man of few words.* He went away to help secure the horses.

"Ah, hell. You're telling me I'm seeing imaginary birds? What next? Fake gorillas? Fictional buffalo?" No, joking about it didn't make it go away. "That damn eagle was real."

Sarange looked up at him in surprise. "Khan, it really doesn't matter."

Was it worth pursuing? Trying to convince her? For some reason, he thought it was. Before he could make any further attempt, a shout went up from the battlements. "They are here! The gray werewolves are just across the valley."

Although the gray werewolves outnumbered them, they had two disadvantages. As far as Sarange could see, they had no clear leader. And they didn't have a tiger on their side. Those were two of the things she was counting on as she surveyed the scene below her.

Emerging from the surrounding hills, they moved closer, their thick fur providing them with protection from the cruel wind that blew off the snowy peaks. It was the same wind that cut into Sarange's skin, blanching her cheeks and bluing her chattering lips. *And this was once my home.* She had obviously once been acclimatized.

At first the gray werewolves were little more than moving shadows, their warning howls carried away on the bitter wind. As they neared, their gray fur became obvious. With the killer instinct of a wolf pack but the intelligence of humans, they communicated in barks and growls, spreading wide and encircling the fortress, cutting off any means of escape.

Where are you, Bora? Because he sure as hell wasn't with them. She could tell because there was no one to whom they turned for leadership. Having formed their circle, they waited. The next move was in the hands of the blue werewolves. *I am leading this.* She gave a bring-it-on shrug. *Not for the first time.*

"Two to one in their favor?" Khan studied the opposition, trying to analyze the odds.

"I rate our chances a little higher than that. And we have you." She spared a moment to glance in his direction. "A tiger among wolves. Always an advantage."

"Except for the time they captured me." His expression clouded. "I wish I could remember how the hell they did that."

"That was then." Knowing her touch soothed him, she took a moment to grip his hand. "This is now. I wish I knew what Bora's game was. Why isn't he here?"

"Could he be down there?" Khan nodded at the waiting werewolves. "Just because there is no obvious leader doesn't mean he's not there. He's already proved he's tricky."

"I remember enough about my past to know that once those werewolves shift, they become a pack of wolves. They follow their alpha." She pointed into the valley. "Look at them. They don't have an alpha. They have been sent here. They formed a circle around the fortress because someone told them to. When we attack them, they'll fight back because they're wolves and that's what they're conditioned to do. But no one is guiding them. They have no one looking out for their welfare."

"You sound almost sorry for them." Khan scanned her face.

"In a way I do. A week ago, I had no idea I was a werewolf. Then I found out that, not only am I a werewolf, I was once a legendary leader who lived almost a thousand years ago. It's taken some getting used to in a short time." She smiled. "But some things were easy, probably because Chinua has always been there inside me. And I know she took care of her troops. There is no way she would have sent them into a battle without being with them. She would call that the sign of a coward." Her lip curled. "And I would agree with her."

"Maybe Bora thinks he's already won this one. He does have a lot more fighters than we do."

"If that's the case, he's making a big mistake."

"So you won't go easy on them because you feel sorry for them?" Khan asked.

Sarange shook her head. "It's sad, but they have to die."

They stepped down from the battlements and she called Galba to her. "Assemble the men. I want to talk to them before we go into this fight."

The blue werewolves gathered in the ruins of the great hall, and Sarange stood on a fallen stone in the area she knew had once been Chinua's place at the head of the table. The thought sent a prickle up her spine. It was a combination of feelings. There was pride, responsibility and honor. Together with a healthy dose of fear. But the fear was necessary. It gave her the edge she needed to remain focused on the task ahead. And she would never show her apprehension to the men who gazed at her with such adoration and respect.

"When we fight, the temptation is to become wolves. To immerse ourselves completely in the fighting mode of the pack. That is what our opponents will do." The warrior spirit of Chinua was strong in her as she spoke. "The way to win this battle is to use your werewolf strength and cunning, but retain your human reason. We know how to do this. It will be brutal. We are not planning to take prisoners. As we attack, keep ahead of the enemy by staying part human."

"What do you mean?" Galba asked.

"If you retain your human senses, you can recall those things that will help you defeat a wolf. The worst thing in the world for a wolf is to be pinned down. Normally, in a fight, both wolves are trying to avoid that. Let your opponent bring you down. It gives you the advantage of surprise and exposes his throat and belly to you. Do what you do best. Claw, bite and tear. But also kick, jump and—" she looked around, unsure how her next suggestion would be received "—consider running away."

As she had anticipated, the proposal that a group of brave warriors should contemplate retreat as a strategy wasn't well received. There were frowns and mutterings.

"Until Chinggis Khan, Chinua was the greatest leader this region had known," Khan said. "Her brilliance in battle was renowned…and she never lost a fight."

"We are outnumbered." Sarange gestured toward the valley. "Our advantage lies in doing the unexpected. I'm not suggesting you run and keep on running." There was a ripple of relieved laughter. "Run and turn when your foe least expects it. Or work together. If you see another blue werewolf being chased by the enemy, seize the initiative and attack the pursuer."

She felt the mood change. Her approval ratings were going up. Khan gave her an encouraging grin.

"One final thing…if they retreat, we will not pursue them." She nodded to Galba. "Let's get out there and start winning."

Before she could step down from her makeshift stage, the entire pack of blue werewolves dropped onto one knee, bowed their heads and placed their hands over their hearts.

Just as they used to before they followed Chinua into battle.

Chapter 17

"You should stay out of the fighting." Galba's face was serious as he accompanied Sarange to the gates. "Every one of the gray werewolves will have orders to kill you first."

"I know." She smiled as she started to shrug off her warm clothing. "It makes it even more exciting."

This time when she prepared to shift, it was like a surge of electricity along every nerve ending. She guessed it was the anticipation of what was to come. She spared a brief thought for her organized celebrity lifestyle. Flowers delivered every Tuesday, workouts with her personal trainer each morning, emails answered by her personal assistant within twenty-four hours, her slightly obsessive habit of organizing her closets according to color *and* fabric. *And all that time I never knew I was a bloodthirsty wolf general.*

As the men around her started shifting, Khan spoke quietly in her ear. "You know I've got your back."

"Always."

"Then let's go."

The blue werewolves exploded out of the gates with Khan slightly ahead of them. As Sarange had expected, the gray werewolves waited for their approach instead of advancing to meet them. Within minutes, they were in the valley. The blue werewolves spread out, charging into the circle of attackers.

The time for thinking of anything except this fight was over. As she had told the men when they were up in the fortress, if they were to win, they needed to take the gray werewolves by surprise. As she darted like a silver streak through the gray bodies that snapped and snarled around her, Sarange felt a rush of adrenaline powering her along. It was like stepping back in time. Or stepping into Chinua's body.

She took advantage of the fact that she was lighter and faster than the male werewolves. Leaping up and onto the backs of the warring males, she used her razor-sharp canines to rip at the ears and muzzles of the gray werewolves, harrying the enemy and moving on before they could respond.

Around her, she was aware of the blue werewolves carrying out her instructions and causing chaos. Throughout it all, there was the giant, comforting figure of the Caspian tiger, plowing through the fight, shredding wolf muscle and bone with his fangs and claws as if he were slicing through butter. Khan tossed the mangled bodies of his victims aside with a triumphant roar. It was brutal, but effective.

Sarange kept going, driving deeper into the enemy

pack. Galba was right, of course. She was the one the gray werewolves were all seeking. As she darted among them, huge jaws snapped dangerously close to her hind legs and she used her superior speed and agility to dodge them.

Before long, the stench of blood was thick and cloying in her nostrils and she had to fight to ignore it. In normal circumstances, blood was a pleasant smell for a werewolf, but when it was the blood of another wolf it was cause for distress. All around her snarls, howls and cries of pain rang out. It was sensory overload, none of it good, all of it distracting.

When two gray werewolves came at her, one on each side, Sarange tried to dart away. Too late, she realized her mistake. A third opponent was blocking her escape. They moved closer, pushing in on her from three sides. Taking her own advice, she dropped to the ground.

The werewolf nearest to her grunted in confusion, his teeth snapping dangerously close to her throat as he stood over her. She pressed herself tighter to the cold earth, waiting for him to attack. When she felt him move, she twisted beneath him, sinking her teeth into the soft fur of his belly and holding on.

The other two gray werewolves tried to come to his aid, but Sarange's position made it almost impossible for them to get to her. As long as she remained crouched beneath her larger adversary, there was nothing they could do. Keeping her teeth locked in place as he writhed and howled, she felt his blood splatter her fur. The harder he tried to shake her off, the worse the wounds she was inflicting became. Eventually, he stopped fighting, flopping onto his side, breathing heavily. Sarange didn't have time to go in for the kill. She had to get away from his companions.

With blood dripping from her muzzle, she darted back into the thick of the battle. Working her way toward the point where she could see Khan hurling werewolf bodies high into the air, she continued to lash out left and right, ripping apart flesh. Moving on without pause.

Teeth closed on her shoulder and she howled in pain and rage. Swinging her upper body around, she was in time to see one of Chinua's tactics in action. One of the blue werewolves threw himself onto her attacker, sinking his teeth into the gray werewolf's neck. Blood, bright red and warm, sprayed in a fine mist, coating Sarange's face and temporarily blinding her. When she blinked it away and cleared her vision, the wolf that had bitten her was lying on its side, gurgling as blood gushed from its wounds.

Sarange continued to dart through the battle, never losing sight of Khan. This strategy began to make sense to her. Although she was in charge, she wasn't as physically powerful as the males. With her tactics, she remained highly visible to her own troops, annoyed the hell out of her enemies and retained an overview of the battle. The only problem was the drain on her energy. She was running on adrenaline, her chest heaving, every muscle aching, heart pounding like the hooves of a wild stallion.

Just as she thought her lungs might explode with her next breath, she realized it was all over. The ground beneath her was littered with dead and dying werewolf bodies, almost all of them gray. The remaining enemy fighters, after giving voice to a united, anguished howl, turned and ran. True to Sarange's orders, her fighters let them go. The valley fell silent as the blue werewolves watched their enemy retreat.

This remembered feeling was in her bloodstream. The movies had it all wrong. There was no elation in victory. No joy in killing. Later, there would be a sense of satisfaction in a job well done, a feeling of relief that, once again, she had kept her pack safe. Right now all she felt was overwhelming sadness. So many lives lost. And for what? Because one man's desire to destroy her was so strong he was willing to send his followers here in great numbers with orders to kill her?

Why, Bora? What did I do to make you hate me so much?

Above all else, there was exhaustion. A tiredness that seeped into her bones. She wanted to lay her head on the hard, cold ground, gaze up at the clear skies and just drift away.

Being in charge brought great responsibility. She shifted back, signaling for the blue werewolves to follow her lead. Blood and gore covered her body as she faced them. *How would I ever explain this to my stylist?* She was able to quash her initial human instinct to cover herself as she stood before dozens of naked men. They were shifters. In that instant, they weren't viewing her as a female. She was their leader. Before she could find the words to thank them, they were bowing before her once more.

The river water had been bone-jarringly icy, but at least it had washed away the blood from their bodies. Sarange had a bite on her shoulder, but the wound wasn't deep. Khan had scratches and bruises. Getting dry enough to put their clothing back on had been the hardest part. Now, at last, the shivering and teeth chattering had stopped.

Sarange and Galba had walked the valley floor, organizing the best way to dispose of the bodies. Khan marveled at the way she slipped into her leadership role. When she talked to the blue werewolves as a group, he had seen tears glimmering in the eyes of many of the big, tough men. Afterward, she found time to speak to each of them individually.

Before Galba and his men prepared to decapitate and bury the bodies, Sarange spoke a few words. Her voice was a soft, soothing sound that carried high on the icy breeze. When she walked away toward the fortress, a new peace seemed to settle over the bloodstained valley.

"What did you say?" Khan asked.

"It was a chant my grandmother used when one of the animals died. It helped them on their way."

A shadow fell over them and Khan looked up. "Still think my golden eagle was imaginary?"

He grasped Sarange's shoulders, pointing at the sky above them. The giant bird circled the fortress several times before swooping down and landing on the outer wall of the battlements. It almost appeared to be waiting for them. As they approached the giant bird, Khan watched in surprise as an incredible transformation took place. The eagle gradually drew its body up, becoming taller and thinner in the process. Its head grew rounder and its wings disappeared, arms appearing in their place. Within minutes, the bird had gone and a woman stood there instead.

Although she was old and lined, there was a vigor about her that energized the surrounding atmosphere.

She wore a dull brown robe with a white sash and a gold silk scarf around her neck. On her feet were reindeer-skin boots and her coat was made of animal hide. She could have been eighty years old. She could have been older than time. Stepping down from the wall, she held out her hands in a sweeping gesture.

Khan's attention was diverted from the woman when Sarange gave a cry and fell to her knees. A suspicion entered his mind. Could it be?

Sarange covered her face with her hands. "This can't be happening."

Khan knelt beside her, wrapping his arms around her in an attempt to comfort her.

"This is the shamanka who told us the gray were-wolves were coming," Galba said. "She is the one who told us Chinua was risen and that we must prepare for battle."

"Golden Wing?" Some deep instinct, the same sense that had drawn him to the bird as it followed them from the ger camp to the fortress, was telling him he was right. That inner pull was so powerful he had blurted out the words before he had time to consider the consequences. If he was wrong, it would cause Sarange pain. She talked about Golden Wing all the time, but she was unlikely to be impressed by him mistaking this mystical stranger for her beloved grandmother.

"A wolf storm brought me back to you, my child." The woman's voice was low and melodic, almost like singing. Ignoring everyone else, she spoke directly to Sarange. "The skies are yours this day."

Sarange uncovered her face. "Is it really you?"

"It really is." The smile on the shamanka's face dispersed the clouds.

Sarange shook her head. "I don't know how, or why, this is happening, but I'm glad it is."

"You can hug me," Golden Wing said. "I am a spirit, but I am not made of vapor."

With a sound between a sob and a laugh, Sarange ran to her and was enveloped in an embrace. She caught hold of her grandmother's hand and drew her forward. "There is someone I want you to meet."

"Khan." Golden Wing took his hand. "You have a tiger soul, but your heart seeks peace. Will you find it?" Coal-black eyes studied his face. "I think the answer lies within yourself."

It was an unusual introduction, but it was the first time Khan had met a shamanka. He didn't know how he was supposed to respond. Casting a pleading glance in Sarange's direction, he encountered only an encouraging smile. "Um, thank you."

In the valley below them, Galba had returned to his men. They were beginning the ritual of disposing of the dead gray werewolves using short, leather-handled silver swords to decapitate the bodies and digging the hard ground to make graves.

"Walk with me, my children. My feet can only touch the land on this day and only while the sun is high."

Sarange cast a fearful glance at the sky. "Can't you stay?"

Golden Wing shook her head as she led them to the highest point on the battlements. The three of them stood together looking out across the sweeping valley to the highest of the snowy peaks beyond. "The spirits may cross into this realm, but we cannot linger."

"Why did you come today?" Khan asked.

"It was not in my power to intervene, but I called upon the spirits of blue wolves past to watch over you."

"It seems they did." Sarange looked back down the curving lines of the fortress at Galba and his men.

"Perhaps, but the strength came from within you. You have grown stronger than Chinua herself." Golden Wing's serene expression clouded briefly. "But the gray werewolf leader was not vanquished in the fight."

"It was obvious they had no leader. I don't know why he chose not to come here today. Can you explain it?" Sarange asked.

"I can ask the spirits."

Sitting cross-legged on the dusty floor, Golden Wing closed her eyes. Swaying slightly from side to side, she began to chant under her breath. Sarange tugged on Khan's hand and they sat opposite her, watching her in complete silence.

After several minutes of her incantation, Golden Wing opened her eyes. Although she looked directly at them, Khan had the strangest feeling that she wasn't seeing them. "The gray werewolf leader wants you to die, but he does not want you to see his face when it happens."

"Is he Bora?" Khan asked.

"That is one of his names."

"Do you know the others he uses?" Sarange leaned forward eagerly.

"I know he is one man who is three."

What the hell kind of answer was that? Khan got the feeling the spirits might be offended if he blurted out that response.

"He has been fighting you for a long time."

"Why did he hate me—hate Chinua—so much?"

"The answer to hate often begins with love." Golden Wing's smile was sad. "The gray werewolf leader wanted Chinua. When she chose the tiger instead, his love became hatred. It turned pack against pack and ignited a feud that has lasted a thousand years."

Sarange turned her head to smile at Khan. "How did I find myself a tiger in a world of wolves?"

"The gray werewolf leader was putting pressure on you to tell him you would be his. You decided to spend some time alone here in the Altai Mountains. It was here you met a man who was good. A man who said 'I am yours' instead of 'You are mine.'"

Khan placed his hand over Sarange's. "I may not remember the details, but I know you made me the happiest man on earth."

"You also made a powerful enemy. From that day on, the gray werewolf leader swore to destroy you." Golden Wing closed her eyes briefly. "He was unrelenting in his desire for vengeance. You found great joy in each other, but he did not allow you to find peace."

"That was why we built this place." Sarange gestured at the mighty fortress around them. "Because we always had to fight, and we had to have somewhere to keep our people safe." Her expression was sad. "Even today, the blue werewolves are persecuted and the wild blue wolves face extinction, because Khan and I fell in love."

"Do you know where Bora is now?" Khan asked.

Golden Wing's black brows drew together and she clasped her hands in front of her as though in prayer. "The spirits cannot tell me his location, but his followers are getting ready to celebrate a great triumph." She shook her head. "It is strange because victory did not come their way today."

"The gala dinner in Ulaanbaatar," Sarange said.

Khan nodded. "Maybe that was the plan all along. Bora didn't want to get blood on his hands. Instead, he gets to put on his tux and deliver the keynote speech."

Golden Wing cast a look at the sky. "The sun is sinking…"

"Don't go yet. Please." Sarange's voice throbbed with emotion as she placed a hand on her grandmother's arm. "There are other things I need to ask you."

"Then you must ask me quickly, my child." There was a note of amusement in Golden Wing's voice.

"You found me miles from anywhere, wrapped in reindeer hide. But you knew I would be there, didn't you?" Sarange asked.

Golden Wing nodded. "The spirits told me where to find you. I know what you are going to ask me next, and I have no answers for you. I don't know who your birth parents were. I only know that you are Chinua born again."

Sarange was silent for a moment or two, considering her answer. "Is it possible that my parents were not human? Could they have been blue wolves?"

Khan remembered her interaction with the blue wolf pack. Recalled the bond between them. The love between them. Could a shifter child be born of wild animals? It made its own kind of sense.

"Anything is possible in this great universe of ours," Golden Wing said.

Sarange bowed her head. With his ability to read her emotions, Khan felt a feeling of peace emanating from her. It was a story come full circle.

When she raised her head, Sarange's expression was serene. "I have one final question for you."

Golden Wing looked from her upturned face to Khan's. "This is not your question to ask, my child. This must come from the heart of the tiger."

Khan regarded them in confusion. "Would someone mind telling me what's going on?"

Golden Wing took his hand in hers. Although her fingers were cool, a curious feeling of heat spread outward from the point where her flesh connected with his, tingling along his nerve endings. It felt as though she was connecting with a deeper part of him than the surface of his skin.

"The question Sarange wants me to answer is one only you can ask me." Golden Wing's dark gaze probed his face.

Khan stared at her, confused and unsettled. How could he ask the right question, when he had no idea what she was talking about? He was a shifter, but the mystical world to which Golden Wing belonged was beyond his experience.

A voice in his head—a voice that sounded a lot like Golden Wing's—prompted him to open his heart. To see what she wanted him to. But he was afraid of what she was offering. There was a strange sort of comfort in not knowing, there was familiarity in the belief that he would never remember it all and there was fear in hearing a shamanka's voice inside his head telling him to let go, to soar with her, high above the earth and into the clear sky.

Without knowing anything about him, Golden Wing was giving him hope and compassion, wrapping him in them as if they were warm blankets. Her dark eyes promised him magic and miracles...if he was brave enough to take them. If he could ask her the only ques-

tion that mattered. Drawing in a shaky breath, he finally found his voice.

"Who is Khan?"

Chapter 18

*W*ho is Khan?

Even though they weren't touching, Sarange felt the tremor that ran through Khan as he asked the question. She saw the pain in his eyes and knew how scared he was of hearing the answer. It was the question that haunted him. The world thought it knew Khan. They saw the image he wanted to project. The flaunting, arrogant egotist. He created a new headline every day, each one more outrageous than the last. That was his hiding place. Because the truth was, he didn't know himself. And he was terrified of what he might discover.

She also knew this was a barrier he had to cross if they were to ever find lasting happiness together. It was a difficult admission. *Because we are happy.* Theirs wasn't even a once-in-a-lifetime story. It was once-in-forever. But no matter how hard he tried to hide it from

her, Sarange felt Khan's pain as if it was her own. And
the source of his hurt was beyond her control. She could
move armies and defeat a centuries-old enemy, but she
couldn't help him with this.

*Maybe I can't help him, but I know a woman who
can.*

Her emotions were still in turmoil over Golden
Wing's surprise appearance and disclosures. Her grandmother's death almost fifteen years ago had left her bereft. Bek and Gerel had done their best to fill the void
in her life, but nothing could really compensate for the
loss of the woman who had raised her. Golden Wing
had been a unique figure. Sarange's guiding light, her
constant companion, and her only family for so long.
Not being able to say goodbye had also hit Sarange hard.
It had been a double blow. Like a death within a death.
First there was the pain of knowing Golden Wing had
gone; then there was the heartache of false hope. Being
so far from home, she hadn't seen a body, hadn't been
part of the funeral rites. Her heart had played a game
of disbelief. What if it wasn't true? Someone had gotten
it all horribly wrong? When reality sank in, grief hit a
second time. She had mourned all over again.

Will this be a third time? She watched as Golden
Wing placed her hands on either side of Khan's face
and pressed her forehead against his. Would the joy of
seeing her again be the roller-coaster high that was followed by a low of sorrow when she left?

And what about Khan? What if his worst fears were
realized and Golden Wing told him something now that
meant they could never be together? If he walked away
from her, the heartache that had sent Chinua wandering
this great land until her spirit faded away would pale in

comparison. *I would not survive.* There was no drama in the thought. Only certainty.

"The spirits speak to me of the Xinjiang region." Golden Wing kept her hands on Khan's face. Her voice was low, almost a whisper.

Khan jerked as though she had delivered an electric shock. "That is where I was held in captivity."

"It is also where you were born." Golden Wing remained silent for a moment or two. "When you shift, you are a Caspian tiger."

"That's what Sarange said."

Sarange knew her grandmother had to enter a mystical realm as part of her shamanistic rituals. Golden Wing's eyes fluttered closed now and her body trembled as she received messages from her spirit guides. "But you were not born a shifter. Your parents were human."

"I don't understand." Khan frowned. "Do you mean I was bitten by a weretiger?"

Sarange cursed her limited knowledge of shifter lore. All she had was what Khan had once told her, but she needed more detail. She weighed her options. While she didn't want to interrupt Golden Wing's vision, these revelations affected her. She needed to know it all, no matter how bad it got. "What does that mean?"

"A shifter is either born or made," Khan said. "Although it is rare, a shifter can be transformed through a bite. It happens in one of two ways. Often the bitten shifter has agreed to the process because he, or she, wishes to make the transformation and live alongside a shifter mate. The other way is during an attack. If bitten humans don't die, they take on the form of the shifter that attacked them."

"So there is a grain of truth in those old movies about

feral werewolves waiting on misty moors to jump out on unsuspecting humans?"

A brief smile lightened the strain on his features. "More than a grain."

Sarange swallowed hard. "Was Khan bitten in an attack…or by a mate?"

She had believed she wanted to know it all, but did she really want to hear the answer to this question? It was all very well to tell herself that Khan had been hers for a thousand years as if that conferred some sort of entitlement on her. Although she didn't know much about shifter tradition, she knew there were creeds and rules that ran deeper than the ties of emotion. Immortality brought benefits and responsibilities. If there was a mate who had a prior claim on him, Sarange didn't like her own chances of holding him. Her inner wolf was already rising in rebellion. Tenacity and loyalty. Wolf traits. *This isn't about my wolf. This is about me. About not letting him go because I love him. With everything I have in me. And I cannot—will not—give up on that.*

"Your story is a strange and tragic one." Golden Wing continued to speak directly to Khan. "You were only eight years old when you were taken from your parents. They called you the Tiger Boys. Children who were converted from human to weretigers by a bite from a rogue shifter."

"Why?" Khan's voice was little more than a croak.

The anguish on his face flayed Sarange's nerves until they were raw. She wanted to wrap her arms around him until the pain went away, but she was afraid of breaking the connection between him and the shamanka. Instead, all she could do was take the hit of physical pain to her chest and stomach and know it was only a fraction of what he was feeling.

"Sometimes evil needs no reason. This shifter kept you as his playthings until, one day, there was a rebellion led by the largest and bravest of the Tiger Boys." Golden Wing tilted her head to one side as though listening to an invisible voice. "That was you, Khan."

"I remember. All of it." Khan's eyes widened in shock. "Twice in my life I have been a prisoner. Once when I was first transformed and then again when I was captured by the gray werewolves."

Sarange pressed a hand to her lips to stifle the sobs that were threatening to escape.

"You killed the shifter who stole the Tiger Boys from their homes. You freed them from their captivity," Golden Wing said.

"And I will kill the leader of the gray werewolves." The strength was returning to Khan's voice, the determination to his features. With his memory, he was gaining resolve. "Both my captors will die."

"Now that you know it all, you have a new decision to make." Golden Wing took her hands from his head. Her voice returned to normal and Sarange guessed that she had parted from her mystical guides.

"I do?" Khan quirked a brow at her. "This sounds interesting."

"It is. Your childhood was stolen from you. This is your chance to turn back time." Golden Wing's eyes rested briefly on Sarange, a flicker of sympathy in their depths. "The spirits will let you remain as you are, or they will reverse the wrong that was done and allow you to return to your human form."

* * *

Khan had his memory back. Finally, he could begin
to understand the events that had shaped him. So much
of his life had been about sadness and despair. He remembered the brief time he had spent with his parents.
His happy family home. Then, when the tiger-shifter
took him and transformed him, it felt like all the hope
and happiness had been sucked out of the world. His
future had been stolen, and in its place there was a
desolate expanse of endless gray. The loss had been
all-encompassing.

Even when he had taken the initiative and escaped
from his tormentor, his life had been empty. He had
felt like an observer watching his own story unfold. No
longer human, he was a reluctant shifter, learning the
lifestyle. Tiger. Shifter. Human. He had become flu-
ent in all three. But human was the one with which he
struggled. Emotions were never his strong point.

Until he met Chinua. She had made him whole. All
three parts of his persona had finally been aligned. He
had made sense at last.

Then the gray werewolves had taken him. Khan
couldn't be killed. That was one of the unique features
of the Tiger Boys. Unlike other shifters, they could be
weakened by silver, but not killed by it. During a battle, his enemies had surrounded him and tied him up
with bindings made of silver, before placing a hood
woven with silver thread over his head. Even then he
had fought like the tiger he was, injuring several of
them. But the silver had done its job. The gray werewolves had taken him back to the Xinjiang region. Back
to a new prison. One that was to be his home for almost
a thousand years.

Although the silver had contained him, so had his own broken heart. His captors had tried everything they could to kill him. In the end, they had resorted to weakening him with the silver and by depriving him of food, water, exercise and sunlight. But it was the loss of his love that had broken him. It felt like they'd taken his heart and dropped it into a bucket of boiling oil. Without her, every part of him had turned to lead and he had been unable to think, to move, to do anything except ache. It didn't matter if that had lasted a minute or a thousand years. It felt the same.

Now Golden Wing was offering him a choice. And he didn't need to think about it. Because the answer was sitting right next to him with a hint of tears and a whole lot of fear shimmering in the blue depths of her eyes.

He reached out his hand and placed it on Sarange's knee. "My *koke gal* is a shifter. My life is nothing without her. I choose to stay as I am."

Sarange leaned closer and rested her head on his shoulder. He felt the quiver of relief that ran through her. As he held her closer, it was as if the pieces inside him that had been broken were gradually coming back together.

Golden Wing got to her feet. "I may be biased, but I think you made a good choice. Although it wasn't the path you chose, you are a strong weretiger who has brought much good to your species. And through your union with Sarange, you have helped save the blue werewolves…many times."

"Why did the Fates bring us back together at this time?" Khan asked.

"I only know there was a reason." Golden Wing looked at the sky. "The shadows tell me I must go."

Khan stood, holding out a hand to Sarange to help her up. "Thank you for giving me my identity."

"It was inside you all the time. I simply helped you find it," Golden Wing said.

He moved away, leaving the two women alone. Golden Wing held out her arms and Sarange stepped into her grandmother's embrace. He couldn't hear what they were saying, but he knew they were both crying. They stayed that way for long minutes before separating.

"I am always here, even though you may not see me."

With those words, Golden Wing's transformation went into reverse, and within seconds, the great eagle was in her place. Spreading its wings, the bird gave a single, harsh cry before wheeling away into the sky.

Khan came to stand at Sarange's side, placing his arm around her shoulder as they watched the eagle until it was a distant speck among the high peaks.

"Does it feel better or worse that you got to see her again?" Khan asked.

Sarange gave it some thought. "Better, I think. She died when I was in America and I never got to say goodbye." She lifted a hand and brushed away a tear. "So, although it hurts that she's gone again, at least I got to hug her and tell her I love her. Speaking of which, if your memory is back, how did you first tell me you loved me?"

"I think I said 'Chinua, I love you.'"

She gave a tearful chuckle. "Mr. Romance."

"My animal guardian is the tiger. They're good at the hunting and killing. They're not big on the romance. But let me try." He turned her to face him. "A thousand years ago, you stole my heart and I will never ask for it back. It's yours to keep. Forever won't be long enough for me to tell you how much I love you."

She gave a little gasp. "Oh, Khan—"

They were interrupted by Galba's approaching footsteps. "The gray werewolves are all buried."

"And I thought tigers were bad at romance." Khan murmured the words into her hair and got an elbow in his ribs in response.

"Thank you," Sarange said. "Your loyalty has been remarkable."

Galba bowed his head. "Is it your wish that my men should return to their tribes?"

"Not all of them." Khan answered before Sarange could speak and she raised her brows in surprise. "We need you and some of your best fighters to accompany us to Ulaanbaatar."

"Do we?" Sarange asked.

"Yes. We have a gala dinner to attend."

By the time they reached the ger camp, the moon was full, the stars were putting on a brilliant display and Sarange was almost asleep in the saddle. Her feet had gone numb in the stirrups, her fingers were tingling inside her gloves and her mind was blank. The well-trained horse was doing all the work. She was certain he could sense her tiredness and was picking his way carefully over the rough terrain to avoid jolting her.

When they finally reached their camp and she slid from the horse's back, Khan was there to catch her.

"Always," she murmured, resting her cheek against the hard muscles of his chest.

"Pardon?"

"Always there to catch me." She was so weary it was hard to put her thoughts into words.

Some of her tiredness melted away at the smell of food coming from the large tent. When they entered, Merkid had made enough stew to feed the entire nomad camp as well. The task of helping to distribute the food and then eating her own meal took some time. During the feast, Jenny emerged from her ger and came to sit with them.

"From her expression, I'm guessing Jiran did a good job of distracting the camera crew," Khan murmured.

"Where did you go?" Jenny helped herself to some bread.

"To the mountains in the east." Sarange bit back a smile as Jiran entered and gave her a cheery thumbs-up. "Did you have a good day's filming?"

"No." Jenny sent a look of dislike in Jiran's direction. "Your friend over there told us he knew where we could find one of the largest blue wolf packs in the area. We spent an entire day following him up and down ravines and valleys. Ask me if we saw a single wolf."

"Did you see a single wolf, Jenny?"

"We may have caught a glimpse of one in the distance. Once. But it was so far away it could just as easily have been an antelope." She took a long slug of Surkh's homemade beer. "If he wasn't with you—" she nodded at Jiran "—I'd be tempted to think he deliberately took us on a false trail just to cause mischief. He certainly seemed to be enjoying himself."

Sarange had grown to like Jenny in the short time she had known her. She wished she could explain that Jiran had saved her life and that of her team with his trickery. He had also protected the anonymity of the shifters in the region, of course, something that Sarange could never reveal.

"How much longer will we need to be here?" Khan's question to Jenny was a key one. If they were to get back to Ulaanbaatar in time for the Chanco Party gala dinner, they needed to leave soon. Sarange knew Khan's choice would be to depart the next day. Every minute they could spend preparing for the coming encounter was crucial.

"I think we're done." Jenny gave a relieved sigh. "A big part of completing this so fast has been Sarange's relationship with the wolves. Everything else is a background to that. We have the two of you together in this glorious setting, some shots of the wolves in their natural habitat, and we caught some wonderful footage of cubs playing near a waterfall. We have a lot of work to do back in the studio, but I know we have the start of something special."

"Does that mean you're ready to leave?" Sarange said.

"First thing in the morning."

Khan beckoned Jiran over. "Can you get us on the first available flight to Ulaanbaatar tomorrow?"

Jiran nodded eagerly. "Three seats?"

"It's not quite that simple." Khan got to his feet, draping an arm around the younger man's shoulders. "We have a few other people coming with us."

She watched as Khan and Jiran walked away. As Jiran's expression became increasingly thunderstruck, she knew Khan was sharing with him the details of the next part of the plan. Since this included taking Galba and twelve of his men to Ulaanbaatar with them, Jiran was clearly trying to come to grips with the logistics of the journey ahead of them.

When Khan returned to her side, she held up her hands so he could pull her to her feet. "Take me to bed, tiger."

"I thought you'd never ask."

She chuckled as they made their way across to their ger. "Khan, I hate to disappoint you, but I may not stay awake long enough to get the entrails out of my hair."

"I love it when you talk dirty to me."

Sarange was still laughing as she switched on the shower, getting the water as hot as she could stand it. As she stepped under the heated jets, she decided her weariness was only partly a reaction to the physical exertion of the day. It was also, she reflected, her psyche's way of coping with the emotional roller coaster she had been on. Leading the blue werewolves into battle, coping with the aftermath, seeing Golden Wing again, discovering the secrets of her own and Khan's past lives... all those things had drained her. And they had happened within the space of a few hours. This intense tiredness was her body's way of giving her time to assimilate everything the day had thrown at her. Sleep was the balm she needed to heal the bruises on her soul.

When she emerged from the small bathroom, warm, clean and scented, her gaze sought Khan. A tender smile curved her lips when she saw him. Sprawled like a starfish across the bed, her hard-living, rock star tiger was sleeping like a baby. Sarange removed his boots, socks and as much of his clothing as she could without disturbing him. Switching off the light, she curled up close to him in the small space available to her, pulling the comforter over them both. Sleep began to overwhelm her almost immediately.

When Khan woke, the patch of brilliant sunlight streaking through the heavy drapes that weren't fully closed told him they'd slept late. Sarange was a sweet, warm weight tucked into his side. They still had a long way to go before this was all over, but it felt like the tide was beginning to turn in their favor.

He had Bora in his sights—even though he had never looked his enemy in the eye—and he wasn't letting this go until the gray werewolf leader had been destroyed. Something about that thought brought him fully awake and he stirred restlessly.

He had never looked his enemy in the eye. Was that true? Had Bora always kept his distance, or had he gotten up close at some point? Was it even possible he was someone Khan or Sarange had met? Even someone they knew?

His restlessness must have disturbed Sarange, because she murmured something unintelligible and opened her eyes. For a moment, she blinked away the remnants of sleep; then she smiled. "I like waking up with you."

She reached up a hand to touch his face, but Khan caught hold of her wrist, kissing her fingertips. "I fell asleep before showering last night. Although I washed in the river, I'm still battle bloody and sweaty."

"I don't mind you sweaty, but bloody…." Sarange's eyes sparkled as she propped herself up on one elbow. "How about I join you while you shower away the blood and the sweat?"

"You have some good ideas, but that has to be right up there among the best ever."

The shower cubicle was barely big enough for one, so some ingenuity was needed to fit them both under the jets of warm water. Once Khan was clean, he pushed Sarange up against the wall. Wrapping her legs around his waist, she wriggled into position until he could feel his cock pressing between her heated folds.

Khan's appreciative growl echoed off the tiles as he lowered his head and bit the tender junction where her neck met her shoulder. Without pausing, he drove into her velvet heat. Sarange's gasps mingled with his urgent groans. Sarange's scent, her taste, her pelvis rubbing and grinding against his own...she fitted him perfectly and drove him wild. Slowly, tormenting them both, he drew out, one hand moving down so his thumb could tease her clit. Then he slammed his cock back into her so hard he almost blacked out. Sarange threw her head back and cried out his name.

Her hips moved in time with his, rocking and pounding, slamming and jerking. She grabbed his ass, driving her nails painfully into his skin. Khan snarled, raking her shoulder and neck with his teeth, before moving along her jaw. When he reached her lips, he plunged his tongue into her mouth, kissing her with an intensity that increased the fire in his blood.

The pleasure building within him was driving him crazy. Sarange pressed her breasts against his chest, sinking her teeth into his pecs. Khan cried out, whether in pain or pleasure, he didn't know. Didn't have time to care. The pressure continued to build, his rock-hard erection driving in and out of her, his thumb grinding out its insistent demand.

She was whimpering now, biting him anywhere she could. He felt the tension spiraling in her as her climax neared. She jerked him closer to her, urging him on with her hands and legs. Khan slammed relentlessly into her, groaning each time their bodies connected. At last it hit, taking Sarange first, and the spasms racked her, stiffening every muscle all the way to her curling toes. She threw her head back and howled. Still Khan drove into her, and still she came, her muscles clenching hard around him. Khan's own harsh growl followed, his release molten heat pulsing deep within her as the world emptied of everything except mind-numbing pleasure.

Sarange went limp and Khan lifted her higher so he could ease out of her. Turning off the water, he wrapped her in a towel and carried her through to the bedroom. Placing her on the bed, he returned to the bathroom and tucked another towel around his waist before he lay down next to her. Drawing her into his arms, he held her close, stroking the long, wet length of her hair.

"What time do we have to leave?" When she finally spoke, her voice was slightly dazed.

"In about an hour."

"You take my breath away. Every time." She traced a finger along the ridge of his abdominal muscles. "You consume me, Khan. With desire, with love, with joy. I never thought it was possible to feel like this. To have felt it twice—" she shook her head "—I must be the luckiest woman alive."

He crushed her hard to his chest, his voice husky. "If we didn't have packing to do, I'd show you all over again how much I love you. Unfortunately, since I don't like our chances of Jiran not bursting in on us to see where we are, this conversation—and any follow-up action— will have to be put on hold until we get to Ulaanbaatar."

Chapter 19

Jiran had taken on the role of tour guide and Sarange had to admit he was unexpectedly—and quite frighteningly—good at it. Since they didn't want to draw attention to themselves, using a hotel such as the one they had stayed in on their last visit to the capital wasn't an option. Thirteen blue werewolf nomads might not have gone unnoticed. With that in mind, Jiran had organized accommodation in a hostel frequented by backpackers.

Before they left the ger camp, Sarange had said goodbye to Jenny. "Is it official that you and the bad boy of rock are an item?" Jenny had paused in the act of loading her cameras into the film crew's hired jeep to give her a searching look.

Sarange had felt a blush warming her cheeks. "I'd appreciate it if you'd keep it to yourself."

Jenny shrugged. "Your business." She frowned. "There is something here, isn't there?"

"I don't know what you mean." Sarange had regarded her warily.

"Oh, you do, but I don't suppose you'll tell me." She had glanced across at where Khan was talking to Jiran. "It's about you and him and the way you generate enough electricity between you to light up a small city…and yet it's even more than that. This is going to sound crazy, but there is magic in this place. I could even feel it coming off your crazy friend when he was leading me on a blatantly false trail yesterday. And don't tell me you have no idea what that was all about, because we both know you do."

Her mock outrage had amused Sarange. "Believe me, it's better if you don't know."

Jenny had given an exaggerated sigh. "Just take care. Khan is too gorgeous for his own good, but rock stars can be dangerous." She had regarded Sarange with bewilderment. "What have I said to make you laugh?"

"You wouldn't understand, but believe me, there are more dangerous things than rock stars in this world."

Now they were back in Ulaanbaatar, planning their next steps, and those words came back to her. Because Bora was the greatest threat to their safety and, on the following night, they would be invading his territory.

Houlun was their source of information on what was happening at the Chanco Party headquarters. While he hadn't been able to get into the building to observe the preparations—security had been stepped up since their last visit—he knew the layout and he had a source on the inside. He had even brought with him a plan of the building.

"This is no ordinary gala dinner. Something big is happening," Houlun said.

The hostel had once been university accommodation. Because Jiran had rented so many rooms, the booking clerk had allocated them their own meeting room. Seventeen people were crowded into a space that contained three sofas and a coffee table. Still in full-on organizational mode, Jiran had ordered takeout and beer. From the stains on the furniture and the lingering smell, Sarange had a feeling this room had seen more than its share of those items.

"How do you know this is out of the ordinary?" Khan asked.

"Security is cast-iron, and not only to prevent unwelcome visitors. Everyone concerned has been vetted to within an inch of their lives. From the caterers to the musicians and serving staff. My source tells me the checks on their backgrounds were more intense than if they'd been working for foreign presidents or royalty."

Khan was silent for a few moments, a faraway look in his eyes. "What are you thinking?" Sarange asked at last.

His wicked smile dawned. "I'm thinking...musicians?"

She caught his meaning instantly, his daring astounding her so much that she gave a little gasp. "Seriously?"

He laughed. "You're the wolf general. When you attack, it's in the open. Let's do this the tiger way. We'll sneak up on them and take them by surprise."

"I have no idea what you're talking about," Jiran grumbled.

Khan turned to Houlun. "I need to know who the musicians are for tomorrow's gala."

Houlun frowned. "I can find that out for you. But why do you need to know?"

"They're going to be joined by a guest duo." He grinned, and caught hold of Sarange's hand. "The Chanco Party is going to get an A-list performance to-morrow night."

"What about the rest of us?" Jiran asked. "How will we get in?"

"Good question. Houlun, find out which company is providing the serving staff."

"Very well, but—" Houlun blinked as he looked at Galba and his nomad companions "—do any of you have any experience serving at a black-tie function?"

Galba paused in the act of tearing a fried chicken portion apart with his teeth, bones and all. "How hard can it be? You put food on plates, don't you?"

Sarange turned away to hide a smile at Houlun's horrified expression. "We'll need to give them a lesson in the basics."

"That's settled," Khan said. "Jiran, your next job is to organize fifteen waiters' uniforms…"

Persuading the band who was booked to play at the dinner to allow a guest duo to join them on stage for part of the performance was surprisingly easy, for one simple reason… Sarange accompanied Khan when he visited their manager.

From the minute they walked into his office, Tod Qatun was unable to take his eyes off her. "This is incredible. Your likeness to her—to the real Sarange—is uncanny. You must make a fortune from your tribute act." Since it was Khan who had made the appointment, Tod spoke in flawless English.

Khan could sense Sarange struggling to contain her mirth. She managed to keep a straight face as she answered, "I do okay."

With obvious difficulty, Tod dragged his attention to Khan, looking him up and down. "No offense, but, although you have a passing resemblance to Khan, this act of yours must rely totally on your partner."

Khan shrugged. "What can I say? She's the star. I tag along for the ride."

"Ah, um…" Tod glanced from one to the other, then relaxed slightly. "I see. You're joking."

"We're a team." Sarange cast a mischievous smile in Khan's direction. "One of us has the looks. One of us has the musical ability."

"And it may, or may not, be the same person who has both." Khan figured Tod was sufficiently confused by now. "We're in town for a few nights. We heard about your big gig at the political function, and wondered if we could get in on that. It's not often you come across such a perfect Sarange look-a-like with whom you can wow your clients."

He could almost see the moment at which Tod's brain kicked into money mode. It was evident in the alteration in his expression, the switch from awed to avaricious. Leaning back in his chair, he studied them in silence for a moment or two. "I get why having a Sarange-a-like—especially one who is almost identical to the original—would be a good idea. But I'll be blunt. I don't see why I also need a second-rate Khan impersonator."

Khan had heard stories about celebrities who jokingly entered look-a-like talent contests and didn't win. Being told he was a poor imitation of himself was a whole new experience. Even though the underlying reason for their presence here was deadly serious, he couldn't help appreciating the humor in the situation. Since he could tell Sarange was close to dissolving into helpless giggles, he decided it was time to get things back on track.

"Maybe the whole Kha-range thing hasn't hit here the way it has in the US, but we're cashing in on the publicity while it lasts," he said.

"Kha-range?" Tod looked bemused.

"Speculation is rife that Khan and Sarange are in a secret relationship," Sarange said.

"Oh, I saw something about that on social media. After that duet they did at the Animals Alive concert. I see what you mean. Very topical." Todd lapsed into silence again. "How much?"

Before Khan could speak, Sarange surprised him by naming a figure. They hadn't discussed this, but when he took a moment to consider it, he saw what she was doing made sense. If they offered to perform for free, or too cheaply, they would arouse Tod's suspicions. With no concept of Mongolian currency, Khan didn't know how reasonable Sarange's suggestion was. All he knew was a hundred thousand togrog amounted to about fifty dollars, so the huge amount she was asking probably wasn't as high as it sounded. From the gleam in Tod's eyes, he thought she had judged it just about right.

"The band isn't going to like the last-minute change. And they might feel you're upstaging them—" It was unmistakably a negotiating tone.

"Okay. Sorry we bothered you." Sarange made a movement as if to get to her feet.

"How about fifty thousand togrog less?" Tod spoke quickly before she could move.

"What time do we need to be there?" Sarange gave him her most dazzling smile. Khan wanted to throat-punch Tod as he almost slid under the desk with a look of pleasure on his face.

The rest of the day was spent in a whirlwind of preparation. Sarange went shopping for a dress. Khan, having no expectation of finding the sort of clothing he wore on stage in the stores of Ulaanbaatar, decided straight-out-of-the-backpack grunge would be his look for the night.

They found Jiran on the point of tearing out his hair. Carrying the wad of cash Khan had given him, he had bribed the manager of the serving company into replacing some of his existing staff with Jiran, Houlun, Galba and the other nomads. He had even ensured that everyone had a uniform.

"As soon as they start serving, the guests will know something is wrong." He pointed at the grass outside the hostel. The nomads had found a soccer ball and were engaged in a noisy game. "They aren't interested in learning how to do it properly."

Khan took charge. Before long, Galba and his men were receiving detailed instructions from Jiran, who had spent a summer working in an upmarket hotel, on how to wait tables at a formal function. Sarange returned while this was going on and stood beside Khan, watching the proceedings for a few minutes.

"This isn't going to work." Her words echoed Jiran's mood.

"The guests will have more important things to worry about than the presentation of their dinner." Khan's voice reflected his grim determination.

What they needed was to get inside that building

when the leaders of the Chanco Party—including
Bora—were there. Everything else was an elaborate
pretense, and possibly also a way of distracting themselves from the reality of what they were about to do.
But walking into a den of wolves? It shouldn't frighten
any of them, not after what they'd already been through.
It's not the werewolves. How could it be, when his companions were werewolves themselves? It wasn't the
thought of another confrontation and the possibility of
more bloodshed. Even the prospect of finally coming
face-to-face with the elusive Bora wasn't responsible
for the curious jittery feeling he was experiencing, one
he knew was infecting his companions.

No, it was the prospect of coming face-to-face with
concentrated evil. That was what the Chanco Party represented. It had been replicated all too often throughout
history. With no respect for time or place, these groups
sprang up. Hiding behind sugarcoated messages and
charismatic leaders, they rose to power on a wave of
false promises. But underneath it all, there was hatred
and poison, old hostilities and new atrocities. Humans
had long memories, but shifters? They could make a
grudge last forever.

The Chanco Party had one policy. To wipe out the
blue werewolves and their descendants. Once that was
over, the Chanco people would move on to another
shifter minority, then another. They were bullies in
suits. They appeared more credible than other extreme
groups simply because most of the world didn't believe
in werewolves. They had been able to rise to power rapidly because they could deliver their popular, second-
ary pledges while all the time keeping that main goal
in their sights. And from what Houlun said, because

they were dirty, using bribery and rigging votes to get to power. Now they were close to their ultimate aim. Government. When they got there, no one would be able to stop them.

No more. It ends tonight.

"Did anyone tell them they lost the battle?" Sarange whispered to Khan as she sneaked a look from between the heavy velvet drapes that spanned the stage. "Because they don't look like a group of people who have been defeated."

The glittering crowd who were assembling represented Mongolia's elite, along with a number of foreign dignitaries. Wealth, fame, political excellence, business acumen...all were present in the huge, lavishly decorated ballroom.

She wouldn't have believed from its ugly exterior that the building could hide such a beautiful venue inside. Sarange had been catapulted into fame at an early age, so she had never earned her stripes the way many artists did. Launching her career on a nationwide TV show meant she hadn't toured small venues building up a name for herself.

Khan had clearly played some unsavory places before Beast made its name, as had Soyombo, the band whose gig they had so abruptly crashed. They were all agreed that this place was the height of luxury.

"I've sung in places where the smell of damp makes you feel sick." Chen, the lead singer, was a beautiful Chinese woman who offered to share her cramped dressing room with Sarange. "Or the plaster is falling off the walls and the dust chokes you."

"You're sure you don't mind us joining you?" Sarange asked.

"No. But I'm going to add to my résumé and say that I sang with Sarange." Chen grinned mischievously. "I just won't mention that you aren't the real one."

Sarange bit back a smile, wishing for a moment that she could tell her the truth. Maybe when this craziness died down, she could do something for her. Offer her an endorsement? Invite her to LA? She was getting ahead of herself. They had a long night in front of them before she could start thinking about "what next."

"We have to get the band, and the other people who have been hired to work here for the night, out before we put our plan into action. I don't want any innocent people to get injured." She whispered the words to Khan when no one else was around.

"I'm already on it. Jiran knows what to do."

"That's a sentence I never thought I'd hear you say." Sarange smiled as she took another quick look through the curtains and saw Jiran surreptitiously supervising the nomads. "Jiran has come a long way."

It was true. Their plans for this night were complicated, but Jiran had followed every one of Khan's instructions meticulously. Getting every piece of equipment they needed, plotting out positions on the floor plan, organizing the getaway vehicle…he had done it all with precision. When they left this building tonight, they wanted to be sure the Chanco Party was destroyed with no danger it could rise again.

Once the guests were all seated, Soyombo took to the stage. Chen sang a few popular songs, both international and Mongolian, while the first course was served. Sarange, observing from the shadows at the edge of the stage, noticed a few minor incidents, but nothing that would draw too much attention to the ineptitude of the waiters.

From her vantage point, she watched Damdid Gandi circulating the room. Focusing on the men, he was patting shoulders, stooping close to his companion's ear to be heard above the sound of the music. Laughing. Joking. Assured. His whole attitude was that of a man convinced he was a winner. It didn't make sense. They had lost the battle…

That was when it hit her. This was the real prize. Seizing power was all that mattered.

"Bora didn't lead his troops into battle because they weren't important."

"Pardon?" Khan bent his head closer so he could hear her.

"They were a sacrifice to keep us away from what was important to him." She waved a hand to indicate the elegant gathering. "From this."

"I don't understand."

Sarange pressed her fingertips to her temple, trying to gather her thoughts. "You and I didn't understand why fate brought us back together at *this* time. All Golden Wing knew was that there was a reason for us to be reunited. The blue werewolves were being persecuted and the blue wolves were facing extinction, so we believed that was why. But it wasn't. At least, it wasn't all of it. Those were consequences of a bigger picture. Our true purpose was to fight these people. This evil. They are going to do anything they can to win this election. When they fight, they are dirty." She turned her head to look at him. "Look at their confidence. They know they have it within their grasp. They will do it if we don't stop them. Once they win, the blue were-wolves will be the first of many groups they come for."

"You think that's why Bora was so determined to kill you? Because he knew why fate brought us together?"

She could see Khan trying to catch up with her thinking. "Maybe he didn't know for sure, but if he even suspected, it would be enough for him to take drastic action."

"How would he know about us?" Khan asked.

"Think about it. He's not just anybody. He has known our faces for a thousand years. We didn't get back together privately. We did it in the most public manner possible, in front of hundreds of thousands of people. We lit up TV screens, the internet and social media." She laughed. "He was onto us the minute we sang that first note together at the Animals Alive concert."

"He let all those gray werewolves die in battle as a diversion?" Khan's growl was only audible to her because she was standing so close. "His own followers?"

"We knew how ruthless he could be when he sent those students to my house simply to test Beast's strength. Or to show us how evil he is."

"But we still don't know who *he* is because he's in disguise." Khan's jaw was tight with frustration as he surveyed the room. "He could be any one of the men here."

As Chen finished her number and turned their way, Sarange took his hand. "I guess we're about to find out."

Chapter 20

No matter the size of the stage, Khan's impulse was to dominate it. It was what he did best. This time, with Sarange at his side, he reined in his controlling instincts and worked with her. Although they were there for a different purpose entirely, he knew the result was incredible. The song was one Beast's former bass guitarist, Nate Zilar, had written at a time when he thought he might lose the love of his life forever. Called "My Only," it was a declaration in which the sense of yearning and hope for the future were palpable.

Clad in a thigh-skimming, backless black dress, with her trademark braid slung over one shoulder, Sarange took his breath away, along with that of most of the audience. The crystal simplicity of her vocals perfectly matched his smoky, rasping growl. The haunting melody didn't allow for Khan's usual acrobatics, but they swayed together in perfect harmony, losing themselves momentarily in the public love letter.

Out of the corner of his eye, Khan observed Damdid. The Chanco Party secretary was a danger. He had met Khan and Sarange before, and knew they were in Mongolia. Sarange had threatened him. Damdid's jaw plummeted as he realized what was happening and he made a move toward the door, presumably to alert security. His exit was halted by a quiet but powerfully effective punch to the throat from Galba. The nomad leader had been warned by Khan at the start of the night to take Damdid out before he could cause problems. Damdid dropped like a stone, and because all eyes were on the stage, he was carried out by Galba and Houlun before anyone noticed.

Khan also noticed there appeared to be a few problems with the food service. One or two of the elegantly clad women were complaining that half their meal had found its way down the front, or even the back, of their designer dresses. Some of the men appeared unhappy at the attitude of the waiters. Luckily, Khan and Sarange's duet was coming to an end.

The closing bars were the cue. Jiran sprang into action, hustling surprised people out of the room. The nomads abruptly stopped serving and started removing their shoes and socks. Khan took Sarange's hand as the last notes died away and thunderous applause echoed around the vast room.

Where are you, Bora? The gray werewolf leader must have recognized them, must have known this was no tribute act. *Nothing.*

"Ladies and gentlemen, I just have one thing to say—" if Bora wasn't coming to them, they were taking the fight to him. And wiping out his evil Chanco Party at the same time. "If you are not a shifter, get the hell out of here while you still have time."

As he finished speaking, he launched himself from the stage, shifting in midair. There were screams of horror as the guests stared into the open jaws of a giant Caspian tiger before scattering in every direction. Sarange was right behind him, the remains of her black dress clinging to her fur as she raced to keep up with him. There was a surreal moment as they faced designer-clad werewolves before the fighting began in earnest.

They had two main aims. Find Bora, and create a diversion while Jiran and Houlun got into the offices. Their job was to get as much evidence as they could. Paperwork, laptops, hard drives. Anything that would damage the Chanco Party forever. Their plan wasn't just about tonight, it was about ensuring that nothing could rise from the destruction they were about to inflict. As for the remaining partygoers? Khan had issued a warning. They were dealing with a weretiger and a pack of werewolves. They knew what to expect and it wasn't going to be negotiation. The gala dinner was about to get bloody.

Most of the guests headed for the exits, which was good and bad. It limited the opposition, but it also meant the police would be arriving soon. There were about twenty male gray werewolves left in the room and a few females. Although Khan figured Bora must be one of the males, he was disappointed when he couldn't feel his presence. He wanted the moment he faced his sworn enemy to be memorable. Right now, he didn't even know who he was seeking.

Galba and his men had shifted and were plowing through the opposition. Khan experienced a bizarre confrontation when a female werewolf in a tiara hurled herself at him. Brushing her aside, he continued on toward the males.

Show yourself, you bastard. Stop hiding behind your disguise.

The ballroom had become a scene of carnage. Led by Sarange, Galba's blue werewolves fought with a strength and fury that couldn't be matched by the shocked gray werewolves. Crushing and slashing, they inflicted terrible wounds on each victim before tossing it aside and moving on to the next. The floor became slippery with blood and littered with bodies.

When he judged the enemy was finished, Khan shifted back and gave the signal for the others to do the same. He wasn't looking for annihilation. Jiran would step up and put the next part of the plan into action.

"Rear exit." Khan jerked a thumb over his shoulder, indicating the direction Houlun had shown them on his plan of the building. He called Jiran's cell phone. "The police are on their way. Make your call, do what you have to and get out."

Sarange cast a look over her shoulder as they left the ballroom. There was no sign of movement. "Bora?"

They piled into the truck that was waiting at the rear of the building. Jiran and Houlun had already stacked the haul of items they had removed from the offices inside. Khan and Sarange jumped into the cab. Jiran joined them a minute or two later. Climbing into the driver's seat, he gunned the engine.

"Everything go according to plan?" Khan asked as

Jiran pulled out of the narrow road at the rear of the building.

"We disabled the security cameras at the start of the night. I just called the police and the fire department and told them there had been a terrorist attack at the Chanco Party headquarters, which was now on fire." After driving for a few minutes, he halted the truck on an incline from which they had a clear view of the area they had just left.

"You're sure the fire you set will spread quickly enough?"

"Look." Jiran pointed at the building where bright orange flame was bursting from the windows and clouds of smoke poured into the night sky. "I used a fast-acting accelerant. Fire investigators will know it was arson, but I already told them that."

Khan viewed the spectacle for a moment or two. "It's a pity Torque isn't here. He loves watching things burn."

Jiran drove back toward the hostel. "We'll never know which of them was Bora." There was a note of dissatisfaction in Sarange's voice that Khan understood. The Chanco Party had been destroyed, its leaders killed, and he was confident that Jiran and Houlun would find evidence of corruption in the items they took from the offices. But it still felt like unfinished business. *We didn't get to look Bora in the eye. That's why it feels this way.*

"It's over. We go home tomorrow." Home. For the first time since his release from captivity, he felt like he knew where that was. It was any place where he had Sarange at his side.

"And I suppose you want me to arrange to get Galba

and his men back to the Altai Mountains?" There was a note of resignation in Jiran's voice.

Khan patted his shoulder. "I knew we could rely on you."

Khan swam several fast lengths of the pool before climbing out and dropping onto a sunbed. There was a misconception among humans that tigers hated getting wet. While most big cats were land hunters and tended to avoid water, the tiger's environment was different. In the wild, its prey didn't form nice, neat herds, which meant a stalking tiger often had to swim long distances.

Not that Sarange's pristine pool resembled a tropical river, or that he was likely to have to hunt down tonight's dinner. The thought made him smile. But he was smiling a lot this afternoon.

The jeweler had dropped off the ring and it was perfect. Khan had designed it himself. The central stone was a sapphire—of course—surrounded by a circle of diamonds that reflected the deep blue color over and over.

"Blue fire." That was what he had told the jeweler, and the guy had delivered a piece Khan would feel proud to place on Sarange's finger.

He had picked up on a hint of impatience in her demeanor lately. Caught her watching him once or twice as though wondering when—*if*, even—he was going to ask. Once or twice he had wanted to confess, to tell her he wasn't being arrogant and doing that whole *"I am Khan"* thing. He was simply waiting for the perfect moment to ask her to be his wife.

Tonight would be that moment. The table was booked. The champagne was chilling. To hell with protecting their privacy. He was going down on one knee in the most public manner possible. He didn't care who saw it.

When Sarange came home, he would tell her they were going out to dinner at her favorite restaurant. He frowned. Where *was* Sarange? She had gone out to pick up a few things to get ready for their trip to New York the next day. Beast was getting back on track with the album, but luckily Sarange had no immediate commitments so she was able to travel with him. The other members of the band were already on their way to the airport. Khan had negotiated with Ged for an extra twenty-four hours.

He reached out a hand for the cell phone that lay on a table at his side and glanced at the time. Sarange had been gone for hours. Far longer than she'd said…

With perfect timing the phone buzzed at that exact moment and he smiled, assuming it would be her. With a frown, he saw it was Jiran's number. As he answered, his mind was registering that it was 5:00 a.m. in Ulaanbaatar.

"Hey."

"Khan? It is Houlun."

The words made his stomach drop as if he were on the worst kind of roller-coaster ride. "Jiran said you don't use cell phones."

"I don't, but this is important." The sinking feeling intensified. No one called at 5:00 a.m. if it was good news. "I have discovered from my sources that Bora wasn't at the gala dinner."

Khan jerked upright, shaking tendrils of damp hair out of his face. "What?"

"He wasn't here in Ulaanbaatar on the night the Chanco Party held its celebration."

Even across the miles that separated them, Khan could hear the other man's distress.

"He was never in Mongolia."

"Where the hell was he?"

"He was in America the whole time. In California."

Khan got to his feet, pacing along the edge of the pool. His thoughts were a whirlwind, but one phrase was pushing itself to the forefront of his mind. He kept hearing Golden Wing's voice. *Bora is one man who is three.*

"Houlun, what is the Mongol word for 'three'?"

He could hear the confusion in the other man's voice as he answered, *"Gurav."*

"Close, but not exact."

"Khan, what is going on?" Houlun was starting to sound concerned.

He's concerned? He should try being me.

"I'll tell you when it's over. Right now I need to call someone else." Khan ended the call abruptly and found the number he needed. Why did his memory still have so many holes? Especially when it came to the ancient language his people had spoken? And why the hell did this have to be one of the missing details?

"Bek? No, Sarange is not here. Look, I'll explain this later, but I don't have time to chat. Sarange said you have a framed document on your study wall with the ancient Mongolian words and symbols on it. I'm hoping that means you have some knowledge of that language. Can you tell me what the number three was?"

When the other man spoke, it only confirmed what Khan had already guessed. *"Gurban."*

He finished the call to Bek, promising he would bring Sarange on a visit soon. Hoping he could make it happen. She had been right. Bora had used the battle against the gray werewolves as a distraction from his bigger plan. More than that, he had *created* the diversion by sending them to Mongolia. Because Bora was Radin. *Gurban* Radin.

I stopped protecting her because I thought we were safe. And now he has her. He was sure of it.

Breaking into a run, Khan was calling Ged on his cell phone as he burst through the bedroom door and grabbed clothes from the closet, pulling them on with the phone tucked awkwardly between his ear and his shoulder.

"Radin has Sarange." The words came out in a garbled *whoosh*.

"Slow down." As always, Ged's voice had a calming effect. "Radin the filmmaker?"

"Yes. I don't have time to explain. All you need to know is that he's Bora. Tell me it's not too late for you to turn around."

"We were just about to board, but that doesn't matter. All that matters is Sarange. Tell me where to meet you."

Khan gave him the address of Radin's West Hollywood office, hoping he was right and that was where he would have taken Sarange. He figured Radin's plan would only work if he got Khan and Sarange together. Destroying one of them wouldn't be enough for the man who had hated them for a thousand years. And Radin would want Khan to see his revenge up close. The thought caused sour, choking panic to rise in his gullet. He quashed it back down. Grabbing up the keys to his rental car, he dashed out of the house.

Golden Wing had been right. Their enemy was one man who was three. First, he was the gray werewolf leader who had loved Chinua and sworn revenge when she didn't return his feelings. He was also Bora, the shadowy figure who had orchestrated the fight against them in this life. And now Khan had the third and final piece of the puzzle. He was Radin, the man who had always looked at Sarange with a mix of admiration and agitation.

Now Khan knew the reason for those glances. Admiration, because, like Khan, Radin had loved Sarange for a thousand years. Agitation, because he was trying to hide his feelings.

He won't harm her unless I am there to witness it. As he pulled out of Sarange's driveway, he kept telling himself that. *He wants to hurt us both.* Khan didn't know how to call on the spirits in the way of the shamans, but he tried his best.

Let me be right about this. Watch over my koke gal.

As she was dragged into Radin's office, Sarange didn't know which emotion was strongest. Yes, she was scared. Now that she knew who he really was, she was very, very afraid. But she was also angry. And most of that anger was directed at herself for allowing him to dupe her this way.

She had been going about her shopping with a slight smile on her face. Khan thought he was being enigmatic. Clearly, he imagined he had tricked her into believing he wasn't going to propose to her. The thought almost made her laugh out loud. A tiger with a secret was something to behold. All the sneaking glances at his cell phone? Jumping up and bolting out of the room for surreptitious conversations when he thought she might overhear? The way he kept watching her as though he thought she might be reading his mind? Then, this morning, he hadn't been able to get her out of the house fast enough. He had practically pushed her out the door. No, either he was having an affair—and, after a thousand years together, she knew him well enough to trust him unconditionally—or he was buying a ring.

Wrapped in her pleasant thoughts, she had left the drugstore where she had called to collect some pain medication for the headaches she recently started experiencing. A brief conversation with the pharmacist had convinced her that she should see her doctor. It was probably nothing. That was what the pharmacist had said. Had she been under any recent stress? That could be the cause. Sarange had bitten back a smile. Yes, there had been a few things going on lately. Stress might just be the reason.

She hadn't heard anyone come up behind her as she reached her car. Hadn't known anything until a hand was clamped over her mouth and her hands were being roughly jerked behind her. As soon as the handcuffs were snapped onto her wrists they burned like red-hot iron fresh out of the furnace. At the same time, the stench hit her nostrils. It was like nothing she had ever smelled before. It was like rotten meat and bad eggs mixed with verdigris. Her werewolf senses told her instantly what it must be...

...*silver*. It was already making her feel weak and light-headed. That was how her attacker had been able to get so close without her noticing.

"If you struggle, the sensations will get worse."

She knew that voice. As she was pulled away from

her vehicle, she fought off the silver fog enveloping her brain in an effort to identify it. "Radin?"

"Don't bring her too close to me, Jason." Radin's voice was sharp.

Sarange tried to turn her head to see who he was talking to, but the mysterious Jason was already placing a dark hood over her head.

"The silver affects me as well."

Radin was affected by silver? Even in her confused state Sarange could work out what that meant. It meant Radin was a shifter. It meant he had tricked her. It meant...oh, hell, did it mean he was *Bora*? One thing was for sure. It meant she was in a whole world of trouble.

The man who had grabbed her had forced her into the trunk of a car and she had been driven across town to the underground parking lot of Radin's office building. From there, they had brought her, still hooded, up to Radin's office.

Now she was seated on a chair near the window. The hood had been removed, but the silver handcuffs were still in place. Radin was standing across the room from her, clearly trying to keep his distance from the effects of the silver. Another man, presumably Jason, stood near the desk. He was a huge, bulky figure with muscles like carved concrete. He had a gun tucked into the waistband of his jeans and Sarange was willing to bet it contained silver bullets. It seemed Radin had thought of everything.

She found if she focused, she could fight off the mind-numbing effects for a few minutes at a time. If she relaxed, the silver acted like a hypnotic drug, pulling her under and making her forget how to think.

"What now?" Her speech was slurred as though she'd had too much to drink.

"Now we wait for the heroic tiger to come to the rescue." Radin's smile was serene.

"Doesn't know where I am." She tried to shake her head, but her neck muscles weren't working.

"I reckon he'll work it out," Radin said. "I may not rate tiger intelligence very high, but he has a sixth sense where you are concerned."

Something wasn't right about this. Trying to draw some air deeper into her lungs was a mistake. The silver scalded as though she'd breathed in acid. Hanging her head, she coughed and spluttered. When she finally regained enough breath to speak, it took her a few moments to remember what she wanted to say. "Bora was here. Attacked you."

Radin laughed. "I thought that was a particularly clever trick. Pretending to have been attacked and robbed…it was just too easy. I was worried that you might start making connections. Maybe even think that my insistence on you and Khan making the documentary together could be more than coincidence. I wanted to kill you, not arouse your suspicions."

"Can't kill Khan."

"Some things are worse than death. For Khan, the worst torture will be to watch you die." The smile deepened. "When he gets here, that is what I will make him endure. Then, when he has nothing left to live for, he can return to his captivity with the image of your death in his mind for all eternity."

"No." Sarange wouldn't plead for herself, but she would do it for Khan. "Don't make him go back there. Please."

The smile vanished. "You think begging for his miserable life is going to change my mind? You are a werewolf—" he spat the words at her "—but you chose a tiger over one of your own kind."

"We don't choose who we love." Her wrists were on fire, her head felt like it had been stuffed full of cotton candy, and all she wanted to do was sleep. But she had led an army against this man and defeated him. She wasn't going to give in easily. Determinedly, she forced herself to focus.

Radin had said he would kill her and make Khan watch. *Get him mad. Make him want to kill me before Khan gets here.* It wasn't much of a plan, but it was the only hope she had of getting him to come close enough so that she could lash out with her feet, maybe even her teeth. Okay, it might provoke the circus strongman into shooting her, but that was going to happen anyway... If only these damn cuffs weren't making it impossible for her to summon the energy to shift.

"You are saying you didn't choose your tiger lover?" Radin sneered.

"That's right. We're mates. The Fates decreed that we should be together." Ignoring the awful silver stench, she drew a deep breath. "But if I lived a thousand lifetimes, I would choose him in every one. Never you."

He lunged toward her, his features suffused with rage. "You will regret those words."

"But not for long." Even though every muscle ached with the effort, she forced herself to shrug. "From what you've just said, I'll be dead soon."

The anger in his face hardened, but another emotion shone in his eyes. "I could make you change your mind."

Dear heaven, did he mean what she thought he did? Snatching victory from the jaws of defeat was what she did best. But this? She had never faced a personal challenge of this magnitude. A man whose arrogance was so great he believed he could make her love him…by forcing her? As the effects of the silver dragged on her psyche, she felt her fighting spirit—Chinua's spirit—surge. "I don't think so."

"Take the cuffs off her and then get out." Radin barked the words at Jason without taking his gaze from Sarange. Yes, she had been right about that gleam in his eyes. It was lust, and it sickened her.

"You said she was dangerous."

"Don't question me!" Radin's growl echoed around the room.

The muscleman hesitated for a second or two, then moved forward to remove Sarange's handcuffs. He did it carefully, watching her the whole time as if she were a coiled snake. She didn't have any energy to waste on him. If she did, she'd have explained that she didn't have the strength to lift her head, let alone attack anyone. Even though the silver was gone, the impact lingered.

When the door closed behind his accomplice, Radin moved closer. Slumped as she was in her seat, all Sarange could see of him was his expensive, handmade shoes. A discordant thought flickered through her mind. As diversionary tactics went, it would certainly be unusual if she threw up over those shoes. And that was exactly what she felt like doing right now…

Radin caught hold of her hair, jerking her head back. The blaze of triumph on his face increased her nausea. He reached out a hand as if to touch her face, but before it connected, the door flew open. Expecting to see

Jason return, Sarange blinked at the unexpected vision that met her eyes. Her sight was slightly blurred from the effects and she decided she must be seeing things.

Because that couldn't be Diablo? And Dev? Could it? As Beast's drummer shifted into a black panther and the rhythm guitarist became a snow leopard, Sarange realized she wasn't imagining this. They were real. The rock-star-shifter rescue party had arrived.

Radin snarled, his hold on her hair tightening as he jerked her to her feet. Sarange's leg muscles refused to cooperate, and she stumbled to her knees. As the two big cats moved closer, she heard a sound from the window. Now things were getting even more surreal. The beating of dragon wings ten floors high was like a small hurricane hammering against the glass. With a single flip of his tail, Torque shattered the window and Khan, ever the showman, leaped from the dragon's back, landing in a crouch in the center of the room.

"You rode on a dragon for me?" Despite her weakness, Sarange couldn't keep the emotion—and a touch of laughter—out of her voice.

"Didn't I tell you I would do anything for you?" Khan swept her up, cradling her against his chest. Immediately, some of the mist swirling in her brain started to clear. She nestled her head gratefully into the crook of his shoulder.

"Jason…" Radin made an attempt to reach the door, but Diablo blocked his path.

"You used the silver trick on me all those centuries ago." Khan's voice was silky smooth and dangerous as he turned on Radin. "That was bad enough. But to try it on Sarange?" He shook his head. "Just one more thing you are going to pay for."

Radin's lips drew back in a snarl so awful it brought a fresh wave of nausea washing over Sarange. "Do your worst, Tiger Boy."

The words provoked a rumbling growl from somewhere deep in Khan's chest. "I intend to. But first…" He raised his voice slightly. "Ged!"

The big werebear came into the office. He was rubbing his knuckles and his expression was one of distaste. "You could have warned me that guy would be carrying silver. Knocking him out was no problem, but that stench lingers for days."

Khan moved toward him. "Get Sarange back to her house. It looks like she's been exposed to a strong dose of silver. Rest is the only cure for that." Tenderly, he transferred her to Ged's strong arms. "You don't need to see him die, *koke gal*. You only need to know it will happen."

As Ged carried her out of the office, she heard Khan growl to Diablo and Dev, "Stand back. This is one kill that belongs to me."

Chapter 21

Khan sat beside Sarange's bed, watching her face as she slept. Exactly the way he had done that first night together. He corrected himself. *The first night of this lifetime.*

He was worried about her. He knew the silver would weaken her, but its effect had been stronger than he'd expected. She had been asleep since Ged brought her back from Radin's office. Khan glanced at the clock. It was now over twenty-four hours.

Her skin was waxwork pale, her breathing shallow and her pulse slow. When he rested his hand on her forehead, she felt cold. The burns on her wrists stood out, angry and raw, scorching into her tender flesh. But it was the injuries to her psyche that scared him. He knew what silver had done to him, but he had an immunity that Sarange didn't possess.

The poison hadn't killed her. That meant she wouldn't deteriorate further from this point. But what if this was it? If this was the damage that had been done? What if she didn't recover from this debilitating weakness? What if his beautiful *koke gal* remained frozen like a statue for all eternity?

He couldn't think like that. It had been a day since he found her. The sun had risen and set once since he finally faced and killed Bora. One thousand years avenged in a single swipe of his claws across Radin's throat. Khan had left his friends to clean up while he raced back to be with Sarange.

Because of everything that had happened in his life, all the barriers that had been thrown up between them, he supposed he was hardwired to believe the worst. By clinging to gloom, he was able to avoid hope. Because faith and belief…they were his enemies. As soon as he went down those twin roads, he was lost. Yet how could he allow his mind to dwell in bleakness when this was Sarange? When his whole life was wrapped up in the slender figure beneath that comforter?

If he gave up on her, he gave up on himself. Lifting her hand to his cheek, he watched her eyelids with their black fan of lashes, willing them to open. "For me, *koke gal*."

He glanced up at a sound from the balcony. Although Sarange felt cool, the day was warm and he had left one of the doors open. Not again. Physically, he felt as strong as ever, but if this was another attack, he didn't feel mentally prepared…

Getting to his feet, he went to the door and pulled back the lightweight drapes that covered it. When he stepped onto the balcony, it was empty. He took a moment to glance back at Sarange before going to the balcony rail and looking out over the yard. Everything was still and quiet.

Paranoia. He shook his head, going back inside. As he reached for the handle of the door to pull it closed behind him, an unmistakable noise reached his ears. Here? In Los Angeles? He would know the sound of those giant wings anywhere. He tilted his head skyward in time to see the golden eagle circle the house once before disappearing into the distance.

Hurrying to the bed, he scooped Sarange up into his arms. Her head flopped against his shoulder as he carried her onto the balcony.

"We are both here." His voice was a croak as he scoured the sky for another sighting of the mighty bird. "Golden Wing and I."

Even before the eagle reappeared, he felt Sarange stir. Her hands came up to clasp his neck. As the great bird hovered directly overhead for a few minutes, casting her shadow over them, Sarange opened her eyes.

"Thank you," she murmured, half raising a hand toward the bird.

The eagle appeared to dip its head in acknowledgment before wheeling high over the rooftops with a single, echoing cry.

When they could no longer see it, Khan carried Sarange back inside and placed her on the bed. Carefully, he lifted the glass of water that had been on the bedside table to her lips and she sipped gratefully.

"How long have I been asleep?" She lay back on the pillows.

"A full day. You went out shopping yesterday morning and it's now four o'clock in the afternoon."

She shook her head, clearly struggling to believe what he was telling her. "The silver...it made me feel like I'd been drugged. I could barely think or move. Every second I had those handcuffs on made it worse."

"What I don't understand is why Radin removed them. He had you in his power, which meant he had control over me. Why would he throw away his advantage?"

Sarange shivered. "He thought—" She paused, clearly struggling with the memory. "He thought he could force me to love him."

"You mean...?" Khan struggled to fight off the waves of fury.

She nodded, her fingers plucking at the coverlet. "I think he was going to rape me. Golden Wing said hate springs from love, and she was right. Radin said he could make me love him, but the only thing I saw in his eyes was hate."

"If I'd known what he was planning—" Khan could barely think, let alone speak. "I wasn't there to protect you from him. I made an assumption that you were safe, and I was wrong."

Sarange reached out and placed her hand over his. "You are always there to protect me and you were again. You arrived in time to save me. Radin is dead and the nightmare is over."

"After all this time, it's hard to believe it's true."

She tilted her head. "The house seems very quiet. Are we alone?"

"Yes, apart from your efficient, unobtrusive staff. Beast has gone back to New York. Ged wanted to stay and help me take care of you, but I persuaded him your recovery wouldn't be helped if you had a shifter rock band living in your house."

Although she still looked weary, some of the magic was back in her smile. "You were right. I am fond of your friends, and grateful to them for rescuing me, but I'm not sure I can cope with too much Beast right now. And even when I haven't been wearing silver handcuffs, I like it best when it's just you and me."

Khan's heart expanded so rapidly his chest hurt. Everything he once thought he could never have was right here in this room. He realized now how frightened he had been. Ged had released him from his prison, but Sarange was the one who had finally freed him from fear. Until her, he had been afraid of living a normal life in case someone discovered he didn't know how to do human emotion, terrified of commitment in case he got hurt, or hurt another person in return. Worst of all, he had been unwilling to give even the tiniest part of his heart because he was scared of losing it forever.

But now he finally knew where all that fear had come from. And he knew how to deal with it. As long as he had Sarange at his side, he could have all the things his heart craved. The life they had once shared could be theirs again, without the need for constant battles…and with one or two obvious, modern-day bonuses such as running water and air travel.

What am I waiting for? The romantic proposal had been a nice idea…yesterday. Before he almost lost her to the crazed enemy who had made their lives hell for so long. After yet another stark reminder of how much Sarange meant to him, perhaps it was time to just get on and do it… "I'll be right back."

He was aware of Sarange watching him in some surprise as he dashed out of the room. He had hidden the ring in a drawer in the kitchen and he retrieved it now, taking the stairs two at a time in his impatience to be back with her. When he burst through the bedroom door and hurled himself onto his knees beside the bed, he was out of breath and could feel his face burning.

Sarange had moved into a sitting position against a bank of pillows. She regarded him in some surprise. "Are you rehearsing a new move for your next tour?"

The question, and the whole situation, struck him as so deliciously funny that he started to laugh. Still kneeling, he leaned his elbows on the bed and kissed her. "This is not a rehearsal. This is the most real thing I've ever done in my life." Flipping open the ring box, he presented it to her. "My Sarange, my *koke gal*, I'm already the happiest man alive because of you. Will you make my life even more perfect and become my wife?"

"Khan..." Her voice trailed off as tears filled her eyes. "Damn. I decided I wasn't going to cry."

He slid the ring onto her finger. "You knew?"

"I had an idea." She smiled through the tears. "You're a tiger. Subtlety is not your strong point." Lifting her hand, she turned it from side to side to admire the ring. "It's the most beautiful thing I've ever seen."

"Is that an acceptance?" Khan tried to growl, but his emotions were still on high alert and his voice was too husky.

Sarange held out her arms. When he rose and went to sit next to her on the bed, she slid her arms around his waist and rested her cheek against his chest. "You are all I have ever wanted. We complete each other. This—" she held up her hand, and the ring sparkled its blue fire just as he had hoped it would "—just makes it even more special." She tilted her head back, the fire in her eyes even brighter than that of the stones on her finger. "I love you, my tiger."

Khan managed the growl he had tried earlier. "And I adore you, my *koke gal*."

One Year Later

Diablo regarded the baby in Khan's arms with interest. "So, what is she? A wiger? Or a tolf?"

"She is Karina, and she's unique," Sarange said. "And we won't know what her inner animal is until she shifts. She could be a tiger, or a wolf, or she may be a hybrid. It doesn't matter." She smiled up at Khan. "After everything that has happened to us, she is our reward."

"And there were no ill effects from the silver to which Radin exposed you?" Gerel asked, when Diablo had gone. The change in Gerel over the last year had been remarkable. Now that she had embraced her shamanistic abilities instead of subduing them, her health had improved steadily so that she glowed with vitality.

"Fortunately not. Of course, I didn't know I was pregnant then because it was at such an early stage. Strangely, I was already experiencing some symptoms. My human hormones hadn't reacted, but my inner wolf had registered the change and I was getting headaches. Once I knew for sure, I was worried that the silver could have harmed the baby, but the shifter doctor Ged recommended did some checks and everything was fine." She stroked her daughter's head and Karina gurgled with pleasure. The baby was a perfect combination of them both, with Khan's red-gold hair and Sarange's light blue eyes. "More than fine. She's perfect."

Everyone who mattered to them was gathered here

for the baby's dedication. It wasn't in any sense a traditional ceremony. Led by Gerel, it was a simple, shamanistic statement of thanks to the spirits for the gift of their child. And there were special thanks for one particular spirit. *I am always here, even though you may not see me.* Golden Wing's words. Sarange felt her grandmother's presence more strongly today than ever.

As well as Gerel and Bek, Ged and the other members of Beast were gathered on the lawn of the Los Angeles house. Sarange was delighted that Jiran, Houlun and Galba had agreed to make the long journey. Getting her personal assistant to ensure that their journey and accommodations were first class and luxurious had given her immense pleasure. She could never thank the three men enough for what they had done for her and Khan. An all-expenses-paid vacation was minor in return.

Jenny was also present. Leaving her movie cameras behind, she had taken one picture of Khan, Sarange and Karina. They had agreed to release it to the press in return for donations to the Animals Alive Foundation.

"I'm just sorry I never got footage of the story everyone has been talking about for months." Jenny's eyes quizzed them over the top of her champagne glass.

"What story was that?" Khan asked.

"The one about a dragon flying up to Radin's office block with you on its back. That was the same day Radin disappeared. He hasn't been seen since."

Khan shrugged. "Must have been some sort of stunt."

"Right." Jenny gave them one of her piercing stares. "Strange things always seem to happen around the two of you, don't they?" She went away and started to talk to Jiran.

"She is frighteningly observant," Sarange said.

"Is it just me, or is she not as hostile to Jiran as she'd like us to believe?" Khan asked as he watched them.

Sarange regarded him in surprise. "Since when did you turn matchmaker? Anyway, Jenny is not a shifter."

"That's true, but she may well be talking to a future president of Mongolia."

The demise of the Chanco Party had caused a major stir in Mongolian politics. No suspects had ever been identified over the attack. Several weeks later, evidence of widespread corruption, vote rigging and voter intimidation within the party had been made public by an anonymous source. Since then, Jiran's interest in politics had become serious.

Sadly, the ger camp was fully booked for the next few months and Surkh and Merkid had not been able to get away. Sarange, who kept in touch with them by email—erratically because of the signal problems in the Altai region—promised them pictures and a visit when Karina was old enough. She and Khan would take their daughter to see the fortress where it all began.

"We will have quite a story to tell her," Khan said.

"Did you read my mind?" They stood slightly apart from their guests, content to spend a few moments alone. Just the three of them.

Their wedding had taken place soon after Radin's death with no fuss or frills. Just the two of them with Bek and Gerel as witnesses. The simple ceremony had been a final confirmation of the commitment that had begun a thousand years ago. Sarange hadn't been sure how much it would matter to them. They already had so much history, so much depth of emotion. Their legend was told and retold as one of the greatest love stories the world had ever known. Could a few words and a piece of paper make a difference?

In many ways, it didn't. In one way it did. It brought the peace they had been seeking. Maybe it was wrong to place too much emphasis on the wedding. Perhaps the peace came with Radin's death, but Sarange liked to think it had started the day they exchanged their vows. She wanted to forget the blood, the fury and the vengeance and focus on the fresh start. It worked for her.

Since then, there had been logistical details to take care of. They had made this house their home, but they both needed to travel for work. After a few months of barely seeing each other, they sat down one day and reorganized their lives. The strategy had coincided with Sarange's pregnancy. They had come up with a strict policy that they wouldn't be apart for more than two nights at a time. And now that Karina was here, Sarange wasn't prepared to accept any work that took her away from her daughter.

"She's beautiful, isn't she?" They never got tired of rejoicing in the perfect little person they had made.

"Like her mother." Khan leaned down to kiss her. A thousand years and that kiss still had the power to weaken her knees. "And Karina is the first of many."

"Whoa, easy, tiger." Sarange placed a hand on his chest. "When were you planning on discussing this with me?"

"You don't want more children?" He raised his brows in surprise. "I thought you'd want your own pack."

"Yes, I want more. It's the 'many' part that's bothering me." She smiled. "Can we negotiate? Maybe bring it down to 'several'?"

The smile in his eyes contained just a hint of something that made her glad they were standing away from their guests. It was a little too Khan, just the wrong—or maybe the right—side of carnal, for sharing. "As long as we can get started on making the next one while negotiating each time, that's fine by me."

Sarange wondered how it was possible for her heart to hold so much love without overflowing. This was her forever. Her husband with their child in his arms. Their journey to this point had been long and tortuous, and every step had been a fight. Now that they were here, it felt like the iron hand that had gripped her spine and propelled her onward had eased. She could finally relax.

"Always."

* * * * *

We hope you enjoyed this story from

Unleash your otherworldly desires.

Discover more stories from
Harlequin® series and continue
to venture where the normal and
paranormal collide.

Visit **Harlequin.com** for more Harlequin® series reads
and **www.Harlequin.com/ParanormalRomance**
for more paranormal reads!

From passionate, suspenseful
and dramatic love stories
to inspirational or historical...

With different lines to choose from
and new books in each one every month,
Harlequin satisfies the most voracious
romance readers.

www.Harlequin.com

HNHALO1018

Read on for a sneak preview of
Healer's Need,
the next chapter in the Ancient Ink series
from Rhenna Morgan!

"Unless you stop me, I'm going to kiss you." He shifted one hand and gently dragged his thumb along her lower lip. "Do you want that, *mihara*?"

Want? Was he joking? *Want* was staring at your favorite dessert when your belly was already full of grade A fillet, tossing aside guilt and not caring how uncomfortable your waistband would feel on the way home. Feeling his mouth on hers was *necessary*. A primal connection she had zero experience knowing how to claim for her own, but knew on the most intrinsic level would re-chart every truth in her life.

"Elise?"

"Yes."

She was pretty sure the word made it past her lips. Tried to at least pair it with a dip of her chin. Whether either worked was hard to tell. Not with the prickling anticipation skittering across her skin and his hot gaze holding her rooted in place.

He slowly lowered his head.

Her heart kicked and thrashed like a frantic animal desperate to escape a trap.

But her lips parted.

Willing.

Desperate.

Ready.

His warm breath fluttered against her skin a second before contact, her lungs reflexively drawing in the unexpected gift along with his earthy scent.

And then was *there*. The full press of his mouth fitted perfectly with hers. The soft whisper of his beard. The teasing glide of his tongue along her lower lip, coaxing her to open. His soft groan as she gave him what he wanted, and the wet heat of their kiss.

She was lost. Floating through a riot of sensations she'd never dreamed existed. Drowning in all that was Tate. Absolutely nothing else mattered except the taste of him. In following where he led with each slick glide of his lips against hers. In savoring the decadent feel of his tongue sliding against hers.

He angled his head and deepened the kiss, sliding one hand to the back of her head and holding her firm as his other hand slipped around her waist and anchored just above her ass, pulling her flush against him.

So much muscle and heat. His arms banded around her. His muscled torso against her breasts and questing palms. His powerful quads pressed against her hips and—

She gasped and jerked away, the startling realization of what she'd felt hard against her belly knocking her headfirst back to reality. She staggered back a step. Then another. Willing her lungs to function despite the air thick with need around her.

A low growl surrounded her before she could take a third. "Don't run." Chest heaving and chin lowered as though he were seconds from charging forward, Tate pumped both his hands in fists. "I won't hurt you. Not ever. But you can't run."

Something in his tone suspended her fear. A desperation that put the brakes on all thoughts of distance and made every protective instinct fire bright. "What's wrong?"

"Just promise me, Elise. Whatever you do…*don't run*."

Find out what happens next when Rhenna Morgan's Healer's Need goes on sale October 22, 2018. Look for it wherever books are sold!

www.CarinaPress.com